Iris & Lily
Book Three

Angela & Julie Scipioni

ACKNOWLEDGMENTS

Cover art by Pietro Spica
Used with permission

Lyrics from
"Lift Me Up," "The Path," and "Halfway Round the Moon"
© Rick McKown
Used with permission

Iris & Lily: Book Three is the third volume in the *Iris & Lily* series.

ISBN-13: 978-0692482179

To sisters and friends, mothers and daughters everywhere,
may you find strength in unity, and serenity in forgiveness

Book Three

From: Iris Capotosti <iris.capotosti@gmail.com>
To: Lily Capotosti <lilycapotosti@gmail.com>
Sent: Sun, November 28, 2010, 12:14 PM
Subject: There's no escaping the turkey talk

Dear Lily,

I have to admit, I enjoyed taking a couple days off from chasing ghosts to do some serious cooking. It always relaxes me, and feeding people still gives me a sense of purpose and fulfillment. Old habits die hard, don't they?

Thanksgiving really is my favorite holiday. I guess that's because it's not celebrated here in Italy, and that means I get to do my own thing, without worrying about conforming to the traditions of anyone else's family (no need to mention any names). For once I am the authority, the one who knows how to stuff and roast a turkey to perfection and can spin stories about the Pilgrims over pecan pie.

I'll never forget my first Thanksgiving here. It was just a regular Thursday, Gregorio was at work, and I had a turkey breast roasting in the oven when the cooking gas ran out. I called the guy down in town and begged him to bring me a new cylinder right away. Meanwhile, I went ahead with my other preparations, then made myself pretty for Gregorio. When the delivery guy finally rang the buzzer, I went to open the door in my high heels, all made up and dressed up for my intimate little holiday celebration, holding a bottle of Berlucchi I was going to put on ice. The delivery guy checked me out, glanced at the candles on the table and the bottle in my hand, dropped the cylinder on my doorstep, and ran off without stopping to count the liras I gave him. What a giggle I got out of that! He must have thought I was a frustrated housewife trying to lure him into a love trap or something. Of course, the laugh was on me when Gregorio walked in a few minutes later enveloped in that hospital smell that always surrounded him like a force field. He snuffed out the candles, asked what was for dinner, and told me he hated turkey.

Well, I could give up a lot of things to appease Gregorio, but certainly not Thanksgiving. That was when I started a new tradition. As of the following year, I decided to move the holiday to Saturday and invite a few friends for dinner. Friends have come and gone over the years, but whoever they are, it always makes them feel special to play American for an evening, and it makes me happy to cook for them.

You probably think I'm stalling for time with these frivolous stories. You're probably right. At the moment, I'd rather extol the merits of Mom's stuffing recipe than expose my demerits as a wife. But let's get on with it, shall we?

Love,
Iris

Dear Iris:

Of all the holidays I hate (which is all of them), I think I might hate
Thanksgiving the most. It's rude and presumptuous and maddening that
someone along the way somewhere decided that we should all stop and
be grateful on the same day. What if I'm not thankful on Thanksgiving?
The only choice I have is to be a big hypocrite.

I'll save you some time writing back to me - I know the spiel. Every day
that we wake up and have life and food and shelter is a day to be
grateful. Survival is not what I am going for here.

Turkey-schmurky. I think God packed it with tryptophan because He
knew that after spending an entire day working in the kitchen and then
sitting down to eat with our families, we'd all need a little anesthesia.
Maybe Gregorio had the right idea.

Personally, I'm thankful it's over.

Yes, let's get on with it. "I can't wait for what comes next," she said
sardonically.

Love,
Lily

1. IRIS

One of the advantages of having a flexible schedule, which in reality meant that Iris knew what time her day would begin, but never when it would end, was that if she needed to step out for an hour or two, she could do so without feeling guilty. As the days grew warmer, and the emerald waters of the cove more inviting, Iris dreamed of using her lunch break to have a swim. A bag containing two bathing suits, a pair of swimming goggles, a cover-up, and a change of underwear sat in a closet in her office, waiting for the midday dip to become incorporated into her routine. Each morning, as she smiled at the guests setting off for a day of leisure or relaxing by the pool, Iris was heartened by the fact that in just a few hours, she, too, would strip off the tailleur that constrained her, body and spirit, into the role of *Direttrice*, and slip into her swimsuit, to enjoy an hour of splashing about as just plain Iris.

In the days following Vanesi's impromptu visit to the hotel, the prospect of her noon plunge was sunk by a series of requests from the other members of the Leale family, who also thought she was entitled to a long lunch break, and happily took advantage of it. Isabella had announced earlier that spring that driving now made her nervous, and had handed her car keys over to Gregorio. Fortunately, the family concurred, Iris worked close to home, and could easily skip out at noon, go fetch the newspaper and whatever items were required by her mother-in-law before the shops closed, and deliver them before resuming work for the afternoon. At the same time, Iris could conveniently run errands for Cinzia, who had sprained her ankle falling from a rubber step during an exercise class she had joined in a spurt of determination to beat her body back into shape before it was too late for her to find a new man. Cinzia had only recently begun to consider replacing her wayward husband Franco who, despite Isabella's prediction that he would soon be running back home with his tail between his uniformed legs, was still missing in action with his cruise ship croupier.

The only slot of time that no one had yet managed to steal from Iris, the only moments when she could puff on a cigarette in peace or listen to music as loud as she liked, were the fifteen precious minutes it took her to drive to and from the hotel. Behind the wheel of her nimble Seicento, she navigated the hills and bends of her daily routine, propelled by the car's spunky engine and the daydreams she tucked away for just such moments. Her latest series of open-eyed fantasies starred none other than the cameraman Massimiliano Vanesi; the setting was the exotic island of Pantelleria.

The morning after receiving Max's email, Iris had read about Pantelleria on the Internet. Apart from guessing it was somewhere in the deep south, she could not say where exactly the island was located and had been surprised to learn it was actually closer to the shores of north Africa than it was to the southwestern coast of Sicily. Reading on, it occurred to her why the name of this island had rung a bell: one of the dessert wines featured at the Dimora was the sweet Passito made from the sun-dried zibibbo grapes that grew there. She also recalled buying Pantelleria capers; they were the best, thanks to the sunny, arid climate of the volcanic island, where they ripened to savory plumpness. Yet the piece of trivia that held her interest wasn't found in the web pages about Pantelleria, but rather in the email from Max, informing her he was there, now, and wanted her to join him. Perhaps he was lodged in a *dammuso*, one of those romantic whitewashed abodes she had seen pictures of, perched on the ragged rocks overlooking waters even more temptingly transparent than those of Paraggi. She imagined his tan deepening in the strong southern sun, the salt-laden breeze tousling his long, thick hair.

It was obvious he had only been teasing when he said she should come down, or he would have called and tried to convince her. How he expected her to pull off such a feat wasn't even mentioned, of course. Not that the logistics of getting there would pose a problem, she was confident she could figure out that aspect. It would be such an adventure, setting off on her own like that. Just for fun, she had checked out how one would get to Pantelleria if one were free to do as one pleased. She discovered there was an airport in Trapani; she could fly there, then board the first ferry for the island. Ships sailed from Genoa to Palermo daily, too, but that leg alone would take over twenty hours, and she would still be far away. She wouldn't mind, though. She would love to stand alone on the deck of a ship, the wind whipping her hair, the immense blue sea and sky surrounding her, blotting out the faces of everyone who thought they knew her, and the demands of everyone who said they cared for her.

The blare of a horn recalled Iris's attention from the imaginary sea crossing, and she was slightly surprised to find herself in Santa Margherita, still circling the open air market in search of a parking spot. She usually enjoyed going to the market and picking out fresh fruits and vegetables, planning dinner menus according to what was in season. But today there would be no time for that; she had received precise orders for her mission to stock up on produce for the entire Leale family. Spotting a freshly vacated spot, she made a sharp turn, and slipped her agile vehicle between the lines, sending into an apoplectic fit the driver of a silver Alfa Romeo Giulietta who attempted to squeeze her out. Whether it be behind the wheel of her little car or seated on the scooter which she refused to give up entirely, driving in Italy was one of the rare situations in which Iris was adamant about protecting her rights. She switched off the engine and pulled the handbrake, glimpsing the still gesticulating red-faced man in her rearview mirror. She waved at him with a raised index finger and pinky, mouthing the word *"Cornuto!"* making sure he could read her lips, which incited him to punch his horn furiously, stopping only when a traffic cop blew his whistle and waved him on. Meanwhile, an insistent beeping from her purse announced the arrival of a text message. It must be from Cinzia, adding another item to her or Isabella's shopping list. Iris had already received three messages since leaving the hotel, and she was fed up; this time she would not even acknowledge it. You would think Cinzia and her mother could pool the brains and education they bragged about long enough to compile one, definitive list instead of pestering her like this. Why, she and Lily had done a better job of keeping the cupboards at Chestnut Crest stocked for an entire household of Capotostis, back when they were still teenagers.

An hour and fifteen minutes later, Iris was relieved to be back at work. Her nerves were frazzled, her armpits sweaty, her throat parched, her stomach growling. She rang the snack bar and ordered a Caprese salad and a bottle of San Pellegrino to be delivered to her office. She couldn't bear the thought of spending even fifteen minutes eating out on the terrace, where she would be forced to watch bathers glide over the surface of the shimmering water or snorkel among the rocks. Sighing, she switched on the air conditioning, wondering whether the whole summer would be as hot and sticky as these early days of June.

Settling in at her desk for the afternoon stretch, she took her cell phone from her purse, opened the messaging function to obliterate the day's chapter of the Leale marketing chronicles, stopping her thumb just as it was about to delete the last, unread message, which wasn't from Cinzia at all, but from a number she did not recognize.

ciao capo! if ur not coming im leaving. u get 1 more chance nxt wk. shooting near rome. it would be good 4 ur eyes or r u 2 married?

Though there was no name at the end of the message, it bore the unmistakable signature of Max Vanesi. He might as well have signed it "trouble," because that's what the man spelled. In big block letters. He was so damn sure she wouldn't do it, wasn't he? Well, maybe she would surprise him this time. She had been putting off a trip to Rome to see some people regarding an affiliation for the Dimora. Maybe the hotel and Gregorio and all the Leales would have to manage without her for a day or so; maybe it was time for a trip beyond those same few kilometers she traveled over and over again, back and forth between house and hotel. An overwhelming desire to escape took possession of her fingers, tapped out a reply:

Email me details.

She was trying to think of something witty to add when the waiter knocked on her door, making her jump in her chair.

"*Mi scusi, Signora.* I didn't mean to startle you. I brought your lunch," he said from the doorway.

"Thank you." The waiter set down the dish of juicy sliced tomatoes, creamy buffalo mozzarella and fresh basil leaves, but the fluttering of butterflies in her stomach caused by Max's message killed her appetite. As the waiter made his exit, Iris stared at the phone in her hand, watching her finger hit the "send" button, then gulped down a glass of water so quickly it felt like the bubbles would blow a hole through her chest.

Iris knew her response could set the cogs in motion for a ride that might spin out of control. She also knew the question was not whether she would ever betray Gregorio, given the chance. She had already flunked that test; she had already discovered that she was capable of shameful deeds, that she could be coaxed into the role of adulteress when coached by an expert like Claudio Olona. Of utmost importance, Claudio had taught her, was to choose your partner wisely, as in their case: married people made perfect lovers for married people. There was no overlapping of roles, no pressing for involvement on deeper levels, no squandering of stolen time on futile discussions, no seething resentment or unrealistic expectations, no long faces at the holidays, no phone calls on evenings or weekends. There was just a different set of rules, and if they were abided by, a marriage could actually benefit from an affair. Claudio had said so; even Beatrix said so, and she was a friend, not a man trying to seduce her.

Massimiliano Vanesi, on the other hand, was a wild card. He did not wear a wedding band, but then again, he certainly was not the type to broadcast his marital status. He was pushing forty, however, so if he wasn't married, there would certainly be an ex-wife and possibly a child or two looming in his background, in

8

addition to a string of girlfriends up and down the Italian boot, islands included. She could picture Max sauntering into each new location the way he had at her hotel, his mystique bolstered by the video camera he wielded, a modern-day version of an outlaw drawing his six-shooter as he burst into a saloon, knowing he could grab any girl who struck his fancy. He must be the kind of man who made women happy twice: once when he turned up, once again when he disappeared for good.

She should run as fast as she could from a guy like that, not encourage him. If and when he replied, she would just ignore him. She picked up her fork, stabbed a piece of mozzarella and tomato, and put it in her mouth, savoring the explosion of flavors and consistencies on her tongue, feeling better already for having made the right decision.

The train crawled at an exasperating pace into Rome's Termini station, prompting Iris to glare at her watch, as if her eyes had the power to slow the movement of its hands, instead of only informing her that the forty minutes she had allowed for her connection had dwindled to ten. She carried just a purse and a tote bag large enough to accommodate her necessities for a brief business trip to the capital, plus two novels, one in English (*Cider House Rules*, passed on to her by Violet last time she visited home) and one in Italian (*Tecniche di Seduzione*, on loan from Bea), which she alternated, as necessary, to discourage idle talk from the other travelers seated in her compartment. Her hand already on the door latch, she was poised to sprint, if only the damn train would make a final lurch to the end of the line. She had boarded the *rapido* in Rapallo, but ever since Grosseto, the train had been hiccupping its way south along the coast, accumulating over thirty minutes' delay. If she missed her connection, she would have to wait an hour for the next local train that could take her as far as Priverno. From there, she would catch a bus for the final leg of her trip to Sabaudia.

Things should be relatively calm at the Dimora after the hectic weekend, and by rearranging her schedule, Iris had managed to clear the time needed to set up those long overdue meetings in

Rome. That had been her sole intention right along, that Wednesday when she obtained *Signora* Mangiagallo's permission to go away for two days. That had still been her intention when she introduced the topic of her planned trip to Gregorio on Thursday, surprising him with his favorite dinner of swordfish steaks ("so rich in protein and Omega-3!" he always commented), which she usually served on Fridays. It had been that same intention which suggested she pop into the hairdresser's for a trim and root touch-up that Saturday. (Appearances may not be everything, but the people she planned to meet expected the class of a luxury hotel to be reflected in its manager; if she made a good impression, so did the Dimora.) That intention had still been intact when, walking back to her car, she spotted in a shop window a pretty pink push-up bra with black lace trim and matching bikini panties, justifying their purchase with Auntie Rosa's theory that fine lingerie bolstered both a woman's morale and her self-confidence.

Going to Rome for those meetings had been her intention, all along. Up until the untimely arrival of a text message heralded by the vibration of her silenced cell phone as it sashayed across her nightstand while she and Gregorio were propped up on pillows, reading in bed at a quarter to midnight (they switched off the lights a bit later on Saturdays). Citing as a cause for her full bladder the second cup of chamomile tea Gregorio had forced on her, Iris palmed her phone and ducked into the bathroom. The message was from Max. He was in Rome.

"I honestly don't know what's come over you, *Piccolina*," Gregorio said the next day to Iris, who darted back and forth between the dining room, where she was serving Sunday dinner to the Leale family, and the kitchen, where she scanned the stream of text messages that had begun flooding her cell phone as soon as she had stepped away from the stove, gulped down a glass of wine, and informed Max that she also had plans to be in Rome.

"What do you mean?" she said, her smile twitching as she set down yet another bottle of mineral water in front of Gregorio, though there were already two on the table.

"I mean that you seem unusually agitated for a Sunday. And I'm quite certain it has something to do with that trip to Rome tomorrow."

Beatrix always said that when trying to defuse a potentially dangerous conversation, the best reaction is no reaction, and Iris had witnessed that behavior in her own mother for many years until she had that one big reaction and walked out. Taking a deep breath, Iris sat down, poured herself some water, and raised the glass to her lips. As she drank, a spurt of vibrations from the cell phone in her hip pocket sent waves of panic up her torso and down her arm to her hand, causing her to spill water down the V-neck of her shirt.

"Look at the mess you're making!" Gregorio said, reaching to take the glass from her.

"I'm sorry," she mumbled, though the cool water felt quite nice on her thumping chest. Had all the eyes in the room not been focused on her, she might have grabbed the glass back from him and thrown the rest of the water in her face to douse the burning in her cheeks.

"I'm not interested in apologies, Iris. I'm interested in your well-being. We all are. Just look at yourself. First, you burned the meat, then you can't sit still for five minutes, now you're spilling things. You are over-extending yourself. I've always said you've taken on more than you can handle with that job."

"I can handle my job fine. Really." Her lips quivered as she smiled, her eyes traveling from the parts of her life she was starting to have a hard time handling: Gregorio and Isabella, Cinzia and her sons, the plates on the table, the meat on the plates. Her stomach churned as she stared at her untouched slice of steak. Cinzia insisted her "boys," who now towered over Gregorio, must eat their *fettina* before going to play soccer, and Iris had cooked the thin, flavorless slices of lean beef in a skillet, just the way they liked it. So what if it was a little overdone. Big fucking deal.

"And while we're on the subject," Gregorio cleared his voice, paused, then continued, "I've been thinking about a few things, and talking them over with Mamma."

"What things?" Iris stabbed the bloodless slab of meat with her fork and began sawing off pieces she would later give to Zenzero. She glanced up at Isabella, who sat with raised eyebrows, nodding with the gravity of a nurse standing by a physician's side as he reveals his fatal diagnosis to a doomed patient.

Gregorio set down his silverware, placing his knife and fork side by side, their tips resting on the edge of his plate, then dabbed at his mouth and goatee with his napkin. "Important things. Such as, that you should have had your fill of this hotel nonsense by now. You've achieved your little success - and I'm not saying you don't deserve credit for that. But you've proven your point, *Piccolina*."

"What point?" Iris said, interrupting her cutting, dropping her hands to her lap. She would bet her new lace panties their little talk had been initiated by Isabella. Gregorio hadn't voiced any objections to her trip to Rome, up until just now.

He continued on as if she hadn't spoken, looking at his mother, then at Cinzia, before looking back at Iris. "One thing is keeping yourself busy but depriving your family of your presence is another story altogether. Where is your sense of duty?"

How could he say that when her whole life had become one big, fucking duty? Didn't she cater to their every need? Didn't she spend every evening at home? Didn't she cook for them all every Sunday? Besides, they were his family, not hers. Anger bubbled in her belly, too heavy to rise to the surface. She sat and stared at Gregorio in silence, fists clenched in her lap.

"And now, what with the hospital, and the university, and the clinic, my responsibilities - and my earnings, I might add - have greatly increased. It simply makes more sense for you to devote your energy to our home, to us. I would like what little leisure time I have to be enjoyed in the company of a well-rested, smiling wife, not an exhausted neurotic."

Iris saw herself jumping to her feet, maybe even making her chair topple over when she rose. She saw herself throwing back her shoulders and telling them all that she was earning more now, too. She saw herself looking them in the eye, one by one, and asking them what the hell more they wanted from her. But she just sat there, her legs too weak to stand on, the words trapped in her throat, a cluster of hapless bystanders unwilling to get involved. "The best reaction is no reaction," they murmured. "The best reaction is no reaction."

"Have some of these, *Caro*," Isabella said to Gregorio, passing him the zucchini.

If the phone vibrating again in her pocket flustered her, she was certain no one would suspect the cause; her crimson cheeks were sure to be blamed on the slap of disloyalty delivered so masterfully, in front of everyone, by Gregorio.

One thing she had to say about Max Vanesi was that he was optimistic. "Near Rome" turned out to be a hundred kilometers south of the city, and the "hour at the most" it would take to reach Sabaudia from the capital mushroomed with each delay accrued on the public transportation system until it had doubled. Evidently, Max's estimate that the location checks would be wrapped up "by six-thirty at the latest," at which time he would be free to meet her in Piazza Regina Margherita, had also been calculated on that same scale of optimism. There was still no sight of him, and she had been standing right there, in front of the boxy-looking brick church he had described to her, ever since a quarter past. She had even had time to stop at a café to use the ladies' room and drink an herbal tea in the hope it would calm her nerves, and take a short stroll around the center of this unusual town she had never heard of until the previous day, when she had finally agreed to the rendezvous. Pacing back and forth in front of their designated meeting point, she studied the impressive mosaic depicting the Annunciation at the entrance to the church.

If Rome and its splendors had not been built in a day, the construction of this city had come close to that time frame. Iris had read on a plaque by the tower at the town hall that Sabaudia was inaugurated in 1934, less than a year after its foundation upon the malaria-infested swampland that had rendered the territory uninhabitable since the times of the ancient Romans. In over two decades in Italy, Iris had never seen anything like this city, so eerily devoid of ancient history, intrinsic charm, and decorative elements.

The rationalist architecture had an unsettling effect on her; the linear, unadorned forms staring stonily down at her laid bare the premeditated motives for her presence there, stripped of any possible mitigating factors in the form of romantic vistas, rosy sunsets and candlelit dinners that might justify a slow surrender to temptation.

At six forty-five, Max sent her a text message saying he would arrive in "about five minutes." She realized he was working, of course, and didn't want to rush him, but the longer she waited, the more she wondered what she was doing there. She was weary from traveling six hundred kilometers after a night of fitful sleep and frazzled from the surges of adrenalin which had been pumping through her body since early morning. A drizzle was starting to fall when the church bells began ringing in the tower. As she debated whether to seek shelter inside, her phone rang. *"Numero privato"* flashed on the display. Max must be calling from another phone.

"Finalmente!" she answered, hunching over to shield her face and phone from the sprinkle that was quickly turning into a shower, just as a black scooter whizzed by her to overtake an orange bus, which blared its horn in reprimand.

"Piccolina!" said the voice at the other end. "I was expecting you to call."

"Gregorio! Hello … sorry… yes, of course."

"I assume you got there all right?"

"The train was late, but yes, I got finally here." Never mind that his "there" did not coincide with her "here." She quickly added, "Where are you calling from?" Better to be the one asking the questions than answering them, that was what Beatrix always told her.

Gregorio said something, but she could not make out his words among the din of the bells striking the hour of seven.

"What did you say?" she said in a loud voice, huddled over the phone, her left hand covering her left ear.

"I said, never mind where I'm calling from. But I know where you are." Gregorio's voice came over the line plenty loud this time, and his words rang clear in her ear as the bells fell silent. She was a rotten liar, and out of practice as well, but she had said she was taking the train to Rome, and she had. How could she have possibly screwed that up? She scanned the square, half expecting to see her husband walk out from behind a building. Her pulse accelerated, as she searched for something to say. She recalled Claudio's golden rule in matters of conjugal deception: Always deny everything; if your husband wants to believe you, he will.

"Of course you do," she blurted out. "I told you where I was going."

"Rome, yes. And right now? I know you, you might as well confess."

She jerked the phone away from her ear and stared at it. She wanted to smash it against the church, then run and hide inside. She heard Claudio's voice again, offering another nugget of advice: Never volunteer information; let him do the explaining. She brought the phone to her ear again.

"What are you talking about?" she said.

"Hearing that crazy traffic and all those church bells, I can picture you perfectly. You're window-shopping in Via del Corso."

"Oh…!" she whinnied. "You do know me! But I'm not really in the mood for shopping." In fact, her legs felt weak, and she felt like throwing up. Stick as close to the truth as possible, Claudio would say. (Or was it Bea who said that?) "It's been a long day, now all I want is a nice hot shower, then have something to eat."

"See? I knew all that travel would exhaust you. Are you having dinner all alone?"

"Um, I'm not really sure yet. I did have plans to meet someone I've been talking to about an affiliation, but maybe I'll just grab a bite on my own." True again. Especially if that someone never turned up.

"Well, if you're eating all by yourself, why don't you go to that *trattoria* we had dinner at last time we were in Rome? It was just off that little piazza, behind the Temple of Hadrian, remember? You loved the *bucatini all'amatriciana,* and they had delicious artichokes *alla romana*. Almost as good as the ones Mamma used to make before we got married. Plus, it was well frequented, as I recall - lots of clergy. I think there must be a seminary or something in the area. You should be safe enough there."

"Good idea. I'll keep it in mind." She was so relieved by Gregorio's small talk that it didn't even annoy her. He tended to grow quite chatty after coming down hard on her, and although she hadn't responded to his comments at the dinner table the day before, she knew he knew that they had upset her.

"What are you having for dinner?" she asked, glancing up at the passing traffic, again on the lookout for Max, now that she knew Gregorio was not lurking in the shadows. She wasn't really concerned about what her husband would eat, but Gregorio would be reassured by this type of question, asked by mothers and wives and sisters and girlfriends all across the country. It showed men that you really cared if you reminded them to eat, or asked what they had eaten, or whether it had been cooked to their taste, and digested in a satisfactory manner. The rain was coming down harder now, the drops pelting her neck, chilling her spine.

"Mamma is making tripe today. She knows you can't bear to look at it, let alone cook it, so she figured it would be a treat for me." As he launched into an explanation of the little shop in the old backstreets of Genoa where he had procured the very best tripe, which he had delivered to Isabella on his lunch break, and how enthusiastic his mother had been about locating the old recipe she used to prepare for Gregorio's father, a beep in Iris's ear signaled another incoming call. Never having mastered the skill of swapping calls without hanging up on one or both of the parties, she felt pressured by the beeping and grew curt with Gregorio. She danced impatiently in the rain as he summarized more of the day's non-events in the Leale household, sparing her the Policlinico chronicles, which he was probably saving for Isabella, always his most rapt audience. By the time Iris managed to terminate the call, the beeping had ceased, and the rain had begun to fall steadily. She scanned the square again: no cars flashed lights at her, no male figure rushed toward her with an open umbrella. The doors to the church must be unlocked at this hour; she had seen people going in. She made a dash for the entrance and ducked into the vestibule to wait before the rain could soak through her clothes to her new underwear.

Though it was a mild evening, the combination of the unexpected rain and Gregorio's unnerving phone call made her shiver. She shook the drops from her bare arms, wiped her phone across the front of her shirt, checked the display; the missed call had been from Max. She tried calling back, but a recording informed her that his phone was switched off. She wondered what criteria had led her to conclude that a man she barely knew would be reliable, considerate or even punctual. She would give him another ten minutes then she would catch the first bus to the station and head straight back to Rome. In fact, the more she thought about it, the more convinced she was that the best thing now would be for him to not show up at all.

Iris had a low threshold for inactivity, and in moments of stress, not being able to do anything added to her agitation. Drawn by the drone of low voices, she inched open the massive wooden door to the sanctuary. A couple dozen heads, prevalently snowy, female heads, were scattered in the pews closest to the raised altar. A few turned stiffly at the sound of the groaning door. Iris dipped her fingers in the holy water font and made the sign of the cross. She recognized the words to the Confiteor being recited by the superannuated congregation gathered for the evening service. Her lips began moving automatically as her voice pronounced the Italian words to the Act of Contrition, which she had learned years ago at the church in Santa Ida "… *ho molto peccato in pensieri, parole, opere e omissioni, per mia colpa, mia colpa, mia grandissima colpa.*" She beat her chest with a clenched fist each time she said the words "*colpa,*" then dropped her head as the prayer finished. She wandered over to a side aisle, pausing by a statue of the Madonna. In keeping with a promise made to Auntie Rosa when she had first moved to Italy, she dropped a coin into the offerings box, lit a votive candle, and said a prayer for her. "Please God, watch over Auntie Rosa," was the best she could manage, what with all confusion churning around inside her, and all the noise of the soon-to-be-committed sins of the flesh and already committed sins of lust and false witness pounding nails into her soul. She quickly touched the fingers of her right hand to her forehead, to her heart, to her left and right shoulders, then turned to leave. She had been wrong to come to Sabaudia, and more wrong to enter the church in such a state. But the rain had been providential: it was God's way of telling her what she must do. She pushed open the door, stepped outside, and hurried down the steps toward the road, just as a white van with a blue RAI logo on its side pulled up to the curb through a puddle, splashing her with rainwater.

"Hey, there!" Max shouted from the open window of the passenger seat. "I've been looking all over for you!" He unlatched the back door from inside without getting out of the van.

Iris stood and stared at him.

"What are you waiting for? Get in!" he said. "It's pouring!" Not wanting to get into a discussion while standing in the rain, she obeyed and slid into the back seat. The least he could do was give her a lift.

"I said in front of the church, not inside the church, *salame!*" Max chided her, grinning as he turned to face her.

"I was getting soaked," Iris said. "And I was also getting ready to leave."

"Leave? What are you talking about? You just got here!"

"It's been an hour," she said. "That's enough."

"Hey, it wasn't my fault. I tried calling you, but you didn't answer. Then my battery died. I must have gotten fifty phone calls this afternoon. *Cazzo.*"

"You could have borrowed a phone," Iris suggested, though it didn't really matter, did it? Not at this point.

"But I didn't have your number. It was on my phone. Who memorizes phone numbers anymore?"

"I do. Yours is 3256643..."

"I'm impressed, Capo," Max cut her off. His playful grin turned into a smile: warm, engaging, provocative. Then he settled back down in his seat, facing forward, and crooked his thumb at the guy behind the wheel. "By the way, that there is Peppe." The stocky mustachioed man with a shaved head smiled in the rearview

18

mirror and reached his left hand over his right shoulder.

"*Piacere*," Iris said, as Peppe's thumb and fingers locked around hers in a soul shake. "Would you mind dropping me off at the bus stop, Peppe?"

"What bus stop?" Max said, half-turning to face her again.

"I'm going back to Rome. I can take the bus to the train station."

"That's ridiculous, you just got here," Max said, his tight laugh attesting to her silliness.

"Like I said, I didn't *just* get here." There was no irony in Iris's voice; she was merely stating a fact.

"Look, we got tied up," Max said. It wasn't exactly an apology, but Iris was not fishing for one. She just hoped he wouldn't turn all the way around and smile at her point-blank again. She had fantasized about those full lips too many times not to be affected by the sight of them, just inches from her face.

"That's OK, really. It gave me time to think. And what I think, is that coming here might not have been such a great idea. But if it's too much trouble for you guys to drop me off, I'll get out and walk."

Peppe's grin told Iris he was amused at seeing Max put on the spot. Max's snort told her he wasn't taking her seriously. He nodded at Peppe, who shrugged his thick shoulders and pulled away from the curb.

"Look, Capo," Max said. "Right now, we're all going for a drink. You can dry off, relax a little. If you still want to leave after that, you can hitch a ride with the limo we have going back to Rome later. You don't really want to take the train, do you?"

Iris looked out the window fogged up by her quickened breath and damp clothes. She could already feel the grimy vinyl of the second-class train seat sticking to the clammy backs of her thighs; she could already see the longing in the falsely virtuous eyes staring back at her as she watched the rain streaming down the windows, wondering what might have been. Going back by limo would certainly be more comfortable, and definitely less depressing.

"You're acting real uptight, Capo," Max said when she didn't reply. "A drink will do you good. Or isn't this place fancy enough for the hot-shot American boss lady of a posh resort?"

"Of course that's not it," Iris said, shaking her head. As if she ever expected royal treatment from anyone; as if she had grown up in the lap of luxury. What did he know about her, anyway, besides the fact that she could really use that drink?

Max turned around to face her again, finger-combing his thick, dark hair away from his tanned face. She had thought of running her own fingers through that hair countless times; it looked so wild and tangled, yet so silky. She remembered how it had smelled on the hotel terrace, how it brushed against her when he leaned close.

"I'll introduce you around to my crew. We'll have a few laughs, relax a little," Max said.

The last time Iris had come across a film crew, which certainly didn't happen often, they had been the enemy, wreaking havoc in her hotel. But when the end of the day rolled around, they always looked like they were having a good time together. It might be fun getting a glimpse at what happened behind the scenes while she dried off a bit. Images of herself as part of a lively crowd, sharing a laugh and a drink or two with TV people in the convivial atmosphere of a local bar elbowed their way into her mixed-up mind.

"And while we're at it, maybe we can put a little sparkle back into those sad eyes," Max said.

There he went again with the story about the eyes. He was the only one who had ever told her that; every other person she knew always commented on her bright smile and sunny disposition. Maybe this was the time to show him that Iris Capotosti knew how to have fun, when she wanted to.

Peppe double-parked in front of a bar, nowhere near the bus stop. Max got out of the van, opened the door for her, and said, "Let's go!" Iris found herself obeying, relieved that any decisions about returning to Rome were deferred, at least for the time being.

Half an Americano later, Iris was beginning to mellow out; by the time her glass was empty, her second thoughts about being there were giving way to speculation as to what surprises the evening might hold in store. As she sipped the strong red concoction in her tumbler, she caught her reflection in the mirror behind the bar and was reassured to see her smile in place, and her eyes twinkling with amusement at the lively banter between Max and Peppe and the owner of the bar. Bubbling with enthusiasm at the prospect of having his business featured in the segment of *"Buona Mattina Italia"* that Max and his crew were taping, the man had invited them all over for drinks on the house. Soon after arriving, they had been joined by Marcello Mezzamanica himself, the host of the morning talk show, together with three other men with Roman accents who did not bother with introductions. Cinzia and Isabella were great fans of Mezzamanica and his program; wouldn't they be in for a shock if they could see her now, having drinks with him in person? The thought made her chuckle. Seeing Max smile back at her, Iris recalled everything that had both attracted and frightened her when they had first met: the sexy allure, the childlike playfulness, the cocky self-assurance. He placed a thumb under her chin, lifted her face to his.

"I'm glad you came, Capo," he said, bending to kiss her. His lips were warm and fleshy and unexpected. The kiss made her feel giddy and giggly and girlish. "That's it," Max said. "You deserve to laugh like that more often."

Yes, actually, she did. Even if this wasn't the romantic encounter she had envisioned, she actually preferred the way things were working out. Having a few drinks with a fun group of people had relieved her tension, and knowing she could not possibly run into anyone she knew here had further relaxed her. As did knowing that she had the option of speeding back to Rome in the comfort of a limo.

"Peppe and the guys are nice," she said.

Max made a yes-and-no movement with his head. "As crews go, I could have done better, but this time I had to take what they gave me. Some asshole at RAI has a brother who has a friend who has a son, and before you know it, you're on the road teaching a bunch of rookies the ropes again."

"Those people must figure you're a good teacher, then. But I imagine it must be frustrating. I'd be curious to hear more about how things work in your business."

"Basically, the bottom line is, you have to learn not to give a shit. You get the job done and have as much fun as you can while you're doing it." Max tossed a handful of peanuts into his mouth and drained his drink. "But what I'm doing now is just a filler, really."

Iris tilted her head. "What do you mean?"

"You don't really think I plan to spend my career filming travelogues for couch potatoes, do you?"

"I don't know, the segment you shot in Portofino was really nice," Iris said.

Max snorted and rolled his eyes. "'Nice' is not exactly a filmmaker's idea of a rave review."

Iris blushed, hoping she hadn't insulted him. She thought the segment was great, and she really did think he had talent.

"I've actually got a couple of projects of my own I'm working on," he said. "There's this screenplay ready to go, as soon as I nail down the right backing."

"You mean, like a real movie?"

"Yeah, it's a feature film. I already have a few shorts to my credit."

Iris didn't really know much about films, and wasn't exactly sure what he meant by "shorts," but what she did know was how to dig for details without looking dumb. It was always a matter of asking and listening.

"Really? I'd like to hear about that," she said.

"It was some experimental stuff I was shooting a few years back. I took a film to the Torino festival, and there was talk about a screening in Venice, too."

"Venice? Really?" She wasn't really up on film festivals, apart from what she picked up from some of the celebrities she had come across at the hotel. She didn't know anything about Turin except for the fact that they made Fiats there, but she figured anything going on in Venice must be pretty prestigious. "How did it go?"

"My work got noticed all right, but by all the wrong people. Those things are totally rigged, and I've never been into kissing ass. Or bribing," Max said. "I figured I'd give it a rest, do some cushy freelance work while I travel around. That leaves my brain free to

22

work on more important stuff."

"Sounds like a good plan," Iris said. It was certainly commendable to aim high and refuse to play into the hands of a few corrupt people. Sometimes it seemed like Italy was crawling with them.

"But that's enough about me for now," Max said. "Are you hungry?"

"I wasn't really thinking about food," Iris said. "But apart from these peanuts and potato chips, I haven't eaten anything since dinner yesterday." An image of the leathery steak sitting on her plate flashed through her mind, made her stomach do a flip.

"What? Don't tell me a wholesome American girl like you skips breakfast?"

"Not usually," she said. "But I have to confess, I was too nervous to have anything except coffee this morning."

"Nervous about what?"

"About this. About coming here, seeing you." She hated to admit it to him, but she might as well be honest. The alcohol was definitely starting to affect her, loosening her tongue, infusing her cheeks with color.

"That's a new one. I haven't met a woman who could get nervous over a date in a long time. I thought the function had been genetically deactivated."

"You must be meeting the wrong kind of women, then," Iris said. His comment made her feel slightly antiquated, but on the other hand, his use of the word "date" to define what they were doing had an old-fashioned ring to it, too. She knew he must be a bit of a romantic, between the things he had written to her, and the work that he did. Anyone sensitive and talented enough to bring out such beauty in the images he captured on film could not be otherwise.

Her considerations were interrupted by Marcello Mezzamanica, who was making the rounds, shaking hands, slapping backs, surprising Iris by stopping to kiss her on her cheeks, as he prepared to leave. "His driver's here," Max said. "Now's your chance if you still want to go, and I'm sure Marcello would love to have you along, especially now that you're all bright-eyed. You don't get to ride in a limo with a TV star every day, do you?"

Iris felt a twinge of disappointment. Max knew she hadn't eaten, but instead of trying to convince her to stay, now it almost sounded as if he wanted to send her away, like some little kid who was out past her bedtime. She would actually be quite happy to hang around for a while longer, now that she had loosened up; Peppe had a gift for telling stories that really made her laugh, and she was learning a lot of interesting things about Max. Plus, there was something about the way Max looked at her, his eyes slanted, his mouth twisted in wry half-smile, that made her heart race and her palms sweat, and her lips crave another kiss. Finding herself at the center of his attention made her feel special. Better than special. Max made her feel attractive, desired.

"I was probably wrong about you, anyway," he said.

"Wrong? About what?"

"That you would have the guts to come."

"But as you can see, I am here."

"Yeah, well, earlier you said you didn't think it was such a great idea after all. I can't blame you for wishing you were back in your cozy villa where you belong, making dinner for that nice husband of yours."

Why did he have to bring Gregorio into this, just when she was starting to warm up to him? Did he think she lacked the nerve to stay? She was tempted to tell him this was not the first time she had strayed from her sweet little home, but what business was that of his? And why should she feel like she had to prove anything to him? She looked out the door at the limo glistening in the rain, its engine running. She would have to decide quickly, which shouldn't be all that difficult, considering she had already made up her mind back in the church. Maybe if God wanted her to leave, He could find a way to push her out the door.

"Then again, as long as you're here, maybe you should have something to eat," Max said. "I'd hate for you to go away on an empty stomach."

"Maybe," she said, wishing the car would speed away, taking

her option of leaving with it.

"Dinner is at Donna Amalia's, down by the seafront," Max said. "It's the best restaurant in town, owned by the same family since it opened for business, three generations ago. The upcoming generation is a pair of fifteen-year-old Chinese twin sisters, adopted when they were two. I thought it might give an interesting angle to our story. The owners invited us to talk over dinner. I figured, why refuse a free dinner, you know? Unless you prefer to go somewhere else, just the two of us." He kissed her on the mouth again, parting her lips with his tongue, finding hers, barely touching it with his, retreating. "If you still want to leave after dinner, I'll get Peppe to drive you back, how's that?"

Iris readjusted her imagined scenario of the evening once more to adapt to the constantly evolving reality. Max ran his fingers through his hair, leaning back against the bar as he waited for her answer. His thick hair was so black as to appear blue in the harsh fluorescent light, like the hair of a comic book Superman. She thought of Gregorio's receding hairline, wispy and greying, with the same mixture of sadness and affection she had felt while riding on the train across from her father and noticed for the first time that he was growing old.

"Promise?" she said.

"Promise," he said.

She relaxed; he did want her to stay but was still giving her a way out. An uninvited thought of Gregorio eating tripe with his mother, and in turn thinking of Iris twirling *bucatini* around a fork with the seminarians skipped across her mind, making her feel slightly guilty, but mostly it made her giggle again. She would worry about the guilt later; it had a habit of hanging around.

During the brief drive to the restaurant, Iris listened to Max and the crew rehash the day's events and swap derogatory remarks about Mezzamanica. Craning her neck over the other passengers to observe the landscape, she was surprised to see that there were more appealing aspects of Sabaudia to be found in nature, with sand dunes and the open sea on one side, and a small lake on the other; the restaurant was located in between. There was still

25

enough light to admire the luxuriant swath of vegetation growing along the shore as far as the promontory of Monte Circeo, whose massive silhouette could be seen to the south.

Over dinner, everyone had something to share with Iris, who was eager to learn more about this strange little city. She learned that Sabaudia had become quite popular with writers and intellectuals back in the Sixties, and one could still encounter celebrities on weekends and during the summer when they buzzed down for a break from the heat and hustle of Rome. Many lived in impressive villas tucked away from view by lush gardens.

Soon after they had eaten their first course of spaghetti with clams in the shell, followed by an immense grilled seafood platter, all of it washed down with several bottles of chilled Cori Bianco DOC, the rain finally stopped, and Iris asked if anyone minded her opening a window. There were seven of them at the table, Iris being the only woman; most of the men had been smoking throughout dinner, and the combined smells of fish and tobacco prevented her from desiring either. Meanwhile, the men kept topping off her wine, joking and flirting and prying, but by responding to their quizzes with questions of her own, she got away with revealing little about herself. Max seemed to get a kick out of watching Iris interact with the other men as they teased her about her accent, and made her blush by attributing double meanings to everything she said. After coffee and a few rounds of digestive liqueurs were consumed, and not a drop of any substance in liquid form remained on the table, the men pulled themselves to their feet.

"Let's go, Capo," Max said, hiking up his jeans as he stood. She had never noted the pudginess around his midsection before, probably because he was so tall; but then again, maybe he was just full. Iris had hardly been able to touch her food, and he had done a good job packing away her share as well. It was a pleasure to eat with someone who had a hearty appetite for once and didn't count how many sips of wine she drank.

"But don't you have to talk to the owners?" Iris said, standing.

"About what?" Max said.

"About the shoot tomorrow? Isn't that why they invited you

guys here?"

Max laughed. "Don't worry about it. No one gives a shit. We get our dinner, and they get to go on TV. We'll wing it like we always do."

"I'm sorry, I didn't mean to butt in, it's just that..."

"Everything's cool, Capo," Max said. "Now, we can lose these guys and concentrate on us."

All Iris really wanted to concentrate on at that point was the feel of a soft pillow beneath her head. After all the travel and tension and cocktails and food and talk and wine, she was bone-weary. It was odd that the farther away she was from the comfort of her own bed, the more it appealed to her. That was where Gregorio had been with his tummy full of tripe when she had exchanged good night messages with him from the toilet of the restaurant, before switching her phone off.

Outside, everybody kissed everybody else's cheeks good night; Peppe handed Iris her tote bag, then slid behind the steering wheel of the van. He looked exhausted, too, and in no condition to drive all the way back to Rome, even if Iris had been heartless enough to have Max ask him. Before the subject could be brought up, the van was in motion, and Peppe drove off with the rest of the guys.

"How are we getting back to town?" Iris asked, watching with mixed feelings as the taillights receded into the darkness, together with any illusions that she could still back out of spending the night with Max.

"We're not," Max said. "Come with me." He took her hand and led her down a walkway that passed behind the restaurant to a little marina on the lake, where a small fleet of sleeping sailboats bobbed in the water. It was a weekday, and not yet high season. There was no one else in sight.

"How peaceful this is," Iris said. Though spoken softly, her words were loud enough to send a large bird flapping away. She jumped. "What was that?"

"I'd guess it was a heron," Max said, as they reached a floating dock. "All kinds of birds nest here."

Woozy from the wine, Iris focused on following Max's steps as he walked down the dock. She nearly tripped over him when he stopped suddenly, crouching by the bollard to which one of the sailboats was tied up.

"Is this your boat?" she asked.

Max chuckled. "I wouldn't be caught dead with a boat here. Let's just say it's a little perk that comes with the job." He untied the moorings, then tugged the ropes, pulling the boat closer to the dock. "Hop aboard, Capo!"

"You want to take me out on this little boat? In the dark?"

"A surprise loses its surprise if you ask too many questions. Hop on. You'll see."

If someone had told her that morning that Max was planning to take her on a moonlight cruise, she would have thought it incredibly romantic and adventurous. She loved anything romantic and adventurous, as much as she loved surprises, at least that was what she always said. Maybe she was just out of practice, but honestly, a boat ride was one of the last things she was in the mood for, especially after all she'd had to drink. Especially when the sky was pitch black, without even a sliver of moon.

"Go ahead. Obey your *Capitano*. Or are you one of those *rompipalle* women who puke on boats?"

"Who, me?" She hopped onto the bow, then stepped aside to make room for Max, holding on to the mast for balance. The owner of the boat, whoever that may be, would want her to take her shoes off, but at least she wasn't wearing high heels. Those were ruled out by her practical sense when she had set out that morning and were packed in her bag together with the little black dress she had never managed to change into.

"Just sit down and relax, while I take care of everything," Max said. It wasn't clear where she was to sit; the deck was still soaked with rain. She looked up at the inky, impenetrable sky, then down at the water, just as black and mysterious. She felt so vulnerable surrounded by all that darkness; that was one of the reasons why she never went swimming at night and had always refused to go scuba diving with Gregorio. She hoped to God Max wasn't planning to cruise out of the lake and into the open sea. She also hoped he didn't want to start screwing around out there; she would be terrified of ending up in the water. The boat did have a cabin, but it looked small and was certainly dank. She could see herself throwing up as soon as she went below. Driving to Rome in a van with a drunk was starting to look like the safe bet. Too bad she had passed. Too bad the outboard motor sputtered to life.

"Where are you taking me?" she called to Max.

"It's a surprise, remember?" Max said. "Trust me."

He looked reasonably capable of handling the boat as he maneuvered it out of its slip - but trust him? What did she really know about him? The very characteristics that had attracted her to Max were what worried her now. He had no use for all those rules that suffocated Iris and dictated her daily existence, but what if his recklessness went well beyond his lack of discretion when writing to a married woman at her place of business? What if he turned out to be some kind of psychopath?

"I don't really like the water at night," she said, crouching low on her haunches as they picked up speed.

"It's just a lake. Doesn't get any deeper than ten meters."

Ten meters were plenty enough to drown in. That is, if he didn't rape her first, then chop her body into little pieces, then dump them into the water. Who knew what strange creatures were lurking below, waiting for some fresh flesh to nibble on? If the crew asked about her tomorrow, Max would just say she had left first thing in the morning. She had cancelled her meetings in the city, so no one would call the hotel looking for her. Gregorio would call in the morning, but her phone would be at the bottom of the lake. He would never know what had happened to her after her alleged dinner of *bucatini* with the seminarians. No one knew where she was. Not a soul. She should have told Beatrix of her plans, but she was in Milan, and something had held Iris back from calling. She hadn't wanted to be encouraged or discouraged; she had wanted to follow her instincts and leave the rest up to fate. Except now, a very different fate might await her. A shiver of fear ran up her spine.

"Hey, Capo!" Max shouted over the putt-putting of the engine. The totally natural sound of his voice as he called out his pet name for her calmed her slightly. No, Max did not sound like a psychopath. Then again, the best psychopaths probably never did, did they?

"See those lights over there?" He pointed straight ahead, to a shore where flecks of brightness blinked at her, intermittently hidden by a thicket of trees whose branches swayed in the wind. "That's part of the surprise!"

His voice sounded playful, but Iris remained on guard, a she-cat ready to pounce, her hands gripping the rails, her tote bag clutched between her ankles. It was difficult to discern the distance to their destination, impossible to know how much safer it would be than the boat. From her perch, the place looked rather desolate, even sinister. The cool night air washed over her, and she drank it in, hoping it would clear her head of unsettling fantasies, and sharpen her ability to recognize real danger.

She glanced over her shoulder at Max, who smiled and gave her a thumbs-up. Tilting her head back, she scanned the sky, where she could now pick out a few scattered stars, and a half-moon playing peek-a-boo through the clouds. The briny, marshy smell of the air, though different from the scent of a Ligurian sea breeze, was not altogether unpleasant. The water, though frightfully dark, was calm, and snatches of peace settled over her as they motored along at a slow and steady pace. By the time Max came alongside another floating dock, tied the boat up, and cut the engine, she was breathing more easily. Maybe she would live to see another dawn, after all.

"So, what do you think, Capo?" Max said, pushing his way through the heavy wooden doors. They were the last obstacle to be overcome by the ring of keys that had granted them passage through the massive wrought iron gate and a series of smaller gates in the park surrounding the villa.

Iris peered through the dark interior at the vast marble foyer which appeared unfurnished, save for an immense crystal chandelier hanging at its center. She had not expected anything to happen when Max flipped the switch but, miraculously, the fixture lit up, instantly exposing an ostentation of austerity similar to the style Iris had noted back in town. The chandelier's many bulbs cast fragmented shadows on the high marble walls, which she could now see were lined with a series of glass cabinets and frames displaying what appeared to be documents, military medals, photographs, and other memorabilia.

"What is this place?" she asked. She had not enjoyed the walk through the dense, dripping vegetation of the dimly lit park leading to the entrance, nor did she feel at ease once inside. There was something inherently disconcerting about the setting, the atmosphere, the feeling.

"Actually, it's a museum," Max said. "This is where we're shooting tomorrow morning."

"Are we allowed to be in here?"

"We didn't break in, did we? I have the keys." Max dangled the key ring in front of her face.

"Where did you get them, anyway?"

"From the woman at the town hall. I told her we had to start at first light. So I gave her the choice of either coming to open up at five o'clock, or giving me the keys. She gave me the keys."

"But are you sure it's all right for me to be here, too?" She still felt like a trespasser but was reassured by the fact that other people would be turning up first thing in the morning.

"Relax, Capo. You've gotta stop thinking about rules all the time. They're for idiots who aren't smart enough to think for themselves, not for people like you and me." He took her by the hand and led her over to a wall. "See that?"

Max pointed his finger at a framed black and white photograph portraying a balding man in riding clothes on a white horse, and a dark-haired woman looking up at him in obvious adoration.

"Guess who they are," Max said.

"I don't know." The man looked like a proud landowner, sitting tall in the saddle of his steed, his head held high, his chest and chin thrust out. "The owners of this place?"

"You're half right," Max said. "The woman was Marianna Guidoboni Moldrone. *Contessa* Guidoboni Moldrone. A Roman noblewoman whose family was related to some pope. Not sure which one, so don't ask me."

"And that was her husband, I take it?" Iris said. "The Count?"

"Not quite. He was her lover. One of them, anyway. You want another clue?"

Curiosity whittled away at the discomfort Iris felt at being in this rambling relic of an estate, studying a picture of dead people she didn't know. "Go ahead. Give me another clue. I've never heard of this Contessa before, so I doubt I can figure out who he is. But he does look vaguely familiar."

"Read the dedication. The handwriting is illegible, but there's a typewritten label. See it?"

"Yes. It says, '*Ringrazia ogni giorno devotamente Dio perchè ti ha fatta italiana.*'"

"Do you recognize that phrase?"

"Give devout thanks to God each day, for He has made you Italian," she repeated. It sounded familiar. Like something Isabella may have said to Gregorio or Cinzia or her grandsons (but never to Iris), when she clucked her tongue at events being broadcast on the evening news, especially when they occurred in the United States. "Actually, I think I may have heard someone say that before."

"He's the one who said it first." Max pointed to the man. "The Duce."

"The Duce? You mean Mussolini? Oh, my God, that's him?"

"You got it! Come over here, look at these," Max said, leading her to another group of black and white photographs of the Duce standing by or sitting with the Contessa in a series of old Italian automobiles. "He loved Alfa Romeos. Everyone knew about his passion for cars, but not so many knew about his passion for the Contessa or his little field trips to Sabaudia. She kept it quiet until her death, but the story came out when her heirs discovered she had left the villa and everything inside it to the town, as long as they turned the place into a museum. You can imagine how pissed off her family must have been!"

Iris shook her head; history could be pretty interesting when it was brought down to a more personal level. She had a fact of her own to share with Max. "Mussolini ruined my grandparents," she said.

"In what sense?"

"Well, my Grandma Capotosti had a breakdown when one of her daughters drowned, and the doctor thought it would be a good idea for her to be close to all her relatives. So Grandpa loaded them all aboard a steamer and brought them back over here, to Abruzzo. He had some savings and used the money toward opening a hotel in Avezzano. Albergo Italia. I remember seeing this picture of my Grandma seated in a horse-drawn carriage in front of the sign."

"So the hotel business runs in your blood."

"Unfortunately, they didn't exactly end up like the Hiltons. The story goes that the hotel was taken over as some sort of barracks for Fascist soldiers, only no one ever paid the bill. Grandpa's business went bust, so they sailed over to America a second time, broke but not broken."

"Sounds like you come from pretty tough stock."

"You don't know the half of it. Fortunately, we Capotostis don't get discouraged very easily. But I wish I could get back at Mussolini for what he put my poor grandparents through."

"Well, Capo. You just may have come to the right place."

Max took her hand and led her across the foyer, pointing out a framed letter along the way, signed "Gabriele d'Annunzio," by the hand of the great Italian poet, and dated 1915, in Rome. When they reached the grand staircase, Max unhooked the red velvet rope that cordoned off the entrance and gestured for Iris to pass. She hesitated on seeing a *"Privato"* sign hanging from the rope, but by now she figured it was useless to ask whether they had permission.

"Go on!" Max said. He placed his hands on her buttocks, and pushed her up the stairs, then took the lead again, using the flickering flame of a cigarette lighter he took from his pocket to find his way down a dark corridor, pulling her along until they reached the entrance to another cordoned-off room. He removed the velvet rope and nudged her inside with such unexpected force that she stumbled in the dark, landing on a bed.

"Make yourself comfortable." Max laughed and lit a candle that stood on the bedside table, then took a cigarette from his shirt pocket, and lit that, too. The pungent odor of pot snaked into the room. He offered the joint to Iris, who shook her head. What she craved was a cigarette, but she wouldn't feel right smoking in the bedroom of a museum. She wanted to tell Max not to either but doubted it would do any good.

"Shall I tuck you in and read you a bedtime story?" he said.

"I love stories," Iris said. She would actually enjoy snuggling up with Max as he told her more of his many stories, although this particular bed, covered in a scratchy, musty-smelling brocade fabric, was not very inviting. "But I hate canopy beds. They give me the creeps."

"Well, this is not just any canopy bed. It's the one where your friend the Duce screwed the brains out of the lovely Contessa."

"You're kidding me!" Iris said, jumping to her feet. Fear, in one form or another, had been stalking her all day, straining her, harassing her, scaring her, but now the danger of being caught or killed in the immediate future was retreating. She felt more thrilled than threatened.

"Apparently it was a turn-on, having that De Chirico staring down at them," Max said, pointing to an enormous canvas depicting two faceless mannequins in the shadow of an imposing tower. "The one hanging there's a copy, though," he added. Iris thought that anyone who could feel pleasure looking at that painting must be deeply disturbed.

She looked back at Max, who squinted through the smoke at her. Holding the joint between his teeth, he unbuttoned his shirt. She dropped her eyes to his chest; it was tanned, hairless. He drew on the joint again, then placed it between Iris's lips.

"Take a toke," he said. "You still seem kind of uptight."

The entire situation seemed so surreal. For all the meandering of her imagination, it never would have found its way here, to this villa, to this bedroom. Maybe a toke wouldn't hurt. The smoke burned her throat, but almost instantly, her head seemed to float away, up to the vaulted ceiling.

"Wow," she said. It felt good to not have her mind tell her mouth what to say.

"It's pretty decent weed," Max said. "You feeling good?" Iris nodded. Something in the painting caught her eye; Iris wondered how the figures could move around like that. She opened her mouth to ask Max, and he placed the joint between her lips again. She took another hit. That should keep her head up in the ceiling for a while, so the rest of her could do what it wanted. Like run her hands over his Max's bare chest, and slide the shirt from his shoulders, for starters.

Max spit onto his thumb and index finger, used them to snuff out the joint. He stood facing her, tracing a line with his damp finger down the middle of her forehead, along the slope of her nose, over her lips. Her skin tingled beneath his touch as he parted her lips with his finger, then placed his mouth over hers. He grabbed her buttocks with both hands, pulled her body close to his. Her tongue was hungry for his, her hands ran over his bare chest, pushed his open shirt from his shoulders, helped him shake his arms free from the sleeves and throw the shirt to the floor. She moaned when Max pulled away from her and looked into her eyes with an intensity that made her shiver. His stare told her he would probe every inch of her body, and still want more. He would get inside her, possess her body, penetrate her heart, bare her soul. Pushing down on her shoulders, Max made her sit on the bed. He remained standing in front of her, his legs slightly parted.

"You do the rest," he said to her, dropping his arms to his sides.

Seeing him standing there in this room where they shouldn't be, waiting for her to strip his pants off while she was still fully dressed, Iris experienced a type arousal she had never felt before. She was crossing new boundaries, entering a new territory where neither Gregorio's scientifically proven preliminaries nor Claudio's well-rehearsed finesse had ever had the power to take her.

She reached out and unbuttoned his fly. His stomach muscles twitched as she lowered the zipper slowly, then slid the worn denim down over his hips, to his knees. Max kicked off his shoes and let Iris free his legs of the jeans. His underwear was tight-fitting, unlike the baggy boxer shorts worn by the only two other men she had ever seen take their pants off. Max placed a hand behind Iris's head and pulled it toward his crotch. He was hot and hard and full of that smell she had picked up the first time she stood near him.

"What were you doing in church?" he asked her, his voice low.

Iris tilted her face up to him. "What?"

"In church, when you were waiting for me," he said, staring down at her.

She heard the voices of those breast-beating old ladies. *Mea culpa, mea culpa.*

"Nothing, I ..." He pushed her head against him, forced the words back into her mouth with the penis still stuffed inside his underwear.

"Did you pray?" He relaxed his hold on her head to let her speak.

"I was only inside a minute."

White-haired heads snapped around to look at her, their mouths moving with words she could not hear.

"Did you pray?" he repeated, in a louder voice. He grabbed a fistful of her hair, pulled her head back so she would be forced to look up at him. The light of the votive candle flickered on his face.

"Yes, I prayed."

Mother Mary came to her in a statue, whispered something she couldn't quite hear, then disappeared.

"I knew it. You should always pray." Still holding her hair with one hand, he slid his underwear down with the other. He released his erection, shoved it into her mouth. Iris gagged. He pulled her head back by the hair again and took his penis in his free hand. "Will you pray for me?" he said.

"What?"

"Next time you go to church, will you pray for me, too?" He thrust himself at her, moving his hips, holding his penis over her upturned face.

"Yes, Max," she whispered. Her throat was tight, her heart racing.

"Somebody has to save me," he said, panting, thrusting. "Are you gonna save me?" he cried. He was getting close.

"Yes, I'll save you!" Iris dug her nails into his thighs.

Max's scream echoed through the deserted villa, as a spasm shook his body. When he released his hold on her, Iris stood up, trembling with confusion, wet with arousal. Max pulled her close, rubbing his liquid into her face and hair.

"Take your clothes off," he said.

She undressed and stood before him in the flickering candlelight. She had never felt so exposed in her nudity, so consumed by desire. Max ran his fingers over her girlish breasts and pointed nipples, down her flat belly, along the curves of her full hips, then lowered himself to his knees before her naked body, and toyed with her need until she, too, begged to be saved.

2. LILY

Nick was the owner and chief engineer at Black Rose Studio. He spent ten minutes on the phone with Lily, asking her what kind of music she liked to sing and patiently explained the recording, mixing, mastering, and duplication process to her.

"I tell you what," said Nick. "I have a soft spot for new artists. If you can get down here this afternoon, I have a nice blues band coming in. I let them use the space to rehearse. If you guys hit it off, maybe they would be willing to accompany you on your demo. Can you come by around two?"

Black Rose Studio was newer, cleaner and sleeker than Owen's studio. The walls were painted a dark gray, with light gray trim around the doorways. With no windows to the outside, the reception area was dark, but the track lighting from the ceiling gave the room a subdued, sophisticated feel. The reception desk was occupied by a stylishly dressed woman of about twenty-five, who greeted Lily as she entered.

"Good afternoon! Welcome to Black Rose Studio." The woman's face seemed to get swallowed up in her enthusiastic smile.

"Hi," said Lily. She was impressed with herself for getting back into an old pair of jeans, but as she looked down at what she referred to as her "rock star" boots, she wished she had taken the time to at least remove the scuffs. With any luck, they wouldn't bother paying attention to her feet.

"How may I help you?"

"I'm here to see Nick. My name is Lily. Lily Diotallevi."

The woman picked up the receiver of the telephone and pushed a button with a long red fingernail.

"Lily Ditelli to see you."

"Diotallevi," said Lily.

"Dovtelli," the woman said into the headset.

She led Lily down a long hall that was adorned with photos of people posing with musical instruments, framed handwritten letters, and one gold record.

"Welcome, welcome," said Nick, extending his hand to Lily. "Have a seat - we're just finishing up here."

Nick was about sixty-five years old, with a scraggly white beard and a few lonely wisps of hair floating just above his scalp, like a cloud. Cirrus. Fair weather cloud. It was a good sign. He sat in a large black leather chair on wheels - no doubt purchased at La Casa Bella, from Joe - and glided himself back and forth along the long mixing board in front of him. He reached over his protruding belly to adjust the levers, which Owen had taught her were actually called faders, as the band on the other side of the glass cranked out their version of "The Things I Used to Do." Another good sign.

When the song was over, Nick flipped a switch on the microphone in front of him. "Guys - hey guys - " he called as his voice was piped into the booth. "This pretty lady here is Lily, and she'd like to record a vocal demo one of these days. I thought maybe you could help out. Her husband is the one who gave me a great deal on that fine leather couch you guys are always crashing on."

The musicians all waved and shouted hello. One of the guitar players, who Lily assumed was the leader, leaned into his mic and said, "C'mon in, Lily - let's play around a little."

Shit. What? Right now? She could hear Uncle Alfred, coaching her when he had first put her in front of an audience at The Luau restaurant. "It's no big deal - anyone can sing. You just have fun, keep the beat, and no one even notices if you do it right or not. It's music, not brain surgery. You're supposed to have a good time."

"So what song do you want to record?" The guitar player placed his pick between his front teeth and extended his hand toward Lily. "I'm Tommy, by the way."

"Hi, Tommy. Well, I was thinking of this song I have from church." She was sure she sounded like Laura Ingalls Wilder from *Little House on the Prairie.* "I didn't know we were going to work on it today. I don't have sheet music - just the lyrics and the chords, and a tape of me singing it at Easter Vigil."

The drummer and keyboardist exchanged smirks.

Tommy looked up at Nick, who shrugged.

"Well, boys, it looks like we're doing a church song."

Lily wanted to explain to them that it wasn't really a church song - like it wasn't the "Ave Maria" or "The Lord's Prayer" or anything like that. She knew she could explain what it wasn't, but she had no idea how to explain what it was.

"Tell you what," said Tommy. "I'll have Nick pop this tape into the deck, and you can start singing along while we get a feel for it, OK? Then, when we're all synched up, I'll have Nick pull the tape, and you just keep going. We'll catch on and see what we end up with - how would that be?"

"OK." Lily felt drunk with exhilaration and surprise, anchored to the floor only by the heaviness of her anxiety.

Lily slipped the headphones on and adjusted the mic stand. She was grateful for the meager experience that Owen had given her; maybe it would help prevent her from looking like a complete moron.

As she sang along with the recording, Lily was comforted by the waves of Jeffrey's familiar piano accompaniment. At the second verse, Nick pulled the recording out, and the band began to improvise. Tommy played an achingly sweet guitar line, and then George came in with a soulful drum beat, followed soon after by the tinkling of the keyboard and the gentle pulse of the bass guitar. She was singing, and they were all there following her - growing more dynamic as she did, pulling back when she backed off. The musicians supported her, and she felt safe in their care as they played with the spaces between her words, filling them with flourishes of melody and percussion, thrilling her and lifting her out of her inhibitions.

Lily's voice gained an autonomy of sorts, continuing under a power and force of its own, without her conscious thought directing it. When she sang in church, she was always so careful not to call too much attention to herself. The music was about God, not about her. But here, it was about her and the song, and this was her chance to show this somewhat reluctant troupe of Samaritans - and herself - that she was talented, and serious, and in charge - as far as any of them knew, anyway.

Lily abandoned her tentative approach to the higher notes in favor of boldness and risk, and she hit every one of them with strength and clarity. When the song lingered in the lower registers that she loved so much, she played with her breath, sometimes releasing it into the note, making the tone fuzzy and warm, and at other times, holding her breath back, letting it slowly wind out, sustaining the notes, stretching them thinly across the room. On the final verse, she improvised the vocal line, the way Uncle Alfred had taught her to do on the guitar when they played blues. As the song ended, Lily's voice trailed off to a whisper, the final keyboard chord hung in the air, the drumbeat tumbled away, and the studio dropped into complete silence. The band erupted into applause.

"Boy, you nailed that," said Nick, from the control room.

"No shit," said Tommy. "Hey, Nick - any chance you were rolling tape on that?"

"No, man," said Nick. "I thought you guys were just going to mess around a little. Then I guess I just got caught up in it."

"Too bad," said Tommy. "I gotta say, Lily. That didn't sound like any song I ever heard in church - that was a freakin' soaring ballad." He shook his head. "Man!"

Lily thought she should say something in return. Tell them how great they sounded, make a semi-intelligent remark about their ability to come together cohesively so quickly on a song they hadn't even heard of fifteen minutes earlier. But she couldn't form the words. She didn't want to soil the sanctity of the moment with ill-formed amateur judgments.

"What do you say, guys?" said Nick. "Wanna back her up?"

"Absolutely," said Tommy. "We have a lot going on for the rest of the summer, what with all our gigs, but we could do this in a couple months - can you check in with us after Labor Day? That'll give us some time to work on punching it up a bit."

"Yeah, sure," said Lily. She could use the time to rehearse

anyway. "If you're sure you don't mind. I don't want to take advantage."

"Are you kidding?" said Tommy. "It's an honor to work with someone as talented as you." He smiled and winked. "Just don't forget us little people when you get to the top."

Lily drove home feeling warm, happy, disassociated from the past, excited about being alive. It reminded her of the way she felt the first time she and Iris smoked pot in high school. She wondered what Iris was doing now. Lily wanted to share this exciting news with her. It would be a chance to show Iris that she was not just some boring old housewife. She might not be as sophisticated as Iris, or as wealthy. But she could sing. That had to be worth something.

Lily spent the summer busy with the boys and adequately distracted by anticipation, which took enough of the pressure off to enable her to slip back into the mechanisms that allowed her to cope with Joe's behavior. She could put up with just about anything as long as she had the demo to look forward to - and this certainly was not the time to rock the boat. As she worked with her song, she became sensitive to how religious the lyrics sounded, and embarrassed at the recurring memory of Tommy saying, "Boys, it looks like we're doing a church song!" As it was, the song was nice for Easter, but Lily wanted to give the tune more of a contemporary feel, so she drafted a modification to the lyrics that came to her one afternoon, and she emailed them off to Jeffrey with a request to get permission from the songwriter to record the demo and to modify the lyrics.

In his reply, Jeffrey wrote:

Dear Lily, Jackson said he's cool with you recording the song as a demo and he said he loves what you did with the lyric - says it's even better than the original. He wants a copy of it when you're done - so do I!
Peace,
Jeffrey

42

September arrived, Pierce entered school full-time, and Lily was ready to embark on a new adventure of her own. She contacted Tommy as promised and they booked a session.

When Lily's recording date arrived, Joe announced, "I'm coming with you."

"What?" Lily said, alarmed. "Why?" Lily had not ever imagined Joe would want to go with her, and the prospect caused her to tremble. She and Donna had the whole thing planned out. Donna would come with her so Joe wouldn't be uncomfortable and to provide Lily moral support.

"I'm coming to support you," Joe said, slamming the red toolbox onto the floor. "Jesus Christ, how did you let Pierce break this door handle again, anyway?"

"He likes to slam things." Lily raised her brow. "And it's been broken forever. I keep fudging it fixed, and he keeps breaking it again. When you try to fix it, you're only delaying the inevitable; it needs to be replaced. Joe, I was counting on you to watch the boys for me when I went to the studio. That's really what I need from you."

"Donna's gonna watch 'em. I just went over there and set it up. You said you wanted me to be supportive. I got you a studio, and I agree to come with you." He turned the screwdriver with a grunt. "Now you're telling me you don't want me there? You don't even know what you want. Why don't you want me there? What is it that you don't want me to see?" Joe was leaning his weight into the screwdriver as he turned it over and over, the screw endlessly spinning in place.

"I think it's stripped," said Lily, fighting her own confusion. She did ask him for his support. But she did not want him to see her singing. "I do want your support, Joe - and I appreciate everything you're doing to help, but I really need to know that the boys are home with you so I can relax and not be distracted during my session."

"Your 'session'? Who do you think you are, Cher? 'My session'... Jesus Christ." The screwdriver slipped, catching Joe's finger and taking a chunk of skin with it. "Fuck!" he shouted. "Maybe if you were spending as much time watching your children as you do working on that fucking demo, I wouldn't be spending my day off fixing doors!"

Lily and Joe dropped the boys off with Donna, and as though he knew they harbored a secret, Joe would not leave the two women alone together. Lily hoped the panic in her own eyes was as evident as the helplessness in Donna's.

"God has this situation in hand," whispered Donna, kissing Lily on the cheek.

Lily was grateful that at least Joe had agreed to take separate cars to the studio. "I have no idea how long this is going to take," Lily told him. "And this way, if you need to leave for any reason, you won't get stuck driving all the way out there to pick me up again."

Lily used the ride over to warm up her voice and to try and settle her frazzled nerves. "I sure hope you know what you're doing," she prayed.

Lily said hello to Nick as he and Joe shook hands.

"Wow, the place looks great," said Joe. "Are you happy with your room design?" Joe asked him.

"It's great, just great. Love it - thanks again for all your help."

"My pleasure - and thanks for helping my wife out with this little project."

"Not at all - she's got a great voice. She should really do something with it."

"She does," said Joe, reaching down to scratch his crotch. "You should hear how she screams at home." Nick chuckled nervously, and Lily escaped into the recording booth where the band was setting up.

"Hey, Lily!" called Tommy. "Good to see you! How are the pipes?"

"They're fine," Lily replied without looking up.

Lily looked back through the glass as she distributed the updated lyric sheet to everyone, and it was evident from the look on Joe's face that the microphone between the two rooms was open. She would have to be very careful not to be too friendly with the band.

Joe burst into the room, stalked by a cloud of English Leather cologne. He stepped between Tommy and Lily, grabbed Tommy's hand and shook it vigorously.

"I'm Joe, Lily's husband."

"Nice to meet you," Tommy replied, looking past him to catch Lily's eye. Lily looked away.

"I'm here to support her, you know, let her get this out of her system and whatnot."

"Cool... cool," said Tommy. He looked back and forth between Lily and Joe as if trying to imagine them together but being wholly unable to come up with a believable image.

"You can take a seat right in the control booth with Nick," Tommy said to Joe. "We've just finished putting a rough mix together, so we'll be leaving Lily in here to do her thing."

"I'm staying in here with her," said Joe.

Tommy looked at Lily. Lily averted her gaze, unsure of what to say or do, not wanting to make Joe angry in front of everyone.

"Oh. Well, OK. I guess you can have a seat, then."

Joe dragged a chair to a spot along the same wall as the control booth window, sitting down directly across from where Lily's microphone was set up, and outside the line of sight from the control booth. He adjusted the bloody bandage on his finger, sniffed, and crossed his arms over his chest.

The band members and Nick situated themselves behind the glass of the control room. They were talking among themselves. The drummer laughed. Lily felt like an exhibit at the nature museum, where all the children were gathered around to see what happens when you put a rat in the snake den.

Nick leaned into the microphone in the control booth and said, "OK, Lily - go ahead and put the 'phones on, and we'll run through a few bars just to get a sound check."

Lily's mouth was dry, and her tongue felt sticky. She took a sip of water from the glass on the music stand, then adjusted the headphones. The click-click of drumsticks counted off four beats, then four more, and Lily glanced over at Joe, who was glancing at his watch.

"That was your cue, there," Nick said.

"Oh - sorry... sorry... Can we start over?"

"From the top," said Nick.

Lily squeezed her eyes closed, trying to recall the way she'd felt the first time she was here, the way she would be feeling right now if Joe were not sitting over in the corner, legs crossed, right foot bobbing up and down arrhythmically, intent on getting home in time for kick-off, tip-off, or face-off - a problem she'd hoped they'd avoided by driving separate cars. She realized now that he had no intention of leaving her here alone.

"OK, OK," said Nick after she finished. "That's our warm up. Let's take it from the top. Lily, do you need anything? More water?"

"No," said Lily. "I'm OK." It helped for her to think of the first pass as a warm-up. Sure. Of course. No one just walks into the studio and gets it on the first try.

The music began a second time.

"When you look at me tell me, what do you see?

Would you be surprised to learn, that in my heart desire burns?"

Nick interrupted before Lily could sing another line. "I think you've got a little bubble in your throat," he said. "Take a drink maybe."

"OK," said Lily. She picked up the glass and took another sip. Joe rolled his eyes. "Can we try it again - from the top?"

"Absolutely," said Nick. "From the top."

Lily took a deep breath and closed her eyes, trying to pretend that Joe wasn't there. But even then, she could smell him. She could feel him. And she could hear him in her voice as she opened her mouth to sing.

"When you look at me, tell me what do you see?

Would you be surprised to learn, that in my heart desire burns?

If you look inside my soul, let go of all you think you know

You'll find that I'm a lot like you,

Just someone who hopes their dreams come true."

Lily opened her eyes when she heard Joe clear his throat. He checked his watch, then shifted his body in the chair.

Nick cut in. "I think you missed your entrance on that last line,

46

sweetie."

Joe straightened his body and craned his neck to look into the control booth. Was Nick crazy calling her "sweetie"? Nick looked at Joe, and then at Lily. She looked away.

"Lily," said Nick. "Let's take it from 'you'll find that I'm a lot like you,' – we'll feed you the line before so you can sing along and pick up the same tone and feeling, OK?"

"You got it," said Lily. She tried to sound professional and carefree, but her anxiety and embarrassment mounted with each take.

Lily struggled through the song three more times, stopping and starting, taking instructions from Nick and from the band members who intermittently shared tips for how Lily could relax and let go. Each suggestion was met with a grunt or a sigh, or a facial expression by Joe that only Lily was witness to, each one making her more nervous and self-conscious.

They ran through the song a total of five times, and by the final time, Lily still had not been able to capture the easy soulfulness she'd felt the first time she met Nick and Tommy, or when she sang it at Owen's studio – or when she sang it in church. No matter what she tried, that feeling of bliss was usurped by an arid self-consciousness. By the time they added a few punches to correct a flat note here and an errant breath sound there, Lily was exhausted.

"I think we have enough here to put together the foundation," Nick said over the microphone. "We'd better stop for now."

Lily struggled to tame the lump in her throat. She doled out quick "thank yous" to each of the band members, and while Joe and Nick settled the bill, she grabbed her purse, stuck a Merit between her lips and slipped out the front door. The cool evening air did little to soothe her irritation. She lit her cigarette, took a deep drag, and walked around to the side of the building.

"God, I am just so pissed!" she called out into the night air. "And mortified. So embarrassed..." She held her hands over her face, the lit cigarette between her fingers, hoping to muffle a scream.

"You coulda used a little bit of that in there," said George, the band's drummer.

"Shit!" said Lily. "I didn't even see you there. You scared the crap out of me."

"I'd say you're an easy scare tonight."

Lily tossed her purse onto the asphalt and sat down on the ground, leaning her body up against the building. The rough brick felt good against her back. Solid.

"Boy, I really screwed that up."

"You?"

"I *was* the one singing - if that's what you want to call it."

"What was your old man doing in there, anyway?"

Lily looked up at George. "Helping."

"No shit?" George ran his fingers through his thick black curls, blew a stream of smoke overhead, then tossed his cigarette butt onto the ground and crushed it with the tip of his boot. "Does he help you a lot?"

"Yes," Lily said. "He's quite helpful."

"That's a bitch."

"Will you tell the others I'm really sorry?"

"You don't need to apologize to us. It was your gig."

It was her gig. And now it was over. Lily ground her cigarette under the heel of her shoe, and as she moved to get up, George extended his arm out to her. She grabbed his wrist, and he pulled her up just as Joe came around the corner.

"There you are honey," he said sweetly. "I've been looking all over for you. I paid your bill, and then I looked around and I said, 'Where the hell's my wife?'"

"I just needed a smoke." Lily brushed the dirt from her behind with her hand.

Joe walked over and put his arm around Lily. "We better get home. Those sons of ours are probably driving Donna nuts." Joe steered Lily around toward the parking lot, sliding his hand down her back to rest on her buttocks, looking back over his shoulder toward George as they walked away.

As soon as they were out of sight, Lily shoved Joe away from her side.

"What's up your ass?" he asked.

"You are, OK? You are! You had to go and ruin this for me, didn't you? You couldn't just let me have this one thing. You have no idea... "

"What are you talking about?"

"I - you made me nervous by being here, by sitting in that chair, staring at me. I screwed up, I did an awful job, I am so ashamed! And pissed!"

"Hey - if you messed it up, don't go blaming me. I did everything I could to support you. Didn't I set this whole thing up for you? Didn't I come here with you, and sit with you, and pay for the whole thing?"

"Yes," said Lily. "Yes, you did."

"It's not my fault if you don't have what it takes, Lil. I know that's hard to hear right now, but I'm the only one who's going to tell you the truth because I'm the only one who loves you and doesn't want to see you get hurt. What do they care, anyway? What reason do any of them have to be honest with you?"

"They said I was good and they wanted to help me."

"Lil, Nick was doing me a favor because I saved him a shitload of money on his new place. Those other guys? They just want to get in your pants; that's how musicians are."

"That's not true," said Lily. "It's just not," she said weakly, wondering who she was trying to convince.

"Well, it's over now," said Joe. "At least you gave it a shot, right? Now you can put it behind you and focus on being a wife and mother again."

The idea of having life go back to what it was terrified her. Fear and frustration and regret lingered there.

"Don't feel bad, Lil. I'll be right here with you, no matter what. I promise."

Lily's gut lurched. Joe took her into his arms, and she sobbed into his T-shirt. Because she needed to cry and he was the only one there.

"So let's go get the boys and put them in bed." Joe glanced at his watch. "Then maybe you and me can mess around in between quarters. Before you know it, things will be back to normal."

Lily wiped her eyes with her fingertips and ran her sleeve across her nose. She looked up at Joe - Joe, who was always there no matter what she did or where she turned; Joe, who always knew right from wrong without question and who masterfully traded one for the other as it suited him; Joe, who told Lily where her world began, what it contained, and where it ended. Solid, unmovable Joe. Anger bubbled up from deep inside Lily. Memories and images of all the times Joe had belittled her, lied to her, made her feel inadequate, and made her doubt her own sanity, gathered up into a hot ball of indignation. All the anger that she had stuffed down over the years came looking for a way out, now ignited by sparks of humiliation and disappointment.

Lily sniffed, looked deeply into his eyes and whispered, "Fuck. Normal."

Joe pushed Lily away and held her by the shoulders at arm's length. "What did you just say to me?"

"Fuck," said Lily, placing emphasis on the k. "Normal. And while you're at it, fuck you!"

Lily stomped over to her car, got in, slammed the door, and screeched out of the parking lot, leaving rubber tire marks behind her. Joe got into his car and followed. Tears streamed down Lily's face as she recalled take after take, her throat closed up like a vise, her body shaking, the band exchanging quizzical looks behind the glass. She stopped at a red light and yelped as her car lurched forward toward the intersection of oncoming traffic. She looked up into the rearview mirror, to see Joe pushing her with his car from behind. Her entire body clenched as she gripped the steering wheel, locked her elbows, and drove her foot into the brake pedal. The light turned green, but Lily was frozen in place. *Honk, honk!* cars in line behind her wailed impatiently. Lily punched the accelerator, and her car lurched forward with a squeal. Joe zoomed up quickly behind her, the grill of his car too close to be viewed in her mirrors. *Boom!* Again he hit her from behind, causing her to swerve out of her lane.

"Son of a bitch!" she cried. "Cut it out!" she called as she pounded on the accelerator in an attempt to create distance between her rear bumper and Joe's grill. But Joe came up behind her just as quickly and bumped her again, this time with more force.

"Hey, buddy!" A man shouted out his window. "What are you trying to do, get someone killed?"

"Jesus!" cried Lily. "Are you insane?" Joe was so close behind her that she could clearly see his face in the rearview mirror. His eyes were vacant, and he wore the hint of a smile.

Lily sped up again. Joe matched her speed, jarred her from behind again, causing Lily's car to swerve in its lane, taking her right tires up onto the curb. She had to get away from traffic before she ended up hitting someone.

An expert at beating the clock to get home by whatever curfew Joe had set for her, Lily knew how to use the secondary roads to get anywhere in town in fifteen minutes. She took a right turn into a system of side streets that she used when she was late coming home from church. Joe followed her. She wound through the maze of streets, with Joe slamming her bumper whenever she slowed down to take a corner. When Lily noticed two young girls riding bikes in the road, she headed back out toward the main thoroughfare. She didn't even know where she was trying to get to - she certainly couldn't go home; Joe was out of his mind. She decided to drive to Violet's house, hoping that Todd would be home and that Joe would be too embarrassed to act out in front of him. Once Joe calmed down, Lily would go to Donna's and figure out what to do from there.

Joe's minivan bore down on Lily. She stopped at a stop sign, and frantically searched for an accommodating break in the stream of traffic, but there was none. She wondered if Joe would follow her into the unbroken line of cars on the thoroughfare. It was dangerous, but maybe she could find a tiny opening for her small car. If he pursued her in his van, he would be the one to get t-boned by one of the vehicles whizzing past. No one would blame her - he was chasing her after all. All she was doing was trying to get away. She found herself wondering how fast the traffic was moving and if the impact would be enough to kill him. One thing was certain -

she didn't need him to get injured or paralyzed, God forbid. Then she would never be free. At that moment, Joe came up behind her again and ran into her, forcing her out into the road. Lily yelped, then slammed the accelerator to the floor, to get out of the way of a red pick-up truck that was headed straight for her driver's side door. Flashing lights erupted in her rearview mirror, and she swerved as she slammed on the brakes with a screech and pulled over to the shoulder. The police car turned down the side street, blocking Joe's way.

Lily watched in her mirror as the policeman walked over to Joe's window, shined his flashlight onto Joe's face, and then swept the car with the light beam. The two men exchanged a few words, and then the policeman headed toward Lily.

Lily's heart pounded, its rhythm reverberating in her head. *Oh, shit - I am so screwed. Can this night get any worse? Can my life get any worse?*

She rolled down her window. "Good evening, officer."

"License and registration, please," said the policeman.

Lily leaned over and retrieved a leatherette portfolio from the glove compartment.

"Do you know why I stopped you?" said the policeman.

"Because I cut into traffic?" Lily swallowed, hoping to ease the burning in the back of her throat. "Or was it because I was speeding back there?"

The policeman read Lily's registration by the light of his flashlight. "Is that your husband back there, in that van?"

"Yes, sir."

"I'm going to go take care of him, and then I want you to follow me, understand?"

"Yes, sir."

The policeman walked back to Joe's window, scribbled something on a pad of paper, they talked briefly, and then Joe turned his car around and slowly drove away. The policeman drove past Lily and signaled her to follow. Lily had never been "taken in" before; she knew she should be terrified, but she moved as though possessed by an alternate self, one who was much more composed than she. *I can do all things through Christ, which strengthens me.* Either it was the power of the Spirit or the dullness of shock. She didn't care what was causing it, as long as she didn't have to feel what was happening to her now.

Once at the police station, the policeman offered Lily a cup of tea, then escorted her to a side chair at his desk.

"Mrs. Diotallevi, I'm Officer Schickler. I'm going to ask you a question, and I want you to be honest with me, OK?"

"OK," said Lily. Was he going to ask for a confession? What was it that he thought she'd done?

"Does your husband hit you?"

"No," Lily replied, relieved that she was not being accused of anything. After a pause, she added, "He does throw things."

"Like what?"

"Ice cubes. Shoes sometimes." Lily blew on the hot tea and bobbed the bag gently up and down. "Books."

"Does he throw them at you?"

"Sometimes. He's got a good arm, but I'm quick." Lily giggled nervously.

Officer Schickler did not smile or laugh. He looked intently into Lily's eyes. "Are you waiting for him to kill you?"

Lily opened her mouth, but she didn't know what to say.

"'Cause that's what comes next, you know. Throwing things, yelling, playing a little chicken with your car - do you have any idea how much danger you're in? He's a time bomb."

"He is?"

"I've seen it a hundred times. I'm going to have you speak to someone here, and she is going to explain your options to you."

"My options?" Lily didn't want options. This was getting too scary. She had a longing to go home but was suddenly aware that she wasn't sure what was so great about being there, especially tonight.

Officer Schickler left, and Lily rummaged through her purse for a stick of gum. She picked through the trash at the bottom, stopping to toss assorted papers, wrappers, and tissues into the aluminum garbage can next to the chair. She finally found a stick of gum, half-wrapped and peppered with flecks of tobacco. She wiped it off and popped it into her mouth. A pair of navy blue patent leather pumps appeared in Lily's view. Lily's gaze followed the legs up to a stocky white-haired woman who extended her hand to Lily.

"I'm Marilyn," she said. "I'm with the Rochester Police Department's Victims Assistance Program, and I'm also the Director of Intake at the battered women's shelter."

Victim? Battered? "I'm not sure what I'm doing here," said Lily, "but I'm fine, really. Can I go now?"

"You can go anytime you want," said Marilyn, "but if you can spare just five more minutes, I'd like to show you something." She pulled a sheet of white paper out of her briefcase and laid it on the desk, turning it so Lily could read what was written there. Across the top were the words, "Power and Control Wheel."

"Have you seen this before?" Marilyn asked.

"Uh... no, I don't think so." Lily clutched her purse to her chest.

"Each spoke of the wheel depicted here represents abusive behavior. I'd like you to review this, and just take stock of how many of these behaviors your husband exhibits."

Lily read through the wheel. "Using isolation: Controlling what you do and where you go; limits your outside involvement. Using economy abuse: Preventing you from getting a job, making you ask for money. Using emotional abuse: Putting you down, making you feel bad about yourself, calling you names."

Spoke after spoke, round and round she went, like an unwilling contestant in a twisted game show. *Yes, yes, yes - he does that, and he does that - yes, that too.*

She had to stop reading, as the words on the page became blurred through tears.

"How many of these things does your husband do on a regular basis?" Marilyn asked the question with detachment similar to that of the man at the deli counter when he asked Lily how many slices of turkey she wanted.

Lily wiped her eyes with the tissue Marilyn offered. "All of them." She cleared her throat. "All of them."

"Your husband broke the law tonight, Mrs. Diotallevi."

"Please call me Lily."

"Officer Schickler ticketed him for the traffic violation, and there's a new law that will allow us to press charges on your behalf, but you'll have to sign a complaint to enable us to do that."

"Press charges? Wouldn't he get into serious trouble?"

"He's already in serious trouble, Mrs. Diotallevi. And from the way you've described his behavior, he is on the fast track to something much worse if someone doesn't stop him now."

Lily blew her nose.

"What would happen if I did that? Would he be arrested or something?"

"There would be a hearing. In Family Court. Most likely, you would be awarded an Order of Protection, and he would have to get court-mandated counseling. There's an anger management class the judge will probably send him to."

Anger management sounded good. It would almost be like doing him a favor or something.

"How does an Order of Protection work, exactly?"

"It's a court order, signed by a judge, stipulating that your husband cannot come within fifty feet of you. If he does, all you have to do is call nine-one-one or come in here and file a complaint. He would be arrested, no questions asked."

"How long is it good for?"

"It's usually six months, sometimes longer. Let me ask you this. In light of what happened tonight, do you feel safe going home now and being alone with him?"

"Well, I'll have my kids..."

"Even worse - would they feel safe?"

Lily recalled the look in Joe's eyes when she saw him in her rearview mirror. She remembered the way his rage erupted when she first brought up recording the demo, how it was like he couldn't even hear what she was saying. She thought of the way he attacked her tree the morning after he came to hear her sing at the Easter vigil. She remembered the wild look in his eyes, his violent determination.

"No," said Lily. "I would not feel safe tonight."

"Then what are you waiting for? I've seen women in your position who tell themselves that they will wait until next time. Some of them don't get a next time. If they're lucky, they end up in the hospital, or at the shelter. This is your chance if you want to minimize the trauma to yourself and your children. We'll help you."

"What do I do about my kids?"

"Where are they now?"

"They were with my next-door neighbor, but I'm sure my husband has picked them up by now." Terror swept through her body. He wouldn't hurt the boys, would he? He wouldn't punish them for her actions. Would he?

"Officer Schickler will follow you home, and when he gets there, he will ask your husband to collect a few things for the night, and he'll wait and then he'll escort him out of the house and present him with a temporary order to stay away from you until after the Family Court hearing."

"It seems so harsh," Lily said.

"Wouldn't you say that having your husband intentionally rear-end you into traffic is harsh as well?"

Lily caught a glimpse of what it must look like to Marilyn. But it's just Joe, after all. The two women sat in silence. Arrest, Family Court, Order of Protection. All she'd wanted to do was sing. How the hell did she get here? Lily considered her other choices. Go home? What else was there? Even if Joe was calmed by the time she arrived, he would grill her about what had happened here, and there would be another endless sleepless night of tortuous argument ahead. She couldn't bear another night of that. She needed a little space, a little time to think. None of this even seemed real.

Lily looked up as Officer Schickler escorted a woman down the hall, just on the other side of the glass from where Lily sat. Her skin was the color of caramel, except around her eyes, which was blue and purple. Her lower lip was split down the center, and a trickle of blood had dried upon her chin. Her arms were behind her back. Time slowed as her gaze locked with Lily's. Lily wondered how many times the woman had been here before, how many chances she'd had. The woman closed her eyes and hung her head, as she was escorted out of sight.

I'm not like her.

Marilyn held a pen out to Lily. "You still have choices, Lily. She doesn't."

Lily read over the Power and Control Wheel again. She thought of the boys, of Pierce taking a stance between Lily and Joe as they screamed, his only regard for an end to the fighting. She thought of the dark cars that continued to crawl by the house at night, of the ringing phone, she unable to answer for fear of encountering yet another bill collector. She thought of Owen, of James, of George the drummer. She thought about what tomorrow might be like if she just got up and went home.

"What do I have to do?" Lily asked.

"Fill this out," said Marilyn, placing a blank form in front of her.

Lily tossed her tissue into the garbage pail and positioned the tip of the pen next to the line that read, "Enter victim name here."

3. IRIS

The hands she clasped were still warm, the fingers supple. Maybe if she just stayed there like that, holding them real tight, she could stave off the cold, stop the stiffness from setting in. But no, death was greedy; it would suck the warmth from the flesh, the way it froze the features on the face. The face she could no longer recognize. Grief came in great, swelling waves, washing over her, dragging her down to where it was deep and dark, drowning her in a sea of blank, dead faces.

"Who are you?" she cried. *"Who are you?"*

Iris was drenched in sweat, her cheeks wet with tears. Gregorio was sitting next to her in his striped pajamas, gently jostling her shoulder, softly slapping her face. "Wake up, *Piccolina*," he said. "Don't worry; I'm here with you."

Iris blinked her eyes with the confusion of a newborn, unsure of which world she belonged in. Ragged sobs pumped air in and out of her lungs as the images blurred and faded from her waking mind. Dreams mixed with reality, relief with despair.

"You were having another bad dream," Gregorio said, pushing her hair back from her damp brow. "Here, drink this." He took a glass of water from the bedside table and handed it to her.

Like a wave washing over a rock, one dimension slipped away, and another remained: the solid, the real, the immovable. She blinked again, in the dim light of the reading lamp. Gregorio was still there, and so was their bed, and their home. She gulped the water down. *"Piano, Piccolina, piano,"* Gregorio said, taking the glass away from her.

"There was a dead man, but I couldn't see his face," she whispered, knowing the few words would suffice as an explanation. Her husband would not encourage her to share the details of the dream, he never did. No one was really interested in anyone else's dreams anyway, and no one's dreams meant anything to anyone else.

"We can't go on like this, *Piccolina*," he sighed, his hands smoothing his pajama top to straighten out the stripes. "We haven't slept through the night in months." He rose from the bed, put on his slippers, and shuffled out of the room. He was right. She couldn't go on this way, dreading her dreams and dreaming of dread.

Ever since sleeping with Max that night in Sabaudia, Iris found herself with two uninvited bedfellows: the insomnia that snatched away her sleep like a blanket too skimpy to be shared, and the nightmares that trampled the territory once belonging to sweet dreams. She buried her face in her pillow, thinking back on the morning she had traveled back north after that encounter. Determined to use the train ride to process her feelings, she had postponed dealing with the guilt, knowing all too well it would still be there later. Punchy from the tension and excitement, giddy from the lack of sleep, she had sat back in her seat to relive the adventures crammed into the twelve hours spent with Max. Her head lolling as she stared out the window, she was filled with the sensations of the strange, intense evening. Her pulse quickened when she recalled that peculiar way Max had of looking at her, how he could make her blush or giggle without saying one word. Replaying the scene of the nighttime boat ride from the safety of her train seat, she thought it one of the most romantic things that had ever happened to her. Max made her laugh; he surprised her, he took her by the hand and led her through uncharted territories to places deep inside herself that no one had ever dared explore, not even she.

As views of the same Mediterranean coast she had first seen on another train trip with Auntie Rosa so many years earlier flashed in and out of view, as people entered and exited her compartment, as stops were made and the whistle blown, Iris reflected on her final pre-dawn hours with Max, when he had clung to her in the musty darkness of the Countess's bedroom, and whispered confessions of his profound loneliness and battles with depression. She had always sensed that there was a deeper side to Max than met the eye and that he wanted more from a woman than someone to have fun with. She had always known that beneath the willfulness and sensuality of this apparently self-assured man lay a sensitive soul, a vulnerable boy who needed someone to bring happiness into his life, just as much as she did.

In the ensuing weeks, communication with Max had been sporadic. She couldn't really blame him if she was never available to talk when he was, he being constantly on the road, and she sandwiched between the duties of home and hotel and the demands of their respective residents. Each time she was sure she would not hear from him again, a message or email arrived, describing an incredibly romantic sunset or inspiring seascape, a spectacular mountaintop or a picturesque countryside that he wanted to share with her. Though joining him was for the most part out of the question, they did pull off the occasional encounter - brief, spur-of-the-moment escapades she conceded to when Max was within range. Each time she managed to join him, Iris was astonished by how conniving and inventive she could be when it came to overcoming obstacles to her adventures, in particular, one named Gregorio. Like an undercover agent, she kept all channels of communication open at all times. Her cell phone never left her side: it was in her pocket when she ate, under her pillow when she slept, on the ledge of the sink when she went to the bathroom. She was obsessive about constantly checking for instructions regarding her next secret assignment. One last look at her computer before going to bed revealed an email suggesting skinny-dipping at sunrise in Sestri Levante, followed by freshly baked croissants on the beach. One buzz of the cell phone in her suit pocket during a business luncheon announced dinner reservations at a chic new *pieds-dans-l'eau* restaurant being filmed in Tellaro. One message received while she was at the green grocer's, debating over whether Isabella would still want the cantaloupe she had ordered even if it wasn't ripe, unsettled Iris with the touching news that Max was feeling lonely. The frustration she felt at knowing he must miss her as much as she missed him, the resentment she bore toward the responsibilities and commitments that did not allow her to be with Max when he needed her most, inspired her to drop the hard, green melon into her shopping basket without further thought.

The emotional anticipation and last-minute strategies that preceded their clandestine encounters, the doubts about what she was doing and where it would lead that followed each rendezvous, the bouts of growing guilt that pounced on her unannounced at all hours of the day or night, the impenetrable silence that accompanied Max's downward mood swings - those were the real culprits responsible for robbing Iris of her sleep. Never knowing if and when Max would contact her, in which soon-to-be-televised restaurant he would invite her to dine, or on which borrowed bed or boat or beach they would make illicit love, infused their affair with an excitement that exceeded all supportable limits. Iris was ecstatic, desperate, confused. If losing your dreams could make you lose your mind, so could pursuing them drive you crazy.

Feeling a presence in the bedroom, she rolled over onto her back and saw Gregorio looming over her. She rubbed her puffy eyes, sighed, blinked.

"Open your mouth," he ordered.

She did; he popped something inside.

"What is it?" She stretched her tongue out below her nose, her eyes crossing to take a look for themselves.

"A little something to help us both sleep."

"But I don't want a sleeping pill."

"I'm afraid I have to insist, *Piccolina*. Now be a good girl, and swallow. We need to get you under control, and the first step is proper rest. Leave it up to me. I'll find a way to bring our old Iris back."

"*Signora* Iris, I know you said not to disturb you, but your brother is on the phone."

"My brother? Which one? I have seven of them." None of whom would ever call her at the hotel. No one in her family had ever phoned her there, not even Auntie Rosa, or Lily, or any of her sisters.

"I'm sorry, he didn't tell me his name, just that he was your brother," the receptionist replied. "He said it was urgent."

"Put him through, Monica," Iris said. Ever since her father's sudden death, unexpected overseas calls from family immediately made her panic. She turned to *Signora* Mangiagallo and said, *"Mi scusi, Signora.* I have a call from America." Her voice was curt, but still on the right side of courteous, despite the fact that the old woman had been sitting in her office for the past hour, complaining about the color of the new uniforms Iris had selected for the chambermaids, while stroking the constantly yelping mini Maltese terrier her son had given her for her birthday.

"Hello?" Iris said into the receiver.

"Hi, Iris," said the man on the line. The connection was good, but she couldn't figure out which brother the voice belonged to.

"Who is this?" she asked, purposely ignoring *Signora* Mangiagallo, who rolled her eyes, stuffed the squirming puppy into her Louis Vuitton Speedy Bag, and walked out of the office in a huff.

"Sono io, Capo."

"Max! Why did you say you were my brother?" Iris asked. "You nearly gave me a heart attack."

"How would I know the girl would believe me? I wasn't even speaking English."

Hearing Max's voice instead of bad news from home did not calm the thumping in her chest. "What's going on? Why didn't you call my cell phone?"

"Because the goddamn number of your goddamn cell phone is on my goddamn cell phone, which I can't fucking find. I got a girl here to look up the hotel. I know, I know, I promised not to call you at work, but like they say, promises are made to be broken, right? Anyway, are you coming or not?"

"Coming where?" Iris asked, not sure whether to laugh or bang her head against the wall. No one on the face of the earth confused her like Max.

"Here, that's where. We should be done shooting in about an

hour. If you leave now, you should get here right about that time. Don't make me watch the sunset alone again." Once Max had sent an email to Iris telling her he remembered every sunset they had seen together, and although they weren't all that many, he had surprised her by describing every single one in minute detail: where they had been, what they had been drinking or eating, what she had been wearing. She had reread the message dozens of times.

"But where is 'here'?"

"Monterosso."

"Monterosso? You didn't tell me you were going to be in the Cinque Terre!" In fact, she knew precious little about what Max had been up to lately. She hadn't heard from him in over a week and was beginning to worry he was suffering from one of his depressions. She had caught her finger hovering over his phone number more than once but already knew that Max wouldn't answer her calls or messages when he was down, which would only make her worry more. Besides, she had worked out a deal with herself to limit her sense of guilt. One thing was caving into his crazy proposals; another was actively seeking him out. She promised herself she wouldn't. For now.

"I thought you liked surprises," Max said.

"You know I do, Max," Iris said. "But you also know I need a little lead time. How long will you be there?"

"Only till tomorrow morning. I have to be in Positano by dinnertime."

"Positano?" The Amalfi coast was so lovely, so romantic - so far away. She would never be able to meet him there for the day like she had when he was working in San Remo, or in Fiesole. Not that it had been an easy trick to pull those times, either; it never was. But she didn't want to think about that now: she didn't want to pop open the lid of the jack-in-the-box where the all lies and scheming were coiled up, ready to jump out at her. Another promise she had made to herself was that she would stop lying, very soon. She just had to figure out how.

"Yep, Positano. But that's not until tomorrow. Tonight there's still a sunset in Monterosso. I have a table and a complimentary seafood dinner awaiting me and my guest at this spectacular place where we shot Tuesday's segment. Are you in?" Iris glanced at her watch; soon the *Signora* would be retreating to her villa for the evening. She looked at her cluttered desk; how urgent could next year's advertising budget be, when compared to a sunset that would be here and gone within a few short hours? And how would she ever be able to sit through dinner at home, thinking of Max all alone at that romantic restaurant? Or worse, *not* alone. The invitation was for two; she wondered who he might share his table with if she did not go.

"I'll be there," she said, her pulse quickening, the wheels of her mind spinning. "Give me an hour and a half." That should be enough time to wrap things up and drive the sixty-some kilometers to the fishing village turned tourist town, just in time for sunset. And, of course, figure out what to do about Gregorio.

"Where are you?" Iris asked Bea as soon as she answered her phone.

"Milan. Everything OK?"

"Great. Listen, Max is in Monterosso. I'm meeting him for dinner."

"You're driving to Monterosso for dinner?" Beatrix asked.

"It's only an hour away. I've already decided. Can I use you again? I have to tell Gregorio something."

"It would be so much easier for everyone if husbands would simply learn to die when they start getting in the way," Bea sighed. "Widowhood is such a respectable state. How did it ever go out of style?"

"Bea!"

"Just kidding. Sort of. Go ahead and tell him I'm a desperate wreck, no lie there. And since you're such a good friend, you would never leave me alone. Would you?"

"Never. Thanks, Bea. I owe you another one."

"No, you owe it to yourself, Iris. Have fun. Drive carefully. And remember to send me a message when you get home. You know how I worry."

Iris and her Seicento were already entering the southbound A12 motorway when she finally got through to Gregorio, who had just finished making afternoon rounds at the Policlinico.

"I'm worried about Beatrix again," she said to her husband after each had inquired about the other's well-being.

"What is it this time?" Gregorio's voice tightened ever so slightly; she imagined him rolling his eyes and clenching his jaw like he always did when his patience was about to run out. He probably still bore a grudge against Beatrix for her role in helping Iris land the job at the Dimora. Or maybe he just didn't like her. He had never come out and said so, and Iris had never asked him, but he had other ways of showing his disapproval. Although Gregorio's less than friendly attitude toward her didn't seem to faze Bea, it bothered Iris, who could never quite accept the fact that not all the people she cared for cared for each other. Like her mother and her father. Like Lily and Auntie Rosa.

"She's devastated." The image she conjured up of her friend sobbing was so realistic, tears sprang to Iris's eyes. "Something to do with that man she's been seeing, but I didn't get the details. She was crying too hard to explain over the phone. She needs to talk. And since, well, I'm really her only friend here..." Iris was amazed at how convincing she sounded; she would have embellished her story further, had she not been approaching a tunnel. "Wouldn't you say it's my duty to be there for her?" That sounded good; Gregorio loved it when anyone talked about duty.

"I respect your sense of duty, *Piccolina*. That's commendable. Though if Beatrix were such a good friend, she would think about you, too. She would remember that you have a husband and that your primary duty is toward him." Gregorio paused. She could picture him grinding his teeth, waiting for her to react. When she remained silent, he added, "Will you be home for dinner?"

"I was thinking of taking her for a pizza. Eating always calms her down."

"It is a work night, you know. You need your rest."

"I won't be late." Iris slowed down, hoping to close the deal before she entered the tunnel and the connection was cut off.

"Promise you'll be home by eleven," Gregorio said.

"I promise," Iris said, then lost him. She wondered whether he had heard her. She hated making promises when she didn't know if she could keep them.

A soft haze floated down from the hills and hovered over the sea at sunset, smudging the burnt orange mélange that streaked the sky in front of Monterosso al Mare. There were few tourists milling about on this mild evening in early autumn, though Iris found this time of year much more suitable than summer for exploring the scenic trails that wound along the rugged coast and steep terrain, connecting each of the five villages. Not that it affected her personally; when would she have time to hike?

By the time Max joined Iris on the veranda of the restaurant, the brilliant hues had waned to pastel, then faded. He cursed the production office at RAI TV for providing him with such a lazy assistant and told Iris she had them to thank if he was twenty minutes late, then proceeded to blame the sun for setting earlier every day. Iris smiled and said not to worry; it obviously wasn't his fault. Of course, he wouldn't make her rush in time for sunset, then intentionally turn up late. True, she regretted not sharing the beautiful display of colors with him, in addition to losing a little of their limited time together, but apart from that, Iris wouldn't have minded the wait at all. In fact, as she had sipped her Cinque Terre *bianco* and contemplated the seascape, she reflected that she ought to use her burgeoning talent for fibbing more often, even when she didn't have anyone to meet. Lying to steal some time for herself was surely a venial offence when compared with lying to rendezvous with a lover, and what was a little guilt trip if it earned her the freedom to hop in the car and drive away to enjoy an hour or so on her own in a magical setting such as this?

Max ordered a bottle of *bianco,* and as they sipped, he teased her with little kisses on her neck and ears with lips made cool by the wine. Her giggling turned to laughter as he entertained her with a story of his trip in the cargo bin of the ropeway conveyor he pirated to cart him up the mountain to the terraced vineyards where they were filming footage for the segment on Sciachetrà wine. His descriptions were so colorful and vivid, he made listening to the episode as much fun as if she had experienced it personally with him.

Part of her couldn't resist comparing the two men, while part of her felt it was unfair, but she couldn't help thinking that if she had remained home tonight, at this hour Gregorio would be droning on about the day's events at the Policlinico. Of course his work at the hospital was indisputably more important than Max's, and of course the events in the operating room infinitely more significant than grapes growing on a hillside. But that realization was of little consolation to Iris all those evenings as she sat across from Gregorio at the dinner table, watching him drink his way through his nightly liter of still mineral water at room temperature, hoping he wouldn't notice her pouring herself a second glass of wine.

This evening the wine flowed as Max polished off Iris's share of the house's special seafood stew cooked according to an ancient recipe in a terracotta amphora. When the bottle was empty and Max's tummy full, he rose from the table, took Iris by the hand, and led her to his accommodations above the restaurant. Iris glanced at her watch as Max pulled his shirt over his head without unbuttoning it, and when he grunted and collapsed on her a few minutes later, she was actually relieved that he had been so quick, and rather flattered to think how much he must have been desiring her. There wasn't really time for anything else, but that was fine with her, other things were more important to her than the sex and the wine and the food. She quickly calculated how much time she had left, and was happy to realize she could afford another ten minutes before she would have to wash up and be on her way. A few cuddles and sweet words would keep her company during the drive home, and help her fall asleep once she got there.

"Summer's finally over," Max said. He stretched out on his back, crossed his arms behind his head.

"Yes, I guess so," Iris said.

"Summers are hard as hell for me. That's why I always travel."

"Rome must be pretty unbearable in the summer," she said, wondering why they were talking about the changing seasons when there were so many more important things to say. She wanted to talk about how she never stopped thinking about him. She wanted to ask how they might find a way to spend more time together, and whether they could try planning things in advance once in a while. But there was no time to get into that now; she'd have to write him an email. She had always been better at writing than talking, anyway, and Max had once told her he kept all her emails, which she thought as romantic as Bea thought worrying.

"Rome's not the problem," he said. "Summer is just so fucking depressing."

"But it's the best time of year," Iris said. "Everyone loves summer."

"Not everyone has been through what I have," Max said, his eyes fixed on the ceiling.

"What do you mean?" Iris said, pulling herself up to a sitting position. She should start easing her way out of bed, even though she did not like the idea of leaving Max lying there, staring at the ceiling, thinking depressing thoughts.

Max drew his knees to his chest and turned on his side, nestling his head in Iris's naked lap. She began stroking his hair, and said, "Is it something you want to talk about?" Max sighed, his breath moist and warm on her thighs, rekindling her arousal. She wished she could hold his head there forever.

"I was ten," he began, his voice as spindly as he must have been at that age. "Ten fuckin' years old, *cazzo*. You know what it's like to be a ten-year-old kid on the last day of school?"

"I sure do," she said, recalling how her hopes would soar like a kite into a cloudless sky at the beginning of each new summer.

"I couldn't wait to get out of that fucking prison," Max said, the vibration of his low voice tickling the tender skin of her inner thighs. "I kept looking at that clock, waiting for that fucking bell to ring. It was right next to the cross, I remember because whenever that bitch of a teacher yelled at me for watching the clock, I told her I was praying."

68

Iris slid a bit lower in the bed, her knees turning outward, her legs falling slightly open. She remembered how she used to look at the crucifix and the clock at the same time, too, and pray for the ticking to slow down or speed up, depending on how much she liked the class. She wished time would stop altogether now.

"My family always rented this place in Gaeta for the summer. It was probably a shithole, but I didn't care where I slept. All that mattered was being by the sea."

"It must be great for a kid to spend summers by the sea," Iris said. All she had ever longed for every summer was to swim in a clean, cool lake, but all she ever got was that stinking mud hole. Those memories should make Max thankful, not depressed.

"I slept in a sleeping bag sometimes, out on the balcony by the kitchen," Max said. "I loved doing that."

"I loved sleeping bags, too!" Though she and Max had drastically different backgrounds, the more she learned about him, the more she realized how much they had in common. She adored the sense of adventure combined with coziness she had felt when zipping herself into one of those Army green sleeping bags, even if it was full of the musty smells and crusty memories of other bodies, even if it was only to sleep in a tent her father pitched in the backyard. She had longed for a sleeping bag of her own, one in which none of her brothers had slept. Maybe she should buy herself one now, and one for Max, too. Maybe they could camp out one night under the stars.

"It was always too hot to go inside the sleeping bag right away, so I stretched out on top of it. I'd try to stay awake as long as I could, listening to my parents talking and playing cards with my aunt and uncle at the kitchen table," he said.

Iris could imagine curious little Max, trying to hear what the adults were talking about. It reminded her of when she would stay at Auntie Rosa's, sitting quietly on a chair in the corner so the adults wouldn't notice her listening in on their conversations.

"The gulls always woke me up real early, but I liked just lying there thinking about what I would do that day, even though it was the same old shit over and over again, swimming and fishing,

fishing and swimming. Today I'd rather shoot myself in the balls, but back then I could never get enough of it. My dad used to take me out in this little blue and white rowboat that came with the place. That thing had so many coats of paint on it, it always got all gooey in the sun, you know? It always smelled like paint and cat piss."

Iris did not say anything but wondered where Max was going with this, and how long it would take him to get there. It was getting late, but she sensed she should not rush him. A mixture of growing impatience and unfulfilled desire made her legs twitch; she loved the way his head felt in her lap, she loved running her fingers through his thick hair.

"That feels great," he sighed to her thighs. After a moment of silence, he said, "I lost it for a minute. What was I saying? Before Gaeta?"

"You were telling me how you were waiting for school to get out."

"Oh, yeah. I couldn't stop looking at the goddamn clock on the wall. When the principal opened the door and called the teacher out into the hallway, I thought for sure they were gonna let us out a little early. As soon as she left, everyone started horsing around, then the teacher leaned in, and called me out to the hall. I saw my uncle, Zio Luigi, out there, and I was thinking, all right, fantastic, he came to spring me. I stuck my tongue out at all the other suckers that were still sitting there, and ran out to the hall."

Max fell silent again. This was turning out to be a lot more complicated than a complaint about the stifling summer climate in Rome. "And then what?" she prompted him.

"Then Zio Luigi put his hand on my shoulder and told me some shit about how I would have to be a man now. I looked at my teacher and at the principal, trying to figure out what the fuck he meant, but they just stared at me." Max paused.

"So did he get you out early?" she asked, hoping to move things along.

"He got me out early, all right. But there was no fucking vacation that year, or any other year after that." Iris felt a tremor pass through Max's body. "All because of some fucking asshole in a truck."

"What do you mean? What happened?" She stiffened, fearing what was to come.

"The guy ran a red light. His truck sliced my old man's car in half. Both my parents were killed on the spot. *Fuck them!*" Another tremor shook Max's balled-up body, as he began sobbing.

"Oh, my poor Max! I'm so sorry." She rocked his head in her lap; she felt his tears flow and mingle with the sticky remnants of his desire, with the warm dampness of her own. Pain and loss were one, joined by a common need for love. Only love could heal Max, and Iris had so much of it to give; she felt it flow from her as she held him close, weeping with him and for him, longing to draw the little orphaned boy into the shelter of her womb. She yearned to tell him she would never leave him, that she would always be there for him. She would, if he wanted her to be. Only not now. Now she had to go.

After a few moments, she tried to speak. "Max, I ..." Her throat was too tight with emotion for the words to pass. She couldn't stay, but neither could she go. A few minutes more. Just a few.

The sobs gradually subsided, and Max rolled onto his back again, returning his eyes to the ceiling. "You're gonna go," he said.

"I have no choice."

"Right."

How could he think she would leave if she didn't have to? How could he think she had a choice? She trembled with sadness and anger and frustration as she prepared to go.

"*Ti voglio bene,*" she said because she needed to say something, anything but goodbye. Max was staring at the ceiling when she kissed him on the forehead before hurrying to her car.

"*Merda!*" Iris gripped the shimmying steering wheel, using all the strength in her arms to guide the wobbling Seicento across the bridge which spanned the hills and valleys of the coastal highway. The bright lights of passing vehicles approached like missiles from behind, exploding in her rearview mirror, blinding her as she struggled to stay in control of her car. She managed to activate her flashers as she slowed down, and the car finally came to a lopsided stop just inside a two-lane tunnel with no emergency lane.

She knew she couldn't stay in the car, but was terrified to get out. Cars and trucks swerved to avoid hitting her, blaring their horns, flashing their lights, shaking her little Seicento as they roared passed her. Her heart raced, but she knew she must calm down if she wanted to get out of there alive. She pulled the lever to pop open the rear hatch, grabbed her purse, waited for a break in the traffic, then dashed out into the road and to the back of her car, where her fears were confirmed: her left rear tire was blown to shreds, the ribbons of rubber hanging limply from the wheel like overcooked fettuccine.

She opened the hatch and took out the emergency triangle she kept there together with jumper cables and a toolbox and set the triangle on the asphalt. There was a spare, too, but this was sure as hell not the place to test her memory for the tire-changing lesson her father had given each of the girls when he taught them to drive. On legs of jelly, she sidled toward the entrance of the tunnel, sticking close to the grimy wall. "Thank you, God!" she shouted each time a car sped past without killing her.

Once she reached the relative safety of the open highway, Iris sat down on the guardrail, her hands shaking as she made the sign of the cross. The story of Max's parents' death was fresh in her mind, and she knew her flat tire could have ended in tragedy. Not that she was safe yet, far from it.

She had just passed Sestri Levante, meaning she was still about twenty kilometers from home, where she had promised to return by eleven. That only gave her fifteen minutes. She reviewed her options. She could call Gregorio, who would be in bed reading by now, awaiting her return. She would have to explain why Bea wasn't with her, and why they had gone so far to eat a pizza when there were a dozen pizzerias right in Rapallo. Or maybe she wouldn't explain anything. Maybe this was a sign that she should stop lying and start telling the truth. Or maybe not. Decisions like this were not made when one was stranded on the highway. Max was the one she should call for help. He traveled all over the place, and was used to all kinds of situations; he'd know what to do.

"*Pronto?*" Iris could barely hear his voice over the roar of the highway. She hoped he hadn't been sleeping. Or worse, crying.

"It's me, Max. I'm in trouble. I have a flat tire, and my car is stranded in the tunnel!" Iris shouted over the noise.

"*Merda!*" Max said.

"That's what I said! I don't know what to do. I'm scared, and it's late!"

"You shouldn't have left," Max said.

"But Max, you know I couldn't stay!" As if she didn't already feel wretched enough.

"What the hell do you want me to do?" Max said. It was hard to hear his tone of voice with the traffic rumbling by, but he sounded angry. Or maybe he was just shaken. Maybe after reliving the story of his parents' death, he just couldn't handle the fact that she was in danger.

"I don't know! But I need help!" What she wanted was someone to tell *her* what to do.

"Aren't there any of SOS phones around?"

"I don't see any. And I'm afraid to go looking for one in the dark! Besides, it would take ages for them to come and tow me."

"Well, you can't just sit there all night. You're gonna have to call your husband," Max said. "Doesn't he always figure everything out for you?"

"I can't call Gregorio! I told him I was out with my girlfriend!"

"You'll think of something by the time he gets there."

Iris didn't want to think of something. She was tired of always trying to think of something. Tears sprung to her eyes, blurring the headlights of an oncoming car that headed straight for her. For a moment, she wished it would hit her. But then it slowed to a stop. A robust figure got out of the car and hurried toward her in the dark. Maybe the man would help her. Or abduct or rob or rape her. Whatever happened, it would get her out of her current situation.

"*Sta bene, Signora?*" he called. "Are you all right?"

"*Sì, sto bene!*" she replied to the approaching silhouette. "Thanks anyway, Max," she said into the phone. "You better get some sleep." Iris did not wait for an answer and again could not say goodbye. Using her knuckles to wipe the tears from her eyes, she turned to the man now standing in front of her. He was close enough for her to see the lines of concern in his forehead.

"Thank you so much for stopping," she said. "I'm not hurt, just stranded. Flat tire." She jerked her thumb in the direction of the tunnel.

"Let me have a look there," he said. "You must have a spare, right?"

"Oh, yes!" Iris said, nodding her head.

The man went back to his car, returning with a battery-operated flare. "You wave this to warn other drivers we're here," he said, handing the flare to her, "while I see what I can do."

It made her nervous to stand on the side of the road facing the oncoming traffic, but it made her more nervous thinking of that kind soul risking his life to save her. She waved the flare madly, screaming, "Slow down!" and "Look out!" and "Danger!" though she knew no one could hear her warnings.

"You can stop now!" a voice called from behind her less than ten minutes later. "You're all set."

"You mean you fixed it? Really? I can't believe it." Iris was weak with relief.

"What good are forty years as a mechanic if I can't help a lady in distress?"

"I don't know how to thank you!" Iris said. "Can I pay you for your trouble?"

"Absolutely not!" the man said. "It's my duty. I couldn't take money for helping out the wife of *Dottor* Leale."

"You know my husband?" Iris asked, her overtaxed heart thumping in her chest, her smile freezing on her face.

"*Certamente, Signora!* I'm Mario Triboni? Autofficina Triboni?" Looking for signs of recognition in her face, the man held up his hands, smiling apologetically at the fact they were too soiled with grease for a handshake. Iris kept smiling her frozen smile, nodding her head.

"*Dottor* Leale brings in all your family's cars for tune-ups. One of my best customers. I tell him once a year is fine, but he's there like clockwork, every six months, changing the oil or the filters or whatever needs changing. We've never met, but you're the only Leale without a white car. When I got a closer look at that Seicento in there, I put two and two together. You got that funny bumper sticker in English. Don't see many of those around here."

"Yes," Iris said. People often commented on the "Failure is Impossible" bumper sticker her mother had bought for her at the Susan B. Anthony luncheon they had attended together. It made her car easy to recognize, but that had never been a problem before. What if this nice man couldn't wait to tell Gregorio about his good deed? What if it was already time for a six-month check-up and this whole episode came out, as it surely would?

"Mind if I ask you something, Signora Leale?" The man said, looking a bit embarrassed. Maybe he was wondering what she was doing out by herself at eleven o'clock. Should she tell him it was none of his business? Or should she repeat the pizzeria story, but ask the man to not mention where he had found her? Would that satisfy his curiosity, or make him more suspicious?

"Not at all," she said. She'd think of something. She always did. What happened, happened. They would cross that bridge when they came to it, right Mom? Failure is impossible, right Mom?

"I don't really know how to say this," the man said, headlights flashing across his face.

Iris wished it were all over; she wished she were safe in her bed. She wished she had never taken such a risk tonight.

"Is there a problem?" she said.

"Well, Signora, when *Dottor* Leale brought in your Seicento last month, he wanted me to put on a new set of tires, but I told him it was a waste of money." The man looked at the ground, then back up at Iris. "Those tires didn't even have fifteen thousand kilometers on them, and when he told me you only drive from the house to that hotel where you work, I convinced him we should just rotate them."

Iris let her lungs expand with relief, suck in a deep breath.

Asphalt and exhaust fumes had never smelled so good.

"That was very honest of you," she said.

"Like I said, *Dottor* Leale is a good customer, and I'd never take advantage of him."

"Of course not."

"A tire can blow anytime, you see, but I feel responsible, you see?"

"But you shouldn't," Iris said. How she loved this Mario! "I'll tell you what. How about I stop by your shop tomorrow for a new spare? My husband doesn't really need to know, does he?"

"*Signora*, I would have never asked you, but would you really do that for me?"

"*Signor* Mario, it will be my pleasure."

"I probably shouldn't have any more," Iris said without much conviction, her head lolling on the overstuffed cushion of Beatrix's sofa as her neighbor poured another round from the chilled bottle of Ribolla Gialla.

"What's with you tonight?" Beatrix asked. "I'm not used to seeing you so down."

"They aren't really calling it 'down.' They're calling it 'depressed.'"

"Depressed? You? Says who?"

"Says Gregorio's colleague at the Policlinico. He took me in for an evaluation."

"You've got to be kidding."

"Nope. Apparently, I am suffering from work-related stress, possibly combined with hormonal imbalance, maybe even the onset of premature menopause. Add to that the unresolved issues of my infertility, my father's sudden death, my parents' messy divorce, my screwed-up childhood, and so on. Apparently, I have not grieved properly over the years, and now my exhaustion is exacerbating the symptoms."

"And Gregorio buys into that? Doesn't he think therapy is a bunch of bunk?"

"Yes, but this guy is a psychiatrist, not a therapist.

"And what did you say to this so-called diagnosis?"

"Well, since I couldn't tell them it was bullshit, and I couldn't tell them about Max, I told them not to worry about me. I told them I learned pretty early in life that you just have to keep smiling and move on."

"So we are looking at childhood-related causes, and work-related causes, and physiological causes, is that correct?" Bea asked.

"Correct."

"No mention of marital problems?"

"The doctor asked us, but Gregorio said everything was fine in that department, so I just nodded."

Iris studied the wine she swirled around in her glass, then took a sip before continuing. "Gregorio was kind enough to sum it up for the kind shrink, as if I weren't there." She lowered her voice to a conspiratorial whisper. "'The patient is displaying a marked alteration in character and habits, manifesting irritability, loss of appetite, forgetfulness, and insomnia. Daily activities such as cooking and cleaning previously performed with diligence and cheerfulness are being grossly neglected. Third party observations made by members of the patient's family support this.'"

"I can totally hear him!" Bea said.

"And I can totally hear what Isabella and Cinzia must be saying behind my back. Oh, by the way – you didn't get left out of the discussion, either.

"I'm honored."

"Yes, Gregorio expressed a concern that I am 'developing a dependency on alcohol and tobacco.' And we all know who my pusher is."

Beatrix waved a dismissive hand in front of her face, then reached for her cigarette case, took out two cigarettes, lit them both, and passed one to Iris. "So how do these luminaries plan to fix you?" she asked.

"The psychiatrist prescribed an antidepressant and something to relieve my anxiety, so I can sleep." Iris drew on the cigarette and coughed. She didn't need Gregorio to tell her she was smoking too much. She would definitely cut down. Soon, but not now.

"An antidepressant? What exactly?"

"Sero-something-or-other, I don't remember. Gregorio holds onto it for me."

"I've only been gone a month - when did all this happen?" Beatrix asked.

"Gregorio was getting pretty insistent, so I finally let him drag me in about ten days ago. I felt so close to breaking point, I really didn't care. All I wanted was a good night's sleep."

"You're actually taking the drugs?"

"Gregorio made me. But I discontinued the antidepressant right away. It made me feel confused, and detached, as if I were walking around with my head inside a big glass jar.

"What did Gregorio have to say to that?"

"Oh, he doesn't know. We haven't gotten to the point where he actually straps me to the bed and watches me swallow the pills." They both giggled. "I've grown quite attached to those little blue ones, though. The pharmacist down in Rapallo scored me an extra box, so now I have a secret stash in the office. I take half a pill just before I head home if I'm feeling edgy. Then Gregorio doles me out a whole one when we drink our chamomile. It's an express train to la-la land. Safe and restful dreamless sleep."

"Do you really want to stop dreaming, Iris?"

"Not if I could choose what to dream about, but I can't. That I can only do when I'm awake. And nobody better mess with my daydreams."

"Iris, this is no way to solve your problems," Beatrix said.

"I know. There is no way. But maybe the pills will help me accept them."

"What you have to accept is that you have a choice, Iris. This is your life, and you have to take control over it. There is a solution if you want it badly enough."

"I could never leave Gregorio if that's what you're hinting at again. I can't stand the thought of hurting him."

"Oh, come on Iris. You're talking to me. Of course you don't want to hurt Gregorio. But that's not the crux of your problem, is it?"

"I don't know. I'm so confused."

"Just look at yourself! You're scared shitless, aren't you?"

Iris dropped her eyes and began counting the squares in the geometric design of the floor tiles. She already knew there were twelve squares per tile, one for each Capotosti; she had counted them many times before. She inhaled sharply, her breath colliding with a sigh escaping in the opposite direction.

"Yes," she said. "I'm terrified."

"The only way to beat fear is to face it, not run away from it."

"I'm just afraid of doing the wrong thing. Of hurting people who don't deserve it. You know those dreams I was having for a while? About the dead man? I'm pretty sure they weren't about my father; they were about Gregorio. That's the only way out I can imagine. Isn't that awful?"

"Have you fantasized about killing him, like I used to when I was married to my second husband?"

"Of course not!"

"As I've said, the world would be a better place if more husbands were thoughtful enough to die," Beatrix tiled her head back, and blew smoke into the air. They both smoked in silence for a bit before Iris spoke again.

"I know I've told you all this before, Bea. But that night in Monterosso when Max told me about his parents' accident, it was such an intense moment, I can't even describe it. It just came pouring out, without warning. I thought maybe he would never refer to it again, especially after the way I ran out on him. But he sent me a long email a couple of days later saying nothing like that had ever happened before. He hadn't spoken to anyone about it in years, except for his analyst, but for some reason, he felt the urge to open up to me. Max needs me. Gregorio doesn't."

"It sounds like your friend Max needs lots of things, and it doesn't take a shrink to realize he may pose a challenge when it comes to developing attachments. The fact that he never got married or had kids worries me a tad."

"He just never found the right person. Someone who could

really understand him, like I do. I know what it's like to be deprived of a family. The Leales aren't my family, they're Gregorio's, and no matter how hard I try, they'll never truly accept me."

"You're a good catch for a man like Max. You certainly wouldn't be lugging into the relationship any of that oversized baggage that makes men jittery – no in-laws, no kids, no pressure to have a baby together. You have the maturity and depth of a forty-year-old, the body of a thirty-year-old, and the spirit of a twenty-year-old. He has everything to gain: a mother, a lover, a playmate. But what about you?"

"Max makes me feel *alive*, for God's sake! I experienced more emotion in those few hours than in the past ten years with Gregorio. I felt this incredible intimacy, like a communion of the souls or whatever you want to call it. And I'm so glad he did share those things with me. It makes it easier for me to understand him if I know where he's coming from. I think he was hiding behind an emotional barrier, you know? It was all sex and jokes before, but now he sends me the most incredible emails. And look at this romantic message he sent just this morning." Iris scrolled down the messages on the cell phone which never left her side. "'I need your kind of good.' And how about this one, from yesterday: 'I feel empty tonight.'"

"Iris, really?" Bea exhaled smoke through her nose, then crushed out her cigarette in the ashtray. "That's romantic?"

"To me it is. Max is expressing all these individual needs to me. It's his way of telling me he needs *me*."

"I'm not really worried about what Max needs. I'm worried about what Iris needs. You know my rule of thumb: the farther a man is willing to travel to be with you, and the more money he spends trying to make you happy, the more you know he's worth it. Until men make some kind of an investment, they don't have anything to lose. That does not seem to be the case with Max, but if you're so taken with him, he must be doing something right. And regardless of what happens, it's better than being stuffed with pills and locked up in your ivory tower with the Leales. So I say, let's do it," Beatrix said.

"Do what?"

"Find a way for you to spend more time with him." She stood up, lit two more cigarettes, passed one to Iris, and began pacing the living room floor.

Iris fought against the cushiness of the sofa to sit up straight, then poured more wine for both of them. Screw the Xanax.

"And just how are we going to arrange that?" she asked.

"Talk to Max," Bea said. "Find out when you can spend a week together, and I'll take care of the rest."

"A *week*? Now you're the one on drugs!" Iris said.

"I'll request a private audience with Doc Gregorio, tell him how worried I am about you. I know taking sick leave is against your religion, but we'll get that psychiatrist to prescribe a week off work, and I'll convince Gregorio to let me take you somewhere to unwind. I'll tell him some bullshit story about you missing your sisters, add some stuff about your need for female companionship."

"That part's not bullshit, it's true," Iris said, tears springing to her eyes. They came so easily these days. But at least part of the lie would be true. And if Bea was willing to provide Gregorio with a complete, alternative version to the truth, Iris might not need to lie at all. She would just have to go along with it. The hotel would be closing for the season at the end of October, so things would be calming down there. She would get the medical certificate for Gregorio's benefit, but she wouldn't use it; that would be dishonest. She'd take vacation time, and keep that detail to herself. This was actually starting to sound possible.

"But if you say we're going away together, you'll have to hide out," Iris said.

"I'll just say we're leaving from Milan, then I'll stay there. The peace and quiet of this bourgeois hilltop get on my nerves when you're not around, anyway."

"Isn't it too evil? Too daring? Do you think we can really pull it off?" Iris asked.

"No, it isn't. And yes, we can. What ails you can't be cured with antidepressants. Believe me, I've been there. It's time for action. Action, reaction. Action, reaction."

"Whatever happened to 'the best reaction is no reaction'?"

"Do your homework, Iris. That one's for when you get caught."

Iris shook hands with the Italian representative of Delightful Hotels and Resorts, then stepped out into the golden Roman afternoon. Sunshine bathed her side of Via Veneto, stimulating whatever receptors or glands were responsible for producing enthusiasm. She was utterly brimming with it: for the deal she had just closed, for the marvelous city she was in, for her exciting plans for the evening. She had concluded the negotiations swiftly and favorably, officially making the Dimora Baia dell'Incanto the newest member of DHR, then politely refused an invitation to dinner and a complimentary night at Rome's flagship DHR affiliate, the posh hotel where the previously cancelled meeting had at last been held. She had plenty of time to get where she was going and planned to enjoy a long walk through the city, trying to imagine how it would feel if she were to spend more time there in the future.

As she set off, Iris was grateful for the upbringing that had engrained in her a practical sense which not even moments of sheer folly could ever completely obliterate. A lightweight change of clothes, a black silk peignoir, and some basic toiletries were stowed in a compartment of the briefcase she slung over her shoulder. That was the extent of her baggage, and the sensible pumps she favored for business attire would be reliable walking companions. At five-foot-seven, with a husband just two inches taller, vanity rarely lured Iris into high heels, even when she wasn't working. She wondered how the high-heeled women she saw managed to fight their way through the undisciplined traffic and the throngs of pedestrians that clogged the streets of the capital. Consulting the creased and worn city map which she had hung onto as a souvenir of her very first trip to Rome, Iris decided that instead of going back down Via Veneto the way she had come, she would cut through to Via Sistina, and from there to Trinità dei Monti. Walking down the impressive Spanish Steps to the piazza below always filled her with wonder and an exhilarating feeling of traversing history. She had seen a fashion show televised from there once, and as she walked, she wondered how the models could have descended with such grace the one hundred and thirty-five marble steps trodden to buttery smoothness over the centuries. At the bottom of the stairs, she paused to look at the little house on the corner, where the twenty-six-year-old John Keats died of consumption, a victim of the doctor who bled him and fed him only one anchovy and one piece of bread each day. She supposed her antidepressants and anti-anxiety medications were no more likely to cure her of her ailments than bleeding and starving might have cured the poet.

As she crossed Piazza di Spagna to Via Condotti, Iris was caught up in a drove of German tourists wearing white socks and sandals. The warm October day made them prefer gelato to the roasted chestnuts sold on the street corner, and they licked their cones happily, pointing and chatting as they admired the fashions in the famous boutiques. It was quite impossible to imagine any of them clad in the prêt-à-porter creations of Gucci or Valentino, Armani or Prada, but clothes like that did make one dream, she thought, as she looked over a strapless red Valentino gown. As a little girl spinning fairytales in bed with Lily, she could not have known anything about Rome or designers, yet that red dress was precisely the one she wore in her fantasies.

At the end of the street, she turned right onto Via del Corso, where the merchandise was decidedly more suited to her budget and lifestyle. She felt a stab of guilt, recalling that Gregorio had imagined her there the evening he phoned her in Sabaudia. She spotted a church and ducked inside with the excuse of lighting a candle for Auntie Rosa, but while she was there, she offered up a quick prayer that the Madonna, or maybe Mary Magdalene, who was probably better at understanding the mind of an adulteress, would help her find her way before she cracked up or screwed up. And though she blushed at the circumstances in which the promise had been extracted from her that night in the Countess's bed, she also said a little prayer for Max, and for the souls of his parents.

There was still a spring in her step when she reached Piazza del Popolo, and from there headed across the bridge over the Tiber river. Never had the air been a more perfect temperature, never had Rome been more stunning or full of promise than today. This girl from Rochester was far from depressed; indeed, she could barely contain her excitement as she ventured into the residential streets of the Prati district, just blocks from St. Peter's Square, reflecting it might be a very nice place to live if one were inclined to set up house in Rome.

"Hey, so that's where you've been hiding!" Max called out, cutting a swathe in the *aperitivo* crowd. Iris had already noticed on other occasions that when Max entered a room, something indefinable happened, something destabilizing, energizing. The man behind the bar nodded and smiled at him, a handful of other people drinking and chatting waved at him, shouting out comments. "*Ciao Maxi*," cooed a leggy brunette sitting on a barstool with her back to Iris. "*Come va, stronzo?*" said the skinny guy with gelled hair and an earring. "*Che cazzo di fine hai fatto ieri sera?*" demanded a stocky man whose tattooed arms stuck out of a muscle shirt, holding a tall glass of beer. It was strange to think that all these people knew Max, that they were part of his everyday life, the one he led without her. It gave Iris a thrill to push back the curtain on that life and take a peek inside.

"Isn't this the place where you said to wait? I've been here since seven, just like you told me," she said, acting more amused than annoyed. The only way to deal with all his last-minute changes of plan and delays was to keep a sense of humor.

"Stop bitching and give me a kiss, Capo," Max said, leaning over the barstool where she had been sitting in her business suit nursing a glass of white wine for the past half-hour, pretending to review the contract she took from her briefcase to stave off undesired attention. She didn't want Max to walk in and find her talking to another man, but now that she knew these people were his friends, she regretted not having socialized with them; she might have gleaned some interesting information about life in his Roman neighborhood. Maybe he would have gotten a charge out of walking in and find her laughing and joking with his friends;

maybe he would have even been a little jealous of the guy she had caught leering at her crossed legs.

Not that it mattered anymore. Max was already pressing his lips against hers, grunting as he shoved his tongue to the back of her mouth, then just as quickly pulling away. He threw back his head, combing his fingers through his hair and laughing, while she sat there looking shocked and embarrassed. She couldn't get used to being so demonstrative in public, but something pleased her about the fact that Max wanted to kiss her like that in front of all these people he knew. She touched her fingers to her mouth, wiping the saliva from her lips, glancing around to check whether anyone had been watching. The leggy girl was staring at Iris from over her shoulder, and the look on her face was not friendly.

Max pulled off the ribbon that held Iris's hair in a ponytail, then tousled her curls with a hand. "Hey, Beautiful," he said, in English.

"Hey, Handsome," she replied in English, tossing her head. Max didn't speak much English, but he sometimes made her speak the language to him when they were in a crowd. A number of people turned to look at them, no doubt wondering where she was from, what she was doing there, how she knew Max.

"I hate to tear you away from this lovely little group," he said, now speaking loudly in Italian, "but I have other plans for the night."

Iris reached into her purse to pay for her drink, but Max stopped her. "*Passo dopo, Luca!*" he called to the man behind the bar.

"*Sì, sì, va bene, passi sempre dopo!*" the man said, shaking his head, wiping a glass with a towel. "Sure you will. Why pay now, when you can pay later?" Another round of nods and waves and ciaos and amiable insults were exchanged as Max led Iris out onto the sidewalk, across the street, and into an apartment building. He opened the wrought iron gate to an old-fashioned elevator, and once inside pressed the little black button with a "6" on it: they were going to the top floor.

A few days after her conversation with Bea, Iris decided that the best way to devise a plan for a week together would be to speak with Max in person. She let him know that she would be in Rome on business, and he immediately suggested he join her at the hotel after her meeting. Besides being risky, Iris did not think that would be very professional on her part, so she told him it wasn't possible. She spent her life in hotels, anyway; what she really wanted to do was share a piece of Max's life in Rome. She wanted to sleep in his bed, have morning coffee in his kitchen, and shower in his bathroom. He said she could crash at his place, informed her of the dates he would be in town, and she set it up.

Max unlocked a series of bolts and kicked open the door with a sneaker-clad foot. "*Voilà*," he said. The apartment was dim, but enough light came in through the undressed windows to see that the living room if you could call it that, was crammed with boxes and cases and half-packed duffel bags whose contents spilled onto the floor. A bicycle leaned against a scuffed wall, and video cassettes were piled on every surface that was not occupied by magazines, newspapers, dirty dishes, overflowing ashtrays, pizza boxes, or soiled glasses.

"It's not usually such a pig-pen," Max said, flashing the same sheepish smile he used on her when he was late. "I'm hardly ever here, and that bitch of a cleaning lady left me a note saying she refuses to come back until I clean. I mean, what the fuck does she think I pay *her* for?"

It was unmistakably the home of a single man, totally devoid of any female touch, and Iris didn't mind that one bit. A desire to create here the atmosphere of domesticity she rarely experienced in her own home these days made her arms twitch and her fingers tingle. Her muscles literally ached to dig into this mess; if only she were free to stay a couple of days, she would turn the place inside out. What she could see of the furniture beneath the clutter seemed chic and contemporary, a combination of black leather, steel, and glass. It looked like Max had a nice entertainment system, too. If they cleared off a place to sit, they might even watch a movie later, or maybe he would show her some of his work, one of those short films he was always talking about. Then they could listen to some music while they talked about their plans, like a real couple spending an evening at home, without having to watch the clock.

She was curious to check out the kitchen; his cupboards were probably bare, and she'd be willing to bet that his fridge wouldn't contain more than a few cans of beer, an opened bottle of wine, and some moldy cheese – unless of course, he had a bottle of spumante chilling to celebrate the occasion.

Before she could verify the accuracy of her speculations, Iris found herself face-down in her bra and undies on the unmade bed, her hands tied behind her back with one of her lace-top stockings, her skirt and jacket and blouse entangled in the rumpled black sheets. The tired texture of the low-quality cotton against her flushed cheeks combined with the stale smell that reminded her of used gym socks and popcorn made Iris wonder when the linens had been last laundered. Max, in the meantime, had already begun licking and sucking and gnawing at her.

"Please Max - not there - " she said more than once, hoping to stop him from leaving his mark on visible areas of skin. Whenever she scolded him for the blemishes and bruises she found on her neck and shoulders and tummy after their encounters, he always laughed and said she hadn't seemed to mind at the time. Since her honeymoon, Iris had come up with several arguments to convince herself that the lights-off policy Gregorio enforced during sex was not such a bad idea, but Max was by far the most compelling.

All attempts at caution, all further reflections of any sort were swiftly beaten back by the riotous impulses that commandeered her body. Iris succumbed to her captor, submitting to his titillating tortures, whimpering and begging for more. Even the bed was whipped up to a frenzy, banging and groaning until Iris's shrieks and Max's screams flew out the open window and into the street. Max collapsed on top of her, his slippery, hairless chest pressing down on her back, crushing her bound arms between their bodies.

"What do you say, Capo?" he grunted.

"Wow," she croaked. "Except I can't breathe."

Max laughed. "I mean it!" she said. Max began tickling her ribs. "Don't!" she said, squirming under his weight. "I hate being tickled!" He tickled her more, his pudgy fingers flying up and down her sides, reaching under her arms. "No!" she cried. "Stop!"

She was giggling uncontrollably, gasping for air; she was little Iris forced to play tickle torture with her brothers when her parents were away, skinny little Iris laughing herself to death while everyone thought she was having fun.

"STOP!" she screamed.

"OK, OK!" Max laughed, rolling onto his back.

"Untie me!" she cried.

"What do you say?"

"Please!" Iris said.

Max untied the stocking, and she rolled over heavily, panting and rubbing her throbbing red wrists and sore shoulders. Her heart pounded as she lay flat on her back, her chest rising and falling as she caught her breath, her eyes staring at the ceiling, watching an enormous cobweb hovering above her. It must have taken months to grow one that big.

"Hey, we better get going," Max said, jumping out of bed.

"Go where?" For once, Iris did not have to rush, but Max was already pulling on his jeans. It wasn't the first time she noticed him dressing without underwear, and wondered how comfortable it was for a man.

"To a party."

"A party? Really?" Iris blinked as her View-Master mind ejected a series of previously imagined images and flicked through the new. Gone were the quiet evening, the talks, the plans, the cuddles, all replaced by scenes of her and Max going out as a couple, Max escorting her by the elbow through a roomful of interesting people, Max introducing her to his friends, holding her hand, whispering in her ear, laughing.

"What's the occasion?" she asked, wishing she had come equipped for a party.

"Nothing special. Just some people I have to see."

"Does it have anything to do with your film project?" Every time Iris asked him how things were progressing, Max said he was ready to roll. All he needed now was the backing of a couple more of the right people. With his talent and determination, she knew he'd make it, sooner or later.

"In the industry, everything has to do with everything else. It's all about connections, staying in the loop, you know? You always run into the same bunch of fakes, but you never know when someone will introduce you to someone else who doesn't have his head up his asshole. You gotta be in the right place at the right time."

"It's like that with everything." Iris sat on the edge of the bed and smiled up at him. "Look at how we met."

"That's what I mean. You never know who you'll run into. And they'll have good food, and plenty of free booze."

"Can I take a quick shower first?" Iris said.

Still buckling his belt, Max leaned over her and sniffed. "Mmmm - you smell like fresh sex," he said. "Don't wash it off. Men can smell that, you know? You'll drive them all crazy."

"You're kidding, aren't you?" Iris said, fishing her rumpled blouse out of the twisted sheets.

"I'm dead serious, Capo. You always smell way too clean. Don't you know that body odors are a turn-on?" Iris had grown so accustomed to the scent of disinfectant on Gregorio that she often felt slightly stinky by comparison; she had been showering twice a day for years. She had already taken one that morning, so maybe she should humor Max and go along with his suggestion; did she or did she not want to experiment with his alternative lifestyle? How "alternative" would it be if she never deviated from the same old rules she always followed?

"And forget about that blouse," Max continued, pulling on his shirt. "Grab something to wear from the closet. Last door on the right is for visitors. Someone about your size left some stuff here once. Expensive stuff. They always give models a shitload of free samples."

Her blouse still clutched in her hand, her mind still processing the extra information that came with her orders, Iris got up and walked to the closet. It took an effort for her to open the door, and she wanted to slam it shut again when she saw the collection of skimpy dresses dangling from wire hangers, the shelf full of balled-up lingerie, the dozen disjointed pairs of high heels lying on the floor.

Ten minutes later, Max called the elevator to the sixth floor. Iris stood shoulder-to-shoulder next to him on the landing, an additional eight centimeters added to her height by the spike heels of sandals a size too big. She was glad she had painted her toenails red (another detail that complicated her life: Max thought varnished nails sexy, Gregorio thought them cheap). At least her toes, if not the rest of her, matched the short dress Max had made her squeeze into while banning the panties whose unsightly lines he said ruined its sleek, smooth look.

The elevator door groaned when Max pulled it open, and the couple stepped toward their reflections in the mirrored wall of the compartment. Max laughed. "I wonder what your old man and his mamma would think if they could see you now."

Iris knew what they'd think: they'd think she looked like a slut. For an instant, Max's cockeyed smile made her want to side with the Leales. She did feel a little embarrassed going out in public in such a skimpy dress, but she certainly wouldn't be running into people she knew. She would pretend she was going to a costume party, that would help her loosen up. And this was Rome. She would have fun.

"You look good enough to eat," Max said, tousling the curls Iris had adjusted minutes earlier in front of the bathroom mirror, telling herself that all three toothbrushes standing in a cruddy ceramic glass could easily belong to Max, then forcing herself to run away before peeking into the medicine cabinet in search of tampons or birth control devices, or whatever other horrors it might hold.

The elevator jerked and began its descent. Iris and Max cross-studied their reflections. Iris did a half-turn, wondering whether her butt looked outrageously big. Max jutted out the jaw of a face darkened by day-old bristle and a season-old tan, tilting his head first to the right, then to the left. He rolled up the sleeves of his wrinkled silk shirt to just above the elbow. Iris was glad they were in a rush, otherwise, she might have offered to iron it for him, and even she knew that would have sounded ridiculously wifey.

"We make a great couple," Max declared to their reflection. Iris smiled. She would have walked the five hundred kilometers to Rome in those absurd heels to hear him say that.

Iris grabbed Max's elbow. "Oh, my God! That's ... oh shoot, what's her name? I know I've seen her somewhere before." Iris pointed her chin at a sparrow-like redhead across the room who was also wearing something that didn't quite fit her: her boobs. They were at least three sizes too big for her scrawny frame, making her look like she might topple over at any moment.

"Marinella Arquati. She has a morning show," Max said, his eyes darting around the room as he nodded at a balding man with sloping shoulders and glow-in-the-dark teeth, who gestured for him to go over.

Iris never watched morning shows, and doubted she ever would, even if she didn't have a job.

"She wrote a few cookbooks, too," Max added. "Made a bundle with them."

"That's where I've seen her picture! On the cover of that cookbook, *Mangiamo Insieme?*. She looks just like that picture, the way she does that thing with her hair draped over her cleavage like a veil. Except without the apron. Someone gave me a copy for Christmas one year." That someone was Cinzia, and the year was the same one Iris had been accused of ruining the Leale Easter dinner. But Iris mentioned neither the name nor the incident. It seemed disloyal to talk about Gregorio or any member of his family when she was with Max, even if she didn't say anything bad about them. Maybe it was just the fact that Max even knew about them, while they didn't know about Max.

"Too bad the slut hasn't cooked a meal in her life," Max said.

"Who?" Iris asked, distracted by her mental meanderings.

"Marinella, no? I went to her villa in Trastevere for a party a couple of months ago. Every single thing was catered. She had a state-of-the-art, professional kitchen installed for free by the suckers that equipped the set at the studio, and it still had stickers on it."

Iris had never tried out any of Marinella's recipes; she always cooked according to her inspiration and what was available. And with all her years of practice, she certainly didn't need any step-by-step illustrated recipes to tell her what to do. "I don't know about her cooking," Iris said, "but it sure doesn't look like she eats much. The only meat on her is her boobs. I don't think I've ever seen such big ones in real life. Except maybe my Auntie Rosa's, but she never showed them off like that."

"That breast meat is not exactly of the corn-fed variety. Marinella's last husband was a plastic surgeon, so those knockers were freebies, too. She better be careful not to bend over any lit burners on that show if she doesn't want those girls to melt right on the air."

Iris giggled at the image; it was so much fun to be with someone who made her laugh, just by the way he said things. Max's language was a bit more vulgar than she was used to, but that was how they all talked in his circles. She knew it wasn't fair to make comparisons, but Gregorio always used such dry, clinical terminology, even with her. If he were to make the same comment about Marinella, he would call her boobs "prostheses" instead of "knockers" – it just didn't sound as funny.

Iris looked around at the stunning penthouse with its polished hardwood floors, beamed ceilings, and walls covered with what Iris bet were valuable works of original art.

"Shouldn't we say hello to the hostess, and thank her for the invitation?" she asked. She would like to compliment her on her lovely home.

"Nah, who the hell knows where she is - probably blowing coke in the bathroom. We'll bump into her sooner or later." Max snatched two glasses of bubbly from a tray carried by a Filipino manservant in a white uniform. "How about a drink?" he said, handing one to Iris.

"I'd love one!" she said. Iris touched the rim of her glass to Max's, and said *"cin cin!"*. He smiled and shook his head. It must be his crowd didn't think it cool to toast, the way Isabella's crowd didn't think it proper say *"buon appetito"* before eating. Iris didn't really care, not enough to feel stupid, anyway. She was too happy to be there with Max, rubbing elbows with famous people. Not that she didn't deal with her share of VIPs at the Dimora, but mingling with them socially was different from being responsible for their comfort as guests of her hotel.

She raised her eyes over the brim of her glass and spotted a man walking in the door. Now if he wasn't important, someone should tell him so, because he certainly acted the part. His practiced smile was as stiff and out of place at a party as the hulk who trailed him in a dark suit and sunglasses, with a hand cupped over one ear. Judging from the way the man panned the room with his beady eyes, left to right, right to left, without ever turning his head, never pausing or looking anyone in the eye when they greeted him, Iris guessed he was a politician. She couldn't quite place his face, but several names came to mind. It was easy to learn them all; there were never any new politicians in Italy, only ones that died.

"Who is that man?" she finally whispered to Max. He was watching him, too.

"Giulio Canestrato. He's whatever he needs to be to protect his slippery little ass. For now, he's a head honcho at Viale Mazzini."

"Where's Viale Mazzini?" Iris asked.

"From which planet doth thou hail, Alien?" Max said. "It's here, in Rome. That's where RAI has its headquarters. Viale Mazzini *is* RAI, remember that if you hear it again. Because you will."

"Sorry," Iris said, blushing. "I'm still learning."

"Yes, you are learning," Max said, running his fingers down her spine, then giving her silky red rump a squeeze. Max downed the rest of his spumante and grabbed two full glasses from the Filipino passing with his silver tray, still nodding and smiling. Iris smiled back at him, wondering vaguely whether his wife was helping in the kitchen, and what comments they might exchange at the end of a party.

"Come on," Max said, putting a hand on her butt to push her along. "I'm gonna introduce you around to a few people." Crossing the room on her borrowed stilts, Iris was grateful for having learned to dance *en pointe*.

"Hey, Tony, how's it going?" Max said, punching the sloping

93

shoulder of the balding man with the bright teeth who had been gesticulating for him to come over.

"Ciao, Max. Who's your little friend?" The man looked up at her face, then let his eyes roam over the short red dress, continuing down her long legs to her red toes. She blushed at the way the man looked at her, but if he was out of line, she was sure Max would take care of it. After all, the clothes had come from his closet, and the man was his friend.

"I'm Iris," she said, as Max turned to whisper something in someone else's ear.

"Nice to meet you, Iris." The man extended a hand. "I'm Tony." Of course. He was *that* Tony. He had been hosting game shows ever since television had made its debut in the homes of Italy. His teeth were indeed very white, his skin very tan, and his dyed hair frozen in time by massive quantities of hairspray. Just like he appeared on the screen.

She took his hand, and said, "It's a real pleasure to meet you." She couldn't very well tell him that she never watched his show unless she was forced to, or that he was a favorite of her mother-in-law and sister-in-law, which would imply that her opinion was not included in the consensus.

"So are you Max's new sidekick?" Tony asked.

Iris smiled. "It depends on what you mean by 'sidekick.'"

"He told me he had a new assistant."

"Well, I'm not his assistant. I'm his - just a friend of his." Iris wondered how Max would have introduced her, and what the new assistant he had never mentioned looked like.

"Gotcha. So what's your line of business, Iris?"

"Hotels."

"Gotcha," Tony said, nodding. Iris did not want to get into details but wondered what he thought she did. Whenever she gave that same generic answer, people's reactions varied according to their perceptions of her. The owner of a dry goods store in Rapallo, always seeing her dressed in sneakers and jeans when she came to stock up for the Leales the first Saturday of every month, thought she was a maid. Once, when she was dressed in a suit and flying to

London in business class, the gentleman seated next to her, after receiving the same answer to the same question, assumed she owned a hotel. The way she looked tonight, Tony might mistake her for an escort, or worse.

But Tony's attention had already been diverted by a cluster of pretty young things - probably aspiring showgirls – throwing their scantily clad bodies at him. Iris cringed to think that she was probably old enough to be the mother of any one of them. She didn't feel that old, but since she was, she thanked God she didn't have to worry about a daughter like that.

Iris glanced around in search of Max, who had wandered away. She spotted him in a far corner of the room, huddled together with a couple of long-haired men of athletic build. One looked like the Italian soccer player featured in a poster hanging in the bedroom of Cinzia's youngest son, and the other one with all the skinny black braids might have been Brazilian. She didn't know or care anything about soccer and didn't want to have to pretend, so she watched Max in action from a distance. He snatched three glasses from the Filipino, then said something that made the other two guys toss their heads back and laugh. She decided not to interrupt his networking, and practice being a little more outgoing; maybe she should roam about a bit and see who else she might recognize.

She did spot someone – it was that singer everyone talked about after she won the San Remo Festival back in February. She had the name of a stone - Turchese or Onyx or something like that. And the man she was chatting with, he was a Minister of Education, or maybe that was in the previous government, maybe now he was Health - either way, she recognized him right off the bat. His picture had recently been in all the papers as the alleged perpetrator of a sex crime involving a minor. Of course, he had no intention of stepping down, and no one was about to force him. It would take years for any kind of ruling, and in the meantime, judging by the smirk on the man's face and the look of adoration in the singer's eyes, he seemed to have reaped considerable benefits from the publicity.

Iris felt awkward standing there all alone, in a room where

everyone else seemed to be engaged in several conversations at the same time. She had seen people walking up and down the stairs off to the right, and decided to investigate. Gripping her sandals with her toes and pressing her knees together to avoid exposing herself, she cautiously climbed the stairs. Stepping onto the terrace, she swooned in the seductive embrace of the Roman night.

Thanks to the opportunities first presented to her by Claudio Olona, Iris had sipped cappuccinos by morning and champagne by night on the terraces of some of the city's most luxurious hotels. She had enjoyed the views of Roman rooftops and cupolas, of the Pantheon and the Colosseum, of Piazza Navona and Piazza di Spagna, of Via Veneto and Via Nazionale. But this was the first time she had set foot on a private terrace, where the atmosphere was animated by the voices and gestures of glamorous people having a good time, or doing a superb job faking it. The atmosphere here was softer, the stage less grandiose as if the pulleys and ropes holding the backdrop in place were left slack. Loud voices and bursts of laughter rode bareback on the mild night air, mingling with the sounds from adjacent terraces, before dropping like crumbs to the crowds milling below.

Iris had always loved strolling through Campo Dè Fiori by day. The square pulsated with the colors and sounds and smells of a picture-perfect Roman market, where buckets of fresh cut flowers vied for attention with the exotic spices that tickled your nostrils, and just looking at the succulent fruits bursting out of their skins made your mouth water. At this hour, the hawkers and their goods had long since abandoned their stalls, and the sunshine had been replaced by soft amber lights that washed over the slowly crumbling buildings.

Clusters of young people gathered around the hooded statue in the center of the Campo, doing what they did best on a lovely Roman night: talking, flirting, smoking, drinking, laughing. Their rowdy socializing was unaffected by the hooded stare of the monk immortalized in bronze, who had been burnt at the stake in that very spot for saying what he thought, or by the scrutiny of the American woman in borrowed clothes gazing down upon them from the terrace of a penthouse, who wondered if she would ever find the courage to speak her mind as that monk had done, and what her punishment would be if she did.

4. LILY

After what seemed like endless days of struggle and exhaustion, Lily didn't feel any closer to understanding what was going on in her life. She still felt constantly sad and continually challenged. Day-to-day demands teased the limits of her stamina, and the boys tested the limits of her patience. They had been told only that "Mommy and Daddy needed a time-out." Which they apparently interpreted as meaning that their father had misbehaved, and Lily was punishing him by putting him in a naughty chair in a far off corner to think about what he had done. They begged her to let him come home, stating that they were sure he was sorry, and whatever it was, he would never do it again. They were especially insistent on the matter after returning from spending time with Joe, which made their short visits with him less of a break for Lily, and more of another crisis that needed her time and attention. Everyone was confused and quick to anger, as the family sat on the edge of their collective seat, anxious to know what life might be like in six months. Or six weeks. Or six days.

Lily felt immobilized, curled up on the couch in the living room, smoking with the drapes drawn. Just to catch her breath, she reasoned. The routines that she had so valued and adhered to so strictly for so long were now too flimsy to provide her life with any sense of structure. Put the kids on the bus, do the breakfast dishes, clean the bathroom, sweep the kitchen floor. Stop and have a second cup of coffee. Put a load of laundry in. Run the errands. Stop at the grocery store. Put the clean clothes into the dryer. Eat lunch. Take Wishes for a walk. Fold the clothes, get the kids off the bus. She knew the drill as she knew her own face. The tasks of her past had been sufficiently demanding to inhibit the meanderings of a discontented housewife but were not now enchanting enough to constrain the footsteps of a wandering soul seeking life's meaning.

She silently praised the increasingly darker colder days for granting her permission to send the boys down into the family room to watch TV after dinner, while she sat and prayed for bedtime so the guilt of not being more engaged with them would ease, for just a few hours.

Ever since the night at the police station, Lily felt like she was living someone else's life. She wondered who was living hers. Each day, she vowed to herself that she would find a way to launch herself into action. And each day she promised she would try again tomorrow. She would certainly have to fill her mother in soon on what was going on. At the very least, she could probably help Lily navigate some of the legal issues. She had built an avocation out of helping destitute women make their way through divorce court. Even if blood hadn't qualified Lily for assistance, surely the depth of her desperation would.

The Family Court waiting area smelled of rubber erasers and body odor. Testament, no doubt, to those who had agonized here over the negotiation of their lives. Lily toddled along behind her mother, the way she imagined she must have on countless Sunday mornings when the Capotosti family trailed down Rugby Road to St. Augustine's for Mass. In the same way, Lily was unconcerned about where to go and what to do once she arrived. The intensity of her anxiety was rivaled only by the gratitude she felt for her mother, knowing that she did not have to face the ordeal alone.

Over the years, Lily had criticized her mother's casual parenting style, a style that hadn't adequately prepared Lily for her first period, or taught her social graces - a lack of which had caused her embarrassment on more than one occasion - a style that had made her look the other way when Lily stood at the altar as an ignorant bride of nineteen years. Yet all was forgiven in the moment that Lily and her mother stepped off the elevator and into this strange land of litigation and Latin. This was Betty Capotosti's playground, and Lily was content to let her lead the way. More than content, she was desperate for the company, the expertise, and the sense of protection her mother offered, if not for the homemade cowboy cookies that she always stashed in her purse in a plastic zipper bag. The two women sat side by side, waiting for the bailiff to open the doors to the courtroom, where they would bring Lily's petition for an Order of Protection before a judge.

"No thanks, Mom," said Lily. "I'm not hungry."

Her mother waved the opened bag under Lily's nose. "Just smell that," she said. "Oatmeal, raisins, brown sugar... it's practically like having a bowl of oatmeal. You need to keep your energy up, Lily. Have one. Tom pulled them fresh out of the oven this morning." Tom Bailey was a man that Lily's mother had met the previous year through the personal ads. He was a quiet man who loved to play jazz piano, cook and bake, and firmly believed in the powers of food and music to soothe the soul.

Lily obediently took a cookie from the bag and nibbled on the edge of it. *Home baked cookies. Just like Mama's live-in boyfriend used to make.* She looked up at her mother, who was doing her best to don a look of reproach - without much success. Her face had only grown gentler with the passing years, her skin more translucent, her wavy hair softer and lighter, having been tempered by time so that it appeared more the color of sandy earth than of smoldering fire. The only hardness that could be found was in her eyes. They seemed a darker green, the result of the defenses she had erected for herself, the walls she'd built during her long and arduous battle with the world, a battle that started with Lily's father and wound through her life like a vine seeking out oppression and injustice, encircling itself around the cause of every abused woman who crossed her path, as if by helping them she might somehow settle the rage that still paced about inside of her, even after all these years.

"I can't tell you how many hours I've sat in this spot, Lily." Her mother looked around the room with a sense of wistfulness that might have been reserved for discovering the height markers of a growing child on a forgotten door jamb. "So many women have gone through what you're going through, yet so many more have not because they are too afraid. I'm so proud of you. You are brave."

"I don't feel brave," said Lily. "I feel nauseated."

"Lily," said her mother, shifting her body in her chair so that she was directly facing her. "You are not the one who should be worried. Joe broke the law - you're the victim here. Remember that: You're the victim." She faced forward again. "I'm so glad that this didn't happen until after New York State changed its laws. I've known women who were threatened at knifepoint by their husbands who still couldn't get the police to do anything about it. They would call nine-one-one and by the time the police arrived, they would lose their nerve and wouldn't sign the paperwork, or would recapitulate after their husbands calmed down and got all lovey-dovey." She took a bite of a cookie, then brushed the crumbs from her lap. "Now with the new law, once the complaint has been filed, the police take over, and it becomes a matter between the state and the abuser. A lot of women - including me - made a lot of sacrifices to make that happen. We paved the way to make it easier for abuse victims. Like you."

"It doesn't feel easy," said Lily.

"I know, honey. I know." Her mother patted Lily's hands. "But your willingness to do this and to be strong when we go in there is going to make it easier for the women who come along after you."

That probably should have meant something to Lily, but it didn't. She didn't care about those other women and their sorry-ass problems. All she cared about was getting through today. Often, Lily would catch herself holding her breath, and then realize that she was thinking about what lay in wait in the days, weeks, and months to come. Wrangling her awareness back to the present moment provided little relief.

"I think we should move over there to the corner, Mom," said Lily. "Every time that elevator door opens, my stomach jumps. One of these times Joe is going to be standing there. I don't want to see his face."

"Nonsense," said her mother. "That's exactly why I chose this bench for us. The first thing I want him to see is us sitting here, unafraid and ready to fight."

"But I'm not unafraid," said Lily. "I'm not ready to fight; I don't want to."

"He doesn't know you're not unafraid," said Lily's mother. "And it doesn't matter if you want to fight or not. You have to. If they sniff out ambivalence or weakness on your part, they will destroy you. Just sit up tall now. Throw your shoulders back and keep your chin up. Just like on that deodorant commercial: Never let them see you sweat."

Lily followed her mother's instructions, and as if on cue, the elevator chimed, the doors opened, and Joe emerged, walking and talking with a man who was carrying a leather briefcase and wearing a three-piece gray pin-striped suit.

"That bastard," said Lily's mother.

"Mom, please, don't start calling Joe names. What if the judge hears you?"

"I'm not talking about Joe - although he is a bastard. I'm talking about his lawyer. That guy is a sonofabitch. He would rape his own mother to win a case."

"Mom! That's an awful thing to say."

"Maybe. But it's true. I was helping this one woman who didn't have money for a lawyer, and that guy actually counseled the husband to perjure himself - right in front of me. He dared me to bring it up during the hearing, but I didn't know the proper protocol. Since the wife didn't have any proof that she was telling the truth, it became a case of 'he said, she said,' and was left up to the judge's determination."

Joe and his lawyer took chairs on the other side of the room, directly across from Lily and her mother. The lawyer leaned over and said something to Joe, and they both laughed.

"What happened?" asked Lily. "To your friend?"

"The judge slapped the husband on the wrist by assigning him to some ridiculous anger management program and then sent everybody home. Since my friend didn't have any money or family, she had no choice but to return to the marital home. That night, her husband beat her to within an inch of her life."

"You're kidding?" Why was her mother telling her this story? Lily didn't need to hear more horror stories; she needed one with a happy ending. Or least one with an ending that didn't cause her gut to clamp more tightly in fear.

"I wish I was kidding," her mother replied. "Except this time, a passing neighbor heard the commotion and called the police. The husband was arrested, and my friend got her Order of Protection."

"That's good," said Lily, looking to her mother for some reassurance. "Right?"

"The only thing good about it is that he didn't kill her first."

Lily's mother twisted her mouth into a knot, the vein at her temple swelled and throbbed. Lily wondered if her mother was quietly enraged at the memory of the story she told, of her own wounds, which she still tended, or at the fact that her youngest daughter was now facing a similar horror. Maybe they were all the same story, but with different endings. She shuddered at what her ending might be.

"I can't face him, Mom. Every time I think of it, I just want to get up and run out of here." Lily considered the option. She could just walk out of here and go home, couldn't she? She could tell Joe it was all a big mistake, that she didn't know why she was acting so strangely, but that she was sorry and just wanted things to go back to the way they were. Back to life as she knew it. It wasn't perfect, but it wasn't the worst, either. There were lots of other women living in worse situations than she was. She could find a way to focus on the good things, couldn't she? On her children, on their beautiful home, on the precious moments when they were all huddled around the woodstove watching a movie, or hanging out in the backyard, Pierce and Joseph playing tag with Wishes at their heels, chortling at the delight shared by dogs and their little boys. Were there enough of those moments to sustain her, to keep the sorrow and the fear at bay? Could she string them together and stretch them out long enough to get her past these difficult years? When the boys were grown, it would be easier to leave. The idea of facing this process and this place later on, when she would be a different person, maybe a stronger one, was certainly worth considering. Wasn't it?

Lily was aroused from her reverie by the cries of a little girl who trailed along behind her mother, the two of them tethered to each other by hands and tears.

"Mommy!" cried the little girl. "No, Mommy, no!" Snot streamed from her nose, and she paused her cry to lick it from her lips, her gaze briefly meeting Lily's before she resumed her mission and her wails. She was a couple of years younger than Pierce. In ten years, the two of them might end up in the same high school. Maybe even go to a dance together. In twenty years, they could fall in love. In thirty years, they could be here, staring each other down from across the Family Court waiting room.

Lily suddenly understood that this was not just about her and Joe. It was about her boys, and what they would learn about being men and husbands in the years to come. It was about what Joseph and Pierce would come to think of her as they watched her endure the indignities and humiliation that were part of her relationship with their father. And it was about the two little girls out there somewhere who would one day share their beds, their homes, their lives.

"May I have your attention," called the bailiff. "All those who have hearings at one o'clock, please come to the desk and check in." One by one, people rose from their seats and took their places in line. Once everyone was checked in, the bailiff ushered them into the courtroom. The long wooden benches smelled of oil soap like the pews at St. Augustine's; they creaked and groaned under the weight of each new person who sat. Uniformed officials stood post at a humongous desk, which sat on a platform at the front of the room. People spoke in whispers. Signs and statues and banners adorned the walls, and all the trembling transgressors sat waiting to be heard and sentenced.

The judge entered the room. The people all stood; the people all sat. The judge spoke; the people answered. Two cases were heard prior to Lily's: both of them were women seeking Orders of Protection from their husbands.

"What is it, an epidemic?" Lily whispered to her mother.

"It'd be considered an epidemic if the men were the ones getting abused," said Lily's mother. "Since it's women getting hurt and killed, it's treated more like the common cold."

"Diotallevi versus Diotallevi," announced the bailiff.

"That's us," said Lily's mother. She grabbed her tattered attaché, popped up out of her seat, and nudged Lily toward the aisle.

Lily and her mother took their seats at the table at the front of the courtroom. Lily noticed Joe's lawyer as he spun the combination on his briefcase and extracted papers from within, making three neatly stacked piles on the desk in front of him. Lily looked at her mother's faux leather portfolio with the broken latch and the manila folder that had been used and reused every time she'd had occasion to appear in Family Court on her own behalf or someone else's. It bore the markings where names had been written and erased, where labels had been affixed and torn off, and upon which dribbling mugs of coffee had been rested. Lily found herself wishing she had a real lawyer - someone with a real briefcase and a success story or two to share. Since the initial separation, however, Joe had not been forthcoming with any financial help, the matter being completely voluntary in the interim between his arrest and the hearing. The last time Lily had used her credit card at the grocery store, it was rejected, and when she tried to get cash from the ATM, the machine sucked her card up and displayed a phone number for her to call to diagnose the issue. There was no need to call the number. Lily knew what Joe was thinking: If she wouldn't take him back for love, she might do so to keep from starving to death.

"Family Court is not a difficult thing," Lily's mother had told her. "I've been through this process so many times; I can do it with my eyes closed." The only other option Lily knew of was to show up alone.

The judge addressed Lily. "Please state your name."

"Lily Diotallevi, sir."

She was pretty sure she got that one right. But what if he asked her a question and she didn't know what to say? Lily thought of the story in the New Testament of Saint Stephen's trial, and how he relied upon the Holy Spirit to inspire him with the right words. Of course, Saint Stephen was rushed by an angry crowd and stoned to death in the streets. Not exactly what she was going for.

The room fell away as Lily's responses to the judge's questions floated in the air around her, as if being spoken by someone else, or as if being answered from within a dream.

"No, sir."

"She's my mother, sir."

"Yes, sir."

"Two children, sir."

"Yes, sir."

"No, sir."

The judge removed his tortoiseshell glasses and set them on his desk. He raised his head up from reading the papers in front of him and looked directly at Lily.

"Mrs. Diotallevi, are you afraid of your husband?"

Lily looked at her mother, and then back at the judge. She didn't want to turn toward Joe, but she caught sight of his form with a timid sidelong glance, and despite her will to face forward, her head betrayed her and followed suit. Joe's gaze chilled her. She'd seen that look before - most recently in her rearview mirror that night after her recording session. There was a darkness in his eyes, a vacancy. In that moment, there was no other answer but the one she was terrified to utter in his presence.

"Mrs. Diotallevi?" the judge repeated. "Are you afraid of your husband?"

Lily's mother nudged her in the ribs with her elbow.

"Yes, your honor," said Lily. "He scares me."

"You've gotta be freakin' kidding me," said Joe, throwing his hands into the air.

Joe's lawyer leaned over and whispered something to him. This time, there was no laughter, just a single grunt. Lily enjoyed the idea that she could say whatever she wanted, and Joe had no choice but to stand there and take it. It was like jumping into the deep end of the swimming pool with one of those inflatable rings around your waist. What you were doing was technically dangerous, but you weren't really scared. Is that what power feels like? Lily wished she had said more, wished she had told the judge not only that she was afraid of Joe, but that she sometimes stayed up all night, hovering on the couch, looking out through the slats of the mini-blinds that covered the front living room windows - just to make sure he didn't try to break in while they were sleeping. And she wished she told him that Joe had driven past the house nearly every night - sometimes at midnight or one o'clock in the morning. One night, she dozed off and woke at four a.m., to find his car parked across the street, puffs of cigarette smoke spilling out a crack in the driver's side window.

The judge turned to Joe's lawyer. Lily had her attention trained keenly on them, and while she could hear the words being spoken, she struggled to discern their meaning, trapped as she was behind a haze of confusion and anxiety. She sure hoped her mother knew what was going on.

The judge gently tapped the gavel and called the next case. Lily's mother squeezed her hand under the table and whispered to her, "Great job - you made it through your first court appearance." The idea that she would have to attend more of them was at first softened by the realization that Lily had been awarded a six-month Order of Protection, and then magnified by the fact that she had reached the point of no return. Joe could forgive her crazy ideas and schemes. He could learn to overlook her occasional outbursts of indignation, and she could even imagine a world in which he might be able to forgive her infidelity; at least that would give him lifetime leverage against her. That was more plausible than him forgiving her for placing a court-ordered injunction against him, keeping him from doing what he wanted with her when he wanted. From this moment on, she was on her own. She had no money, no means of support, and no one to watch the boys even if she could get a job. It would take weeks before a child support order could be processed. Assuming she could hang on until then, she had officially less than one year to get on her feet and put her life back together. Her saliva felt hot in her mouth. She looked around the room for a garbage can in case the cowboy cookie decided to make its way back up.

"Mom," said Lily, gripping her mother's sleeve as they walked through the parking garage. "Now what do I do? How are we going to survive?"

"You'll have to get legal separation papers drawn up to protect yourself. Legal aid can probably help you with that, but one day at a time," said her mother, patting her hand. "Today is a huge victory for us, Lily. For now, let's get out of here, and go to my place." Rubbing the palms of her hands together, she added, "We can brainstorm about next steps."

Lily bristled at the way her mother seemed to be enjoying the whole process. It wasn't a party, after all. If anything, it was more like a funeral. One for which it wasn't completely clear who the corpse was.

"Mom, I really can't stay to visit," said Lily as she pulled her car into the parking lot of the condo her mother shared with Tom. "I have to get home before the school bus drops the kids off."

"You have ten minutes for a cup of tea," said her mother. "I'm sure Tom has been in there whipping up something delightful for us."

"Here's a little snack," said Tom, placing a small blue plate of sliced banana bread in front of Lily. He patted her on the head. "It's still warm." Then he disappeared again into the kitchen.

Lily watched as globs of butter on the brown surface of the bread first melted into tiny glistening pools and then disappeared. Except for half a cowboy cookie, she hadn't eaten since last night when she'd nibbled on Pierce's leftover fish sticks. The aroma of the bread swirled its way up into her nostrils, arousing memories of Iris' passion for making baked goods in the winter. Her best memories always included Iris. At least they always used to.

Lily's stomach growled. She picked up a slice and bit into it. It collapsed in her mouth, sweet, warm sponginess, laced with salty butter, the first communion of her freedom. In a good, small way, it renewed Lily's faith that even now, when there was so much to be afraid of and worried about, even as the ground itself seemed to be disintegrating beneath her, there was this moment of respite and home-baked banana bread.

Lily offered a prayer of thanks for Tom, for her mother, and for the comfort of a hot cup of tea with milk and sugar. As she took a gulp from the mug that her mother had set before her, a faint groan escaped from her throat.

"I only have about an hour," she said, picking up a second slice of bread.

The phone rang, and as was their custom, neither Tom nor Betty moved to answer it. They were staunch screeners - they always waited and listened to see who was calling and what they had to say before deeming the communication worthy of a trip all the way across the room.

When their recorded greeting finished playing, the voice on the other end was broadcast over the speaker, "Mom - are you there? It's Violet. Pick up. Mom, there's been an accident." Violet's voice disappeared into a muffled cry as Lily's mother launched herself from her chair and lunged for the telephone. "Mom, please pick up the phone if you're there."

"Violet? Violet?" said Betty as she raised the receiver to her ear. "What's happened?" She listened with a furrowed brow. "What?! Oh, dear... Uh-huh, OK, well, what... oh... uh-huh..." She plucked a tissue from the box next to the phone and dabbed at her eyes.

Lily froze, taking fragile shelter in her ignorance. For as long as her mother stayed on the phone, Lily would not have to face whatever news Violet was delivering. In this instant, Lily's pain and sorrow would be limited to the demise of her marriage, the terror of her unknown future, and the reality of her poverty.

"Of course, of course," Lily's mother said. "Lily is here with me; we will head right over." As if in slow motion, she returned the telephone to the cradle. Lily held her breath.

"It's Henry, your brother," said Lily's mother, as if Lily would not know who Henry was. "He's had a very serious car accident," said Lily's mother. "We have to get over to Strong Memorial Hospital."

Lily picked up the phone and dialed. "Let me see if I can get a hold of Donna so she can take the boys off the bus for me." Part of her hoped that Donna would not answer the phone; she wasn't sure she could handle any more tragedy today.

"Mom, no one is answering," said Lily "I have to go home. If I can, I'll catch up with you later."

Betty already had her coat on and was fishing through her purse for her car keys.

"OK," she said. She absentmindedly kissed Lily on the forehead. "You stay and finish your tea. Tom, don't wait dinner for me."

"Call me later," said Lily as her mother closed the door behind her. Lily felt a small rush of relief at being left behind, quickly followed by sharp pangs of shame and guilt. She looked down at the half slice of banana bread in her hand and returned it to the plate.

Lily's mother called late that evening to tell Lily that Henry had survived but was in a coma. Family members were encouraged to come to the hospital at their earliest convenience, and many were starting to gather. But Joseph and Pierce were already sleeping, thank God. She would come down in the morning as soon as she got them off to school.

The next morning, Lily followed the lines that marked the linoleum tile, as the woman at the front desk of the hospital had instructed her. *Take the red elevator to the orange level and then follow the blue lines to the intensive care family waiting area.* With each new color, she prayed for tears to come. Ironic. She'd spent the last few years of her life doing nothing but unsuccessfully trying to squelch tears, and now that she really wanted to cry, she couldn't find any sadness inside. How would it look to show up at her comatose brother's bedside with dry eyes?

Lily arrived at the family waiting area and discovered Henry's wife Diane emerging from his room.

"Oh, Lily!" cried Diane. She threw herself into Lily's arms. In the five years since Henry had married Diane, it was the first time Lily could remember ever touching her. Her stiff body was bony and cold; her pin straight blond hair smelled sterile, like rubbing alcohol.

"Any change?" Lily asked.

"No," said Diane. "I've been by his side all night, but he hasn't responded at all." Diane's sunken eyes and pale skin bore witness to her vigil. "In fact, I was just going to go join the others in the cafeteria to get a quick bite to eat, but I hated the idea of leaving him in there alone. Would you mind staying with him for a bit?"

"Absolutely," said Lily. "That's why I came down, to see him." It was true in one sense, but the whole truth was that she came down because she knew it was expected of her. And because she was still afraid to stay home alone. After all, as her mother had reminded her, an Order of Protection was still just a piece of paper.

"You're an angel," said Diane. "I won't be long."

"Take your time," said Lily, hoping that she wouldn't.

Henry was laid in the bed, swaddled in white sheets. His exposed arms were tucked in closely at his sides. Lily had expected to see tubes coming out of his mouth and his nose, like in the movies, but the only machine was a heart rate monitor that was attached to his index finger with a small blue clip. It steadily blipped out the tenuous rhythm of his life. Lily had never seen him so quiet and still. So benign. She stopped a few feet from the bed. The heart rate monitor blipped. Telephones faintly twittered at the nurse's station down the hall. A woman laughed. Lily took a step closer to the bed and placed her open purse on the bedside table next to a bottle of lotion and a box of tissues.

"Hey, Henry," said Lily.

The heart rate monitor blipped.

"I'm sorry about your accident." She was.

Lily looked about the room, noticing her reflection in the screen of the silent television that was mounted to the wall.

"I hope you're not in pain," she said. Of course. Goes without saying, doesn't it?

The heart rate monitor blipped.

Lily and Henry had barely spoken to each other as adults. Lily had always assumed that their continued mutual indifference - which manifested itself in the way they simply pretended not to notice one another - was the preferred course of action over talking about what had transpired between them in the chicken coop those many years ago. Small talk hardly seemed like the next step. Yet neither did death.

The landscape of their family would be forever changed in many subtle ways if Henry died. When asked how many children were in her family, the answer would be reduced by one. There would be a hesitation in their voices whenever they obliged friends by rattling off the names of their brothers and sisters; the list would shorten, but almost imperceptibly. Would Lily still be the ninth child in a family of twelve? Or would she now be the eighth in a family of eleven?

Was that all? Just the names and numbers would be different? Wouldn't her life change in any real way if Henry never woke up? Lily scanned her memory for an image of joy or a remnant of tenderness, for a single happy scene from her life with Henry in it. But all she could feel was fear. All she could sense was the dank hard floor of the chicken coop against her back, the dead fly suspended in a cobweb over her head, the weight of Henry's body thrusting all of the air from her lungs.

Henry's face was still and had Lily not known he was in a coma, she may have mistaken his state for one of peaceful rest. Didn't seem fair, though. For him to rest peacefully and leave her carrying the burden of her memories, of her shame.

"I wish I'd had the nerve to ask you about that," said Lily, surprised at this burst of courage. "Maybe if I'd gotten some answers from you, I would be able to find my peace, too."

Lily was buoyed by the resulting silence, emboldened by the realization that she could say whatever she wanted and he couldn't do a damned thing about it. He couldn't tell her to shut up or dispute her. He couldn't hit her or run out of the room. He could no longer ignore her; he could no longer hurt her. It seemed to be an emerging theme.

"Why did you do that to me, Henry?" she blurted. "Why? What did I ever do to you?" She rifled through her purse and then plucked a tissue from the box on the bedside table. "You were three times my size, Henry - you were heavy, and every time you laid on top of me I thought I was going to suffocate. I was terrified that you would forget I was there, that you would fall asleep, trapping me, crushing me." Her voice grew louder. "I was just a little girl, you know?" With a stomp of her foot, Lily grabbed the bedside table with both hands. She shook it and cried, "You were my big brother, Henry... Big brothers are supposed to protect you!"

Lily's face burned white hot. "I thought you loved me - I thought I was special! I didn't even realize what you were doing. I was nothing more to you than some kind of a toy, like nothing, like a rag doll!"

Using the full force of her body, Lily shoved the table, sending it flying on its wheels across the room. It collided with the wall, dumping the contents of Lily's purse, the lotion, and the tissues onto the floor. Lily froze, seized by the thought that Diane might return at any moment, or that a nurse could come running to investigate the racket. Yet she was unable to focus on anything except the purging of her pain.

Lily reached into her coat pocket and retrieved a brand new pack of Merits. She fumbled with trembling hands to pull the tiny cellophane tab, finally abandoning the effort and ripping the pack open with her teeth. She placed a cigarette between her lips and frantically patted down her pockets for a lighter before she realized that she could not smoke there.

After several minutes, her sobs waned, and she said, weakly, "You were my big brother." Were. My big brother. Lily looked down at Henry. His face remained unchanged, but he seemed more vulnerable than before; fragile, but she did not feel sorry for him. The heart rate monitor blipped, then blipped again. This time, Lily had been the one with the power, and this time, she was the one who used it to discharge her pent-up tensions while Henry lay defenseless. Yet somehow the score seemed no more settled; they were in no way even now. Lily would not be able to scream loudly enough or cry deeply enough to satisfy the debt he owed her.

Lily was exhausted but strangely energized. She felt different in a way that she didn't recognize. She crossed the room to retrieve the bedside table and collect the items that had scattered themselves around the floor. She wheeled the table back toward the bed. Sunlight strained to wriggle its way through a crack in the heavy drapes covering the window. She stopped and considered opening them before leaving the room, but decided against it.

It was the sort of cold that made you want to wail. It drilled right through your coats and layers and clothes, past your skin and blood and bones and stripped you of warmth at your core - which was just as well because it helped you find the tears you knew you needed to cry. It was perfect weather for burying a sibling.

Lily ran her hand along the smooth cold surface of the casket, wondering what it looked like from the inside - and why they lined them with all that fancy draping when the only person who might really enjoy it never would.

Lily envied the way all of their brothers and sisters stood under the tent at the cemetery gushing love for Henry, though it seemed to her that no one had much of anything good to say about him before his accident. Now he was the star of the family, suddenly sweeter and kinder and funnier than they had ever deemed him in life. The least you could do when someone leaves this world was agree that their presence was worthwhile. Lily was glad that it didn't even really matter if it was true.

They all told their favorite Henry stories. Laughter mingled with tears and rain and ice fell around as they stood there, no one wanting to be the first to walk away - as if he wasn't really dead, but only sleeping in that box, and could be awakened again by the clatter of memories.

Lily surveyed the circle of siblings gracing Henry's coffin like a garland of wildflowers. As a group, their accomplishments were impressive; the desperate cultivation of the independence that had enabled them to survive their childhood and scratch and borrow their way into adulthood had sent each of them off in a newly forged direction, bearing less and less resemblance, as the years went on, to the simple river from which they flowed.

Alexander had worked his way up through local politics and was currently engaged in a campaign for Congressman - as a Republican. Betty Capotosti was incensed by her eldest son's rejection of her values; he was embarrassed by her misguided loyalty to them. John was the first to fulfill Carlo's dream of having a doctor in the family by becoming a surgeon. Jasmine - perhaps inspired by being the eldest girl in a family whose children always seemed to need more time, more love, more attention than their mother could give - dedicated her life to the rescue and rehabilitation of animals, feral and domestic. Violet's birthing centers had popped up all over Rochester and in every surrounding town while Marguerite spent her evenings and weekends producing gallery shows, literary readings, and theatre openings, earning her a place of respect in the small but fierce regional artist community. Louis loved working with his hands, but hated classroom study. He had earned a sterling reputation as the best auto mechanic in town, and his stories were about engines and catalytic converters, which he always told with a dimpled smile on his face, gesticulating with hands that were permanently stained with grease. Charles and William, adrift in the aftermath of their parents' divorce, had wandered into government-funded degrees in engineering at the nearby Rochester Institute of Technology. Ricci was the only one who figured out that intelligence and accomplishment were not the antidotes to the Capotosti legacy; money was. He obtained his undergraduate degree in Global Finance, and then his M.B.A. He'd made plenty of money for others in his career as an investment banker, as well as for himself. Iris was still living in Italy, working as Director of the *Dimora Baia Dell'Incanto* hotel, still the cherished wife of an adoring husband still graced and blessed and special, simply by virtue of being Iris.

Catholics, atheists, evangelical Christians; Republicans, Democrats, and anarchists - the Capotosti siblings were a community unto themselves bound together now only by blood and so by grief. Just six weeks ago they had celebrated Thanksgiving together, and now there Henry lay, sealed away, by all accounts - except Lily's - as innocent as the day he was born.

Despite the years of arguments, childhood cruelties, and divergences in careers and systems of values and faith, they all stood shocked at their newly discovered impotence against nature

- an impotence that was never more evident than it was at that moment, in the cold truth that no amount of love or laughter or happy memories could ease their pain or change the fact that one of them was no more.

When Lily was small, and she'd say her bedtime prayers, *If I should die before I wake, I pray the Lord my soul to take,* she'd often wondered if she would be the first of the Capotosti children to die. The only thing worse would be to be the last. The thought of attending all eleven funerals filled her with overwhelming sadness; the thought of having all eleven of them attend hers, with terror. Lily couldn't help but wonder what her brothers and sisters would be saying about her if she were the one who was leaving them behind.

"Remember how Lily married that asshole and spent twenty years living in hell?" Iris would say.

"She should have protected herself better," Marguerite would say. "Or at all."

"Oh," Violet would chime in, "How about when she went bankrupt? That'd be the day I'd let anyone ruin me financially."

"I tried to tell her," their mother would say. "But she just didn't listen."

"And now she's gone," Jasmine would say. And then they would all go out for lunch.

That was Lily's legacy: Disaster, pain, failure. Unless of course, she contracted a dramatic disease that took long enough to kill her so that her siblings would have ample time to forget her countless shortfalls and crises, using their great capacity for compassion to fashion the image of a gentler, kinder Lily.

As his state had declined and it was clear that Henry would never regain consciousness, Diane had given the order to remove the feeding tube, according to the instructions left by Henry in his Living Will. One at a time, the Capotostis found their own way to say good-bye. Violet and Todd sat with him one Sunday afternoon and played CDs of old Beatles' tunes, leaving Henry's old Gibson guitar propped up in the corner when they left. Marguerite stopped by during the week and read to him - sometimes from Hemingway or Thoreau, and sometimes from a book of dirty limericks. Betty Capotosti simply sat with her son afternoons and held his hand as she recalled to him the stories of how, when he was small, he would spend entire afternoons building elaborate castles out of Lego blocks and then use her meat mallet to knock them down again.

Iris was the only one who didn't get to say good-bye to Henry while he was still alive. She'd arrived in town the night before the funeral. Since Auntie Rosa had moved into the senior living facility, Iris had developed a custom of staying with Violet whenever she came home. After all, Violet had a guest room, a hot tub in the backyard, and an extra car to loan - the sort of hospitality that Lily could never provide. So her time with Iris was limited to the one or two authentic pasta dinners that Iris would whip up for whoever happened to be around - and when Iris was home, there were many. Because of the crowd that Iris magnetized, she and Lily rarely had the chance to sit down together, just the two of them. But it was better that way. If Lily were alone with Iris, and if they shared a bottle of wine or a quiet dinner, Lily might tell her about the darkness that dwelled within her. She might tell her how she understood why Dolores left this world as she did - whether it was a desire to permanently escape or to temporarily anesthetize herself, Lily understood; Iris never could. Such darkness did not exist in Iris' world. It would only irritate her and augment the distance between them.

After the graveside ceremony, Lily exchanged a flurry of obligatory kisses and "I love yous" with her sisters before they all darted away through the chill rain across the parking lot to their cars.

"Lily, are the kids staying overnight with Joe?" Violet called out the driver's side window of her two-seated sports car.

"Yeah - why?" Lily shoved her hands into her coat pockets, making a mental note to buy a pair of gloves.

"Come on over to Violet's," called Iris from the passenger's seat. "We'll have some hot tea and a little lunch, and then maybe later we'll force ourselves to go out for a while. We've all been crying for days, and we need to let loose a little - I think Henry would be mortified at the thought of causing all this sorrow." Lily doubted that. She thought it would make Henry glad to lash out in such a grand and sweeping way, affecting all of his brothers and sisters with one act while depriving them of the opportunity to retaliate.

Regardless of what they would end up doing, it didn't take a great deal of skill in math to figure out that the price tag for any activity that Iris and Violet had in mind would far exceed the ten dollars in Lily's purse, which needed to last her through the weekend. Anyway, when the sisters were together, they often chatted about vacations in the tropics and compared new pieces of jewelry their husbands had given them. Lily tried to smile and coo and offer congratulations, but as the years passed, time spent with them only accentuated her own feelings of inadequacy, and it became increasingly difficult for her to enjoy their company. It would be too hard. Especially now.

"Maybe I'll come by for a little while, but then I really have to get home. I have to go let the dog out."

By the time Lily pulled into the housing development where Violet lived, the street was lined on both sides with the cars of family and Iris' friends. Lily parked three blocks away and tried to tiptoe through the wet snow that had begun to accumulate on the sidewalk. As soon as she stepped inside the house, she kicked off her shoes and sat on the floor by the fireplace to warm her numb toes.

"I think the last time we were all together like this was when dad died." Iris sat down next to Lily and offered her a plate of food.

"Death has a way of making people appreciate each other. That's the good thing about it." Lily surveyed the assortment of salami, provolone cheese, olives, and boiled fava beans that Iris had selected.

"Is there any real food over there?" She placed the plate on the floor.

"Sorry," said Iris, the smile falling from her face. "I didn't know what you liked. Why don't you try it? It's good."

"That's OK - thanks anyway. I guess I'm just not hungry." Lily's stomach rumbled.

"Listen - we decided to have a family bowling night tonight. We need to be together, and since Henry absolutely hated to go bowling, we thought it was the perfect activity."

"I'm not much of a bowler," said Lily. Recognizing that was a weak excuse for getting out of it, she added, "Anyway, I really can't afford it this week." It was so much easier to plead poor and stay home. Who could fault you for not having money?

"It'll be my treat - you just come and have fun."

"I don't want you to pay my way, Iris. It's embarrassing."

"But it's me... there's nothing to be embarrassed about." Iris picked up the plate of food and handed it to Lily again. "I know you at least like salami."

"Of course it's not embarrassing - for you," said Lily. "Ever since we were little you've been paying my way. Remember Grandpa Capotosti's spittoon? He would only allow you to earn the twenty-five cents to empty it, and so you were the only one who ever had any Christmas money. Even then, I was embarrassed to have you put 'From Iris and Lily' on all the gifts. I knew they weren't from me."

Lily brought a slice of provolone cheese to her nose, sniffed it, scrunched up her nose, and then returned it to the plate. "I was a tagalong then, and I'm a tagalong now." She set the plate back onto the floor. "Let's be honest. I don't fit in here with you and the other sisters. It's better if we stop pretending that I do."

"All I wanted to do was pitch in five bucks for you to come bowling so we could all be together! And now you're blaming me for trying to help you fit in? For signing your name on the gifts I bought with the money I earned? For bringing you to play with my friends because you never made any of your own? For convincing Mom to let you stay home sick when I did? For convincing Auntie Rosa to let you come for a weekend sleepover?"

"Well, I am so sorry I was such a drain on you."

"Please don't be like that, Lily." A droplet emerged and perched itself at the tip of Iris' long slender nose. She daintily dabbed at it with the tissue she had wadded up in her hand.

"Be like what?"

119

"First of all, you're remembering it the way you want to. I only got a nickel for emptying out the spittoon, and you wouldn't have done it for a dollar."

"How do you know that? How would anyone know unless they bothered to ask me? Besides, a nickel or a dollar - it doesn't matter. The money was never the point, was it?"

"No, the money isn't the point. The point is, you are feeling sorry for yourself like you always did."

"Someone's got to do it. I'm the only one who seems to notice - who pays any attention to what's going on with me. Just as it's always been. I don't know why I'm so surprised." Lily sidled up closer to the fire and crossed her arms over her chest.

"How could anyone know what's going on with you if you don't tell us? I tried so hard to stay in touch, I used to write to you all the time when I moved, but then you stopped answering, and I didn't know what to write anymore." Iris reached back and pulled an afghan off the couch, and draped it over Lily's shoulders. "Why didn't you tell me about what was going on with Joe? Why did you shut me out like that? I have a hard enough time keeping up with everyone else's problems from halfway across the world, do you expect me to be a mind-reader too?"

"Don't worry, Iris. I don't expect you to keep track of my problems. And when am I supposed to have the chance to talk to you about anything? The only time I see you, there is a crowd of people around, or you, Violet, and Jasmine are going off on one of your spa weekends or vacation trips that I can't go on."

"So now I'm supposed to feel bad if I take a vacation? Well, you'll be happy to know that I already do feel bad. Even though I work ten-hour days six days a week, I still feel guilty if I come here, and do something you can't do. I even take off my jewelry when I know we are going to see each other because I feel bad about having things you don't have. I suppose you think I always got whatever I wanted, without working for anything?"

"Believe me, I don't want you to be burdened by going through all that trouble of taking off your diamonds. And no one is asking you or expecting you to feel guilty." Lily shrugged, and the afghan dropped to the floor. "All I'm saying is, it is clear what your priorities are when you are here. That's all. And that's your choice. Nothing I can do about it anyway. Let's just forget it; it doesn't matter."

"Yes, it does matter. My priorities when I am here are to see you all. I spend every holiday missing my real family, and I'll never have a family of my own like you do. Just try sticking your head out of your own little world long enough to realize how hard it is for me. I go crazy trying to make the rounds to see everyone! Auntie Rosa expects me to visit every single day, and every single day she asks me when I'm moving back home. When I try to see Mom, instead of asking about my life or telling me about hers, she drags me to some luncheon or conference where I have to listen to a stranger rant on about some women's rights issues. I have this whole family to see, and I end up spending time with the ones who make more of an effort to see me. What effort do you ever make? Have you ever once invited me over for dinner in the past ten years?"

"Oh, be honest - you don't want to have dinner at my house."

"How do you know if you don't ask?"

"Believe me – if you knew what it was like at my house these days, you wouldn't want to come in for a drink of water, let alone for an entire meal. I don't even want to have dinner there half the time. Anyway, who ever has a chance to invite you to do anything? From the minute you get off that plane, there's a mad dash for your time and affections. I'm not going to compete for your love." Lily turned from the fire and looked at Iris. "Don't you get it, Iris? I don't want to be clumped into your 'rounds.' When did I slip down the list to those that you'll make time to see if you can fit it in? As far as Mom is concerned, she does that with everyone. That's what it's like to be a daughter in this family. And just once, I'd like to hear you tell Auntie Rosa 'no.'" Lily stood. "But then again, I guess if you were capable of doing that, you wouldn't have had to run away in the first place."

Iris shot up from the floor. "I didn't run away!"

"Of course you did!" shouted Lily. "And everyone knows it!"

"I can't believe you're doing this to me! I'm on the other side of the world and find out my brother is dead, I rush over here to make it for the funeral, and you won't even let me grieve in peace. You'd think you'd want us both to have the chance to do that, but maybe you're not grieving at all; maybe you're glad he's dead!"

Lily opened her mouth, but nothing came out. Her body trembled from the cold that still chilled her and from the rage she felt at Iris for breaking the silence they'd kept about what had happened between her and Henry. Lily couldn't bring herself to even look at Iris. She was afraid she might see a reflection of the pain she still carried in her sister's eyes. Then she might be forced to look at it when all she really wanted to do was forget.

Finally, she said, "I am not glad he's dead. I thought I would be. I used to wish for it, pray for it. I used to think that if Henry died, he would finally get punished and I would be free from the memory of what he did to me. But as it turns out, whether he's alive or not does not change the past; there is absolutely nothing I can do about it. And whether you're here or whether you're in your own fairyland in Italy it does not change that you just don't get it. You never did. And you probably never will. So go on - go do your grieving. Far be it from me to get in your way."

"You think I live in a fairyland? You think I'm so lucky - you always have - but that's not how it is! All I do is try! I try so hard, but it doesn't do any good. You'll never understand!"

"You're right. I'll never understand, that's for sure. So just do me a favor and go back to your perfect little world with your rich husband and your resort hotel on the sea. Just go."

"And you just stay put, wallowing in your pool of self-pity! But be careful, if you stay in there much longer, it's going to stink so bad no one will want to get near you!"

Iris stormed from the room in tears. Lily listened as Jasmine and Violet tenderly consoled her, assuming she was crying over Henry. Lily took her tears into the bathroom where she stayed until she heard the clinking of silverware against stoneware and the rumble of conversation from the kitchen. She then slipped out the back door and drove home. She trudged up to bed and disappeared under her covers, imagining her sisters on their seventh frame, chatting derisively about her absence before turning to order another round of beers.

Dear Lily,

I've been looking at this computer screen for about half an hour, but I keep running away to Facebook to postpone writing. It's not that I don't want to, it's just that I don't know where to begin.

I knew we were getting uncomfortably close to that horrible time of Henry's death and our quarrel, but I wasn't sure whether you would skip over it, deal with it, or expect me to. Sugar coatings were never your forte, and true to form, there's not a trace here. Just the bare bones served up on a platter of bitterness.

When I read those pages yesterday, all the shock and pain and sadness of that time came rushing at me. I sat here alone, staring out my window, in an awful state. I was glad no one was around to look back at me, except the olive trees. I spent the night alone in mourning. For Henry, for you, for me, for us, for our disappointments. For the fact that I couldn't protect you, even though I was your big sister.

Henry didn't exactly pick a good time to get himself killed, did he? You were desperately trying to figure out what to do with your life, and so was I. I guess I never fully realized to what extent you were actually struggling to survive on a practical, physical level until you blurted out that you didn't have the five bucks to go bowling. I always wished you had shared more with me. I would have helped you if you had only asked. I thought it was just your Capotosti pride, but I know now that I was the last person you would have confided in. Boy, does that sting.

My fairytale life strayed from the plot back then, too, but I didn't tell anyone what was going on with me, either. Not even Gregorio, and it was his life, too. I was too embarrassed, too terrified, too uncertain.

Our fight really shoved me over the edge. I was in a horrible state when I returned to Italy, and I felt such pain every single time I relived the experience in my mind. Until somehow it scabbed over in my memory. The little blue pills did their part, and so did Max.

That was until yesterday. I never want to feel like that again.

Love,
Iris

P.S. Did I really make that nasty comment about you being glad Henry was dead? I can't believe I would say something so cruel.

From: Lily Capotosti <lilycapotosti@gmail.com>
To: Iris Capotosti <iris.capotosti@gmail.com>
Sent: Sun, December 19, 2010, at 12:12 AM
Subject: Re: There are chapters, and there are chapters

Dear Iris:

I got your note last week. I just haven't had the time to write back. Well, I guess I had the time, but then every time I tried, something would happen. I can't even tell you what. I've just been really tired lately, and for some reason, I've been having the strangest dreams. It's gotten so I'm afraid to fall asleep.

I know what I wrote about Henry's funeral, and the big fight we had wasn't fun, but I'm just so sick of everyone trying to pretend that everything's OK when it's not. I feel like if we were going to gloss over the truth, our whole story would fit on one page. Or even within a paragraph. It might read, "I was born, some shit happened, and then I got over it." But getting over it and healing aren't the same thing. Still, I don't feel like I'm healing either. I feel like I keep ripping open the same sores over and over again. I have to admit to a kind of morbid fascination with my own emotional pathology, you know? It's like when you're trying to get a knot out of a gold chain or something. You know that there is a real possibility that you could make it worse by messing with it, but at the same time you keep thinking, "If I could just pull that part through this loop, I am sure I could fix it." I never do though. The knot just keeps getting bigger and more complicated. (If you tell me I mixed my metaphors, I swear I will get on a plane and fly over there just to slap you.)

Don't take my reticence about my situation back then too personally, Iris. I can't even tell you how confused I was. Before Pierce was born, I was volunteering at church to provide food to the needy, and by the time Joe and I split, I *was* the needy. I still remember trying to figure out what time of day to take my trip to the food cupboard so as not to be seen.

Funny, but for someone who once dreamed of being an actress, I spent an awful lot of time and energy hiding. I still do. Back then, it was because I felt so ashamed, and now it's more a matter of survival I guess. I got pretty good at putting on a front because people tend to not want to hire you if they think you're a basket case. So I learned to coil it up and shove it down inside for the sake of the paycheck. This twisted little trip down Memory Lane has awakened the viper, so to speak. Maybe that's why I keep having these spasms in my chest. My doctor says it's esophagitis. I can't imagine letting our story drop at this point - I certainly don't want to remain suspended at this awful juncture, but I can't honestly say I see it getting easier any time soon.

Don't feel bad about what you said about me being glad Henry died. Maybe you weren't being cruel; maybe you were the one being truthful.

Love,
Lily

From: Iris Capotosti <iris.capotosti@gmail.com>
To: Lily Capotosti <lilycapotosti@gmail.com>
Sent: Sun, December 19, 2010, at 8:05 AM
Subject: Re: Re: There are chapters, and there are chapters

Dear Lily,

I was relieved to hear from you. I was beginning to worry.

I'm sorry you're not feeling well. I've heard esophagitis can develop into a chronic problem if you don't take care of it.

Bulldozing down Memory Lane definitely leaves tracks, and we've each been churning out a chapter a week for a while now. Why don't we take a breather over the holidays? 'Tis the season to be jolly, after all. Maybe it will do us both good. I'm getting into a funk about missing Christmas with the family this year, but by now I know being there in my dreams is sometimes better than the real thing.

Since it will just be the two of us, we were thinking of having a picnic on the beach in Camogli if it's a nice day.

Love,
Iris

From: Lily Capotosti <lilycapotosti@gmail.com>
To: Iris Capotosti <iris.capotosti@gmail.com>
Sent: Sun, December 19, 2010, at 1:12 PM
Subject: Re: Re: Re: There are chapters, and there are chapters

Iris:

Taking a break won't make any of this go away.

I'd rather just keep going. Let's get this over with.

Enjoy your picnic.

Love,
Lily

5. IRIS

"Stromboli!" Max said, as soon as she answered her cell phone.

"What do you mean, Stromboli?" Iris asked, determined to keep the irritation sizzling in her nerves out of her voice. She swerved over to the side of the road, as an Alfa Romeo passed her on the curve, blaring its horn. Was that all he had to say when she had been waiting for his call all day? It was half-past seven on a Friday evening, and she had promised Gregorio she would be ready to leave the house for a dinner with hospital colleagues by eight. She had no time to waste on guessing games.

"That's where we're going," Max said.

"We are?" Since they had first discussed the possibility of spending an entire week together, Max had come up with a dozen different proposals, sending Iris's imagination soaring all over Italy to explore the majestic beauty of the Alps, the quaint charm of the countryside, the art and architecture of the cities.

"Yes, Capo, we are!" Max sounded genuinely enthusiastic. "The Sicilian tourist board has even agreed to cover expenses for my new American assistant. How about that?"

"Your what?"

"My American assistant! And the only thing she - that is, you - have to do, besides pretending to help me, is write the copy for the new promotional video I'll be shooting. We'll do some work during the day, but the rest of the time, it will be like a honeymoon."

The word "honeymoon" might have blocked out all the rest, but Iris's instinctive prudence forced her to at least ask what Max was getting her into. "Wait … what do you mean, 'write the copy'? What copy?"

"Don't worry, for you, it'll be a cinch. It's for the American market, so it's all in English."

"Just because I speak the language doesn't mean I know how to do that stuff," Iris said.

"You'll do great. You should see some of the crap those people write," Max said. "Anyway, I'll email you the schedule so you can get yourself organized. But now, I gotta run. I should've been out the door ten minutes ago."

"Where are you going?" For each time Iris got up the nerve to ask the question, there were ten times when she didn't. The last thing she wanted was for Max to mistake her curiosity for jealousy, or her interest for an interrogation.

"Flavia's picking me up. It's too fuckin' beautiful to spend the weekend in Rome. We're going to her place in Capalbio." Iris felt her pulse quicken. She had met the chatty, olive-skinned quiz show hostess at one of the parties she had attended with Max in Rome. Afterwards, when Iris had remarked upon her quintessential Mediterranean beauty, Max had immediately agreed the woman was incredibly attractive and then gone on to admit that he himself had been in love with Flavia briefly a few years back, though they had soon discovered they were totally incompatible as lovers. He said they had been the best of friends ever since, once the issue of physical attraction had been resolved. Iris knew she was being old-fashioned, and to be fair, Max had introduced her to Flavia as his girlfriend, but still, she just plain didn't like the idea. She would have to keep her misgivings to herself, however; after all, wasn't she still sleeping in the same bed as her husband, and still having sex with him every other Saturday night? She was starting to understand why Claudio Olona was convinced that married people should only have affairs with other married people. Weekends they were at home and accounted for, not out gallivanting.

"Have a good weekend," she said, already thinking she might indulge in an extra little pill before bed.

"You, too, Capo," Max said.

"Stromboli?" Beatrix lit two cigarettes and held one out to Iris, who was pouring them each a glass of wine. Sunday nights were so much more bearable when Bea was in town. And tonight the two women had plenty to discuss.

"Yes, can you believe it?" Iris said.

"Frankly, no. Why the hell would you go all the way down there to that pile of ash and rubble when you can fly almost anywhere in Europe from Milan in under two hours?"

"It's not a pile of rubble; I've done my research, and it looks absolutely astonishing! This is a great opportunity to go somewhere I doubt I would ever go otherwise."

"But at this time of year? The place will be deserted. Everything will be shut down."

"We're not going as tourists. Max has an assignment there, and I'll be helping him, like an assistant." Iris refrained from telling Bea that she would have a job of her own to do, or that all expenses were being footed by Max's client. Her friend had that asinine rule about measuring a man's interest by the amount of money he spent on you, but until she got to know Max in person, she would never understand that rules like that simply did not apply to men like him. Not many rules did. Plus, not to criticize or anything, but what kind of men had Bea found for herself, when it boiled right down to it?

"The whole idea was for you two to enjoy a vacation together," Bea took a drag on her cigarette, tilting her head back to exhale. "To take some time to relax, you know? You're a wreck."

"This will be much more than a vacation, Bea. We'll be working on a project together. And get this – Max said it would be like a honeymoon. He used that exact word!"

"My idea of a honeymoon is slightly different, but then again so was each of my ex-husbands'. Do you still get to have sex, or isn't that part of the job description?"

"I'm not going for the sex, Bea," Iris said. "At least, not only. I'm not interested in fueling some pointless affair that will eventually fizzle out and die. What I want to do is see where we are going with this relationship. I want to see how it feels to be a real part of Max's life."

"I know exactly what you want to do," Beatrix said. "You want to hedge your bet, see what cards you're holding before making any decisions. But I can't say that I blame you."

"That sounds so cynical, Bea!" Iris said. "I'm in love with Max. But I love Gregorio, too, in a different way. I'm just so confused and scared."

"Scared will get you nowhere. Now is the time for nerves of steel. To stick with the gambling jargon, you'll be upping the ante with this trip, Iris. It'll make the game even more interesting."

"I know." Iris gulped down her wine. "So can I still count on you, for the alibi?"

"A promise is a promise," Beatrix said. "I'll handle Gregorio for you. You have enough to worry about with Max."

The Piaggio Ape crawled up the old mule path in pursuit of the dim headlamps feebly leading the way. The vehicle's three bald tires slipped and spun, determined to get a grip on the semi-paved surface of the track whose bumps, cracks and potholes jostled the grogginess from Iris, still recovering from her four o'clock wake-up call. Sitting in the cargo bed with her back against the minuscule cab, she used her legs as stabilizers to cushion the shocks that jarred her tailbone and shot up her spine, ricocheting off each vertebra along the way. Despite her discomfort, she couldn't help but admire the vehicle's "I think I can" attitude; it reminded her of the spunky little locomotive in a book her mother used to read to her when she was a child. The book was one of Iris's favorites, and she checked it out each time she was lucky enough to accompany her mother to the town library. Whenever they read the part where the tenacious locomotive made it to the top of the hill, she and Lily would clap and cheer and jump up and down on the sofa. But what really fascinated Iris was the way her mother told the tale, the inflection in her meek voice steeled with an uncharacteristic tone of obstinacy, her face flushed with effort, as if she herself were the locomotive as it willed its way uphill, instead of Mrs. Carlo Capotosti, mother of twelve, sitting on the cushion of a sprung sofa sprinkled with cookie crumbs, her varicose-veined legs propped on a footstool, with Iris tucked under one arm, Lily under the other.

The Ape driver jerked the handbrake and unlatched the door to his cab, growling an incomprehensible comment Iris took to mean the ride was over. His short, stocky form waddled away on thick legs toward the edge of the clearing. Max unfolded his long limbs and hopped down from the cramped flatbed where he had been wedged in the corner across from Iris. He yawned, stretched, scratched his crotch, and walked to the other end of the clearing. Iris took a moment to let her ears adjust to the silence after the constant grating of engine gears; it was so quiet she could distinguish each man's tinkle as he peed. She wondered whether men actually had a physiological need to urinate so often, or if theirs was just a dog-like instinct to establish their presence and assert their masculinity wherever they went.

She lowered two backpacks and a tripod to the ground, then hoisted herself over the edge of the Ape, hopped down to her feet, and walked in the opposite direction of the men. She inhaled deeply, raising her arms to the inky sky, joined her hands as if in prayer, then bowed low at the waist, exhaling. She placed her open palms on the soil, introducing herself to the ground on which she stood. She slowly inhaled and exhaled a second time, then straightened up and brushed the grainy black dirt off her hands. Its color and texture reminded her of the ashes she had received on her forehead all those first Wednesdays of Lent. She could recall the haunted, holy feeling that descended upon her when the priest thumbed a black cross in the center of her brow, whispering the Lenten reminder: "From dust thou came, to dust thou shalt return."

This ash was different, though; it had come from the bowels of Stromboli. *Iddu*, to the locals. Familiarity, fear, and a pagan form of reverence convened in the islanders' name for the volcano in whose shadow they scratched out their existence. As a child, Iris had perceived her father in a somewhat similar manner: a solid, benevolent presence when respected; a formidable fury-spewing force when angered. If Carlo Capotosti could see her now, he would certainly wonder what business she could possibly have here, atop a volcanic island, in the company of a blue Ape, a native with driving habits as rough as his dialect, and a Roman filmmaker. She could describe to him in detail the fifteen-hour train ride south to Sicily and the day of ferry-hopping through the archipelago she had endured to get there, but as for the why, well, that was something she was still trying to figure out herself.

Yet there she stood, enveloped in a velvet cloak of darkness. The only lights were those of the Ape's tail lamps blinking their farewell as they were dragged out of sight by the rotund man and the cantankerous engine grumbling its way back down the hill. At first, the darkness seemed absolute, but soon Iris could make out some forms emerging from the shadows. Her eyes first discerned the leafless branches of a gnarled fig tree, then a colony of prickly pear cacti waving their thorny pads at her, and a whitewashed abode squatting on the hillside. Nature murmured all around her, each sound piercing a pinhole in the silence which had at first seemed impenetrable. A breeze rushing in from the open sea breathed freshness into the air, rustling from slumber the island which blocked its path. A rooster crowed in the distance, impatient to start the new day. A gang of gulls screeched as they cruised the coast in search of breakfast.

As she stood there, Iris focused on absorbing the sensations and impressions she would later record in her journal. Writing about a totally new place would be stimulating, and the challenge excited her. She hoped she would be able to translate her perceptions into words, to make viewers feel and taste and hear the things they would be seeing in the video. During the endless train ride south, the nebulous notions about her future that had been floating aimlessly around in her mind started clustering together. Ideas began to form and latch onto one another until she had strung together a surprisingly credible theory of a new life - her new life, on the road with Max. So much depended on this assignment; if she did a good job, it could all begin right here. There were many more islands to visit; many more stories to write.

The snapping of a twig interrupted Iris's reverie. She spun around. "Max! You scared me!" she shouted in a whisper, the way her parents used to scold their chatting children in church.

Max drew her close and kissed her, his stubble scratching her chin as he flicked his mint-flavored morning tongue at hers. When

Iris had caught him earlier in the bathroom with her toothbrush sticking out of his mouth, he just grinned through the froth, then spat into the sink and shrugged, saying he had forgotten his. It was ridiculous that it should bother her to share her toothbrush with Max when they were already on far more intimate terms, and surely it was not his fault that the vision of him catapulted her back to another time and place where she often found the bristles of her toothbrush wet with someone else's spittle. The memory still filled her with disgust.

A thunderous rumble followed by a loud clap brought Iris back to the present. "Look, Capo!" Max cried, pointing to the mountaintop.

"Wow!" Iris exclaimed. Incandescent chunks of matter soared high into the air, tracing a red arc against the black sky before disappearing into nothingness.

"How'd you like that?" Max asked, as if he were personally responsible for the pyrotechnic display.

"It was amazing!" Iris said. "But isn't this dangerous? Shouldn't we be on the lookout for lava?" She knew what volcanoes could do; she had visited the ruins in Pompeii with Gregorio once on their way to Ischia.

"Don't be stupid," Max said. "Lava flow is rare, and anyway it always runs down the *sciara*, on the northwest flank of the mountain." Iris searched his face for further reassurance, some sign that he knew what he was talking about, but found nothing there except that smirk he always wore when he teased her.

"Anyway," Max continued, "it's time to move our asses if we want to get some footage. Once day breaks, all we'll see is the smoke. You got your flashlight?"

Iris nodded, smiling proudly as she unzipped a pocket of her new backpack and extracted her new flashlight, switched it on and shone it in his face. Her secret shopping trip to a sporting goods store in Rapallo had filled her with an inebriating sense of adventure, and she would have bought a sleeping bag, too, had it not been winter, and had Max not told her that all their accommodations would be paid for. But she hadn't been able to resist purchasing one of those red pocket knives with a dozen different tools she had always wanted to own but never had an excuse to buy. "I'm all set!" she said, feeling like a full-fledged assistant as she hoisted the backpack laden with half of Max's paraphernalia onto her shoulders.

"Move it, then!" Max said. Shouldering his own bulging pack, he prodded Iris's butt with the tripod, nudging her to the trailhead. Half an hour into their uphill trek, Iris was sweating but proud of her ability to keep up with Max, thanks to her refusal to give up jogging despite Gregorio's warnings about saving her joints for old age. Fuck old age.

"Hey, where are you going?" Iris called, seeing Max squeeze through a jagged opening in the barbed wire fence at the side of the track. "That sign says 'VIETATO ALLONTANARSI DAL SENTIERO.' We're not supposed to leave the trail."

"That's just for tourists, Capo," Max replied.

"Well, what are we? I don't know about you, but I'm not exactly a volcano climbing veteran," she replied.

"Oh, come, on!" Max said. "The tourism board is paying for us to be here. And the way I want to frame this, I have to shoot from over there, off to the right." He pointed into the darkness. "It's not like I'm planning to climb into the crater or anything."

"I know that. But I just don't think we should. If there are signs and barbed wire, there must be a reason," Iris said, kicking the dusty gravel with the toe of a sneaker. She didn't like the idea of passing for a coward, but she liked the idea of leaving the authorized path for an off-limits danger zone even less. She was pretty sure she could feel a tremor beneath her feet at that very moment.

"Listen, I don't have any time to waste," Max said. "We only have about fifteen minutes until the next eruption. So let's say you follow the rules like a good girl, and wait for me here. Give me that backpack." He reached over the fence, and Iris obediently shrugged the pack off her shoulders and handed it over. Maybe she was being overly cautious, but maybe Max was being reckless. If only he would reason with her, convince her, give her a minute to get used to the idea - but he was already on his way. "If I'm not back in an hour, go for help!" he called over his shoulder as he marched off into the darkness.

Iris cursed herself for being such a coward; she should have gone, she would have felt safer with Max than she did standing there all alone in the dark. Especially once she realized that her phone and water bottle and survival knife were all in her backpack, and her backpack was with Max. Thank God she at least had the flashlight, she thought, playing the beam over the rocky slope on the other side of the barbed wire, as she debated whether she should try and catch up. But Max was nowhere in sight. She climbed up on a boulder that stood to the side of the path and sat down on it. It seemed like a safe, solid place to wait.

She couldn't figure out why exactly she had been so reluctant to follow Max. If she hadn't seen the sign, she probably would have gone, which made her wonder whether it was a fear of physical danger or a fear of breaking the rules that held her back. As a child, her behavior was expected to conform to the rules of her home and school and religion. As a young married woman, new sets of rules were generously provided by her husband, his family, and the culture of their country. Wasn't her relationship with Max all about breaking some of those rules that had been stifling her for so long? Wasn't she already violating far more serious rules – the laws of the state and church and her own morality - by simply being with Max? There must be some way to balance things out, some way to reconcile her need for new experiences with her upbringing and beliefs.

Reflections on who she had become and why led her to think back on who she used to be - before Gregorio, before Italy. Things were easier back then when rules were not open to alternative interpretations, and breaking them was not an option for Iris or her siblings. Except for Henry, of course. There wasn't a rule that he respected or a punishment that he feared. While the other kids were filing onto the school bus, he was sneaking out of line and hopping onto the rear bumper where he would ride all the way to school, clinging to the bus like a monkey. When the other kids were outdoors playing ball in the sunshine, he was playing his guitar down in the basement. When the other boys his age were holding hands with girls at school dances, he was lying on Lily in the chicken coop.

Despite all the times she felt nostalgic about the past, she was saddened by what it had done to Lily, and to their relationship. She could still see her sister's face the day of Henry's funeral, so devoid of expression that Lily herself looked like a corpse. Tears of hurt filled her eyes when she recalled the way Lily had lashed out at her later that day, and how viciously she had reacted to Iris's efforts to be nice. She knew Lily couldn't have meant what she said; it was just all the strain she was under, and that strange way she had of reacting to death. Like when she had burst out laughing on learning of Dolores's suicide. Like when she had stood dry-eyed and stone-faced at their father's burial.

Iris lowered her head to protect her eyes from the grainy dirt swirling in the wind. Gathering herself into a ball, she felt incredibly small sitting there on her rock, totally exposed to the elements of nature. The earth rumbled, and Iris looked up as the volcano belched again, spewing out its fiery stones. She stared in awe until the activity ceased, then turned her gaze to the sea below, where a lighthouse winked at her through brightening shades of grey tinged with rose. She was relieved that the night was over.

Once upon a time, Iris had looked forward to nights. Nights when she would lie on her side of the imaginary line that divided the bed she shared with Lily, while the lovely fairies of their homespun tales hovered above them, whispering of happy endings. Nights when she would slip between crisp sheets to snuggle up to Auntie Rosa, her head cradled between fluffy pillows and plump breasts. Nights as a young bride lying in her husband's embrace, feeling loved and protected and full of hope, imagining his seed seeking out the egg that would become their baby. It was difficult to pinpoint the moment when his arms had started feeling like a vise squeezing the air from her lungs, clamping her in place as she lay awake in the lonely hours before dawn.

She couldn't take many more nights like that; she needed to have hope in the future, she needed to believe in a love that would last forever, like she had back in those days when she still had Lily, and they both still had their dreams. Lily had found the courage to leave Joe, but now her life was a mess, while Iris was still stuck in a life as confining as Stromboli.

Iris recalled when she had first heard of Stromboli, the year when she was halfway through high school, and halfway through the dog days of a sweltering summer, wishing they would both end soon. She had seen the advertisement for the matinee at the Little Theatre, where they were screening an old flick, *Stromboli Terra di Dio*. She had asked Lily to go with her, but Lily was not enthusiastic about sitting through a film in black-and-white, where everyone spoke Italian. There would be subtitles, Iris argued, and with an outside temperature of ninety-five degrees, accompanied by the same percentage of humidity in the air, the cool, dark cinema would be a good place to kill a couple of hours. Plus, it would be Iris's treat; she would pay for the movie, and the popcorn, and something to eat afterwards. The girls re-emerged, squinting, from the movie house a couple of hours later, to see that although the sun had sunk lower in the sky, nothing else seemed to have changed during their absence. This impact with reality frustrated Iris, who was reluctant to abandon the sense of adventure the film had stirred in her. She was in no mood for their usual diner, and convinced Lily they should stay downtown, and go try one of those Garbage Plates at that Nick Tahou place her older brothers were always talking about.

"Why aren't you eating?" Iris asked her, watching Lily toy with her macaroni salad, while she sank her own teeth into one of those famous white hot dogs she had heard so much about. It really was delicious, she thought, wiping away the condiments dripping from her chin with a paper napkin.

"I *am* eating, Iris. See for yourself." Lily held up a cheeseburger that had been nibbled around the edges. What Iris could see was that the food was giving Lily no pleasure. It worried her that so few things did.

Iris took another bite of her hot dog, savoring the combined flavors and textures of the meat with the tangy pickle relish, the spicy ketchup and mustard, the pungent onions and soft bun. She was as ravenous as if she herself had endured the harrowing experience of the Nordic beauty trapped on a remote Mediterranean island with a jealous husband.

"They fell in love, you know. In real life," Iris said, dipping a French fry into the ketchup and cramming it into her mouth. It was hot and crispy, greasy and salty, the way a fry should be. Not limp and soggy like the ones they served at the suburban family restaurant where they usually went for coffee.

"Who, Karin and the fisherman?" Lily asked, a forkful of macaroni salad poised in front of her mouth. "I'm not surprised. He was handsome." Iris was about to push the fork those last three inches toward Lily's lips when her sister finally delivered the food to her mouth on her own.

"No, Karin and the director," Iris said. "Actually, Ingrid Bergman and Roberto Rossellini. She stole him away from another actress, also his lover, who was supposed to get the part. And from his wife. Ingrid was married, too. They fell in love while they were shooting the movie, then they both got divorced so they could marry each other. Isn't that romantic?"

"How can you say that, Iris? What's so romantic about wrecking a marriage?" Lily asked.

"Well, what would you do if you married someone you thought you loved, then you met someone else who you really loved and who really loved you? You could never be happy with your husband again. Would it be right to suffer for the rest of your life?" Iris asked.

"Well, in a way. It might be kind of romantic, like being the heroine in one of those love stories you're always reading," Lily said. "But it would never happen to me. You'd have to be crazy to marry someone if you weren't in love in the first place."

"Of course you would. But sometimes people get married for other reasons," Iris had said.

"Such as?" Lily had asked.

"Such as, in the movie. Karin married the guard at the prison camp because it was the only way she could stay in Italy. It was a matter of survival. And *he* really was in love with *her*. She didn't know that in civilian life, he was a stinky fisherman from some hellhole of an island," Iris said.

"I dunno, Iris," Lily said. "I mean, you don't just go marrying the first person that comes along and asks you, do you? Just because *he* loves *you*? Can one person love enough for both?"

"I'm not saying it's right, Lily. I'm just saying you could *convince* yourself you are marrying the right person for the right reasons. But then you could realize later, even *much* later, that you married the wrong person for the right reasons, or the right person for the wrong reasons, or the wrong person for the wrong reasons. Maybe that's what happened to Mom and Dad."

"Well, when I get married, it's gonna be for good," Lily said.

"Me too, Lily. And it's gonna be for love," Iris said, wiping her lips with the napkin, now crumpled and soiled.

"To eternal love," Iris said, raising her glass.

"To eternal love," Lily repeated, raising hers.

The sisters toasted, their plastic glasses touching with a dull thud: they sucked up the last of their diluted root beers through melting ice, then pushed away the remains of their Garbage Plates. Not even Iris could finish hers.

"Hey, Capo!" a voice called out from behind her. She turned to see Max jogging toward her in the pale morning light. "Race me to the beach!"

"You're on!" Iris said, hopping down from her perch.

"Then move that pretty ass of yours!" He tossed Iris her backpack as he jogged past without stopping. Iris managed to catch it on the fly, nearly falling over in the process, but was quick to regain her balance. She slipped the straps over her arms and began chasing Max, her sneakers skating over the gravel, her backpack riding her shoulders like a jockey on a trotter, already distancing herself from the worries that had assailed her on the boulder. She had spent far too much time thinking; now it was time to start living. And that, ladies and gentlemen, would be her last thought of the day, she decided, as she careened down the hill, her heart pumping, her thighs shaking with the effort of balancing speed and safety. Running made her feel free and alive, and now, for the first time, she finally had someone to run with.

"C'mon Capo! Faster!" Max called from over his shoulder, leaving the gravel path for the semi-paved road they had climbed earlier in the Ape.

Iris giggled and pushed herself harder, her heart racing as she rode the wave of energy and optimism gushing inside her. Panting and sweating, she followed Max down a series of steep stairs and shortcuts, arriving at the rocky beach just behind him, her toes sore from banging against the insides of her sneakers, her legs burning with lactic acid, her shoulders strained by the bouncing backpack. But she loved the aches and pains; each was a confirmation that all this was real and not another one of her silly daydreams. Throwing her head back, she looked up at the gulls circling in the clear morning sky, and laughed; she looked at Max, sweaty and winded, and laughed; she looked out at the sea and laughed.

The beach was deserted at this time of day and year, save for a straggly bunch of displaced hippie types, probably German or Dutch, judging from their long blond hair, who waved at them from beside a couple of tents where they had evidently camped for the night. Though it was chilly, three of the women were stark naked, performing what looked like some kind of a ritual in honor of the rising sun. Iris and Max dropped their loads on the beach, kicked off their shoes and socks, and went to the water's edge. The sea was smooth and thick, its opaline surface reflecting the iridescent hues cast by the early morning light. Iris wriggled her toes in the coarse black sand.

"What are you waiting for?" Max said. "Jump in!"

"But it must be freezing!"

"Didn't that run warm you up? Or do you want to race again?" Max pulled off her windbreaker, grabbed her wrists with one hand, and began poking her in the ribs with the fingers of the other, hitting all her most ticklish spots.

"Please, Max! Stop!" she giggled.

"Nope! Not until you take off your clothes and jump in!"

"You go first!" she howled.

"No, you go first!" His fingers scurried up her sides to her armpits, making her laugh so hard she doubled over. "You lost!" he reminded her.

"OK, OK!" She would do anything to make him stop tickling her. The sweat was already drying on her skin; if she must jump in, she should do it before she cooled down too much and lost her nerve. An early morning swim in such an incredible place was something she would remember forever - and it would be a perfect way to show Max what a fun-loving travel companion she was. She stripped off her T-shirt, wiggled out of her jeans, and dove into the water before Max could make her take off her underwear.

The shock she felt when she hit the water stopped her heart, sucked away her breath, froze her skin so badly that it burned. She thrashed about to warm up, but instead of subsiding, the paralyzing effect of the initial impact spread, increasing in intensity, producing a painful stinging sensation on her arms, on her chest and neck, on her legs. She splashed her way to the beach, where a fully dressed Max laughed at the sight of her hopping about, dripping in the sand.

"*Merda!*" he said, pointing at her. "Jellyfish!" She looked down at her wet, pink skin, and saw that it was covered with angry red welts. "Good thing you went first!"

"I don't know, *Piccolina*," Gregorio said. "That trip doesn't seem to have done you much good. If anything, you seem more depressed and absent-minded than before." He tilted his head back to scrutinize through the half-lenses of his reading glasses the label of the second bottle of mineral water Iris gave him to set on the table. He had finally succeeded in converting all of the Leales to still mineral water, which, backed by scientific evidence he was prepared to cite (and did), he deemed more salubrious. Iris usually preferred to go along for the sake of avoiding unnecessary discussions, but today she wanted to drink some fizzy. She had stuck a liter bottle in the freezer to make it extra cold, additional insurance against the possibility that someone else in the family would try to drink it. All of them agreed that cold beverages blocked one's digestion; all of them would stare at Iris in disapproval, but if she wanted to be reckless with her own digestion today, that was nobody's business.

"Of course, of all people for you to spend some time with, I certainly wouldn't have chosen Beatrix. I still don't know what the two of you have in common."

"It's what we don't have in common that makes us friends," Iris said, spreading whipped cream over a chocolate cake.

"Just the same, I never should have put you in the hands of a chain-smoking, whiskey-guzzling, man-hating neurotic for a whole week. I still don't know how she convinced me," Gregorio said. "And don't go overboard with that cream."

Iris felt her face grow hot. She hated it when he talked about Bea like that, almost as much as she hated the way he referred to her, Iris, as if she were a ward of the court, and he her legal guardian. Everything she had worked out in her mind during her time on Stromboli, all those arguments elaborated in support of her need for more space and freedom, now seemed so vague and weak. Her grounds were shaky, her reasons blurred by insecurity, undermined by fear, silenced by a series of wrong times and places in which to verbalize them. Only the memories of that week with Max remained vivid and continued to feed her tumultuous emotions.

On this rainy Ligurian Sunday, she felt chilled to the core, despite the fact that she had been working in the kitchen all morning. Using the back of a spoon, she created peaks in the whipped cream topping of the birthday cake she had baked for herself, which she would carry to herself at the table at the end of the birthday dinner she had cooked for herself. She insisted on maintaining the birthday traditions she had grown up with, and she was determined to celebrate her special day with the only family she had, even if she had to do all the work herself.

"I think I hear the door!" Gregorio said. "Mamma must be here!" He rushed to the entrance, though Iris didn't see the necessity;

Isabella only traveled down one flight of stairs to reach their door, and she certainly never had any problem letting herself in.

A vibration in the back pocket of her slacks made Iris drop the spoon, which clattered to the floor. Licking whipped cream from her fingers, she pulled out her cell phone and saw Max's name flashing on the screen. What was he thinking, wanting to talk on a Sunday? She refused the call, then tapped out a quick message.

Sorry, can't talk! Miss you.

She was cleaning whipped cream from the floor before Gregorio could scold her for making a mess when the phone vibrated again.

isnt 2day ur bday? i love you even if u r an old lady.

Her hands were shaking as she jammed the phone back into her pocket, pulled it out again, read the message again, shoved it back in her pocket again. She knew it! She had known all along that he loved her. He was just one of those guys who couldn't say it. No wonder, with all the trauma he had suffered as a child, losing his parents like that. He must be terrified of risking deep attachment to anyone. Fear of abandonment, Beatrix said it was called.

Reading those words she had longed to hear for so long made her giddy with joy. This was the most incredible birthday gift she could have imagined! Her soaring spirits burst through the walls of her kitchen; the floor pitched and rolled like the ferry boat that had taken her and Max to Stromboli. She gripped the handle of the refrigerator door to steady herself, then opened it and took out a bottle of her special occasion spumante. No sense waiting for the others, who would only turn up their noses at her frivolous traditions and unhealthy habits, then perhaps humor her with a polite sip if they were in an indulgent mood. She opened the bottle, letting the cork fly where it may, smiling when she saw the black mark it left on the spotless white ceiling. She poured herself a glass, giggling as the froth overflowed and dripped to the floor. She raised her flute in the air, the bubbling rosé infusing her with optimism. She knew she could have a future with Max. Just like she knew dreams could come true, if your belief in them was strong enough, if you held onto them tight enough if you wished hard enough.

"We're ready when you are, *Piccolina!*" Gregorio called. Her head floated in the air like a birthday balloon, tethered to her body and the other bodies in the dining room by the thinnest of strings. Gregorio's voice sounded mushy and lifeless, with the consistency of canned peas. All their voices sounded tinny. All their faces seemed frozen as she entered the dining room with the first course, and saw her husband and his mother and his sister and his nephews sitting in the same exact spots where they always sat, a family of well-preserved vegetables. She went back to the kitchen to get the bottle of spumante.

"Anyone care to join me?" she said, her head looking down on the hand waving the bottle of spumante in the air, but no glasses were nudged her way in acceptance. She saw herself smile and pour another glass, preparing to indulge in the daydreams which would see her through the boring dinner-table conversation made inevitable by the same boring members of the same boring family, who knew every single boring detail of every single boring minute of each other's boring lives.

Iris saw herself serving and passing dishes; no one seemed to notice her silence as they chewed their food and chatted; no one could have noticed the similarity between Iris's faraway eyes and the expression on Betty Capotosti's face the evening she drove away from Chestnut Crest, never to return.

At the end of the meal, Iris saw herself rise and go to the kitchen, where she lit the candles on her birthday cake, then carried it back to the table in silence. She saw herself set it down, and close her eyes to concentrate on her wish. Memories of more joyous birthdays played across the insides of her eyelids and rang in her ears; she saw Uncle Alfred and his Gibson, leading the Capotosti clan in their unique rendition of "Happy Birthday" in her honor; she saw their hands clapping wildly when she blew out the candles then cut the first slice of cake, to be sure that her wish would come true. Iris thought of those who were gone and those who were left in her faraway family, of Max and his precious words, of how her desire to be with Max and with them instead of where she was, might be rolled into one big happy wish. Opening her eyes, she took a deep breath and blew out the four-plus-one symbolic candles. Her head still bent over the cloud of whipped cream, she raised her eyes to look at the small, silent family sitting tall in their chairs, staring at her. The smoke from the extinguished candles tickled her nostrils, and she straightened up to sneeze.

"*Brava, Piccolina!*" Gregorio said, reaching over and taking the knife from Iris's hand. He made a neat, swift slice into the heart of the cake.

"Why did you do that?" Iris said.

"Do what?" Gregorio asked, the guilty hand frozen in midair, still holding the cream-covered knife.

"*Why did you cut the cake?*" Iris screamed.

"What's all the fuss about?" Gregorio said. "We all know you're as bad at cutting as you are good at baking."

"*That's not the point!*" Iris yelled.

"For heaven's sake, Iris! What *is* the point?" Gregorio's eyes darted from Iris, to the cake, to the rest of his family, whose heads bounced back and forth to follow the exchange.

"The point is, it's *my* birthday, and I have to cut the first slice, or my wish won't come true!" Iris replied. "*Everybody knows that!*"

"Honestly, Iris. That may be how you did it in your family, but you're a bit old for that nonsense now, don't you think?"

"No, I don't! And no matter what you think, I'm telling you that's the way it's done! You blow out the candles then you slice the cake. Is that so hard for you to understand?"

"And just what did you wish for that's so important, if I may ask?" Gregorio placed the knife on the table, next to his mother, out of his wife's reach.

"I can't tell you!" Iris said, her chin quivering. "Wishes have to be kept secret. Otherwise, they won't come true."

Gregorio rolled his eyes, then dropped his arms to his sides, palms facing forward, a Saint Sebastian slain by invisible arrows.

"*Piccolina*, there's only one thing you could have wished for, and

148

we all know what that is. But you know what the specialist said. You're not getting any younger."

Iris detested his condescending tone of voice; it made her feel like a stupid child, made her want to pound him, the way she had wished she could have pounded her big brothers when they picked on her. She knew she looked silly standing there, a forty-one-year-old girl ranting on about the power of wishes, pegging her dreams on birthday cakes and candles. For the first time, she didn't care. She had plenty to be ashamed of, but she wasn't going to be ashamed of this.

"You know nothing about my wishes!" she said, her voice shaking as it dragged the words over her surprised tongue.

She could not look at Gregorio. She could not look at the others sitting with their mouths agape. The only thing she could look at was her birthday cake, hoping it could still make her wishes come true. She thought she might go get a spoon to smooth the whipped cream over the knife wound. She thought she might serve the cake before she vomited the rest of the words on top of it. She might have, but she didn't want to.

"People get separated every day," Max said. "It's no big deal."

"I know, but I'm not 'people,' and it's never happened to me before." Cradling the phone on her shoulder, Iris grabbed a fistful of tissues from one of the cardboard boxes that shared the Ikea sofa bed with her, just in time to scoop up the gob of snot bungee-jumping from the tip of her raw nose. The sofa bed and the one-room apartment of which it filled half were courtesy of an ex-classmate of Beatrix's who used the flat on weekends in the summer and had agreed to rent it to Iris until she could figure out her next move. Why anyone would want a pied-à-terre overlooking the railroad bridge in Recco was beyond Iris, but then again, the fact that she herself was living there was pretty unbelievable, too. Bea had been her salvation that first night, letting her cry, but keeping her calm, imposing a twenty-four-hour moratorium on contact with either Gregorio or Max while she thought things through, then pouring her a stiff whiskey. Iris wished she could have stayed with

Bea for a while, but the proximity of her house to the Leale villa did not make that a viable option. She wished she could talk to Lily or one of her other sisters. She wished she could see Max.

She found it hard to believe it was her voice talking about the end of her marriage when she phoned Max the following day to tell him about her impromptu birthday performance. She found it even harder to believe when he burst out laughing and told her she was overreacting. Even if he couldn't drop everything and run to her side, couldn't he just reassure her that everything would be all right, that he would always be there for her, even when they could not be together?

"I have to go, Capo," he said.

"Already?" Before she had walked out on Gregorio, their phone conversations had been brief and to the point. Last minute plans were volleyed back and forth, decisions reached rapidly, desires expressed in feverish whispers. Now she had plenty of serious things to discuss with Max and no one from whom she must hide their conversations.

"We've been on the phone for fifteen minutes. I have people waiting for me."

"Sorry for keeping you, Max," she said, feeling hurt. "You go ahead, don't worry about me."

"What's with that tone of voice, now? If the weather improves, I'll be up there next week. No sense coming with this rain, when all we can do is sit inside."

"Right," Iris said.

"I should be able to wrap up this project by then. I have lots of trips coming up. We'll make plans. How does that sound?"

"Sure, we'll make plans," Iris said. She was in desperate need of a plan, but not just for another trip. A plan for working out some sort of arrangement with Gregorio (she hated the word separation; it sounded so drastic), who after a week of listening to her sob into the phone, begging to be left alone, had done just that. A plan for finding a decent place to live. A plan for telling her family about the nightmare she had made out of her fairytale marriage. A plan for her new life with Max.

"Now that you're free, it will be easier for you to travel with me," Max said.

"Sure," Iris said, sniffling; she alternated blowing her snot onto tissues with snorting it back up into her nose. She sensed this was not the time to remind Max that she still had a job, and better hold on to it tight, now that she had to support herself.

"I'll try to call you later, Capo. Ciao."

"Ciao, Max," she said. "I love you." Her voice was drowned out by the rumble and roar of the eight o'clock Milan-bound *rapido* speeding over the bridge, rattling the window panes, her teacup, and her nerves so violently she thought they would shatter. When the noise subsided, Max was no longer on the line. She wondered whether he had heard; what, if anything, he had replied.

Iris screwed her fists into her itching, burning eyes. She still had a hard time believing that she had found the strength to leave home, yet could not force herself to explain why. Her action, for all its apparent courage, had been a vile act of cowardice. She had preferred to run away from Gregorio, rather than confess her true feelings to him. Sometimes she wished she had a more serious reason for leaving like Lily did. But no: Gregorio was the perfect husband, just not for her. She was the one with the problem.

Iris recalled the hurt camouflaged as anger in Gregorio's voice, how he had pleaded with her to explain. All she had been able to do was cry, and all he had been able to do was flog her with words of reason, in a desperate attempt to convince both of them that her current state was the result of a series of traumatic events, which would quite naturally overwhelm anyone of fragile disposition: the sudden death of her brother, the falling-out with Lily, the stress and strain of her job. She had been tempted, for a moment, to succumb when he begged her to consent to a hospital stay, so that her precarious mental condition might be tended to by professionals before she capitulated to a complete breakdown. He did not think or perhaps dare to ask whether another man was behind her motives, nor did she volunteer the information. It wasn't just about Max, she told herself. Still, she would be mortified if her infidelity were to be discovered. She knew that if the facts were revealed, she would be instantly and irrevocably demoted from the honest albeit pitiable status of *"povera Iris"* going through a breakdown, to Iris *"la sgualdrina."* And a slut must be shunned by such respectable man as Gregorio, and such a respectable family as the Leales.

Iris walked the few steps to the tiny, windowless bathroom where, after hours of scrubbing, she had transformed the dingy, cheap white tiles into clean, cheap white tiles. She opened the hot water tap to fill the half-size bathtub, and after staring at the water trickle into the tub for a while, she squeezed past the sofa bed to the kitchenette, where she washed down a little blue pill with a sip of leftover green tea, before dumping the rest into the stained porcelain sink.

She opened the cupboard and took out an old Nutella jar living its second life as a glass and poured some red wine into it. Judging by the number of jars lining the shelf, Bea's friend, like many women starved for affection, must suffer from an addiction to the nutty chocolate spread. Iris switched on the portable stereo she had bought from a Moroccan down on the boardwalk for twenty thousand lire, but she felt too confused to decide which of the two old CDs she had retrieved from her car best suited her mood. It was only by resorting to a game of eeny meeny miny moe that she was able to pick the Rolling Stones over Béla Fleck. She popped in the CD, then took off her clothes, practicing at being a new Iris by leaving each item wherever it fell, as the beat of "Paint It Black" hammered the air. Another train roared past, causing the compact disc to skip to "Ruby Tuesday," and a nerve-wracked Iris to gulp down her jar of wine. She poured a refill, turned up the volume on the stereo, and returned to the bathroom, where a cloud of steam hovered over the half-full half-tub.

Without testing the temperature, she stepped in, taking pleasure in the pain caused by the water scalding her toes and ankles and calves, then her bottom, and her tummy, and everything in between, until she had lowered herself to a sitting position, drawing her long legs to her chest in order to fit her whole body inside. Sweat beaded on her brow, as she reached for the jar of wine she had set on the edge of the tub. She took a few sips, then set it down again.

So, this was it. This was what she had wanted so badly for so long. Finally, she could talk to Max whenever she liked, sit in the bathtub for as long as she liked, use as much hot water as she liked, drink as much wine as she liked, and no one was there to hassle her. She slid lower in the tub, submerging the upper part of her body until the water covered her pointed breasts, her shoulders, her neck. She formed a tighter ball with her body, sliding lower still until her hair was a curly halo floating around her head, until her eyes and mouth were under the water, until only her nostrils were barely above its surface. She stared at the ceiling through the lens of the water and the filter of steam, then switched perspective, imagining how she would appear from above. If she were in a film, this might be the scene where she had just stopped flailing her arms and legs while someone held her head under the water, except for the fact that she couldn't imagine a movie murder taking place in such a pathetically small bathtub. The image fascinated her, in a morbid sort of way, but then it suddenly frightened her. She sat up, gulping for air, her hair dripping, her heart pounding, and reached for the Nutella jar. The heavy glass slipped from her wet hand, falling into the tub, spilling the Chianti into the water, which triggered images of another bathtub scene, one of those where the female character slits her wrist and sits there watching the blood drain from her body, tingeing the water crimson.

Iris just sat there, motionless, watching the wine blend with the water, listening to the final verse of "Ruby Tuesday." She recalled all the times she had listened to that song and cried, wondering whether her dreams were lost forever, whether she would ever be freed from the chains of her existence. Yet she had managed to break away, after all, and now she had the rest of her life to pursue her dreams. Fat tears rolled down her wet cheeks, making little splashes as they fell into the tainted water.

Hugging her knees, Iris wept for the indecisive-impulsive girl who had fumbled her way into her forties; for Gregorio, as much a victim of his own emotional sterility as of her physical sterility; for her siblings Henry and Lily, both lost to her, in different ways. She wept for Max, whose childhood trauma still caused him suffering, and prevented him from throwing himself into their relationship without reserve. Even though he had not dared to openly ask her to leave Gregorio for him, she knew how he felt; she just wished it were easier for him to tell her.

She sat there sobbing until the water turned cold, then pulled the stopper, and watched the liquid hiccup down the clogged drain. She reached for a towel, thinking she should buy a plunger and some bubble bath, and that she should only drink white wine in the bathtub.

Iris drove her Seicento slowly through the gate, holding her breath as if to lighten the car's tread on the gravel crunching beneath its tires. For the first time, she was unable to park in the spot assigned to her car, now occupied by the Aprilia motorbike with off-road tires and big fenders which the family had given to Cinzia's middle son as a gift for his *maturità*. She smiled ruefully; despite the implications of the term, the high school diploma could not have been bestowed upon a more immature youth. Switching off the engine, she prayed no one would be home. She had sent Gregorio a message the previous evening saying she needed to pick up some things during her lunch break, and he had replied simply: *"Certo."*

Soccer jerseys, shorts, athletic socks, and T-shirts hung limply in the cold drizzle from a clothesline in the side garden. Cinzia, who detested accumulating laundry, had apparently washed and hung her Monday morning load before going to work, despite the weather. "Easy for you to wait for the sun, you don't have three kids," she had snapped at Iris one day, a month ago, a lifetime ago, when they crossed paths by the clothesline, as Iris retrieved the linens that would bring the scent of the sun and breeze to her tired bed. She'd wait a year to do her wash, rather than stink of mildew like Cinzia.

With quick, light steps, Iris walked down the gravel pathway through the small patch of neatly clipped lawn; she could imagine the cool, spongy grass beneath her bare feet, though she could not recall ever straying from the walkway or wandering through this garden without her shoes on. She let herself in the front door and tiptoed up the stairs to the second floor. She felt weak-kneed as she turned the key in the lock, then walked through the door she had walked through thousands of other times, in thousands of other states of mind and heart and body, none remotely similar to her current state.

"Zenzero!" Iris jumped, startled by the cat that appeared out of nowhere to run figure eights around her ankles, purring and arching her back, her quivering tail pointing straight at the ceiling. Iris scooped up the cat and held her to her chest, rubbing heads like she always did (used to) when she came home at night. She held her up in front of her, legs and tail dangling: the cat looked well-fed, perhaps even a tad plumper, Iris noted, half relieved, half regretful, then set her back down.

Iris kicked off her shoes by the door, like she always did (used to), but felt no less an intruder as she padded down the hall to the bedroom, where she found the shutters closed and the drapes drawn. Her nostrils twitched at the antiseptic non-odor she associated with Gregorio; her eyes, adjusting to the dim light, saw the bed was neatly made, the dresser devoid of clutter. The room was familiar yet foreign, slightly smaller and stuffier than she recalled, the way it seemed each time she returned from a trip. She switched on the light and filled two suitcases as quickly as possible, then left the room. On an afterthought, she went back to look for the novel she had been reading, which in her haste and mental state when packing her first bag, she hadn't thought to grab from her night table. But the book was gone. She switched off the light and dragged the suitcases down the corridor to the door, feeling shaky and thirsty.

She decided to drink a glass of water to calm her nerves, so she went to the kitchen and opened the refrigerator, hoping that Gregorio had started living dangerously and drinking his mineral water cold. Individual servings of plain, low-fat yogurt in glass jars lined the top shelf of the refrigerator; the remainder of the shelves were empty. A spasm of sadness gripped her as she pictured

Gregorio here alone in the morning, his teaspoon clinking against the glass jar as he consumed his plain yogurt in silence before leaving for the hospital. After work, he would surely dine upstairs with Isabella. Would they talk about Iris? Would they criticize or pity or condemn her? Or would they leave the talking to that same dreadful anchorman with the mole on his face delivering the evening news, while they ate their food from trays balanced on their knees, chewing in silence, pretending everything was the same as before? Maybe, to them, it was. Maybe, for them, it was better.

Iris closed the refrigerator, ran a glass of water from the tap, drank it down, then dried and put away the glass. As she turned to leave, she saw a white envelope on the table, with the name "Iris" scrawled across the front. She picked up the envelope, her bowels churning and cramping. Maybe she was finally getting her period; it was a week overdue, but that was no surprise, what with all the stress and upheaval in her life lately. Her hands trembled as she slipped a finger under the flap of the envelope and opened it, pulling out a single sheet of fine writing paper. She immediately noticed that the letter had been written with the same antique fountain pen Gregorio had used during their long-distance courtship.

Dear Iris,
I took you into my family in the belief that the sweet American girl I kissed on Lago Maggiore that day would be a loving wife for me, a wholesome mother for my children, a second daughter to my mother, a sister to Cinzia.
You were the branch I chose to graft onto our family tree to make it stronger and more vital, to make its fruit sweeter.
Though your branch bore no fruit, I continued to prune it, and water it, and tirelessly tend to its needs. Despite my care, with each passing season, the branch grew more and more crooked, shooting out in a different direction from the rest, as if it wanted nothing to do with the tree.

I should have realized long ago that the branch was affected by a disease that will always prevent it from becoming one with the tree, but I was blind. It wasn't until you ran off with no explanation that I realized, with Mamma's help, that I have done all I could do. You have begged me to leave you alone, so I will grant you your wish.
It pains me enormously to admit that the time has come to sever the branch, lest your disease spread to the entire tree.
Gregorio

Iris placed a hand over her mouth to stifle her cry. After so many years of trying to conform to Gregorio's idea of a good wife, of believing that making him happy was enough to make her happy, of thinking he would wither up and die if she ever left him - and now he was simply axing her out of his life, out of his home, out of his family? Everyone said a good, clean cut would be less painful, but what did anyone know about her? Spasms gripped her gut, sending her rushing back down the hall to the bathroom. She sat on the same toilet she had sat on for years, the same one Gregorio had used that morning, as tears streamed down her cheeks, and her womb sloughed off its waste. She wept at the sight of the "*Anestesia Oggi*" magazine on the windowsill; and at Gregorio's razor and shaving cream and deodorant and dental floss and toothbrush staring at her from the shelf, reminding her that whether or not she thought of him, whether or not she wanted him, whether or not she was there, Gregorio was carrying on with his life. She sat there until her body had been voided and her tears cried. She opened the medicine cabinet in search of a tampon and found her side had been cleaned out: There was no trace of a wife in this bathroom.

She staggered to the living room, dazed by the rapidity with which the life she had managed to keep glued together for so many years had fallen apart and its pieces been swept away. She stopped to stroke Zenzero, snoozing contentedly on a chair; she wished she could take her away with her, but knew that if she were a cat, she would prefer to stay, too.

She reached behind the sofa and grabbed her dust-covered

guitar, then headed out the door and down the stairs, juggling luggage and instrument, past and present, pain and relief, regrets and dreams. She managed to squeeze her suitcases into the Seicento but had to open the sunroof to accommodate the guitar. Maybe the drizzle would not turn to rain like the forecast said; all she could do was hope. Iris looked back at the house that had (not) been her home for so many years, and could have sworn she saw Isabella peeking out from her upstairs window.

As she drove through the gate, she noticed that the lilac bush she had planted by the entrance to remind her of her faraway birthplace was no longer there.

6. LILY

"If you ever need to establish cruel and unusual punishment later on - as part of divorce proceedings, for example," Lily's mother had told her after the initial Family Court hearing, "having documentation in your medical chart is priceless." Of course, a doctor's visit might also be in order simply because you'd been through hell and might need a little extra care and attention.

Lily's check-up resulted in a diagnosis of anxiety disorder, and a prescription with a name that Lily could only remember as "Xanadu" and that was supposed to "take the edge off," although since she was living her entire life on the edge these days, she wondered exactly what effect it might produce. She had the prescription filled and then tucked the small brown bottle into the back of the medicine chest, behind her diaphragm, relegating both of them to the "just in case" shelf, since the use of either would be, at the least, imprudent at this stage of the game. Being diagnosed as needing medication due to the abuse would work in Lily's favor with regard to divorce proceedings. Actually being on the medication could quite possibly work against her in matters regarding the children. Lily was determined to get through this without the little brown bottle. Even if it killed her.

Donna's friendship had been one of the few things that had managed to traverse the rickety bridge from Lily's perilous past to her fragile present. Lily's life had been basted together at the seam by her visits.

"Can you believe this weather?" said Donna. She stepped onto the mat in Lily's foyer and pounded the snow from her boots. Wishes chomped at the snow with a snuff. Donna's rosy cheeks and cheerful smile reminded Lily of Mrs. Claus, and of Christmas, which was rapidly approaching. With it, there would be demands to make cookies, shop for presents, decorate, and pressure to wax on about joy, peace, and love. Blah, blah, blah.

"Oh," said Lily, from her spot on the couch. "Is it snowing?"

"Old man winter is upon us!" said Donna.

Lily parted the drapes with her fingertips. The bright reflection of snow stung her eyes. "Ugh," she said, letting the drapes fall closed again. "I hate snow."

"Lily, in the summer you hated the heat," said Donna. "Last month, you hated all the rain we had. It's not the weather, you know. Anyone can see that you have a case of good ol' depression. It's plain as day."

Donna scurried about the living room, first picking up a cup with a dried film of milk in the bottom from the coffee table, then an empty can of Diet Coke and three granola bar wrappers from the computer desk, and finally, an ashtray overflowing with crushed Merit UltraLight butts sucked down to the filter.

"Donna, really," said Lily with as much compunction as she could muster. "Don't do that. I can take care of it."

"Hush now," said Donna. "I don't need you to do a thing 'cept stay out of my way, do you hear me?"

Lily happily acquiesced. Who cared about the house anyway?

Lily peeked out through the drapes again to see the mail truck roll by. "I'll go get the mail," she said hoisting herself from the couch. "That'll keep me outta your hair for a minute or two."

Lily pulled on her snow boots over bare feet and stepped out onto the snowy front stoop. The snow completely covered the small hedge of lavender she'd planted along the sidewalk when she and Joe had first moved in. Next summer when she felt better she would clear more space in the garden, maybe even add in some rosemary or thyme.

The melody from "Scarborough Fair" began to play in her head, tempting her to sing along. She refused. She hadn't sung a note since that night in the recording studio. Nick had mixed and mastered her demo and sent it to her in the mail, weeks ago. She had no interest in listening to it, in being reminded of that night and of how it caused her entire world to unravel. As far as she could see, singing brought her nothing but pain and suffering, and she wanted as much distance from it as she wanted from Joe. She hid the unopened package from herself in the liquor cabinet, along with a half used fifth of Cuervo and an unopened bottle of vodka. It was an appropriate place to store the CD; it would be at home with the other devices of addiction that promised escape but that inevitably only delivered on new problems of their own.

Lily stepped down onto the sidewalk. The snow was so deep that it climbed over the tops of her boots and slid down inside, melting against the bare skin of her legs. The neighborhood was covered in white, bright snow. The rumblings of street plows and the *scrape-scrape* of metal shovels against asphalt echoed in the stillness.

She trudged down the driveway and across the road, landing in the tracks left by the mail truck. She opened the door to her box and retrieved the phone bill, the cable bill, the gas and electric bill, the car payment statement, and a brown eight-and-a-half by eleven envelope bearing the return address of Joe's lawyer.

Lily tucked the bills under her arm and pinched the metal butterfly clasp on the larger envelope, which was sure to contain documents written in secret lawyer code that would need interpretation by her mother, but that she was compelled to read immediately nonetheless. Lily reviewed the contents as she made her way back up the driveway, enjoying the iciness against her skin as her boots filled up with snow.

Lily's mother agreed to come by that evening to read the documents and deliver a meatloaf that Tom had cooked for Lily and the boys.

"Can they do that, Mom?" Lily's mouth was still sticky hot with panic.

Betty Capotosti pulled a plate of food from the microwave and set it down in front of Lily. She took a seat next to her, put on her eyeglasses - which dangled from a cord she wore around her neck - then flipped through the pages of the packet of papers.

Without looking up, she said, "Well, they can write whatever they want in a letter. This gist of this is that if you want the separation, you have to sell the house and move – basically, he's saying if he can't live here, no one lives here. Says here you have to be out by the end of April, and that this house will be rented to a third party if a buyer hasn't been found by then."

"Where am I supposed to go? I don't even have a job yet. He is so far behind on his child support I have a hard time keeping food in the house, let alone being able to find money to move."

"Did you report that?" snapped her mother. "They'll put a garnish on his wages if he doesn't pay. You can't let him get away with that, Lily. You have to go down to the Child Support Enforcement Unit and file a complaint."

"And what about his children? Doesn't he even care that this is their home, too?"

Betty set the papers down on the kitchen table and removed her glasses. "Lily," she said. "You have to stop doing that."

"Doing what?"

"Expecting him to act civilly. He is trying to wear you down, flush you out. This is a war, and he intends to win. That's all he cares about."

"No matter what it costs me, or his children?"

"The greater your suffering, the greater his victory. The children are collateral damage as far as he's concerned."

Lily looked down at the dish of food in front of her, a perfect rectangle of meatloaf, covered in a thin mushroom gravy. Mashed potatoes, steamed broccoli. She pushed the dish away.

"Are you going to go to the CSEU and file that complaint?"

"I don't know Mom; I can't think about that right now."

"You can't afford not to think about it, Lily. And you can't afford to just lie down and give up like this."

"Mom - please!" Lily screamed, thrusting her leg out under the table and kicking the chair across from where she sat. It toppled and fell to the floor with a thud. "Call the legal aid office, file a complaint with child support, apply for emergency aid from social services, write a fucking letter to the fucking editor of the fucking newspaper - how about you come over and just be my mother for

162

a change? Hold me, let me cry... tell me everything is going to be alright!"

Lily stood up and stomped over to the counter, shaking the last Merit from a pack that was lying there. With the cigarette between her lips, she turned the knob for the front burner on the stove, and it ignited with a burst. She bent down and lit her cigarette, the end of which caught on fire, singeing her bangs, filling her nostrils with the smell of tobacco and burnt hair.

Any moment now she expected to feel her mother's arms around her. She would bury her face into her shoulder and cry and cry. Her mother would comfort her and dry her eyes, maybe feed her an imaginary "smile pill" the way she used to when Lily was small. Then Lily might even bring herself to eat some of Tom's meatloaf. It would be her first meal in two days.

"Lily," her mother said, putting the papers aside, but not rising from her chair. "Come. Sit." She patted the chair where Lily had been sitting. Lily dutifully walked over and sat down.

"Crying is a waste of energy, and you don't have any to spare if you want to have a snowball's chance in hell of surviving this. I *am* being your mother, and I could tell you that everything is going to be alright. I wish I could promise you that. But I can't. The truth is that you have a long hard road ahead of you, and you are going to have to learn to take care of yourself, to advocate for yourself, to stick up for yourself, for Pete's sake. Otherwise, he is going to eat you alive. Just like your father did to me."

A loud *boom!* shook the ceiling, and was followed by a scream as Pierce came bounding down the stairs, tears streaming down his face, shouting, "Mommy! Mommy! Joseph pushed me off the bunk bed!"

"I did not, you big crybaby!" said Joseph, following his brother into the kitchen.

Pierce scrambled up into Lily's lap, screaming.

"I am not a crybaby!" Pierce wailed, flailing his arms, his clenched fist colliding with Lily's nose with such force that it caused her to lose her equilibrium, and she grabbed for the edges of the table to keep from falling from her chair, with Pierce in tow.

"Crybaby, crybaby," taunted Joseph, as he ran around the table, Wishes at his heels. "PJ is a crybaby!"

Pierce squirmed in his seat, a deep guttural roar rising up from inside him. Lily felt his small body tremble against her belly. He wriggled himself free from Lily's grasp and darted after Joseph, who continued to chant, "Crybaby, crybaby, PJ is a crybaby!" Joseph ran down into the family room, a screaming Pierce and a chortling Wishes chasing close behind.

"I'd better go take care of that before they kill each other," said Lily, relieved to draw a definitive close to the conversation. "Thanks for coming by." Lily sniffed, not sure if her nose was running from the blow that Pierce delivered, or from the realization that her mother was no longer in the business of making it all better.

"There's just one more thing," said Betty, reaching into her purse.

Oh, thank God, thought Lily. It must have finally occurred to her mother to offer Lily some money. A car ride to Dunkin' Donuts for hot chocolate and a stop at 7-11 for a pack of cigarettes would provide a welcome distraction and get her through till bedtime. Another day would soon be done. She had survived one more.

Betty pulled a brochure out of her purse and handed it to Lily.

"Choices for Battered Women?" said Lily.

"CBW. If you only do one thing tomorrow," said Betty. "Call them. They keep records of each woman who attends those support groups. If Joe's lawyer ever questions the extent of the abuse you endured, the counselors there can provide credibility."

Lily tossed the brochure onto the kitchen table. "I hope you don't mind letting yourself out." It was the nicest thing she could think of to say. She hoped her mother would take her up on the invitation to leave before she lost her temper again. Betty closed the front door behind her, and Lily held the plate of food over the garbage can and tipped it, watching as meatloaf, potatoes, and broccoli slid off the plate and into the trash.

The next morning, just after the school bus pulled away, Donna poked her head in through the front door. "I've got cinnamon rolls!" she sang.

"C'mon in - I'll be right down," Lily called from the bathroom. Another sleepless night had sketched a new layer of gray exhaustion over her face, its effect all the more disturbing against her bloodshot eyes. She fastened her belt, feeding the buckle past the spot where it usually landed, to a new as yet unused hole. She was disappearing. If only she really could.

"Coffee?" Lily asked Donna as she entered the kitchen.

"Yea, sure," said Donna. "Thanks." She was reading the brochure for CBW. "Where did this come from?"

"My mother." Lily rolled her eyes. "Apparently she thinks I'm battered."

"You seem irritated."

"I know I've been through an awful time, but it's not like Joe beat me up regularly or anything. He's basically just an asshole with a short temper and a gambling problem."

"Is that all?" said Donna.

"I don't belong with those women, Donna - did you see that photo on the inside?" Lily jiggled the basket of coffee grounds, then pulled it out of the coffee maker and dumped it into the garbage. It landed on top of the meatloaf. She didn't want to have this conversation right now. Or ever. All she wanted to do was put this nightmare behind her, get a separation before the Order of Protection expired, and get on with her life.

Donna unfolded the flaps of the brochure. "I'm lookin', but I don't see where these women look any different than you do, sweetie. They're just sittin' there in a circle, talkin' and cryin'. You're great at both those things."

"Ha ha, very funny," said Lily. Donna was one of the few people who could get away with poking fun at Lily these days. Lily filled two mugs with coffee and brought them to the table.

"I'm serious, Lily," said Donna. The cinnamon rolls had baked themselves into a round loaf. Donna grabbed it with her bare hands, worked to pull a single roll free, and smeared a glob of butter on it. "This CBW might be just the place for you." Donna smacked the icing from her fingertips. "They're having a meetin' tonight - doesn't Joe have the kids on Wednesdays? You should go.

You could use the support."

"I have you," said Lily.

"It's not the same, Lily. Now, I can make you some cinnamon rolls, and I can babysit your kids, and I can even quote you a scripture or two. But I have never walked in the shoes you're walkin' in now. And there isn't anythin' like the voice of experience when you're hurtin' like you are."

Donna took her purse from the back of the chair, extracted her wallet, and pulled out a crisp twenty dollar bill. "This here is for gas and parking," she said, slapping the bill down onto the surface of the table. "Now let's have our coffee." She picked up her cinnamon roll, plunged it into the coffee then retrieved it again, taking a lusty bite as the brown liquid dribbled from her chin, bringing a smile across her face.

Lily looked at the twenty. She could put the gas on her Mobil card (Joe at least allowed her the means to drive - especially since her inability to do so would mean that he would have to provide any transportation the children needed for school, or Little League, or play dates with their friends.). And it was likely that the meters downtown would be free after six at night. With twenty dollars, she could buy cigarettes, a loaf of bread, a carton of milk, a dozen eggs, a jar of tomato sauce, a box of pasta, a couple envelopes of Kool-Aid, and some generic cereal. It would get them through a day or two, at least. Of course, if she took the money, she would have to go to the support group meeting. But at least then she could prove to everyone once and for all that she didn't belong there. She imagined sauntering into the room pictured in the brochure, her hair pulled back into a neat ponytail, wearing fresh lipstick and a smile. She would sit politely and quietly listen as the others told their tales of getting beaten up and cheated on and threatened at knifepoint. Then when she told her story, they would see how different she was, and they would tell her that she really didn't need to be there; she was much better off than any of them. Then Lily's mother and Donna would have no choice but to drop the matter and leave Lily alone.

"CBW hotline," said a woman's voice. "How may I help you?"

Lily could hear the chatter of voices and the muffled ringing of telephones in the background, like when she called the AOL technical support line.

"Hello? Are you alright?" said voice. "If you can't talk, just go ahead and press any button on your phone, and we'll send help."

"No! Oh - sorry," said Lily. "I'm fine, I just, I mean, um, I was going to come to support group tonight, but your address isn't on this brochure."

"May I have your first name?" the voice asked.

Lily wanted to hang up. She didn't want to tell a stranger her name - not this stranger who then might take it and place it there among the sad and beaten women in the brochure. If she gave them her name, she wouldn't be able to get it back.

"It doesn't even have to be your real name, sweetie," said the voice.

"Lily," said Lily. "My name is Lily."

"Thank you, Lily. I'm Sophie. I'm one of the counselors here at CBW. You've read our brochure, I take it?"

"Yes. My mother gave it to me."

"You are welcome to join group at any time. The address isn't printed on the brochure in order to protect our clients and our resident community. If you are certain you are going to attend this evening, I would be happy to tell you where we're located."

They had her name, and now she would have their address. Seemed like a fair good faith exchange.

"Yes, I'm certain," she said, not sure at all.

CBW was in a neglected section of downtown Rochester, the whole of which was itself old and rundown. The building was wedged between the Rochester Gas & Electric Company and the Eldorado Hotel in front of which a sandwich board sign proclaimed, "Rooms: $35.00/hour". Lily circled the block three times, before finding an available parking meter.

A sign posted next to the intercom outside the front door of CBW read, "Ring buzzer for admittance." Lily pushed the small white button. A moment later, a gravelly voice came over the speaker, delivered through cackling static.

"Can I help you?"

"I'm here for the meeting?" *Why did that come out like a question?* Lily wondered.

The door buzzed and clicked, and Lily pulled it open and stepped into the foyer. A stout woman with pock-marked skin, greasy black hair, and wearing a stained white polyester turtleneck emerged from behind a glass encased reception desk.

"Right this way." The woman hobbled over to the elevator. The tattered cuffs of her black chinos dragged on the floor, a chain of keys swayed and jingled at her hip. She selected a key, turned it in a lock next to the elevator buttons, then pushed the "up" arrow. The elevator whirred and bumped, abruptly arriving with a thud. The doors jerked open, and the woman gestured for Lily to get inside.

"Twelfth floor," she croaked.

Lily touched the button marked "12." The woman hobbled away, the closing doors reducing her to a tiny sliver until they sealed shut and the car started up with a lurch, rumbling and moaning as it climbed toward its destination.

"God," said Lily out loud to herself. "I hope when the doors open again I don't find myself in hell." She quietly laughed in spite of her anxiety, glad to know she only had to come here this one time.

Directly across from the elevator on the twelfth floor was a paper sign bearing a large red arrow and the word, "Group." Lily walked in the direction indicated, discovering other signs along the way, each one taking her farther through a system of long narrow hallways marked by grungy carpeting and the faint stench of spoiled infant formula. She stopped and turned to look behind her, realizing she could not remember the direction from which she'd come. She continued down the hall a bit further, straining to discern the sound of voices which might indicate that she was getting closer. She turned right at the next sign, when a searing pain shot up through the center of her body, as though someone had shoved a sharp object into her rectum and up through her gut. She cried out and immediately doubled over. She shuffled forward until she came upon a rest room, and tumbled inside. She kept trying to stand upright, but each time the pain yanked at her, forcing her back into a crouch. Her eyes watered and her breath quickened. She didn't want to die in the bathroom at the battered women's shelter.

She made her way into a stall and sat on the toilet, hoping that what she was experiencing was a simple case of gas pains. But her body was unyielding, her gut clamped in rebellion against itself.

"Attention residents," announced a voice over a speaker in the ceiling. "Group starts in five minutes. Remember, children are not permitted into group. If you need child care, Michelle will be staffing the playroom until eight PM."

Relieved to hear that there were other people in the building besides her and the scary receptionist downstairs, Lily scrambled from the stall and washed her hands. She tried to check her hair and makeup, but she couldn't stand up straight enough to see her face in the mirror. She shuffled out into the hallway, still bent and holding her side. To her right, she noticed a stream of women crossing the far end of the hall. To her left was the dark, fusty maze of corridor. The prospect of following the crowd seemed slightly less objectionable than returning to the toilet to writhe in solitary agony, or wandering through the halls for all of eternity. All she had to do was get to the meeting room and find her way to a chair.

After a few steps, the pain began to loosen its grip on Lily's gut. As she approached the room, she stopped to fish a compact from her purse and discovered that the barrette in her hair had become unclasped and was hanging for dear life by a strand of hair; her lipstick had faded, and her mascara had run. She plucked a used but dry crumpled tissue from her coat pocket, and, wetting the tissue with her saliva, she tried to wipe the smudged mascara from around her eyes as she walked.

"Please sign in here." A woman at the door held a clipboard and a pen out toward Lily and Lily scribbled her name on the line under someone named Kitten. She scanned the room, taking in the new faces, which mostly just looked back at her dolefully.

"Lily," said the woman, reading from the clipboard. "I think you and I spoke on the phone earlier." Lily turned her attention to the woman, noticing her name tag. It read, "Hi! I'm Sophie." She smiled warmly at Lily.

"I'm surprised you remembered me," said Lily. "You guys sounded pretty busy this morning when I called."

"Unfortunately, we're always busy," said Sophie. "But it's not every day you get a call from someone with such a lovely name. It's like Lily of the Valley."

Lily smiled. It had been ages since anyone had called her that. Sophie had a frail build and blond hair that fell to her waist. Her blue eyes were set off by her China-doll complexion. She seemed nice. Too bad Lily wouldn't have the chance to get to know her better. Lily took a chair in the circle, relieved to sit, to at least be somewhere. The pain in her side settled into a dull throb.

Sophie sat cross-legged on her chair, the folds of her patchwork skirt draped over her knees. "Good evening everyone," she said with a smile. She had a slight overbite, with one of her front teeth slightly overlapping the other. It graced her with an endearing childlike quality and made it difficult for Lily tell how old she actually was. "Who would like to begin?"

The women in the circle all looked around at each other until finally a petite brunette timidly raised her hand halfway as if afraid Sophie might actually notice and so call on her.

"Go ahead, Claire," said Sophie. "You don't need permission to speak here."

"I just wanted to say," said Claire. "That I had two pieces of pepperoni pizza last night."

The circle erupted into applause and shouts of, "Way to go, Claire!" and "Woo-hoo!"

"That's wonderful progress, Claire," said Sophie. "Why don't you tell us why that's a cause for celebration? We have a new member with us tonight - everyone say hello to Lily."

"Hellos" tumbled across the room from all points in the circle.

"I'm just visiting," said Lily.

"Me too," said a large African American woman. "For the one-hundredth time."

The circle broke out into laughter.

Sophie smiled gently, and said, "Now Kitten, do you remember our rule about the proper way to respond when someone shares?"

"Yes, ma'am," said Kitten. "Non-judgmentally. Sorry - what's her name again?"

"Ask her," said Sophie.

"What's your name again?" said Kitten.

"Lily."

"Sorry, Lily."

"'S'OK."

"Cool."

"Claire," said Sophie, "Can you tell Lily a bit about why eating two slices of pizza is such a big deal?"

"I'm anorexic," said Claire, folding her hands in her lap and looking down at them. "I stopped eating the day my husband mowed over my flower garden with his lawnmower, and I'm trying to gain some weight so I can get well enough to get my kids back."

Lily wasn't sure if a response was expected, and was grateful when someone else spoke.

"Why they do that, Sophie?" asked the woman. "My ex made me throw all my poems into the fireplace - said he would throw my babies' pi'tchers in there too if I didn't do it. Why they do that?"

"Why do you think they do that, Edie?" asked Sophie.

"I dunno. Maybe 'cuz they think everything belong to them and they kin do whatever they want with it."

"I think it's because they want to break our spirit," said Claire.

"Tell us what you mean by that, Claire," said Sophie.

"It's like with those wild horses in the cowboy movies, you know? They are so beautiful with their long necks and thick manes - with the way their muscles ripple when they run.... but all men want to do is break them, teach them how to obey. Pretty soon, they forget what it was like to run free, and they give up trying."

The circle grew silent. Kitten started to cry. Edie started to cry. Claire started to cry. Lily felt their sadness as it made its way toward her in waves; she felt the familiar sting in her throat, and she steeled herself against it until she realized that for the first time ever, there was no reason to fight the tears. Everyone was crying. And no one was paying any attention to her. She'd shown her face; her name was on the roster as a matter of record. She could even get up and leave if she wanted to. Or, she could let go and grieve with them. Just for tonight.

Lily listened as each woman told her own story of how her husband or boyfriend or girlfriend - or even mother, or son - had tried to break their spirit.

When the sharing slowed, and the room grew quiet, Lily said, "I used to have this tree..." She told the story of her tree and of Joe's furious attempts to keep it from growing. She told them through unabashed tears about the men who roped and cut off the limbs, and about the man who ground the stump with brute force until it was nothing but a hole, just a place where something used to be.

"And now," said Lily, spitting her words out in between sobs. "My husband won't let me and the boys stay in the house - he says if he can't live there, no one can - and I don't know what I'm going to do... where I'm going to go. I don't have a job or any money. We have to put our stuff in a truck and drive away."

Lily looked at the women around her; their reddened saddened faces nodding in sympathy, crying in empathy. She watched and as they cried for her, she cried for them, too. Their common pain traveled full circle back to her, the pain in her side melting in the warmth of their understanding.

"You've all been through so much," said Sophie. "Yet you're still here. You're all still here. Your spirits might be bruised, but the fact that you are still going and still hoping, sometimes even laughing - that is proof that your spirits have not been broken." Sophie glanced around at the faces in the circle. "Where are we?" she asked.

In unison, the women answered, "We are in the presence of many strong and beautiful women."

Lily would have to remember that one. Maybe one day she would believe she was one of them.

While Lily fished her car keys out of her purse, Sophie walked over and handed her a phone number scribbled on a piece of lavender note paper that had the word, "Choices" printed across the top in black block letters.

"This is my direct number," said Sophie. "When we spoke earlier, I was staffing the hotline, but if you call my office and set up an appointment, I can see about helping you find work."

Sophie smiled her charming snaggletooth smile. "You did good by coming here, Lily. Don't think about the entire journey right now." She gestured to the notepaper. "Just focus on taking the next step. And then the next. You'll get there."

The following day, Lily called Sophie and made arrangements for job placement counseling. She would go in one more time, just to see about finding work.

"First let me explain how this works," said Sophie, setting a file box onto the table in front of Lily. "This box is filled with index cards, and each one has a job description on it. Any of the jobs are yours for the taking, as long as I agree that it is a good fit for you. *Choices* acts as a kind of a temp agency. That way, you and women like you who are really in need of a job right away don't have to go through the stress and expense of the whole interview process. But if you report for a job and it doesn't work out, the employer can release you, no questions asked."

Lily lifted the lid off of the box. "I can have any of these jobs?"

"As long as I'm willing to vouch for you," said Sophie, "you can try any one of them. What kind of a job do you think you'd like to have?"

"I don't know, to tell you the truth," said Lily, as she fanned through the cards. "I haven't worked in a long time, and I don't have any college."

"Well, what skills can you bring to a job?"

"At my church I used to volunteer as office coordinator for the food cupboard - answering the phone, setting up deliveries, keeping records... that sort of thing."

"Sounds like an office job. Maybe an administrative assistant," said Sophie. "See if you can spot something along those lines that captures your imagination."

After sorting through about a hundred entry-level job listings, Lily pulled an index card from the box.

"Sophie," she said, holding up the card, "How about this one?"

"Oh, The Fertig School... that's an interesting choice."

"I just saw that it was a school, so maybe I won't have to spend too much on daycare if they keep the same calendar as the public schools. I could start right after Christmas break. Why is it an interesting choice?"

"The Fertig School enjoys a stellar reputation among the elite - it costs almost as much to send a child there for a year as it does for tuition at a local college."

"So it's a school for rich kids?" Lily started to slip the card back into the deck among the others. "Probably not right for me after all."

Sophie reached over and snatched the card from Lily's hand. "Nonsense!" she said. "It's exactly right for you."

"Oh yes," Lily rolled her eyes. "I'm sure I'll fit right in."

"As long as you think you won't, you won't," said Sophie. "Your assignment will be to go and work there until you don't feel out of place anymore. Yes," said Sophie, fanning her face with the card and winking at Lily. "This is perfect."

Lily had been dreading Christmas for weeks. She had managed to buy each of the boys a toy and a new pair of pajamas, but she had neither the money nor the energy to give them the kind of Christmas celebration to which they were accustomed. Nor did she have the strength to fight with Joe about who would "get" them for Christmas morning. She finally decided to order a pizza on the afternoon of Christmas Eve, when she would present them with their gifts and then send them to Joe's for an overnight and the Diotallevi Christmas that had been a part of their tradition. Lily didn't even care if Joe considered it a victory. Even warring countries took a break from hate on Christmas. Her gift to everyone this year was one day of peace.

Lily spent Christmas morning scanning the classified ads for a apartment or house to rent, trying to convince herself that it didn't matter that she was alone on Christmas. After all, she could use the quiet time; she needed the rest. It was just another day. Next year would be different.

The Fertig School was located in Rochester's arts and cultural district - which was barely large enough to be referred to as a district – encompassing a ten-block area where the Memorial Art Gallery, the Museum & Science Center, the Strasenberg Planetarium, the George Eastman House, several historical churches for obscure religious communities, and a spattering of independently owned cafes and boutiques made their home. The area was bordered by the run-down neighborhoods of some of Rochester's poorest residents, as though this city famous for its activists and pioneers wanted to force those who would aspire to the upper echelons to pass through the dregs, to remind them of their privilege, perhaps to humble them and elicit service. As Lily drove to her first day of work as the newest Fertig School "Director of First Impressions" (which, as far as Lily could tell, was a fancy name for a receptionist), she felt at home in neither extreme. She was grateful she did not live in one of the sad, decrepit homes with broken plastic chairs tottering on frozen lawn-bare yards, but she was also nervous and worried about trying to fit into a world that would be better suited to Marguerite, or Iris, or someone more worldly than she - which would include just about everyone.

"Good morning, Ms. Childs," said Lily, extending her hand.

"Windham-Childs, actually." Gloria Windham-Childs was the Director of The Fertig School. Lily guessed that she was in her early sixties. "Mrs.," she added with emphasis. She accepted Lily's handshake as though she had just witnessed Lily picking her nose, and then gestured to Lily to take a seat in the cane-back chair across from the mahogany desk behind which she sat. The desktop was occupied by only a pad of white paper upon which notes had been carefully written in perfect Palmer penmanship, a five-by-seven silver photo frame, a china teacup and saucer, a silver pencil caddy which held a silver letter opener, three number two pencils, and a magnifying glass on an ornate filigree handle. An electric typewriter sat on an adjacent side table.

"Sorry," said Lily. "Well, Mrs. Windham-Childs, I just wanted to thank you for this opportunity. I promise I will do my very best."

"Yes," said Mrs. Windham-Childs. She ran her hands through her salt and pepper hair, which was cut in a bob that fell just below her jawline. "I'm quite sure of it." She managed to curl the edges of her mouth up, but only by the greatest stretch of the imagination could it be called a smile; her blue eyes remained cold and detached.

"Let's review your tasks, then, shall we?" Mrs. Windham-Childs used both hands to gently balance her half-eye reading glasses atop her long slender nose and referred to the pad of paper. "You'll be answering the phones - I'll provide you with a script of how to address whatever questions our callers may have. You'll also be taking orders for our publications - they can't be purchased anywhere else - and then you'll prepare the shipping and the invoices for the orders." Mrs. Windham-Childs made a mark on her paper with a number two pencil. "Do you have any questions so far?"

Lily suppressed a laugh at the idea that there was anything as yet to be misunderstood, but then remembered that Sophie told her that employers liked it when you asked questions. She said it showed curiosity.

"How would you like me to answer the phone?"

"Excellent question!" Mrs. Windham-Childs clapped her hands together. "I've noted it here on the script, but when you answer the phone, you say, 'Good afternoon!' - or 'Good morning!', whatever it happens to be, you see? And do so cheerfully, but with restraint. And then you say, 'This is The Fertig School for gifted children. My name is -'" Mrs. Windham-Childs glanced down at her pad of paper.'" - Ms. Diotallevi. How may I assist you?' "

"Got it," said Lily.

Mrs. Windham-Childs looked up at Lily over the tops of her glasses and raised her eyebrows.

"I understand?" said Lily, embarrassed. She made a mental note to herself to speak formally. Donna was sure to get a kick out of this when Lily told her about it later. Lily suppressed a smile.

Mrs. Windham-Childs nodded once. "In addition to answering the phone," she said, "You will manage my correspondence by processing all of my incoming mail, which includes the opening of all envelopes, extracting the contents, attaching the envelope to the contents with a single paper clip, like this." She paused and clipped a sheet of notepaper to an envelope in demonstration, "And also typing and posting any letters that may proceed from my office that I do not write and address by hand myself." Mrs. Windham-Childs set the pencil down onto the desk, removed her glasses and looked at Lily.

"Is that it?" Lily knew it sounded as though she was thoroughly unimpressed with the job, but the words came out before she could stop them. And the truth was, she was unimpressed. But not dissuaded. She would sit and watch grass grow if it meant she could afford an apartment and deprive Joe of the pleasure of evicting her.

"In addition to your regular duties, I would expect you to learn as much as possible about our school and its founder, Agatha Fertig." Mrs. Windham-Childs picked up the photo frame and handed it to Lily. The woman in the photograph reminded Lily a bit of the photos she'd seen of Auntie Rosa as a nursing student – buxom, determined, proud.

Mrs. Windham-Childs retrieved the photo from Lily, wiped the frame with a white cotton handkerchief, which she pulled from the cuff of her blouse, and set it back on the desk with a sigh. "She was truly a pioneer. She developed the alternative approach to education that is employed by every Fertig School around the world."

"How can I learn about her?" asked Lily.

"You are welcome to borrow any book from our library," said Mrs. Windham-Childs. "As long as you are careful not to soil them with food or beverage. I suggest you start with the series called, *The Fertig Foundations*. Not only will that give you some background about our beloved Founder, but you will gain insight into the Fertig philosophy and why it is effective in the cultivation of exceptional children." Lily imagined a row of rich kids popping up out of the soil, being pruned and watered by Agatha Fertig and Mrs. Windham-Childs. Mrs. Windham-Childs added, "We've even seen some promising results from pilot programs done with the underprivileged children right here in our own neighborhood."

She led Lily out to the front desk, where she would take her post.

"You may store your personal things - your coat and your pocketbook - in the utility closet where we keep the broom and vacuum cleaner and dust cloths - other things you'll need access to from time to time."

"Where's the computer?" Lily asked, glancing around the room.

"Ms. Diotallevi," Mrs. Windham-Childs replied with a *humpf*, "At The Fertig School we do not believe in the use of electronic screens in the education of our children, nor in the work we do to serve them."

"No computer?"

"You will learn about why we do not lean on such crutches here when you study the life of our Founder," said Mrs. Windham-Childs. "For now, all you need to know to perform your duties is that any records you need to access can be found in the file room, and as you can see, your telephone and typewriter are here." She walked over to the floor-to-ceiling bookshelf and selected five books, which she brought over and set on Lily's desk. "When you are not greeting visitors, answering the phone, or providing client service, you may indulge in reading these lovely works. Begin with this one." She handed Lily a hardcover book with gold lettering on the front. "You may need to read through that book more than once in order to grasp it, but it is worth the effort - that is, if you are interested in the art and science of developing the human potential."

Lily had the vague sense that she had just been insulted, but she wasn't sure if it was because Mrs. Windham-Childs didn't think she was intelligent enough to comprehend the material or because she assumed a lack of interest in human potential on Lily's part, evidenced in what could only be an obvious failure to develop hers.

A chime sounded, as a woman about Lily's age dressed in a tailored royal blue jacket and matching skirt entered the building, leading a girl of about six years of age by the hand.

"Mrs. Howe! Victoria! How lovely to see you this fine morning," gushed Mrs. Windham-Childs.

The little girl hid behind her mother, who shook Mrs. Windham-Childs' hand and glanced at Lily. "Good morning," she said with a smile.

"Right this way," said Mrs. Windham-Childs. "I'll have our new girl get you some tea."

"No, thank you," said Mrs. Howe. "I'm afraid I've had quite enough this morning already."

The two women and the little girl disappeared behind the closed door of Mrs. Windham-Childs' office. Lily placed her purse, her jacket, and a brown bag containing a peanut butter and jelly sandwich and an apple into the utility closet, noticing there would still be just enough room inside for her.

January and February flew past as Lily became acclimated to her new schedule, squeezing in apartment hunting excursions on the weekends, and support group meetings on Wednesday evenings, which she decided served a practical purpose, and would be useful to her until she got settled.

"I'm starting to freak out," Lily shared at support group. "I have until the end of next month to move, and I just can't find anything I can afford."

"What's the worst that can happen if you don't move by the deadline?" asked Sophie.

"I signed the agreement," said Lily. "So technically, my husband could have me evicted."

"Would he do that?"

"If you'd asked me six months ago, I would have said 'No, absolutely not,' but I wouldn't put it past him these days. If he evicts me and I don't leave, he could have me arrested. If he evicts me and I do leave, I would have to stay with my mother and send the kids to live with him until I found someplace."

"They stay wit him," said Edie. "You won't never get 'em back."

"When abusers see their victims begin to become more powerful," said Sophie, "they themselves grow increasingly desperate, and their behavior becomes more erratic. Most women think that they are in the clear once they make the initial break, but that's actually when the violent behavior escalates because that's when the abuser realizes he has lost control. They will pull out all the stops, making one last-ditch effort to get that control back."

"Great," said Lily. "That sure doesn't make me feel any better."

"The truth is sometimes difficult to hear," said Sophie. "But that doesn't make it less true."

Sophie was beginning to remind Lily of her mother. She squirmed in her chair.

"All I'm saying," continued Sophie, "Is that you're wise not to get yourself into that situation. Would you like the group to help you brainstorm solutions?"

"Please," said Lily. "I'm all out of ideas."

"OK," said Sophie. "So we are going to have a brainstorming session, to see if we can help Lily find a solution to her dilemma. Just to go over the rules: In brainstorming, there are no bad ideas. Just shout out whatever comes to mind. Remember that even a preposterous idea contains the seeds of possibility. We do not use brainstorming to give advice or criticize others. Everyone's ideas are respected and appreciated." Sophie looked around the circle. "Who would like to be scribe?"

"I will," said Claire, raising her hand.

Lily was excited and humbled. All of these women were going to work together to help her. She couldn't remember the last time she felt so cared for. She would miss them when she stopped coming.

"Who would like to begin?" asked Sophie.

"They's a house for rent near me," said Kitten. "It's on Rosewood Lane, just right near that school where you workin'. I could find out how much they want."

"Oh, I can't live there," said Lily, forgetting the rule to not be critical.

Kitten sat up in her chair and pulled her stained T-shirt down over her round belly. "Why not?"

All eyes turned toward Lily. She looked to Sophie, who raised her brow and cocked her head to one side as if to say, "Yea, why not?"

Because that's where the poor people live, Lily wanted to say. Because my kids deserve better than that. Because we don't belong there. Because I'm not that desperate. A series of reasons paraded themselves through Lily's mind. Some of them were true. Some of them were honest. None of them were defensible.

"Well," she finally said, "I would have to put my kids in a new school if I moved that far. I don't want to uproot them anymore than I have to."

"Kids switch schools all the time," said Claire, with the wave of her hand. "They'll do fine."

"But I just really think it's important for them to have some continuity, you know?" Continuity was one of the tenets of The Fertig School. It was important for healthy self-esteem, which was the basis for a sense of security and confidence. Yes, it was because of continuity.

Kitten folded her arms across her chest.

"What they need is to know that they have a mama who kin take care of 'em and who don't get bullied around," said Edie.

I am not living there, thought Lily.

"Hey – why can't you move to that house Kitten's talking about and then send your kids to that school you work for?" someone asked.

"I can't afford to send them to Fertig," said Lily. "Even with the discount, it would still be way too expensive." *I am not living there.*

"I think you should rent one of those cottages on the beach," said Claire. She looked off wistfully into the distance. "You could watch the sun rise over the lake, and the boys could play in the sand. That would be really awesome." Lily's heart leapt at the image. Kitten balled up a piece of paper and tossed at Claire. All the women laughed. "What?" Claire said. "It's brainstorming! I'm writing it on the list."

After twenty minutes of listening to ideas darting about the room, Lily's head was a swirl of possibilities, hope, and despair. At the end of the session, Claire handed Sophie three sheets of paper filled with handwritten notes outlining all of the ideas discussed.

"Take these papers home with you," Sophie told Lily. "But try not to think about this anymore tonight. If it were possible to name a benefit of being controlled, it's that you never really have to angst over any important decisions. So for most women who leave an abusive relationship, making decisions can be very difficult. The thing to remember is that good decision-making is part logic and part gut. Experience is really the only way to get better at it. You have to make bad decisions sometimes just so you can see what that feels like. And you also learn from the process of making good decisions. So sleep on it, don't obsess, and see how you feel in the morning."

Lily was fairly certain she'd had her quota of experience with making bad decisions, but she followed Sophie's advice and tucked the list away for the night, and avoided it until that Saturday after Joe picked the boys up for their overnight. She watched from behind the drapes of the living room window as Joe buckled them into their seats.

"Nice," she heard Joe say. "Your mother can't even be bothered to come to the door."

As they drove down the street, Lily pulled out the list that the group had created. One by one, she went through and assessed each one from, "running away with the circus" (*Appealing idea, but Agatha Fertig would hardly approve*), to "let the kids live with your ex temporarily" (*Over my dead body.*) At the end of the exercise, only two items remained: "Rent the house on Kitten's street," and "Get a cottage on the beach," which Claire had notated with a smiley face, and which Lily probably should have eliminated immediately, but she liked pretending that she might have such a choice one day.

The rusted muffler on her dented blue LeMans rumbled, as Lily slowly made her way down Rosewood Lane. Lily had decided to sell her car back to the dealer to get out of the payments, and her mother used the opportunity to give Lily her old car and buy a new one. At least this car certainly belonged in this neighborhood. If she ended up here, she wouldn't have to worry about someone stealing it.

She scanned the sad little yards and dirty windows for "For Rent" signs. As she approached each house, Lily thought to herself, *I hope it's not that one. I hope it's not that one,* until she finally came upon a forest green house with white trim - not counting the places where the wood was bare - with a red and white sign on the front lawn that read, "For Rent by Owner" and offered a phone number. She pulled into the next driveway and turned around, this time pulling over to the curb to get a better look.

The side screen door was hanging by one hinge. One of the windows on the second floor was cracked. An old stained mattress was slouched up against the front porch, bearing a sign that read, "FREE."

She wondered if the others on the street were in the habit of leaving such items in the front yard. She imagined Pierce bouncing on it the way he liked to bounce on her mattress whenever she stripped the bed. She imagined him falling onto it, rolling around on it, tumbling onto the front lawn, running into the house, the side door coming off its hinges. She saw Joseph's face through the second-floor window, its image distorted through the cracked glass. There was no fenced yard for Wishes. She would not be able to run here.

Lily looked down at her very short list and then back up at the house again. Surely the mattress would be gone by the time she moved in. If not, she could have it removed. The screen door probably wouldn't be that big of a deal to fix. It would just take a trip to the hardware store and maybe a do-it-yourself book from the library. Same thing for the window. Tears came to her eyes as she realized this was her only real option. She could probably afford it, even on the weeks when Joe defaulted on his child support payments. And it wouldn't have to be forever. She jotted the number from the sign onto her paper.

She put the car in drive as she took one more look. A Calico cat emerged from under the porch. Its fur was matted, and it hobbled along on three legs as it made its way over to the mattress, where it curled up into a bony ball and tucked its head under its haunches.

Lily slammed the gear shift back into park, furiously scribbled lines through, "Rent the house on Kitten's street," threw the car into drive and peeled away, leaving a rubber tire mark in the road behind her.

7. IRIS

Max stretched out on his back, hands locked behind his head, his face bathed in the rosy glow of the setting sun, looking satisfied and relaxed and, Iris might add, incredibly sexy. One of the things Iris loved most about her new apartment high in the hills above Camogli was that it came furnished with a cozy double bed from which you could watch the sunset and that the bed in question was often occupied by Max. Making love on those early spring evenings was simply magical, and the view over the Golfo Paradiso nothing short of divine - though it was a luxury that took away more than Iris's breath. The outrageously high rent gobbled up a hefty portion of her monthly paycheck, but Iris felt it was worth every hard-earned lira. First of all, Max now stayed with her whenever he had time between assignments, whereas he had only visited her twice in her previous digs in Recco. Not that she could blame him; if the one-room flat by the railway bridge depressed her, she could only imagine the devastating effect it must have on someone of Max's moody disposition. The fact that he seemed to prefer the apartment in Ruta to his own place in Rome worked out well, too, since her responsibilities at the Dimora made it hard for her to go visit him. And in addition to it being a perfect love nest for them to share, even when Max was not around, living in an apartment surrounded by natural beauty rather than by man-made horrors had a beneficial effect on Iris's morale, and helped her appreciate the moments of solitude she had often longed for during her marriage. Inspired by the infinite views of sky and sea, her wings of hope grew longer and stronger, propelling her dreams to new heights.

"It just doesn't make sense to me, Capo," Max said, his gaze fixed on the ceiling.

A shiver passed through Iris's naked body, instantly dispelling the delicious afterglow she was enjoying. Pulling the sheet up to her chin, she said, "What do you mean?"

"I mean, things are getting really busy for me now that spring is here. I'll be traveling a lot," Max said. "I have that Italian islands series to finish. By the end of next month, I have to do the Tremiti shoot."

"Where's that?" Max had never mentioned islands by that name before, and Iris had never heard of them.

"Off the Adriatic coast," Max said.

"Oh," Iris said. Everything on the Adriatic coast was far from Liguria, not to mention anything *off* the Adriatic coast. With the hotel gearing up for the new season, there was no way she would be able to get off work to join him there.

"Then we head back to the west coast to do Elba and the Tuscan archipelago." Tuscany wasn't terribly far; she might drive down in the Seicento. Even so, there was no way around the fact that all islands were pretty damn inconvenient to get to, especially if you were in a hurry.

"Then it'll be down to Sardinia, then Sicily. I'm planning to hit Lampedusa and Linosa and Pantelleria, then swing back up to the Egadi islands and probably head over to a couple more of the Aeolians." He might as well be talking about Hawaii, or Fiji.

"God, that sounds amazing," Iris said. Ever since their trip to Stromboli, she kept a map of Italy in her desk drawer, so she could follow Max around with her imagination, even when she was at work. When he first told her of his itinerary, she had highlighted the islands on the map, dreaming of going there with him someday. Someday.

She glanced at Max from the corner of her eye and saw that he was still staring at the ceiling. "So, what is it that doesn't make sense?" she asked.

"I'll basically be gone until the fall, Capo," Max said.

"And so ...'" Iris said, wondering why he was hesitating to just speak his mind like he always did. She was still trying to get her head around the idea of him being gone for so long, but if he had something else to tell her - if he wanted to be cut free for the summer, for example; if he wanted to end things now, if he wanted to wreck her life and destroy her dreams, he should have the courage to come out and tell her.

"What I mean," Max said, "is that it would be a goddamn waste to go to such fucking incredible places all alone."

By now, she knew Max would never be "all alone"; she had seen how things worked. There would be a not necessarily all-male crew, and certainly the latest in his long line of female assistants, whoever she may be. The thought of him spending the coming weeks shooting in all those romantic locations "assisted" by some eager, scantily-clad twenty-year-old, while Iris put in twelve-hour days at the hotel was more than she could bear. And now that she was living on her own, she had no one around to distract her from obsessing about Max when he was away. Each time he set off for a trip in the company of people she didn't know, each time he described to her (when he didn't misplace or forget to charge his cell phone) all the beautiful places he was seeing, and all the fascinating women he was meeting, the precariously balanced bliss of her newly acquired solitude was shattered. Iris was sure there was nothing to worry about as long as he told her about the women, but that did not change the fact that she longed to be with him, to share his experiences, to meet those same fascinating people, and see those same beautiful sights. She could imagine the army of little blue pills she would need to combat her anxiety during such a long absence, just to keep functioning. She made a mental note to get another prescription filled.

"I'll be staying at the trendiest new resorts and eating at the best restaurants, all for free," Max said.

"How lovely," Iris said.

"If you don't find a way to come with me, it just doesn't make sense," Max said. "I mean, what are we doing together if all you do is work?"

"There's nothing I'd love more than to come with you," Iris sighed, relieved to think that he wanted her along, frustrated to know that there was no way in hell she could go. Now that she was officially though not yet legally separated, she could come and go as she pleased. She had no family and no obligations. The only thing holding her back from living the life she dreamed of was her job. Which was not exactly a minor detail.

"But what about my job?" she said.

"Take a leave of absence," Max said. "Or say you're having a nervous breakdown like you did the last time, only make it worse."

Iris was still ashamed of the lie she had used to secure permission to travel to Stromboli, even though Gregorio was the only one to see the medical certificate. She had immediately regretted confiding the details of her scheme to Max, who had laughed and complimented her on her knack for deception, making her feel even more of a despicable cheat. She could forget about Gregorio or his colleagues helping her out this time, or ever again. Besides, there was no way she could take a leave of absence. The hotel needed a manager; surely Max could understand that.

Max turned on his side to face her; propping himself on an elbow, he looked her in the eye and said, "Better yet: Quit."

"*Quit?*" Iris stared at him wide-eyed, wondering whether she had heard right. Could he be offering to support her? This was starting to sound like a serious proposal.

"Why not? And while you're at it, sue them," he said.

"Sue who?" Now she was confused.

"Those bastards you work for. Wake up, Capo! You're in Italy, remember? People don't walk away from their jobs without squeezing a little extra out of their employers, just like they don't vacate rented apartments until they get a payoff from their landlords."

"But I have no grounds for suing anyone," Iris said.

"I can think of plenty, and that's only based on the things you tell me. You're underpaid for the hours you put in, first of all. And that old bitch Mangiagallo and her fucked-up fag son are always on your case. Union reps and labor lawyers call that harassment."

"I accepted the job, Max," she said. "And the pay. I signed a contract, and it's my own fault if I don't have the guts to ask for a raise. And if I stay until late to make sure everything is running smoothly, it's because that is my responsibility."

Max rolled his eyes and snorted. "So in the end, when it comes right down to it, you're no different from everybody else."

"What do you mean?"

"What I mean, is that you sound like all those other poor slobs chained to jobs they hate, who start drooling with envy whenever they meet someone with the balls to live life for real, like me. None of them actually want a different life, or they'd do something to make it happen. All they want is that pathetic little desk. That monthly paycheck. That paid vacation every August. That death by boredom."

"That's not what I want!"

"Are you so sure? Sounds to me like you're looking for excuses. Why should you give a shit about the Mangiagallos, when all they're worried about is sucking your blood."

"Part of me feels sorry for them. They may be rich, but they're miserable. No money can solve the problems they have." Despite Gregorio's reiterated opinions to the contrary, Iris knew that duty and loyalty were fundamental to her character, and she also knew that sometimes people took advantage of that. That was just how she was, how she had been raised: to get the job done and do it well. And be grateful if anyone remembered to say thank you. But maybe Max *was* right about one thing. Maybe forty years of doing what was asked of her was enough; maybe now was the time for her to start doing some of the asking herself.

"But what about the apartment? I'd still have to pay the rent," Iris said. Unless of course, Max was thinking of giving up his place in Rome and officially moving in with her. He'd certainly help cover the expenses if he were living there.

"If you quit, you'll get severance pay, right? That should hold you over for a good six months. Of course, if you were a *normal* person, with an ex-husband like yours making a shitload of money, you'd be getting a nice fat alimony check every month."

Iris pulled herself up in bed to relieve the tightness in her chest. They had already discussed this topic more than once, and always at Max's insistence, but Iris would not change her mind. She simply did not see why Gregorio should support her if she could take care of herself. There were no children involved, and he had already agreed to buy out her share of their apartment in the jointly-owned Leale villa, even though Iris had not made a cash contribution to its purchase. Gregorio was a fair man, and she knew he would want to give her the money, even if it hadn't been required of him by community property laws. She did not want to use those funds to live on, though; the money would be her little nest-egg, her safety net in case of an emergency.

She hadn't told Max yet, but she had earmarked a portion of that money to take him on vacation to America. She was planning to take him to New York City, then maybe even out to California, but first, they would stop and visit her family. Iris was still filled with remorse for not having gone at Christmas, but since she had rushed home for Henry's funeral just weeks before, a holiday visit just wasn't feasible. She cringed at the painful memory of the last Christmas dinner she had prepared for the Leales, while her heart ached for her real family across the ocean, and for poor Max down in Rome, with no family of his own.

Violet and Marguerite and Jasmine had been pumping her for information about Max ever since calling to wish her a happy birthday the day she ran away from home and finding her in a dreadful state. Her three older sisters were sworn to secrecy, and no one else knew about her separation, not even Lily. It wasn't so much that Iris had decided to keep it from Lily, but Lily never wrote, Lily never called, Lily never asked. As for the rest of the family, Iris didn't feel equipped to deal with them yet, and hiding her whereabouts from them was relatively simple now that all communication was via cell phone or email. She planned on breaking the news just before going there with Max. Once they met him in person and discovered what a talented, exciting man he was, it would be easier for them to understand her decision. Gregorio had never really hit it off with her family, anyway. In fact, it became quite clear early in their marriage that the very things that had fascinated him about her larger-than-life clan had soon begun to repulse him. He had been lured out of his den of order and propriety long enough to snatch her up, but in the end, that was where he wanted to stay. Though he never said as much, she knew he considered her family's vivacity vulgar, their unbridled emotions uncouth, their forthrightness unsettling. After their first few visits together, he had stopped accompanying Iris unless the trip coincided with a medical conference or convention to which he could rush off after a day or so.

With Max, it would be different. He had always wished for a large family but had grown up an only child, and an orphan. Max knew how to adapt to any situation, and even if he didn't speak much English, his personality would make up for the vocabulary he lacked. Auntie Rosa would be able to understand him, though, and she would certainly be touched by the tragic story of his parents, having experienced traumas of her own. Perhaps she would be so moved that she would even forgive Iris for walking out on a perfectly good doctor husband. Iris was pretty sure Max and her mother would find some common ground, too. Max was not your typical Italian, and Betty Capotosti was not your typical mother. As soon as there was a break in Max's busy schedule, she would make plans.

"Did you hear what I said, Capo?" Max said.

"What?" She blinked.

"Christ, I could tell by that look in your eyes you were on another planet. Earth to Iris, Earth to Iris: We were talking about your divorce settlement."

"I've already told you how I feel about taking money from Gregorio, Max," Iris said. "He offered to help. He said that unlike me, he respects his marital duty. But why should he pay alimony when I'm perfectly able to work? I would feel guilty taking his money, in addition to ruining his life. After all, I'm the one who left him."

"He'll get over it. And it's not about how you feel; it's about what you deserve. So screw the guilt trip and pay a good lawyer. You have to learn to demand more for yourself, Capo, or you'll never get it."

"Please, Max. Can't we talk about something else?" Iris was

perfectly aware that she was not as wise to the ways of the world as she should be; Gregorio had kept her wrapped in a cocoon for her entire adult life, and now she had a good deal of growing up to do. But she just wasn't a grabber; she never had been, and never would be. Besides, Iris hated being told she should change, even though Max and Bea repeated over and over again that change was necessary for personal evolution.

"Suit yourself. But if you're so hell-bent on wanting to work, you can work with me, like you did in Stromboli. Only this time it would be on a bigger scale. I have approval for a crew of four; if you come, I'd be willing to do without Alicia, but you'd have to give me a hand. You won't get paid for that, but your expenses would be covered, and I can find a way for you to earn some money on the side. You could help the program author write the copy, maybe even narrate the pieces. They got all these speakers imitating American accents, but with you, they'd get the real thing. Maybe we could even do a voice-over in English. We could say we're gonna sell the program abroad, even if we never do."

"Are you serious? You could get me a job in TV?"

Max must really want her to be with him if he would go to the trouble of creating a job for her. It didn't exactly sound like steady work, but if it could provide her with a way to prove to him how serious she was about wanting to change her lifestyle and still allow her to pay the rent without running through her savings, maybe it was worth a try.

"You have no idea how many people live off Mamma RAI, Capo. All the guys bring in their wives or girlfriends or kids under some guise. That asshole director doesn't know shit about filmmaking. I've got him by the balls, he'll do whatever I say. And don't forget about my film project. We can definitely start working on that together. That is, if you believe in me. If you're behind me in this. Because if you're not, you'd better speak up now."

"Of course I'm behind you!" She did not doubt Max's talent or ambition in the least. Iris had always felt the reason the project couldn't seem to get off the ground was because he was surrounded by the wrong people: envious cutthroats who wanted nothing more than to see him fail; smooth operators who sniffed around to see what was in it for them before committing. Not to mention the coke-snorting bimbos distracting him all the time, using him for his connections. She had seen them all and wondered how he managed to develop even a fraction of his potential in such a negative environment. Max was an artist, and everyone knew artists were easily led astray. He needed someone like her to keep him focused, to deal with practical concerns so he would be free to concentrate on his creativity.

"Well, now's your chance to prove it," Max said. "You're smart, and you speak English, so I'm gonna be needing you to make some calls for me, make some contacts. Meanwhile, you'll have the best summer of your life, you'll see."

"But what about next fall? What will I do then?" Iris said before she could stop herself. She hated sounding so insecure. Honestly, what was the worst thing that could happen? That she'd have to find another job?

"We could be dead next fall." Max fingered her tangled curls, ran his hand delicately over her face, down her neck, to her breasts and tummy. His touch sent a shiver through her. "This summer won't come back, Capo. You don't have forever. *We* don't have forever."

Max was right. She had spent far too much time worrying about the future in her previous life. "We'll cross that bridge when we come to it," she could hear her mother whisper in her ear. As for the bridges behind her, what good was burning them if she just stood on the riverbank staring at the smoldering ashes, instead of moving on? *Really* moving on.

"Maybe I *have* wasted too much time. Maybe I *should* start living for today," she said. Her insides fluttered crazily as scores of butterflies took flight, performing loops and spins and figure eights in her tummy. She was past forty; now was the time to dare, not when she was fifty, or sixty, or dead.

"Let's do it!" she said, her heart racing, her hands clapping with such enthusiasm the bed bounced.

"That's what I wanted to hear!" Max said, smiling that smirk of his. "What have you got to eat around here? I'm starving."

"Don't worry, Auntie Rosa, of course I'll be careful!" Her aunt always gave her the same advice every time they spoke, as if Iris were a victim in search of an accident. If she knew what her little Iris had been up to lately, she'd realize that careful was a thing of the past. Sooner or later, the time would come for them to talk about that, too, but for now, she replied, "You be careful, too!"

"Cheerful? I'm always cheerful when you call!" She did sound cheerful, whenever she realized she was talking to Iris. And despite being only a decade shy of a hundred, Auntie Rosa put many younger people to shame with her energy and enthusiasm. There was nothing feeble about her voice, either; it flew across the ocean clear and strong. But expecting Auntie Rosa to understand anything over the phone was another story altogether. In recent years, she had tried three different types of hearing aids, but none seemed to help much.

Iris gave up and followed the flow. "And I'm cheerful when I hear your voice, too! I'll call you again soon. I love you!"

Those were three words Auntie Rosa always understood. "I love you too, honey!" Little kissing noises tickled Iris's ear before the line went dead; as usual, Auntie Rosa had hung up without saying goodbye. Iris wondered whether she simply forgot, or omitted her goodbyes intentionally. Iris still felt terrible that she hadn't been able to make it home for Auntie Rosa's ninetieth birthday celebration, but she hadn't wanted to abandon Max, who was going through a bout of depression, and for the first time had not distanced himself from her. In addition, she had just turned in her resignation at the Dimora, and *Signora* Mangiagallo was intent on making life difficult for her until the very last day, so taking vacation time was out of the question.

There had been a surreal quality to the weeks leading up to her final day on the job. When Max was around, talking incessantly about all the places to which they would travel, the decision seemed so right. But as soon as he went away and she was left on her own, she was assailed by doubts. Ever since her first day on the job, the

Dimora had been to her exactly what the Italian word meant: her dwelling. She had been there since before its opening and put heart and soul into creating the perfect atmosphere, developing business with the just right type of clientele, earning their fidelity. The staff looked to her for guidance and were loyal to her. She was treated with respect by everyone, and despite her aversion to formality, she had even grown into the title she had strove to achieve, and gradually became accustomed to hearing: *"Buongiorno, Direttrice."* *"Posso disturbarla un momento, Direttrice?"* *"C'è un problema, Direttrice."* *"Posso portarle un caffè, Direttrice?"* The Dimora had been more than a job to her; it had been a home, and the staff her family. Families could hold you back from living your life, though. If it hadn't been for Gregorio, she would still be in Rochester doing who knows what. And if it hadn't been for Max, she would never have risked cutting herself free: from Gregorio, from the Leales, or from the Mangiagallos.

Each time the ship pitched and rolled, the plastic water bottle that had toppled to the floor of the cabin followed suit, rousing Iris just as she was drifting off to sleep. Though she had hoped for a smooth crossing to Cagliari, she did not actually mind the rough sea. It lent a sense of adventure to her first overnight voyage, and fortunately, she did not suffer from seasickness. Neither, evidently, did Max, who slumbered in the bunk beneath her. His melodious snoring was juicy and full-bodied, its range and consistency maximized by his fleshy lips and slack jaw, and punctuated by a chewing movement and the heaving of his chest whenever he changed position, as if sleeping exhausted him.

She thought back on her sleepless nights lying next to Gregorio's inert, lean form, of the monotonous sound of his dry snorts followed by an almost imperceptible puff, as air sought release through his thin lips, pursed even in repose. Gregorio's snoring was neat and composed, its cadence so regular it was reassuring, and sometimes actually helped Iris fall asleep. Unlike Max's trumpeting, which with each roll of the ship was complemented by the percussion of the renegade water bottle, the banging of the toilet door, and the swishing of coins and keys on the nightstand.

This disjointed ensemble accompanied the exquisite images collected over the past ten days which flickered through Iris's now wide-awake mind. She had already filled a notebook with her impressions but wondered whether her words could faithfully convey the loveliness of the scenery and variety of sensations she encountered each day. She had never expected to discover such dazzling waters in the Adriatic, the coast she had always associated with mobs of mindless vacationers who flocked there each summer to play cards under endless rows of striped umbrellas, smearing their bodies with creams and oils smelling of tropical fruit, parading their paunches up and down the flat, sandy beaches, wading aimlessly in its colorless, shallow waters by day, and cruising its clubs by night. Further down the coast, just an hour's ferry boat ride from Termoli, she had been delightfully surprised to discover the Tremiti islands, where the green gouache of Aleppo pines was mirrored in the crystal-clear waters of the marine reserve. The same currents that kept the water pristine also kept it cold, and although it was early in the season, she and Max always took a dip during lunch breaks. The water exhilarated her, made her skin tingle and her heart race, made her feel alive and lucky and in love.

After returning to the mainland, they had driven through the Gargano peninsula, and she made everyone laugh by pointing excitedly at what looked like a giant alien spider from an old Japanese horror movie she spotted along the water's edge. Smiling that smirk of his, Max explained that the contraption was a *trabucco*, an ancient system of poles, lines, pulleys and nets used to pluck fish from offshore waters. They were still exploring the coast when the RAI production office called to instruct them they must cut their stay short and leave at once for Sardinia: the tuna were running.

During the drive west, Iris had ridden in the backseat of the van, oblivious to the bedlam of the other passengers shouting into their cell phones, fighting to be heard over one another. With no one calling her and no one to call, she stared out the window as they crossed Italy's breadbasket stretching from Apulia to Campania, marveling at the rolling fields of durum wheat, a landscape she did not know existed in southern Italy. For all its vastness, it was not Oklahoma, however, and within a few hours, they had already reached the outskirts of Naples.

Views of drab apartment buildings with drab laundry hanging from drab balconies overlooking drab roadways infiltrated the harmonious images of the countryside still floating in the space between Iris's eyes and her memory, as the van snaked through the traffic to the port and queued up with the other vehicles waiting to board the ferry. Drivers were leaning against cars in the fading light, smoking, obsessively checking their wristwatches and cell phones, intent on looking as if, unlike the others, they had better things to do than wait. Looking across to the pier where the hydrofoil for Ischia was docked, Iris swallowed, as a surge of sadness tightened her throat. She had waited at that pier many times, after flying down from Genoa with Gregorio and his diving gear. She wondered whether he would go to Ischia this year and whether he would rinse out his own wetsuit and hang it to dry at the end of the day, in the same methodical way he had taught her two decades earlier.

Iris curled into a ball in her top bunk, clenching the rough sheet in her fists; the pitching and rolling was getting worse. Each time the ship listed to one side, she held her breath until the movement was reversed and the cycle repeated itself: inhale-apnea-exhale, inhale-apnea-exhale. If Gregorio were there, he would sense she was awake, and cradle her in his arms. If sleep still eluded her, he would resort to more effective means, and now so would Iris. Lying on her stomach, she stretched an arm down to the night table and grabbed her travel pouch. Her fingers found the familiar package of pills and popped open a blister. Not wanting to climb down from her bunk to chase the rolling bottle of water, she swallowed the little blue pill without drinking. Hugging the flat pillow, she silently recited the goodnight prayer she used to say as a child. All she had to do now was wait.

"*Buongiorno, Bella Addormentata!* Are you planning to come

ashore or are you just gonna stay here and doze?"

Iris forced open her heavy lids, trying to figure out where she was and why. In the dream she had just abandoned, Gregorio was looming over her, holding a baby in his arms, demanding explanations she could not give. But the man standing in front of her in the artificial light was Max, and from her bunk, little more than his head was visible. She could see that he was already wearing a shirt, though, and that his backpack was slung over a shoulder. A deep shudder vibrated through the cabin, through her groggy head, through her lethargic body. The ship was maneuvering into its slip at the pier.

"Where are we?" she mumbled. The last thing she remembered was waiting in the port of Naples, looking at the hydrofoil for Ischia.

"We're there," Max said. Great. If only she could remember where "there" was today. "Now move that pretty little ass of yours!"

Iris raised her sunglasses and parked them on top of her head, bracing her eyes to face the midday sun. The morning had passed in a blur, and she recalled only snatches of the westbound drive from Cagliari to Portovesme in the van. This final crossing to the island of San Pietro would be brief, and she wanted to remember every minute of it. A surge of excitement for the imminent arrival at their final destination ferried the last traces of grogginess from Iris's system; her loose hair slapped her in the face as she stood on the open bridge, inhaling the salty air peppered with the smell of deck paint and engine grease. The thought that she was here, about to set foot on a little-known island, rather than fielding the complaints of the clients, staff, and owners of the Dimora, was as difficult for her to grasp as if it were a dream dangling from the moon. Only this time she was awake, this time she was living that dream in person. Exhilarated by her newfound freedom, Iris tossed her head back and laughed aloud, sharing her joy with the sun and the sky, the sea and the wind. As the ferry approached land, her heart quickened at the sight of a brand new territory to explore.

There was something oddly familiar about the colorful pastel buildings that lined the waterfront of Carloforte, and Iris wished that she knew more about the island and its history.

"Max, it reminds me of home!" Funny, how Liguria was home to her when she was traveling, and Rochester was home when she was in Liguria. It was all relative, she supposed.

"I'm not surprised," Max said. "Wait until you hear someone talk. I'll bet you understand the *Tabarchino* dialect. It's a lot like what you hear in Liguria."

"How can that be? We're so far away!" she said.

"Ah-ha! You mean *Signorina* Capotosti didn't do her homework?"

"I haven't been able to hook up to the Internet for five days, or I would have." Max always teased her for spending more time researching the local history and customs of their travel destinations, rather than where they would be sleeping or what specialties they would be eating. To her, it seemed presumptuous, if not downright rude, to arrive in a new place without first learning a bit about its culture. All she knew about the island of San Pietro was the reason given for this stopover on their itinerary: tuna fish.

"You must know something about this place if you agreed to come here," she said. "You must have learned something in geography class; after all, it is still Italy."

"I don't remember the whole story," he said, shoving his hands in his pockets. "All I know is that the island was settled a couple of centuries ago by a colony of Genoese descendants."

"Really? What did they come here for?"

"They didn't really mean to come here. They went to Tunisia first, to a place called Tabarka, to fish for coral. When the coral ran out, there wasn't a hell of a lot they could do there, so the smart ones left. I guess they just stumbled on this place on their way back to Italy and discovered there was lots of coral here, too. It worked out well, because no one was living here then, and the king was looking for someone to colonize the island."

"How amazing! Where did the name come from?"

"Look, Capo, you're the one who's supposed to be telling

everyone about this place, not me. I'm the movie man, remember?" Max poked her in the ribs.

"OK, OK!" Iris giggled. She couldn't wait to find out more about the island. She wondered whether there was a little museum or library she could visit. With all there was to see and learn in the world, she felt she could travel forever, and never tire of it. All those months spent locked up in the Dimora, all those years spent trying to conform to life as a Leale – they all seemed squandered on the pointless existence of another person she hardly knew anymore. She smiled up at Max, her green eyes sparkling, her pink cheeks rolled up into little balls of joy.

"Thank you, Max! I'll never forget this!"

"What? The history lesson?"

"No, silly!" she said. She gathered her flying hair in one hand, and with the other made a sweeping gesture that encompassed the indigo sea, the fishing boats bobbing in the harbor, the late spring sun shining in the cloudless sky, the palm trees lining the seafront, waving their fronds in the breeze. "All this! If it weren't for you, I wouldn't be here!"

"And if it weren't for you, I wouldn't be so happy to be here, Capo." Max spoke in a low voice as if frightened by the sound of his own words. "The demons don't mess with me so much when you're around." He pulled her close and kissed away the tears of joy glistening in her eyes.

Iris had known it all along: people *could* change. All you had to do was believe in them, and love them with all your heart. Just like with dreams.

The sky and the sea were still joined in darkness when the van parked in the unpaved lot in front of the *tonnara*. The salty morning air was thick with expectancy, laden with the pungent odors of an unfamiliar world. Breathing in shallow sips, Iris identified the smells of manual labor, of physical fatigue, of a perennial dampness that permeated body and soul. A sense of predestined purpose seemed to guide the movements of the muscular men she observed preparing for what promised to be a busy day for the islanders who relied upon the bounty of the sea for their livelihood.

The previous evening, while Iris and Max and the crew were led on a gastronomical tour of tuna-based delicacies under the tutelage of a highly acclaimed restaurateur to be featured in the program, they had all been infected with the excitement reverberating throughout the little island. The tam-tam in town was that the *Rais*, undisputed chief of the tuna kill, had declared the conditions perfect for a *mattanza*.

At the museum in Carloforte, Iris had studied a model of the ancient and intricate system of tuna fishing that still survived in San Pietro and precious few other locations in the Mediterranean. For centuries, man had been using the same method devised to catch the bluefin tuna during its migration. Programmed by a genetic code, the fish followed a route that led them from the North Atlantic and through the Strait of Gibraltar, to the warmer waters of the Mediterranean to deposit their eggs. It was said that the fish followed the land with their left eye as they swam until they reached the waters near Sardinia and Sicily, where they were tricked into following nets which ran perpendicular to the land, mistaking them for the coastline. The nets led the befuddled tunas into a series of other nets, a labyrinth of chambers from which it was impossible for them to find their way out. On the morning of the *mattanza*, they would be led into the final chamber, *la camera della morte*, where they would meet their demise.

It was in the more modern, concrete building of the *tonnara* where the tunas, fresh off the boat, were cleaned and sectioned, so their highly prized meat could be promptly shipped off to the highest bidders, some as far away as Japan. The hearts and egg sacs, traditionally the spoils of the workers who eviscerated the fish, were hung to dry in the cool darkness of another ancient building and later sold to local restaurants and specialty food shops, where they were appreciated as delicacies.

Max and the crew had made previous arrangements to film the *mattanza* but had been forewarned that the indoor work premises were strictly off limits to cameras. Max, never keen on restrictions, ran through his well-rehearsed gamut of persuasive tactics to gain access to the inner sanctum while Iris, the only woman in sight, preferred to stay out of the way of the burly men who glared at her as they went about the tasks performed by generations of men before them. Wandering off on her own, she found her way down to the wharf where the tied-up boats drowsed, rocked gently by the waves, under the soft pink blanket of a breaking dawn. Iris wondered where the unsuspecting tuna might be now; all she could see, off in the distance, were the bright bobbing buoys of the nets.

The early morning hours gently and generously shared revelations with Iris whenever she took the time to listen, and between a thought and a prayer, a regret and a hope, her mind had wandered elsewhere by the time she heard Max calling her name. Everything was set for the departure, and Iris was ordered to board a long, barge-like vessel along with him and the crew. As she hopped aboard, she felt a flutter of the curiosity that had been aroused by everything Max had told her about the tuna fishing tradition, about how exciting and passionate an experience it would be, about how this was a once in a lifetime opportunity to witness the practice firsthand, before it became extinct. As soon as they set off, however, her desire for adventure was eclipsed by a growing cloud of dread, and she began wishing she had remained ashore. She hugged her bare arms, wondering whether she really needed to participate in the *mattanza* to write about it, and why she had not worn something more suitable than the white gauze pants and flimsy top that did little to protect her from the cool morning air out on the open sea.

"You hang on tight, and stay put right here, Capo," Max instructed her when the vessel slowed down and maneuvered into position. "I'll be running back and forth with the other guys. We'll have to move fast once the action starts."

Iris nodded; she had no intention of budging from where she was. She looked around at the other smaller boats, the so-called *bastarde,* which had been towed into place and joined to form a giant square along the perimeter of the underwater death chamber. She admired the agility of the bare-chested men of the *ciurma,* or crew, as they jumped from boat to boat, but she still did not see any tunas.

Maybe there had been a mistake, maybe the nets were empty, maybe they could turn around and head back to shore, maybe ... Her thoughts were interrupted by a piercing cry that made her blood freeze. Her gaze turned to the *Rais*, as all activity came to a standstill, and all men fell silent. The tension in the air was palpable.

"*In nome de Diu, molla!*" he shouted. His men raised their voices in an unintelligible cry and sprang to action.

Based on what she had read, Iris recognized this as the command to drop open the door to the death chamber and let the tuna in. She looked at Max and his crew, eager to start filming; at the *Rais* and his crew poised for the kill; at the deep, dark water, for signs of their prey. The rays of the morning sun grew stronger, bouncing off the sea and warming her face and arms, but still, she felt a deep chill as she waited. At first, there was just a flicker of movement; seconds later, she could make out the shapes of the long, sleek forms and silvery tail fins circling in the deep blue pen. Iris had never seen such enormous fish and would be terrified to be in the water with them, but from the safety of the vessel, she could watch them for hours. They were magnificent.

"*Issa!*" the *Rais* shouted out in command.

Savage cries filled the air as the men of the *ciurma*, lined up along the sides of their boats, began tugging at the four sides of the immense net, grunting and shouting as they heaved. As the net was pulled to the *bastarde*, the floor of the death chamber rose, forcing the tunas higher and higher, until their dorsal fins sliced the surface of the water. The boats closed in on the fish, and they closed in on each other, swimming furiously, thrashing their tails, whipping the water white. Iris could see the shiny skin of the tunas flashing through the foam; she could smell their panic surging in the clear morning air, as they showered her with sea spray. Her heart beat wildly as she watched the fish crash into one another, injuring each other in their frantic efforts to escape, the blood from their wounds tainting the water.

The men chanted and shouted and whistled as they labored, their muscular torsos glistening with sweat and saltwater: round and round the tunas sped, until their movements were crippled by the net closing in on them, making the water too shallow to swim in. Tears blurred Iris's vision as she watched them flail about helplessly, suffocating, bleeding, exhausted, defeated. Prodded by an instinctual urge, they had swum thousands of kilometers to these waters, in this season when their meat was fleshy, and the bellies of the females swelling with eggs, only to be tricked and trapped by these men. Thoughts of the tuna tartare she had been served at the restaurant the previous evening made Iris want to puke. She shouldn't have come to witness this ritual, even though she knew her presence was irrelevant to the tunas and to the men who trapped them with their tricks. She looked up at the cloudless sky, thanking God it was finally over. They had their catch, and they could go.

"*Aaayyy!*" Iris swiveled around to look in the direction of the cry, her eyes widening as she saw one of the men drive a giant hook into one of the fish. The huge tuna, hemorrhaging but still alive, was raised from the bloodied sea amid excited shouts, then laid onto a bed of ice on the deck of the vessel on which Iris stood. One by one, the floundering fish were hooked and hoisted, then lowered to their mass grave, their tails beating out a sorrowful song of betrayal as they bled onto the melting ice. Iris was staring at the scene in horror, not wanting to look, but unable to turn away, when she was showered with the first spray of bloody water by a fishtail. One by one, the captured tunas were forced to join their ill-fated companions, their massive bodies convulsing in the throes of suffocation, their blood spilling onto the melting ice. Desperately flailing tails churned the pool of iced blood, and Iris was doused over and over again, until her clothes and skin and hair were completely drenched, until the metallic stench of blood pervaded every pore. She searched for cover, but there was nowhere to retreat; she was forced to endure the spectacle she had come to witness. She lowered her head in shame and repulsion, closed her eyes, and waited for the massacre to be over, praying for a speedy death to deliver the creatures from their agony.

Finally, like all things, regardless of how beautiful or horrible

204

they may be, it did end, and the expedition headed back to shore. As the boats approached land, they were greeted by the joyful peal of church bells celebrating the successful *mattanza*. As soon as the vessel was moored, Iris jumped off, ran down to the rocks, and dove into the water fully dressed. She rubbed her skin and hair and clothes with water, but no amount of scrubbing could wash away the stains from her clothes, or the tinny taste of blood from her mouth, or the stench of death from her nostrils. She needed to get out of this place; she needed to go back to the hotel, take a hot shower, change into some clean clothes. Her soaked sneakers squished as she trudged out of the water and over to the van, where she found Max and the crew cleaning off their equipment, laughing and talking excitedly about the scenes they had managed to shoot.

"We got some fuckin' amazing footage out there," she heard Max say. "If we got all we need, maybe we can go out again tomorrow just for fun and leave the equipment behind."

He leaned inside the van, then reappeared seconds later, holding Iris's backpack.

He waved at her, calling out, "Hey, Capo! Just in time! Your phone's ringing. Here!" He tossed the backpack to her, but it fell short. "What the fuck happened to you? You're a mess!"

Iris bent over to pick up her backpack, still too shaken to speak. Her hands trembled as she fumbled with zippers and clasps, trying to remember in which of the many compartments she had stowed her phone. Following a trail of rings and vibrations, she finally got her hands on it and saw that the call was from an unidentified number.

"*Pronto?*" she said.

"Iris?" Her sisters all had the same voice, and no matter who this one belonged to, it sounded terribly out of place here.

"Yes, it's me. Who's this?" Whoever it was, she shouldn't sneak up on Iris while she was dripping wet, wearing blood-stained clothes, and on the verge of vomiting.

"Iris, it's Violet. You have to come home. Get here as fast as you can."

8. LILY

The dilapidated houses lining Rosewood Lane passed in a blur as Lily sped away. She breezed through several intersections, each light turning green as she approached, like gates of providence ushering her frantic retreat. Mesmerized by the white lines dividing the lanes, she neared the end of the road, catching sight of the final traffic light changing to red just in time to slam on her brakes. She watched through tears as a white-haired woman, the burden of her years weighing heavily on her back, stepped clumsily off the curb.

Lily dug through her purse for a tissue but came up empty. She swiped at her face with the palms of her hands. The old woman began to hobble her way across the street, pushing a wire cart overflowing with plastic grocery bags filled with food, a loaf of bread precariously balanced on top.

Lily continued to dig blindly through her purse, accidentally jamming the tip of a nail file under the nail of her index finger.

"Ow - shit!" She squeezed the flesh of her fingertip and watched as a bubble of blood rose to the surface. The old woman was nearly halfway across the street. "Old woman, you are never going to make it if you don't get moving," Lily said to herself.

She picked up the tattered pages of the group's brainstorming notes from the passenger seat and scoured the list; every possibility had been crossed off. Every one except for Claire's. The words jumped off the page: "Rent a cottage at the beach."

The old woman was nearly three-quarters of the way across the street when the front wheel of her cart became lodged in a pothole, sending her tottering loaf of bread up into the air and then down into the street.

"Oh, good Lord!" said Lily, more out of exasperation than pity.

The woman steadied her cart and then began to shuffle over to rescue her loaf of bread. The light for the cross traffic turned yellow. Lily threw her car into park and jumped out in a huff. *Like I don't have enough problems of my own right now,* she thought.

"My Monks' Bread," said the old woman. "I need my Monks' Bread for my dinner."

Lily snatched the bread from the street as the light turned green. She held her hands up and shouted to the waiting cars, "Hold on one second... just give her a minute." Lily offered her arm to the woman and using her free hand, she guided the cart up and over the curb.

"Goodness gracious," said the woman. "I wasn't sure I was going to make it today, but it was a very important errand. I have to have my Monks' Bread for dinner, after all." She shuffled away down the sidewalk without a word of thanks, as though she may not have noticed Lily at all, or perhaps had taken her for an angel, sent at just the right moment for the express purpose of saving the Monks' Bread, and as if the appearance of a celestial being for such ordinary purposes was quite commonplace.

The air filled with a cacophony of horns from the early evening traffic that lined up behind Lily, each driver needing to get on with their own very important errands. Lily hopped in behind the wheel, buckled her seatbelt, and headed for the lake.

One of the few times Lily remembered going down to Charlotte Beach on Lake Ontario was when Grandma Whitacre visited Rochester and suggested it as a Sunday ride.

"Now I don't know why y'all don't come down here all the time," she'd said to Lily's mother. "Why if I lived this close to a beach, I would set my lawn chair out on Memorial Day and stay until Labor Day."

But Lily had known that trips to the lake cost money - twenty-five cents for each ride on the antique Merry-Go-Round, fifty cents for an ice cream cone, not to mention the gas to drive twenty miles "for no good reason," as her father would say.

Most of what Lily had seen of Charlotte Beach in recent years had been on the news. The public park had fallen into neglect in the late 1980s, due to a lack of municipal funds for maintenance. Its broken benches and pock-marked parking lots had discouraged families from driving in from the suburbs, making the way clear for the local kids on the other side of the Genesee River to walk across the Stutson Street bridge in determined search of trouble, which they found in the forms of fights, vandalism, and the occasional auto theft. A small industrial park, which sat along the river, was a favored target - especially the Kendall bicycle manufacturing plant, whose front lawn hosted an iron sculpture of an old-fashioned bike. It wasn't uncommon for the local paper to feature photos of the sculpture decorated with toilet paper or adorned with empty beer cans.

In recent years, however, the city had launched an effort to revitalize the area, promoting the assumption that the money invested in cleaning up the beach and developing the surrounding area with restaurants, shops, and lakefront housing would provide a hearty return in the form of tax revenue. The marginalized elements had scattered, finding refuge in the rundown homes that still stood in the few remaining pockets of neighborhood that were separated from the public beaches - and the city's benevolence - by the Genesee River and the borders of a town that grandiosely referred to itself as Summerville.

The fisherman's pier at Charlotte Beach was still deserted this early in the season, which meant that Lily could walk along it at a leisurely pace, without being worried about dodging the baby strollers and rollerbladers that crammed the way during the summer months. As she strolled, Lily could see the modest homes of Summerville along the shore to her right. To her left were the stately new homes that had been recently built or remodeled. It was this concrete slab upon which she walked - so littered with the droppings of seagulls that it appeared to be whitewashed - that separated the haves from the have-nots.

The light tower stood directly ahead, against a blue horizon streaked with pink cotton candy clouds. The further Lily walked out toward them, the wilder the wind grew. The water of Lake Ontario, which seemed calm closer to shore, began to rock and lurch. Like water hands, waves reached up over the guardrail and then slapped themselves down again upon the surface of the pier, soaking Lily's shoes. But she didn't care. She barely noticed; all she could see was the light tower. She set her sights upon it and vowed to keep walking toward it, no matter how wild the wind grew, or how many cold sprays she was caught in. Getting to the end of the pier without turning back seemed like such an insignificant goal given all that she had to deal with in her life, but it was still a goal, and if Lily could make it to the end, at least that was something.

With every step, the trials of Lily's life grew more distant, as though she had left them in the parking lot, locked in the car with the windows rolled up, their screams for her attention drowned out by the roar of wind and waves. Finally Lily found herself standing directly under the light tower. She rested her body against the railing at the end of the pier and looked out over the slate expanse of the great Lake Ontario. Even though she knew that Canada was out there, just beyond the horizon, the lake looked like it might stretch to eternity, even to God. A cluster of seagulls was suspended in mid-air, riding on a current, like a mobile hung from heaven simply for Lily's delight. Lily closed her eyes and took in the pungent scent of fish, seaweed, and the trace of a campfire.

"I sure hope you remembered your gun," said a man's voice.

Lily jumped with a gasp, turning around to discover a man of about sixty-five years sitting on an overturned white plastic bucket, which had presumably been meant to hold a supply of freshly caught fish. His tattered fishing cap sat askew on his head. He was holding a fishing pole off the side of the pier.

A smile came across the man's face. "I see you don't have a rod, so I hope you at least remembered your gun," he said. "For all the good it will do you with the fish in this pond."

"You scared me," said Lily. She placed her hand over her chest. "I didn't even notice you there."

"Sorry about that," said the man. "It is still a bit early in the season for most folks to be out here. That's why I come. I like the solitude."

"Oh, I'm sorry," said Lily. "I didn't mean to bother you."

"Well, aren't we two of the most polite people you've ever

seen?" The man laughed, which provoked a coughing fit that lasted so long Lily wasn't sure if she should continue to stand there waiting for it to be done. She eventually turned away in order to save the man from embarrassment. He finally hawked up one final cough, and Lily heard him spit, followed by the sound of a small splash.

"I beg your pardon," he said, dabbing at his lips with a white handkerchief.

"That's OK," said Lily, turning back around. "What are you hoping to catch?"

"Oh, I won't catch anything. I'm not even using any bait. Only thing that's any good this time of year is trout, except that these waters are so polluted my doctor said I can't even eat it, so what's the point?"

"Let me get this straight," Lily said, "You're sitting there holding a rod with no bait on the hook, not trying to catch a fish that you can't eat anyway?" His plan sounded only slightly less preposterous than her own.

"When you say it like that," said the man. "It sounds downright ridiculous, doesn't it?" He laughed again, which induced another coughing fit, which resulted in another spit into the water. This time Lily watched as a school of tiny fish rose to the water's surface to nibble at the sputum.

"At least I have a rod," said the man, wiping his mouth again. "What in God's name are you doing out here on an evening like this? This wind is likely to pick you right up and toss you in."

"Actually, I'm looking for a house." Lily laughed at the thought of how ridiculous that must seem to him.

"You don't say," said the man. "Haven't you got a home?"

"Well, I have a house, but, well, I'm going through a separation, so I have to move." Lily turned to face the lake, enjoying the sensation of the wind tangling her hair into knots. "It's just a fantasy," she said, "But I have two little boys, and I've been daydreaming about giving them a place around here. It's so peaceful."

"What's your name?" asked the man.

"I'm Lily." Lily extended her hand.

"Hi, Lily, I'm Curtis." His hand was warm; his handshake was weak. "Now, what would you say if I told you that I just happen to have a house for rent right over there?" Curtis gestured to the right, toward the houses in Summerville.

"No way!" Lily's excitement was immediately supplanted by the recognition that she would never be able to afford a house on the lake, on her budget.

"Yes, ma'am, I do," said Curtis. "If you're interested, you can come over and take a look."

"I don't know," said Lily. "I'm sure it's more than I can spend..."

"What can you spend?" Curtis asked.

"I just started working," said Lily. She didn't even want to quote a price since she was embarrassed and worried about offending this fisherman without fish. "And I don't have a very good job yet."

"Just spit out a number," said Curtis. "You never know."

Lily looked down. "I'd only be able to pay about six-hundred and fifty dollars a month - I know that's not nearly enough for a place on the water."

"Well now, isn't that a coincidence," said Curtis. "That just happens to be the exact amount I'm asking."

It was clearly too good to be true. Either this was a cruel joke, or as her mother would say, this guy was up to something.

"Why don't you live there?" Lily asked.

"I'll be living there for another couple weeks, and then I'm headed down to Florida, to stay with my daughter and her family for a bit. Doctor's orders."

"Why haven't you been able to rent it out?" asked Lily.

"I haven't tried," said Curtis. He pushed his cap up away from his brow and looked out over the water. "Renting it out was sort of like saying I'm not coming back. But it seems to me that it would be put to better use by you and your boys than it will be by just sitting there waitin' for me until the end of time."

"But you don't even know me."

"Maybe so," said Curtis, "but I find it strange that on my final fishing expedition here – or," he added with a cough, "should I say my non-fishing expedition – that the only other person I see all evening is someone who is on a fishing pier looking for a house. I'd like to believe that's gotta mean something."

Objections popped into Lily's head faster than she could address them. What school district is it in? How much are the utility bills? How many bedrooms does it have? How long can I stay? How do I ask that question politely?

"When do you expect to return?" Lily asked.

"Oh, I don't know," said Curtis. "I expect I'll be with my daughter six months to a year. My lawyer would let you know in plenty of time when you'd need to vacate the place."

Despite the voices in her head shouting, warning, trying to convince her that something was not right with this whole deal, Lily felt uncharacteristically calm. She looked at Curtis, perched on his white bucket, looking out over the water as though he could see Florida and didn't like it one bit. In a strange way, Lily knew she would be doing him a favor to take him up on his offer and fill his house with life.

"Can't hurt to come have a look," said Curtis.

"No, I suppose you're right about that."

"Is your car parked up in the lot there?" Curtis asked.

"Yes," Lily replied.

"Mine too - what say you follow me over there and I'll give you the nickel tour?" Curtis stood up and gathered his tackle box and rod. Lily picked up the white bucket, and they turned and headed back toward the parking lot.

Lily thought about stopping at a phone booth to call Donna to ask her to come down and meet her. She thought about calling the CBW hotline to see if Sophie was around, so someone would at least know where she was. It just didn't seem necessary. When she thought about going to see the house, a sense of peace came over her. Maybe that was what a miracle felt like.

"Whoever thought that I'd cast an empty line and find myself a tenant?" said Curtis.

"Whoever thought I'd come to the edge of the world and find a home?"

Lily stepped out of the front door of the house on Trevi Way for the final time, carrying a garbage bag filled with bed pillows. There had been a time when she loved the house when it represented safety and joy. But now, everything about it was just a reminder of pain and fear. The broken door jamb in the bathroom. The missing light fixture on the patio. The slip-shod repairs. The bed.

Lily set the bag down as she crouched over to snip several sprigs of lavender from the garden walk, hoping to transplant them at the lake so they would still have time to bloom before fall. She slipped them into a plastic zipper bag into which she had placed a moist paper towel. "I'm sorry I can't bring all of you with me," said Lily to the hyacinths and daffodils. "Anyway, soon someone new will come take care of you and love you - and Donna's going to come by every once in a while and make sure you're getting enough water. Be good. Be beautiful." Knowing that they would be cared for in her absence wasn't the same as being able to see them and care for them every day. A tear trailed down Lily's face and landed in the dirt. She laughed.

"Well, I think that's it," said Lily. She shoved the garbage bag into the trunk of her mother's old LeMans and then used the force of her entire body to slam the lid closed, only to discover a tuft of plastic sticking out through the crack. She thought about opening up the trunk and trying again, but it was just an excuse to avoid doing what had to come next: Turning around and facing Donna.

"I just can't believe you're leavin' us," said Donna, her eyes glistening.

"I'm not dying, Donna," said Lily, with an empty giggle. She knew that in a way, she was. Lily thought of Iris and how they had grown apart over the years. Of course, Italy was a lot farther than Summerville, but even when Iris was in town, she barely managed to traverse those last few miles that remained between them. There just never seemed to be enough to pull them toward one another, to overcome the awkward pauses and the suspicion that the past was the only thing left to share. No matter what happened now, Lily and Donna would not be next-door neighbors anymore. They wouldn't babysit for each other or drive to church together. What use would Donna have of a depressed, scared, impoverished, confused friend on the other side of town? Their daily lives would no longer be compatible; it was only a matter of time before they followed suit.

"What in the world am I gonna do without you?" Donna wrapped her arms around Lily, and both women collapsed into tears. Donna's embrace was soft and warm, like a favorite sweater. The two women rocked from side to side. Lily wanted to climb deeper inside the embrace, curl up, go to sleep, wake up next year. Or last year. Be anywhere but here today, saying goodbye to her best friend – her only friend – in the world.

"You are not going to be without me," said Lily. "I'm only moving fifteen miles away." She understood that Donna wasn't talking about the distance between them. Rather, she was talking about the distance between them.

They continued their embrace.

"You sure you don't want me to come out there with you?" asked Donna. "Help you get settled?"

"I'm sure," said Lily. "I don't think I could bear to say goodbye to you from the new place. It would just be too much." The truth was, Lily couldn't wait to get the good-byes over, get past all the sadness and get on with her new life. She would always have a special place in her heart for Donna, but even if their friendship ended right there on the strip of lawn that separated their driveways, Lily knew she had to do this alone. Lily was the first to release the hug. Someone had to, and Donna didn't have it in her.

"I understand," said Donna, wiping her tears. "But you only have a few hours until Joe brings the boys back - you know I'm just a phone call away if you need help, right?"

"You'll be the first one I call." Lily wouldn't have phone service until the end of the week. It was just as well. Make a clean break.

"Now, don't you take no guff from no one, you hear?" Donna wiped her nose with her sleeve. "And just you remember how much I love you, will ya'?"

"I love you too, Donna," said Lily. "I don't know how to thank you for all you've done for me, I -" the words stuck in her throat.

"Hush, now," said Donna. "You'd better skedaddle, or those movers are going to get there before you do. I wouldn't put it past those guys to dump your stuff on the lawn and drive away."

Lily slipped herself behind the steering wheel, gently setting her baggie of lavender clippings on the passenger's seat. Wishes whimpered from her carrier in the back seat.

"It's OK, girl," said Lily. "Just try not to look back. It's easier to just make a clean break of it. Don't take any expectations with you and you'll save yourself from future disappointments."

The house on Trevi Way, along with Donna, grew smaller in her rearview mirror as Lily drove away.

It was hard to believe that just this morning, home was somewhere else, a place where Lily had been surrounded by things and people she knew, where she could go from room to room in the dark and never stub her toe. Everything at the new place in Summerville was foreign to her. The house itself was built into the side of a hill, separated from the beach by a quarter acre of lawn, half of which had been overcome by tall, reedy weeds. The house was uniquely situated, in that pulling into the driveway brought you to the back door, which opened onto a foyer on the second floor, where the bedrooms and laundry were located. A full flight of stairs took you down to the main floor with a great room lined with windows. When you looked out from them, instead of seeing the asphalt of the road, or the front of another person's house, you could see the endless water of Lake Ontario.

Lily opened one of the boxes marked, "kitchen," feeling disappointed that she had to stack the cupboards with old mismatched, battle-scarred dishes that she had stored away in the basement the last time she and Joe had moved. But she saw that they were also a perfect figure for her life these days. Some of the dishes had come from a grandmother, some from an aunt. Some bought, some given. One chipped, five cracked, one blue, one gold, six floral, and twelve melamine saucers. Remnants. Of a family, of a time. Placed now with love in a new place, a peace place , a place of hope.

Lily was constantly pulled from the work at hand into the great room, out onto the front porch, toward the lake. She stood in the dining area, picking a spot for next year's Christmas tree. Would it go there, in the corner, or in front of the window?

She imagined the laughter she would hear when the boys arrived, as they ran toward the beach, racing, tripping, chasing. She lost track of time standing there, but it didn't really seem to matter much. Suddenly, there was nothing to rush for, nothing to race toward, nothing to fret over. She simply stood in that room, being with her new home, the sun first at her right, then above her, then at her left, until the sound of Joe's horn signaled that the boys had arrived – just in time to watch the sunset.

Lily ran up the stairs and out the back door as the boys burst forth from their father's car and ran to greet Wishes, who was running toward them.

"Mommy – can we go swimming?" shouted Pierce, holding a straw cowboy hat in place on his head as he ran past Lily and down the hill toward the sand.

"The water's still really cold," called Lily. "But we can go wading… maybe we can find some cool sea glass."

"Hi, Mom!" called Joseph, as he and Wishes followed Pierce down the hill.

Joe started to walk toward the house, but then suddenly stopped, as though he collided with a force field, no doubt courtesy of one Order of Protection. Lily wondered what would happen when it expired.

"Hey," called Joe. "Don't you guys say goodbye to your Daddy?"

"Bye, Dad!" called Pierce, waving without turning around. His cowboy hat flew off. He stopped for it, put it back on his head, and continued running.

"Yeah – bye, Dad," echoed Joseph. "See you Saturday night!"

Lily stood by the back porch looking at Joe, who stood at the end of the driveway next to his car.

"This place is sort of far for me," called Joe.

"You were the one who said I had to move," said Lily.

"How are they going to get to school from here?"

"I'm handling it," said Lily.

"What did you do to get this place?" Joe asked. "Or should I say 'who did you do'?"

"I have a job," said Lily, feeling too grateful to bother taking the bait he dangled.

"Yeah, right... how the hell can you afford a place like this?"

"Don't you worry about it," said Lily. "I'm doing just fine."

"Don't you worry about it, I'm doing just fine," Joe mimicked. "I'm living in a two-by-four apartment in the city, like an asshole. If you think I'm paying for this, you're nuts – and by the way, it's going to cost you a fortune to keep this place up. It's falling apart. The wiring is probably older than dirt. If you had a fire, the place would go up like a tinderbox."

Lily turned around to scan the house. According to Curtis, it had been built during the Lincoln administration and had survived two fires and a flood – disasters that had caused the demise of surrounding properties, enabling Curtis to buy up several of the adjacent lots, leaving Lily's stoic but tired old house standing alone on a strip of private beach in quiet isolation, struggling to hold its head high. It might almost seem lonely as the oldest remaining structure of its generation. Some of the stones at its foundation were cracked and crumbling, the window panes hung nonchalantly in their frames, rattling with even the smallest breeze. The porch leaned to one side and swayed in the middle. The roof tiles that remained were worn. But these were the scars of its long and eventful life, which made Lily love it even more.

"Was there something else you wanted?" Lily asked. She couldn't help but enjoy the sensation of dismissing Joe, knowing that he probably wanted to scream or shout or run at her, but also knowing that he couldn't. Except, of course, that there wasn't actually anyone close by enough to hear if he did. She reeled in her bravado. Better not to poke an angry bear.

"I'll have the boys ready on Saturday by six." She turned to walk out to the beach, still feeling the heat of Joe's stare on her back.

Lily's days began by wrangling the boys out of bed half an hour earlier than usual to accommodate for the commute to their school across town. Cranky and uncooperative, they used up most of that time arguing with Lily, often arriving at school with uncombed hair, sleep in their eyes, and rumpled mismatched clothing – concessions Lily accepted as being temporary and that would no longer be required once they all got settled into their new routine. After she dropped them off, she made a mad dash back across town to work, barely making it through the door at The Fertig School by eight o'clock, arriving breathlessly under the disapproving gaze of Mrs. Windham-Childs, who believed that proper control of one's home and family resulted in a calm and self-possessed countenance. From chiding her for her gum-chewing (which Lily did to stave off nicotine fits during work hours), to the way she sat in her chair, Mrs. Windham-Childs often offered Lily tips on how to present herself "in a manner more suited to a professional representative of a widely recognized and globally respected organization such as The Fertig School." Lily did her best to appear interested and compliant (she still sometimes held a wad of gum in between her teeth and gums, sneaking in a chew or two when Mrs. Windham-Childs wasn't looking), because she had the sense that Mrs. Windham-Childs considered herself a bit of a Pygmalion and that the greater portion of Lily's value to her (and so her job security) was in her willingness to participate in the delusion that she was being groomed.

At the end of each day, Lily would rush back across town to pick the boys up from the after-school care program, where they could usually be found in the gymnasium, pumped up on junior surges of testosterone and competition. Lily would settle their sweaty, exhausted bodies into the back seat of the car, and drive across town as they whined in stereo about being hungry, about having homework, and about having such a long ride home.

Dinner, dishes, homework, and showers took up the evenings. Lily collapsed with exhaustion each night. By the end of the first month, she still had not unpacked any boxes except those containing items that were absolutely necessary for daily life.

As the days and weeks passed, the boys' behavior toggled

between what might be considered normal, and what could be called erratic and violent, getting worse and more intense every time they visited their father. At first, they simply refused to obey her requests that they go to bed, or clean their room. Soon, they were talking back, even calling her names, and telling her that they hated her and that it was her fault that their father was alone.

More and more of Lily's time was spent first dealing with their bizarre antics and then recovering from their effects. The boxes remained unpacked. She feared she was losing ground. She thought about asking her mother to come stay for a while, just to act as reinforcement, but that would still only delay the inevitable: Lily had to learn to be strong with them on her own terms. Besides, her mother was likely to tell her that the solution to her problem with the boys was in the law and that she had an obligation to other women to hold Joe accountable through the courts, as part of establishing a precedent for future cases. But what Lily really wanted was to be where she could talk about *her* needs and how *she* was feeling, and didn't place an additional burden on her for the whole of the future of womankind. She hadn't been to a support group meeting in weeks. Maybe it was time to check in.

"I have no doubt that your ex is coaching your boys to give you a hard time. That's alienation of affection," Sophie explained, the following Wednesday. "It's a common tactic used by men to gain residency by creating discord between children and their mothers."

"But our separation agreement stipulates joint custody," said Lily.

"Custody concerns itself with who has legal jurisdiction over the children," explained Sophie. "Residency – where the children live – is a separate issue. The preference of the children is a significant factor in determining residency. What your ex is doing is grossly immoral."

"What should I do? Write a letter to his lawyer?"

"Are you serious?" Edie said. "His lawyer is prolly telling him 'zactly what to do."

"But if it's immoral, then why would his lawyer help him do it?"

"Lily, lawyers are hired to help you win," said Sophie. "They don't keep you from breaking the law; they only protect you from getting caught. With his history of gambling and abuse, your husband knows a judge would never grant him residency, and that the only way to get your children from you is to make them *want* to go live with him. He's doing that by trying to sabotage their relationship with you while making them feel responsible for his happiness - and God only knows what else. I see this all the time. It's entirely despicable. The only way he will be held accountable for this is if you file a petition with Family Court."

"And he knows you ain't gonna do that," said Edie.

"What makes you say that?" asked Lily.

"'Cuz in order to prove your case," said Edie, "you would have to put your babies on the stand, make them testify against they Daddy." Edie reached into her pocket for a tissue. "He knows you kin never do that."

Edie was right. She wouldn't. She couldn't.

"What I am struggling to understand is this: What in the world would my ex do with two little boys, living in a two bedroom apartment in the city, and working at a sixty-hour-a-week job?"

"Don't expect it to make sense, Lily," said Sophie. "His objective is to hurt you. Attack never makes sense."

"Good point," said Lily.

"He could jus' be tryin' to scare you," said Kitten. "Mebbe he thinks you'll come back if you think he will take them boys away from you."

"Yeah," said Lily. "That's probably what it is. I have to say, if he's trying to scare me, he's doing an excellent job."

"When my ex lured my kids away, that's just how it went," said Claire. "First they became belligerent, then they asked for extended visits, then my ex got a girlfriend and the next thing I knew, they wanted to be over there all the time."

"What did you do?" Lily asked.

"I panicked," said Claire. "I went out and borrowed money from everyone I knew, I mortgaged the house, and I took him to court. That was four years ago, and it's still not settled. My kids are still living with him, getting more deeply entrenched. Only now they're so old, that even a judge would agree that they should choose where they want to be. Plus, they're angry with me for causing their father so much trouble." Claire was looking down, winding the cord from her drawstring jacket around her index finger, unwinding it, and then winding it up again. "I've dug myself into such a hole that if they did come back to live with me, I wouldn't even be able to afford to take care of them. I lost my job because I had to be in court so much – my ex and his lawyer kept booking dates and then cancelling them at the last minute - once I had already gotten time away from work. I'm broke, unemployed, and I still have to live with this mess every day. If you want my advice, Lily, just let them go if that's what they say they want. You can use the time to heal and get your act together. In your ex's situation, with his job and all, I bet you'll have them both back by the Fourth of July. And then this matter will be closed forever. You won't have to live in fear of him stealing your boys away, and he will lose his power over you. I say call his bluff and let's be done with it. Otherwise," added Claire, "this is going to eat you alive."

"It already is," said Lily.

After Joe picked the boys up the following Saturday night, Lily walked down to the neighborhood grill and ordered a Philly cheesesteak sandwich and fries to go, which she devoured while sitting on the front porch watching as the moon rose and cast ribbons of silver light on the water. She finally forced herself to go inside where the plan was to enjoy a long hot bath in the deep claw-footed tub before tackling a few unpacked boxes. However, a short rest on the bed to catch her breath turned into a sleep so sound that she didn't stir until Wishes licked at her toes, which had found their way out from under the blanket and were dangling off the side of the bed.

"You're a good friend, Wishes," said Lily, filling her dish with dog food. "And," she added, patting Wishes on the head. "I am grateful for your silence." Lily made her way back upstairs just as the boys came bounding in and ran past her down the stairs.

"I'll be right down," she called to them. Lily peeked out the back window to make sure that Joe's car was gone, then washed her face, brushed her teeth and pulled on a pair of jeans and the first T-shirt she could find. For the first time in recent memory, she wasn't tired.

"Did you guys have fun?" Lily called from the kitchen. She poured herself a cup of coffee, which had gone cold since the auto-timer had switched off more than four hours ago. She placed the "World's Greatest Mother" mug the boys had given her for Mother's Day into the microwave and joined them in the living room, looking forward to planning a day of fun and relaxation with them.

The boys - Pierce wearing his cowboy hat, as he had become accustomed to - were sitting on the floor in front the TV, playing Super Mario Brothers on Nintendo.

"What did you guys do with your dad?" Lily asked.

"Oh – no!" shouted Joseph. "Not Bowser! I hate him!"

"Look out, Joseph!" cried Pierce, covering his eyes with his hands.

"Hey – guys – I'm talking to you," said Lily. "What did you do with your dad?"

"Nuthin'," said Joseph.

"Let's turn off the TV and go for a walk on the beach," said Lily. "It's a gorgeous day!"

Joseph looked at Pierce, and then picked up the game controller and resumed the game. "We don't want to go to the beach," he said.

"Yeah," said Pierce. "We don't want to go to the beach."

"What do you mean? You love the beach. C'mon, let's shut off the TV and get out into the sun and fresh air."

"No!" said Pierce. He picked up his controller and then looked at Joseph, giving him a little nod. "Right, Joseph?"

Joseph nudged Pierce with his elbow, and then looked at Pierce with eyes widened, as if in warning.

"I'm serious, you two. We're going outside." Lily picked up the remote control and turned off the set. "Now," she added.

Joseph folded his arms across his chest. "You can't make us."

Lily reached behind the TV set and pulled out all the cables for the game system.

"Mommy – what are you doing?" shouted Pierce.

"I can't make you go outside, but until you do, there will be no more video games."

Joseph ran for the phone. "I'm gonna call my Dad and tell him that you're being mean to us."

"No, you are not," said Lily. She tucked the Nintendo system under her arm, and strode across the room, pulling the base of the phone from the wall as Joseph attempted to punch out a series of numbers on the keypad.

"Get outside, both of you." Lily's heart was pounding. She had no idea what her next move would be if they didn't comply.

Joseph leaned over and whispered into Pierce's ear. Pierce nodded and smiled at him.

"OK- if that's what you want," said Joseph. "We'll go outside."

"Yeah, we'll go outside!" said Pierce.

Both boys darted out the front door and ran toward the water. Lily ran after them, stopping briefly on the front porch to pull on her flip-flops.

The three of them came to a halt at the water's edge together, the boys seeming to be at as much of a loss about what to do next as Lily was.

"I could teach you guys how to skip stones!" she finally said. "Watch this."

Lily picked up a smooth flat rock from the sand. With a flick of her wrist, she sent it sailing over the surface of the water, skipping every couple of feet until it finally disappeared beneath the waves. "Isn't that cool?" she said.

Joseph raised a large rock overhead, walked over to the water, and let it fall, causing a splash that sprayed Lily with cold lake water.

"Joseph!" she cried.

Pierce followed suit by finding a rock and pitching it into the water, the limited force of his small body creating a much smaller physical effect, though not lacking in fervor.

"Good one, PJ!" said Joseph.

"OK, that's enough, you guys," said Lily.

The boys scurried about the beach, collecting rocks and firing them into the water, giving each other a high-five whenever Lily was caught in the splash.

"Cut it out!" Lily cried. "The next one to pick up a rock is staying in their room the rest of the day!" It was a punishment she wasn't sure she could mete out.

"OK, no more rocks!" cried Joseph. He scooped up a fistful of sand and threw it up into the air. The wind blew the sand back at them.

Pierce then picked up a fistful of sand and released it, only to have it blow back into his own face. "My eyes! My eyes!" he cried.

Lily squatted down and set Pierce on her thigh. She splashed his face with lake water, which only made him angrier. He screamed and wriggled, landing himself face down in the cold, shallow water. He scrambled to his feet, his cries rivaled only by Joseph's dark laughter. Lily grabbed Pierce and held his flailing arms down at his sides.

"Calm down, Pierce," she said sternly. "As soon as you calm down, I will let you go."

"Look!" said Joseph, pointing out toward the water.

"My cowboy hat!" screamed Pierce.

The small straw hat bobbed on the surface of the water.

"I'll get it!" called Joseph.

"Joseph – no!" cried Lily. "You two stay right there. I'll get it."

Lily rolled up her jeans and waded out into the icy water. With every ripple, the lake carried the hat farther from shore, until it became clear that the only way to retrieve it would be to jump in and swim after it.

"My cowboy hat!" cried Pierce. "My cowboy hat!"

Just as Lily resolved to dive into the frigid water after it, the hat tilted and then disappeared beneath the waves.

"My cowboy hat!" cried Pierce. "My daddy gave me that hat! I want it back!" Pierce threw himself into the water. "I want my cowboy hat!" cried Pierce. "I want my cowboy hat!"

Lily wrangled him from the cold water.

"I want my cowboy hat! I hate the lake! I hate you!"

Joseph jumped up and down in the water, clapping his hands. "You tell her, PJ!"

Wet, cold, and covered with sand, the three of them trudged back toward the house, Lily dragging Joseph by the hand and carrying a wailing Pierce in her arms.

After baths and a change of clothes, they were all subdued. Lily made peanut butter and jelly sandwiches and warmed up a can of chicken noodle soup. The three of them sat quietly at the table, as Lily struggled to make sense out of recent events and out of Joseph and Pierce's behavior.

Joseph slurped his soup. Pierce peeled the crusts from his bread.

"Guys, I gotta ask you – what the heck was that all about anyway?"

Joseph and Pierce exchanged a glance.

"What?" said Lily. "What on earth is going on with you two?"

"I want to go live with my Dad," said Joseph.

A rush of heat rocketed up through Lily's body.

"What do you mean?" she said.

Tears came to Joseph's eyes. "My father is all alone, and he won't make it without us."

"Of course he will, Joseph. He's a grown man. He'll be fine, in time. We all will."

"*He* won't," said Joseph, a tear running down his face. "He'll die if he's alone."

"Sweetie, look at me," said Lily, taking Joseph's hand. "Your father is not going to die. Is that what he told you?"

Joseph looked down at his soup, then glanced at Pierce, and then back at his soup. "No," he said, pulling his hand out of Lily's. "I can just tell."

"I want to go live with my Daddy, too," said Pierce. "Then you will see what it's like to be left all alone, right, Joseph? Ow!" cried Pierce. "Why did you kick me?

"I don't know what your father has been telling you," said Lily, "but you are not going to live with him. It is *not* going to happen, so just forget about it." The boys sat staring at her blankly. "Now finish your lunch and go play video games."

Lily returned from group the next Wednesday, just as Joe was dropping Joseph and Pierce back home. The interior lights of the car switched on. There was a woman in the front seat, and she got out to let Pierce out of the back seat. She was tall and thin and wore a short faux fur jacket and high-heeled boots.

"It was so nice to meet you, PJ," she said.

"It was nice to meet you, too, Samantha," Pierce replied.

"Can I have a hug?" Samantha asked. She squatted to bring herself down to his level, and he threw his arms around her neck.

"Lil," said Joe. "I was thinkin' of keeping the boys both days this coming weekend. You got any problem with that?"

Joe, Pierce, Joseph, and Samantha all looked at Lily.

"Sure," said Lily, still trying to put together the picture before her. "I guess that would be OK." Her stomach churned, but she had no legal grounds to refuse.

"Will you be at my Dad's on Saturday?" Joseph asked Samantha.

"You bet she will," said Joe. "Now go and be good for your mother."

Joe looked at Lily, winked, and drove away.

Lily found comfort in telling herself that it might be nice to have the entire weekend alone, but by Saturday night she was inexplicably anxious, and by Sunday morning she found that she was pacing the floors, watching for the boys to return. When Joe finally dropped them off, they burst in through the back door, flung their jackets and backpacks onto the floor of the foyer, kicked muddy sneakers off into the air, spraying Lily with clumps of dirt, before barreling down the stairs, followed by Wishes, with Lily standing dumbfounded in the foyer.

"Wait just a minute, you two!" she called. "Just where do you think you're going?"

"We're gonna play the new video game Daddy bought us at the mall."

By the time Lily arrived in the living room, Joseph and Pierce were planted in front of the television, each with a game controller in hand. On the screen was a graphical display of a war zone, with soldiers in arms running across a bridge, firing at oncoming characters.

"Get 'im, PJ!" shouted Joseph. "Get him - blow his head off!"

"I'm trying," shouted Pierce, as he furiously manipulated his remote.

"Oh, my God!" said Lily. "What in the world are you playing?" She walked over and clicked off the TV.

Joseph got up and clicked it back on.

"You are not playing that game in this house," said Lily.

"My Dad said we could!" said Joseph. "He bought it for us - it cost sixty-five dollars!"

"Yea - my Dad said we could!" mimicked Pierce.

Lily walked over to the game console and pushed the eject button. "Well this is my house, and I say you can't."

"You're a bitch!" said Joseph.

"What did you say?!" Lily started toward him.

"I said you're a bitch," said Joseph, heading for the stairs. "C'mon PJ - run!"

Pierce followed Joseph up the stairs.

"Both of you put your things away while you're up there, and stay in your room until I tell you to come down."

Lily pounded out Joe's number on the phone, but there was no answer. When the beep signaled Lily's opportunity to leave a message, she said, "Joe - it's me. I need you to call me as soon as you get this message. The boys -"

Lily heard a loud thump, and then Wishes came running down the stairs.

"Help!" Lily heard Joseph cry.

She slammed down the receiver and took the stairs two at a time.

"Help!" cried Pierce.

"We're being abused!" shouted Joseph.

Lily flew into Joseph's bedroom to find Joseph straddling the window sill, one foot on the floor of his room, the other outside on the roof. Pierce was leaning out the window, his feet off the floor, as he balanced his belly across the sill.

"Abuse! Abuse!" cried Pierce.

Lily ran over and pulled Pierce away from the window, and then grabbed Joseph and pulled him inside.

"What in the world is going on up here?" she cried. "Why are you guys acting this way?"

"You're abusing us!" said Joseph.

"Yea!" said Pierce.

Lily stood and looked at her sons, their arms crossed over their small chests, looks of defiance plastered across their faces, and she burst into tears.

Pierce ran over to her and wrapped his arms around her hips.

"Don't cry, Mommy!"

Joseph stomped past Lily and back down the stairs. Lily sat on the bed crying, with Pierce at her side.

"It's OK, Mommy," said Pierce. "I'm sorry. We'll be good, OK?"

Lily kissed Pierce on top of his head. "I'm OK," she said, wiping her face. "Are you OK?"

"Yes, I'm OK, Mommy. Don't cry, OK?"

"OK," said Lily, struggling to put a smile on her face. "Just go downstairs and play nice with your brother, alright?"

Pierce hopped down from Lily's lap and scampered down the stairs.

Lily replaced the window screen, closed the bedroom window and securely fastened the lock. She surveyed the vista from where she stood, grateful that none of her neighbors lived close enough to hear the commotion.

When Joe finally called Lily back later that evening, she explained what had happened.

"And this is my fault, how?" Joe said.

"They had just come from a visit with you, Joe. And that video game you bought them is awful - did you even watch it?"

"They play it over here all the time," said Joe. "They wanted one for your place."

"It's no wonder they came home so wild."

"Lil - it's not the video game's fault that you can't handle your own children."

"I can handle them just fine," said Lily curtly. "I just don't want them playing any more violent video games."

"Your house, your rules," said Joe. "My house, my rules."

"Screw you!" said Lily, and she slammed down the receiver.

The following Tuesday night after dinner the phone rang, and Joseph leapt up from his chair to answer it.

"Hi, Daddy!" He spoke to Joe in the syrupy way that children speak to babies. "Aw, nuthin... we just finished eating. What did you do today? (pause) What? You DID?! (pause) You want me to tell her right now? And then do what? (pause) OK, Daddy."

Joseph turned toward Lily, pointed the headset of the phone at her and announced, "Mom, my Dad just bought our house!"

"What do mean? What house?"

"Our house – our house on Trevi Way – my Dad just bought it!"

"WHAT!? Lily screamed.

"He's coming over to get us so we can go see it!"

Lily's stomach roiled, and her knees grew weak. She trembled with anger and panic.

"Let me have the phone, Joseph." Lily extended her hand.

"She wants to talk to you, Daddy." Turning back to Lily, Joseph said, "Daddy said he doesn't want to talk to you, and you can just tell me whatever it is you want to say."

"No, baby, I can't," Lily told Joseph, placing her hand on the receiver. "I need to talk to your father."

"Daddy," Joseph yanked the receiver back and cried into the phone, "she won't let us come over!"

Lily and Joseph wrestled over the phone, Joseph getting control of it long enough to ask, "She's pulling on the phone, Daddy - what should I do?"

Joseph looked at his mother and said, "You don't even know what it means to be a mother! You're just a slut, and no one will ever love you!"

Shocked, Lily instantly released her grip on the telephone.

"Come and get us, Daddy!" said Joseph, banging the receiver back into the cradle. He took Pierce's hand and ran up to the second floor, slamming the door at the top of the stairs behind them. Lily heard the chain lock sliding into place.

She was paralyzed, stunned – first at the news, then at what Joseph had said to her, and finally at the recognition that Joe had supplied him with the words. She wriggled her toes and catapulted herself up the stairs, taking the steps three at a time.

Trying to open the locked door, she called, "Joseph - you let me up right this instant."

"No! We want to go with my Daddy."

"That is not going to happen, Joseph."

"You're not in charge - my Dad is the boss, and anyway he said we can go wherever we want, and we want to go back to Trevi Way. Right, PJ? Don't we want to go back to our old house to live?"

"Yes, I want to!" said Pierce. "I hate the lake – it took my cowboy hat!"

Lily took a deep breath. "Joseph, talk to me, honey - why are you doing this?"

"Because."

"Because why?"

"Because you kicked my Dad out into the street so you can go out and suck some other guy's dick."

"What did you say!? Open this door! Open this door!" Lily pounded on the locked door, and in her rage kept pounding and pounding, until all she knew was that she had to get the door open, with no recollection of why, with no plan for what she would do when she did. The outer edges of her fists grew red and swollen.

"Open this door!" she screamed. She finally stepped back, and with a swift kick, she planted her foot against the door, popping the door latch from the frame and pulling the chain bracket from the wall. As she fell screaming in pain, Joseph stood staring at her, his mouth agape. Pierce started to cry. Lily sat, crying, holding her foot, reassuring Pierce that she was OK, as a set of headlights pulled into the driveway and shone in through the back door. Joseph stood staring at Lily until he heard the car horn, at which he stepped over Lily, grabbed Pierce by the wrist, and ran out into the dark calling, "Daddy!"

Lily remained lying on the landing. The pain in her foot paled in comparison to the agony she felt in her gut - as though Joe had taken a hunting knife, had sliced open her belly, and ripped her babies out from inside her. He was doing more than taking them from her house. He was teaching them to do to her what he could no longer do. This could not be happening. Images of her children flipped through her mind. The day she first held Joseph in her arms. The way he used to laugh when she put on her sunglasses. She must have taken them off and put them back on a thousand times in one day, just to hear the sound. The way Pierce used to hurl himself over the side of his crib, even before he was old enough to stand on his own, and how they had to cover the floor with pillows to protect him from getting hurt. She remembered how he used to sing the theme song from *Winnie the Pooh* incessantly, performing it in the grocery store, at church, anywhere he could find an audience. She thought of the winter nights they spent curled up in front of the fire in the family room, reading stories or watching Christmas specials on TV. She sobbed. Where were her sweet babies? Was this really happening? How could they do this to her?

She kept expecting them to come back, kept looking for the headlights to reappear in the driveway, kept imagining the tearful apologies, then making hot cocoa and cinnamon toast for their snack before tucking them safely into their beds. She could smell their hair, taste the salty skin of their brows on her lips. She couldn't believe that this nightmare was unfolding before her when just weeks ago she had so much hope.

Too drained and in too much pain to move from the spot from where she saw them leave, she just lay on the landing. Maybe if she didn't move, she could keep life from going forward, like pressing "pause" on a movie. She could wait until she was ready, until she knew what to do next. Were they really gone? They had been her life all these years. Did she mean so little to them? Lily sobbed until she fell asleep.

She woke the next morning, hobbled to her bedroom and called Joe.

"I want to talk to the boys," she said.

"Took you long enough to call," he said.

"Put Joseph on the phone, Joe." Her head was pounding, her foot was throbbing, and there was no way she was going to make it to work on time today. A scolding from Mrs. Windham-Childs would surely be called for. In her fragile state, Lily didn't trust that she could handle it with restraint. Knowing that she could lose her job at Mrs. Windham-Childs' whim, she would have to find a way to get there, and then a way to smile, and nod. She would cross that bridge when she came to it.

Lily heard muffled voices coming from the other end of the phone line.

"They're having cereal and watching cartoons," Joe said. "They don't want to talk right now. I'll have them call you after school."

"What do you mean, 'after school'?"

"I mean when they get home from school. Sam is going to hang out here today so she'll be here when the school bus drops them off. I'll have her ask them to call you then."

"I am going to come and pick them up," said Lily. "I'll be there around five-thirty, after work."

"We won't be here," said Joe. "We're taking them out to Chuck E. Cheese for dinner tonight."

"Joe, what are you doing? Why are you doing this to me?"

"What's the matter, Lil? You don't like being kicked out of your house, being left all by yourself? It ain't so great, is it?"

"Joe, those boys belong with me. I'm their mother."

"And I'm their father," bellowed Joe. "They want to be here, in their own home."

"But I would have stayed there with them at the house – you made me leave. You can't just go buy that house and get a girlfriend, steal my children and then pretend like I don't exist." Lily's foot was still throbbing. "You can't do that!"

"I got news for you, little Miss Want-To-Have-My-Own-Life. I already did that." Joe lowered his voice. His whisper had a dark, baleful quality to it that sent shivers down Lily's spine. "You can make this all go away anytime you want, Lil," he hissed. "All you gotta do is come home. Otherwise, you can just forget about getting the boys back. You call me back when you're ready to come home.

232

Until then, the boys are staying with me."

Mechanically, Lily hung up the phone. Home. Wherever that was.

With each passing day, Pierce and Joseph became more securely nestled back into their routine of school, street hockey, and indifference. Samantha and her daughter moved out of their apartment and moved into the house on Trevi Way. The boys visited Lily on Saturdays for a few hours, doing so begrudgingly. But since Joe worked weekends and Saturdays were Samantha's "me" time, they had no choice in the matter. To make up for this and other assorted inconveniences, Joe lavished the boys with gifts and privileges. He bought the latest new video game system, complete with a library of the hottest games. He put in a swimming pool.

Lily moved numbly through her life, which had become an endless stream of work, tearful support group meetings, coffee, and cigarettes. She'd retrieved the little brown bottle that her doctor had given her from the back of the closet several times, yet it remained unopened - the one personal victory she could claim.

The lake house was eerily empty, especially at night. The moonlight that had so recently charmed her and ignited a sense of humility and gratitude now cast spooky shadows around every room. It terrified Lily to know that she was there alone, with no neighbors to call on, her only protection a dog that didn't bark.

Spring on the lake might have been viewed as beautiful by most standards, but no matter where Lily was in the house, she was surrounded by windows, each one reinforcing the sense of isolation she felt in the vistas of endless sea and sky they offered.

She watched one evening as a storm made its way across the water, wishing that life's own tempests were as predictable. Still, would you want to know that a disaster was coming if you were powerless to avert it? Wouldn't it be better to abide in blissful ignorance and be caught unaware than to pace and wring your hands, counting down the hours until your doom?

When the storm hit the shore, the wild sea breeze twisted itself about the house, sending drafts and sprays of rain in through every door and rattling every window, like a thousand angry demons furiously knocking, sending Lily dashing from room to room, staying the window frames with wedges she had fashioned from the flaps of cardboard torn from the unpacked boxes that still laid about. As she pounded a wedge in between the frames of her bedroom window, she noticed the headlights of a car slowly approaching. The car stopped. Lily crouched, lowering herself so that only her eyes peeked over the window sill. The high beams flicked on, and then off again, and then the car crawled away down the street. Lily grabbed the chair from the desk in Joseph's room and hooked it under the knob of the back door. She returned five times to make sure it was securely wedged in place.

Occasionally at night, as she stood in the kitchen washing dishes, or just as she was locking up before going to bed, she would catch sight of a car moving slowly past. She couldn't be certain of whether it was the same car every time. It may well have been some lost soul searching for the pier or the frozen custard stand, or maybe even just a young couple looking for a quiet spot to park and make out. Just the same, Lily kept the chair in the back hall and secured it under the doorknob whenever she was home. Even if someone could get past the barricade, the noise would be enough to wake the dead, giving Lily plenty of time to run out the front.

The first week in June, Lily received a brown eight-and-a-half by eleven envelope in the mail, with an official seal as the return address. Inside was a Family Court document. For this, she needed no interpreter - Joe was petitioning her for child support.

"Are you serious?" Lily screamed at Joe when she finally got him to answer his phone. "Child support?"

"I'm entitled," he said. "The kids are living with me, and that means I'm entitled to like twenty-five percent of your income to help pay for stuff."

"Help pay for video games, and your summer vacation, and your new swimming pool? Joe - I barely make enough to live on. Your salary is quadruple mine."

"Why should I get penalized for being successful?" he asked. "I have that money coming to me."

"Joe... please don't do this," Lily said. "I'm begging you. I don't have money for a lawyer, and I don't know how I'll survive if I have to pay you child support - I'll have to go out and get another job."

"I guess maybe you shoulda thought about that before you left us." Joe sniffed. "By the way," he added, "The kids want their dog back."

The trip down Trevi Way seemed endless. As she passed each house, Lily recalled the faces with whom she once shared this neighborhood. The twins with the speech impediment, the Jehovah's Witnesses, the guy who spent every waking moment cultivating his front lawn - they were all still there. She was the only one missing. Only none of them seemed to notice either. Lily was glad that Donna's car was absent from her driveway. She couldn't handle seeing her now.

Wishes pawed at the door of her carrier as Lily approached the house.

"Yes, girl," said Lily. "I know you can't wait to get back there either."

Samantha was outside scurrying about, buzzing in and out of the garage, setting up tables and display racks, pounding a "Garage Sale" sign into the ground. Lily pulled off to the side of the road, parking her car along with her desire to scream and shout, hoping that she could use this opportunity to capture Samantha's feminine sympathies and avert the swiftly approaching child support hearing.

"Hi," Lily said as she walked up the driveway. She unclipped Wishes' leash from her collar and watched as the dog darted into the garage and slipped into the backyard through the doggie door Lily had put in when she was a puppy. Tufts of purple flowers poked their heads out from among the weeds that had all but overtaken the lavender in the front garden.

"The boys are down the street playing," said Samantha. Her long wavy brown hair was artfully streaked with blond and pulled back with a rhinestone barrette that matched the decorative stones on her sandals. A pair of pink framed sunglasses were perched atop her head.

"I was hoping we could talk," said Lily.

"So talk," said Samantha. She lowered her sunglasses onto her nose and busied herself straightening items on the long folding table.

"It's about this child support thing," said Lily. "As you know, Joe makes a lot more money than I do, and I have the rent, food, gas, utilities – well, you know what it takes to run a home." Lily smiled her best Windham-Childs smile.

Samantha clumsily balanced a pricing gun between long acrylic fingernails. She shot out a label and stuck it to Pierce's old playpen.

"I expect lots of people here very soon - what's your point?" Samantha pulled a stray sticker from her thumbnail and flicked it to the ground.

"Well, I was hoping that we could talk about this - you know, mom-to-mom? I'm sure you can appreciate how difficult this has been for me, and I was hoping, well, that we could come to some sort of an agreement outside of the courts, you know? Maybe I can spare a few dollars a week, and we can just work that out between us."

"Look," said Samantha, removing her sunglasses and turning to look at Lily. "It's not my fault you don't want your kids - why should I suffer because of it?"

"I don't want my kids? Is that what he told you? I *do* want my kids - more than you know. In fact, I'll take them back home with me right now. I would love nothing more. Where are they? Go get them."

"Sure, now that there's money involved you want them back – Joe told me all about you. No way you're getting those kids. They mean everything to Joey, and they are staying right here with us."

"But you don't need my money, Samantha - I wasn't working at all before the separation... you guys have so much. You have this nice house, Joe makes good money, and I'm sure your ex is giving you something..."

Samantha threw the pricing gun down onto the table and placed her hands on her hips. "What my ex does or doesn't do is none of your goddamn business. Do you have any idea how expensive it is to take care of this family? I'm spending three hundred bucks a week on groceries, fifty bucks on gas, then there's the trips to the mall, the movies, having their friends over, going to the amusement park - that costs *a lot* of money, and all you have to worry about is taking care of yourself. Must be nice, that's all I can say."

Lily and Samantha stood staring at each other for a moment. Lily surveyed the items on the table – things that had been stashed in the crawl space and that Joe had put into storage during the separation. Clothes the boys had outgrown, room vaporizers that had been replaced by better ones, baby toys that Lily had always meant to clean and donate. Fragments of her life, available at bargain prices.

Was that all that was left now? Memories of moldy playpens, grimy toys, and the driveways and houses that she used to pass? She wanted to move her feet, but they were lead, weighted in place. Her mind searched for something to say that would bridge the gap between them, that would soften Samantha's heart, that would express the sorrow and fear that Lily had carried around with her since the boys left that night. But how could she find words to explain a pain so visceral, so vile, as that caused by watching your children step over your lame body, and then being forced to pay their father money for having taught them how? It was no use. There were no words to say. At least none that Samantha would hear. How could she ever hear them, and then stay here? Lily turned to go back to her car. "That's my old breast pump," she said, pointing to a box on the table.

"You want it?" Samantha called after her. "It's two bucks."

Lily held the newly issued court order in her hand as she sat with her back against the massive trunk of the ancient oak tree, her tear-soaked T-shirt the only indication of how long she'd been sitting there, lost in her sorrow. Her life had given her many painful memories, but most of them had faded, over time. Through distance and self-examination, she had been able to achieve a philosophical position on most things. But the memory of losing her children would never fade; this she knew. It was a sorrow that would live inside her, slicing her open with every recollection, twisting her gut into a pool of bile. It would be with her tomorrow as immediately as it was with her today, as it had been with her at the moment it had happened. And when was that moment, precisely? Was it when Joseph and Pierce walked out the door? Was it when the cowboy hat finally succumbed to the pull of the chill lake water? Or was it further back, on that day when Lily succumbed to passion in the arms of another man, irrevocably changing her? But didn't that yet have its own cause? Was the fatal moment then when Lily and Joe were married? And what causes and conditions led to that? Maybe it was when Iris moved away. Or when James left. Or maybe it was all because of Dolores. Yet even those events were preceded by others. Like when her mother left, or when Henry cornered her in the chicken coop. As she meandered through the maze of cause and effect, tracing each tragedy back to the one that bred it, Lily discovered her one fatal error: She had come into this world.

Lily imagined all the things she would miss in the years to come: Pee-Wee football games, science fairs, birthday celebrations, first dates, senior proms.

The waves of Lake Ontario rushed towards the shore, the sandy beach clean and unmarked by the footprints of little boys. The house stood watch over the sledding hill, its rooms finally quiet; there were no dirty socks on the floor in front of the TV, no juice boxes in the refrigerator.

Lily freely tumbled into a sense of profound disappointment about her life. She finally understood what Dolores must have felt, what her own mother must have experienced - an all-pervasive pain that Lily herself could never have imagined, a sorrow fashioned by the knowledge that life didn't want you, that you lived in a world that snickered at your failures as it withheld its blessings and capriciously doled out its cruel curses, never providing a clue as to how you might gain its favor.

The sun dipped its toes into the water, blazing orange across the sky. Lily stood up and went into the house, letting the door of the front porch slam behind her.

Lily stood in a scalding shower until her skin was raw and dimpled. She kept waiting to feel better, kept thinking that she should stop the tears, but she couldn't find a good reason to try.

She grabbed her robe from the back of the bathroom door, then opened the medicine cabinet, and dropped the little brown bottle into her pocket. She had lost her sense of time, but since it was dark out, she probably wasn't supposed to be at work. She wondered what Mrs. Windham-Childs would say to her now, what bit of advice about posture or etiquette she may deem applicable to this particular situation.

"We've even seen some promising results from pilot programs implemented with the underprivileged children right here in our own neighborhood," mimicked Lily.

She stood in the hallway between the boys' bedrooms, unable to turn around and face their absence, afraid to inhale the lingering scent of them. She let her body fall back against the wall, and then slid herself down to the floor. She sat at the top of the stairs for hours, unable to proceed from that spot.

She had done the best she'd known how with her own boys, to see that they had as many privileges as she'd been able to give them. When they were babies, she'd read her copy of Dr. Spock until its pages had come loose from the binding. She had diligently created a daily schedule that provided them with consistency, security, and boundaries. Despite Joe's craziness, Lily had always thought she'd done a pretty good job keeping them well and safe. Despite all of her other failures, she'd always thought of herself as a good mother. But children don't leave good mothers. They don't turn their backs on good mothers lying injured and crying on the ground. Lily played the events of that night in her mind over and over again, wondering what she might have done differently, trying to make sense of how things had gone so wrong. If there were answers, they would not reveal themselves to her.

She glanced down the stairs, to the first floor. It seemed so far away, the effort to get there too great. She swung her legs over the

239

top step, grasped the railing, and slid down the stairs to the dining room. She hoisted herself up with a grunt, picked up one of the boxes stacked there and upended it, spilling the contents onto the dining room floor. A dark laugh escaped from her throat.

She kicked at the contents of the box, sorting through toys and books with her foot. She picked up the next box and upended it. Glasses wrapped in newspaper tumbled out and rolled across the floor.

"Well, I was looking for the liquor," she said, "but at least now I have a proper glass."

She repeated the process with each box, dumping the contents onto the dining room floor.

"Who said unpacking is hard?" she laughed.

The sixth box delivered an unopened bottle of vodka, half a fifth of tequila, and a sealed envelope addressed to Lily.

"How perfect," she said.

She tucked the envelope under her arm and placed the vodka and the glass on the end table next to the couch, which had been positioned to provide the best view of the lake. As the horizon warned of a new day, Lily broke the seal on the vodka and poured herself a glass.

"Today is the first day of the rest of your life!" She was unsure of what to expect, never having drunk straight vodka; she winced at the first sip. The second sip went down easier. The third sip was a gulp that drained the glass.

"This party sucks!" she exclaimed. "What it needs is a little music!"

Lily tore open the envelope and shook out the CD. She popped it into the boom box, and hit "play." She poured herself a second glass.

When you look at me, tell me
What do you see
Would you be surprised to learn
That in my heart desire burns

"To Curtis," said Lily, raising her glass. "Who was kind enough to let me stay in his house. Wherever you are, Curtis, I hope to see you again soon. We can go fishing for real next time."

Lily lit a cigarette and filled her lungs with the hot, acrid smoke as she walked over to the window. She watched as the rolling waves of Lake Ontario ended their journey at her doorstep. The grey-blue waters stretched out as far as her vision could take her. She could understand why people thought the world ended at the edge of the sea. She only believed in the beyond because other people had told her it was there. That was the only reason she knew that the currents of this great lake rode out to the St. Lawrence River and into the Atlantic Ocean. She imagined what it would be like to be water, to flow and travel as you pleased, with no body to contain you, no life to limit you. She imagined herself disappearing into it, flowing out across the Atlantic, slipping through the Strait of Gibraltar, and into the Mediterranean Sea. It didn't seem so far away if you could imagine that you were water. Perhaps she would lap at the shore, and Iris would hear her, and come down, and dip her toes in. But Lily wouldn't even know where to begin looking for her, and anyway, Iris probably wouldn't recognize her; she would just see water. Lily would be stuck there, slapping up against the rocky shores she'd seen in photographs, clapping furiously against the stones, "Iris! Iris!" But Iris would just sit, maybe turn to Gregorio and say, "Did you hear something? I thought I heard my name," and he would say, "It must be your imagination, *Piccolina*." Then she would pour two glasses of cognac or something sophisticated like that, and they would resume discussing their plans to go diving in the Mediterranean, or hiking in the Alps, as Iris wrote in those letters she used to send.

Lift me up, take me higher
Feel the power, feed the fire
Lift me high above the clouds
Up to a place where dreams come true
Lift me high enough to touch
The sun, the stars, the moon

"To Iris." Lily raised her glass, forcing the vodka past her tongue and down her throat. She reached into her robe pocket and broke the seal on the little brown bottle. She shook a pile of pills out onto the end table and scooped them into her palm.

You hold the power in your hands
To touch what most don't understand
So trust your heart, you'll know just what to do
Lift me up, I'm reaching out for you

"And this one," she said, raising a full glass to the rising sun, "is for you, Dolores." Lily tossed the pills into her mouth, threw her head back as she drained the liquid, and then lay down and waited for darkness.

9. IRIS

"Beautiful city, isn't it?"

In her whole life, Iris had never told anyone to shut up and leave her alone, though that was precisely what she wanted to do. Instead, she turned to face the woman in the petunia pink warm-up suit who smiled through glistening lips coated in the exact same shade. Iris wondered how some women did that, whether they bought clothes to match their lipstick, or vice versa. She also wondered why, despite the circumstances, she would notice such details, while failing to grasp what the woman had said to her. "Pardon me?" she said.

"Roma, I mean. Beautiful. Isn't that right, Marty?" the woman said, turning to the man seated at her left, who looked up from his newspaper to peer at his plump pink wife over the rim of his reading glasses.

"Too much goddamn walking," the man said. "My feet are one big blister. The food, though. Now that was good." He patted his belly and smiled at Iris. "Met some nice folks from Jersey on the tour bus, too. Got plans to meet them in Atlantic City. Lookin' forward to that, aren't we, hon?" The woman bobbed her head, the dewlap beneath her chin jiggling with enthusiasm. Iris debated briefly whether she should tell the woman she had lipstick on her front right incisor, but said nothing.

She wished she had been quick enough to respond, *"Non capisco l'inglese,"* when the lady started talking to her, but it was just as well; she struck Iris as the type who would go to great lengths to make herself understood in any language by speaking slowly and loudly, which would be even more annoying. Iris leaned into the aisle as far as her buckled seatbelt would allow, craning her neck to see whether she could spot any vacant seats on Alitalia flight 1212, just departed from Rome Fiumicino airport, with non-stop service to JFK, but the only alternatives were middle seats, where she would be wedged between two other passengers. Resigned to spending the next eight hours with chatty neighbors, she plugged in her earphones.

The nervous energy that had been sustaining her bottomed out as she surrendered to the plane the responsibility of holding up her body and getting it to where it needed to be. Shivering with exhaustion, she tore open the plastic bag she had been sitting on, and unfurled a thin green blanket that crackled with static; she tucked it gratefully around her trembling legs.

The shock of her father's unexpected death and, more recently, of Henry's fatal accident, had caused a shift in Iris's perception of permanence. Painfully aware that tragedy could strike at any time, she vowed never to be caught unprepared again, and always carried her passport with her whenever she left home. Though such foresight could do nothing to cushion the blow delivered by Violet's phone call, it had enabled her to catch a plane from Cagliari to Rome the previous evening and secure a seat on the morning's first outbound flight to New York. Too confused to deal with the practicalities of finding a hotel, she had wandered aimlessly around the Fiumicino departures terminal until her indecision became a decision; she ended up spending the night in the airport, where she eventually attached herself to a molded plastic chair riveted to a row of other molded plastic chairs and waited for the check-in area to open.

As the plane circled over the Mediterranean and climbed to cruising altitude, Iris heaved a sigh heavy with impatience and dread, one moment wishing the thousands of kilometers ahead of her were already behind her, the next wishing she could remain suspended above the earth indefinitely. She tucked the blanket more tightly around her thighs, and thought of reclining her seat, but didn't want to bother the person behind her the way the person seated in front of her was bothering her. She wished sleep would come to rescue her from her sadness and restore her strength, but doubted it would be possible without the pills she had forgotten in her haste to leave Carloforte. Neither the dark lenses of her sunglasses nor the puffy lids she closed over burning eyes could shut out the images of the past twenty-four hours which danced across her mind on their way to becoming firmly embedded in her brain.

Was it just the previous morning that she had taken part in the *mattanza*? Despite the rapidly increasing distance between herself and the island of San Pietro, she could still see the tunas thrashing about wildly, still smell their blood in her nostrils, still taste it in her mouth, still feel it on her skin, still see it on the clothes balled up at the bottom of her backpack and on the sneakers she wore on her feet. After that, everything had happened so quickly: the phone call, the discussion with Max, the hasty preparations for her departure.

Tears rolled down the well-traveled path on her cheeks as her thoughts turned to Max. Through the blur of events and emotions, she recalled all too vividly his expressions and comments when she had announced that she must leave at once, and wanted him to come with her, to be by her side, and take his place in her family. First, he had laughed and asked if she were serious. Then he had told her he was sorry for what she was going through, but she could hardly expect him to just drop an important assignment and fly halfway across the world for the funeral of a person he had never met. Next, he had tried to convince her that she should stay on with him, insisting it was pointless for her to rush home, that there was nothing she could do that the rest of the family couldn't. Finally, he had reminded her that he had gone to a lot of trouble to bring her along and that if she deserted him, she would not only be leaving him without an assistant, she would make him look bad.

Iris was too overwhelmed by the news, too stunned by Max's reaction, to do anything but cry. She went through the mechanical motions of packing, while Max arranged for one of the crew to drive her back to Cagliari. The look on his face as she boarded the ferry to Portovesme, had been one of hurt and betrayal. She had seen variations of that same expression in the past, each time they had spent a day or an evening together, at the end of which she had been forced to abandon Max and return home to Gregorio. It was an image that picked at the old scabs of pity and guilt that failed to heal; it made her remember the look on Lily's face when she went away to college, and the look on her father's face when he walked her down the aisle, and the look on Auntie Rosa's face when she moved to Italy, and the look on Gregorio's face when she fled their home. It was the image that accompanied her over France and Ireland, and out across the Atlantic Ocean.

"I'm sorry Ma'am, but this flight is full," the agent at the domestic airline's JFK service desk said with as much courtesy as minimum wage could buy. Sorry her ass. She couldn't care less. All she wanted was to get her fat butt out of there and drive home to some shitty apartment in Astoria or Brooklyn, where some freeloading boyfriend was sitting on a recliner, pumping up his paunch with beer and watching whatever sports it was the time of the year for on cable TV.

"But you don't understand," Iris said. "I have to get there *tonight*. I can't wait."

"Due to weather-related issues, two earlier flights to Rochester were also cancelled. We are doing our best to reschedule all our passengers. We can put you on a flight tomorrow at noon, flying into Syracuse," she said, staring down at her computer as she spoke, her acrylic nails hammering the keyboard.

"But I don't want to go to Syracuse tomorrow at noon! Or ever! I want to go to *Rochester*. Tonight! It's an *emergency!*" She bit her lip to stop it from trembling, determined not to melt into a puddle of tears again, like she had back at the gate when her flight, after being delayed seven times in five hours, was finally relegated to the status of cancelled.

"I'm sorry, Ma'am. That's the best we can do. You're booked on the noon flight." She glanced up briefly to hand Iris a new boarding pass, then turned her attention back to her computer. "Kindly step aside so I can assist the other people in line."

Iris scanned the crowd of annoyed passengers who, like her, had been swept from the departure gates by the wave of delays and cancellations and found themselves like so many pieces of driftwood washed up at the customer service desk. Surely the dismay caused by their thwarted plans was in no way comparable to the anguish Iris was suffering. She wished someone would sense her desperation and offer a solution, but all they would do was check their watches and cell phones obsessively, roll their eyes and glare at her as if she were a madwoman. Mad she was. If the airline had been honest about the circumstances, she could have rented a car hours ago and been well on her way to Rochester. Now it was dark, and from what she could see through the thick glass panes overlooking the tarmac, the rain was coming down even harder than before.

She was beyond exhausted, but there was no way in hell she would spend a second night in an airport. She had to get home. Tonight.

Two hundred miles later, Iris was fighting against the hypnotic effect of the windshield wipers and trying to focus her bleary eyes on the road ahead. Her progress north and west across the state of New York in the downpour had been marked by a succession of coffee counters and restrooms, and now it was time for both; she swerved just in time to catch the exit ramp to a service station. She was just north of Binghamton and estimated she had another two and a half hours to go. She could make it. She had to. She pulled into one of the many empty spots, parked, cut the engine, then checked her cell phone. There was a message from Max.

cazzo capo i cant believe you left

Her heart swelled as she recalled once more the expression of hurt and accusation on Max's face. He was right, it was horrible of her to abandon him so suddenly, but what was she supposed to do? She thought back to just a few hours before the phone call that had changed everything, when the day had seemed so full of promise as she lay next to Max, stroking his thick, black hair while he slept in the early morning hours, smiling to herself as she wondered how many more islands they would visit over the summer, how many other unforgettable adventures they would share in their life together. She typed a reply:

Still trying to get home. Be back asap. Baci.

It would be morning in Italy now. The sun would be climbing in the deep blue sky, its rays already deliciously warm. It hardly seemed possible such a sky could be on the same planet as the one pissing on her head as she sprinted across the parking lot. She made a beeline for the ladies' room, where the sound of her coffee-induced pee streaming into the toilet shattered the after hours silence. At the sink, she splashed her face with cold water, unwittingly catching a glimpse of herself in the mirror. The eyes looking back at her in the fluorescent light were puffy and shot through with red, but the effects of the Mediterranean sun and sea shone in her tanned face, and in the streaks of blond highlighting her tousled curls. It shamed Iris to admit that apart from the sadness and strain in her eyes, she had never looked this good.

All because she had been frolicking around Italy, while the person who had held her hand as she grew up - the person who had encouraged her to dream, who had shared the joys and trials of her childhood - had decided it was time to leave this painful world behind. She wanted to spit at that face but lacked both the conviction and experience to perform the gesture well. She wiped the fine spray of saliva off the mirror with a paper towel and walked away.

"Way to go, Iris," she muttered to herself, stepping up to the only open counter in the deserted food court.

"I'm sorry, Ma'am, what was that?" said the man with caffelatte skin at the cash register.

"Coffee to go, please."

"I'm sorry, I thought you said something else. Will that be a tall?"

"Yes, that will be all." Iris fished through her bag for the envelope of money she had exchanged at the airport.

"But will that be a tall?" The man looked at her expectantly.

"A what?"

"A tall. You know, the size." The guy raised one hand over the other, distancing them at horizontal increments to indicate her options.

"Just make it a large. Or whatever the hell you call the biggest damn cup of coffee you can get in this country these days." Actually, there *was* something else she could use. "Oh, and a pack of cigarettes. Any brand that comes in long and light."

"I'm sorry, Ma'am, we don't sell cigarettes here." The guy looked at her wide-eyed as if she had asked him to score her some heroin. "But there is a vending machine by the door."

The shades were drawn on Violet and Todd's dark house when she pulled into the driveway. No one was expecting her at this hour; Iris had not shared her plan to drive the three hundred and fifty miles upstate instead of waiting for her flight the following day, or today, or whenever the hell it was. She knew Violet would have tried to dissuade her, then spent a sleepless night worrying. Now that she had arrived, Iris couldn't decide whether to ring the bell or let herself in with the spare key she knew would be hidden in a flower pot next to the garage. She stood there for some minutes, trying to decide which option would create less of a disturbance, but couldn't. She was too shattered, too utterly exhausted and grief-stricken to decide anything at all.

Max had stressed the importance of packing light for their trip, but all the fantasies and expectations she had crammed into her backpack together with her flimsy summer clothes, now soiled from her travels, were suddenly too heavy to bear. She shrugged the pack from her shoulder, let it slide to her hand, then drop to the walkway. Her road-weary eyes were soothed by the velvety darkness; they roamed gratefully over the dewy lawn, feasting on the vision of a smooth, natural surface devoid of painted lines, unmolested by the glare of headlights. The heavy rains that had let up just west of Utica must not have hit here, she thought, as she kicked off the sneakers which might have been dry by now, had it not been for all the parking lot puddles she had been forced to dash through. She peeled off the thin cotton socks glued to her skin and sighed with relief when her itchy feet made contact with the cold flagstone.

She took a few steps down the walk, then abandoned the pathway for the grass. Her feet sunk into the spongy earth carpeted with tender tufts of green that tickled her soles and toes. This was the grass of home, of the barefoot summers of her childhood. She looked around at the upscale suburban cul-de-sac, at the lamplights holding vigil over latched front doors, imagining the dozen neighboring families slumbering safely in their beds, and twice that number of cars resting in their attached garages. Why hadn't her home in Italy ever given her the same sense of serenity that she perceived here? What would have been different if she had remained here and married here and lived her life here, in a house like these? For years, Auntie Rosa and her sisters had been asking when she would move "back home." How was she to determine where home really was for her, now that she had complicated her life further? Was it where the Capotosti clan clustered on holidays? Was it where you were born, or where you wanted to be when you died, or where you did all the in-between things? Was it a place you had to look for, or a place that found you? Did you reside in it, or did it reside in you? Or was it the place you ran away from like she had been doing ever since she was a scraggly little girl with a blue valise.

Iris shivered. Her light cotton pullover, still damp from her dashes in the downpour, did little to stave off the early morning chill or the fear that froze her in place on the lawn. She had traveled long and far to get here, and now it was time to face what she had come for. Sneakers dangling from one hand, backpack from the other, Iris walked to the front door, and pressed the bell once, lightly. Seconds later, Violet opened the door to her home.

"Iris!" she cried, her red-rimmed eyes glistening with emotion, as she tightened the belt of her robe around her slender waist and gathered Iris in an embrace. Limp with relief, Iris buried her face in the crook of Violet's shoulder, wishing she had a robe like hers, made fluffy by tumble-drying with lavender-scented softeners, and laced with the homey aromas of the bacon and eggs Todd fried for breakfast on Sunday mornings, and the wood fires he built on chilly nights, for Violet to curl up in front of with a glass of red wine. She let the shoes and backpack fall from her hands.

"Thank God you made it, Iris," Violet said. "But how in God's name did you get here?"

"I drove," Iris nodded in the direction of the rental car parked in the driveway.

"You poor thing, you must be exhausted!" Violet said, running her hand over Iris's hair. How good that felt. How soothing and reassuring. She wished Violet would hold her hand there forever.

"I'm really sorry I woke you," Iris said, averting her mouth as she spoke, realizing her breath must be raunchy from coffee and cigarettes.

"Who could sleep?" Violet said. "I was in the kitchen making some tea."

"So, I made it in time?"

"Of course! I'm brewing a full pot," Violet said.

"No, I meant for ... " Iris broke the embrace and met her sister's gaze. "Well, you know what I meant."

"She's slipping away, Iris. It's amazing she has held on for so long. The woman's a Capotosti, don't forget. She won't go until she's good and ready, and she just hasn't been ready yet. She's been waiting for you, that's what everyone says."

Iris and Violet stood on the threshold clasping hands, their shared pain and love bridging the time and distance which had created the illusion of separation. A sister was never far away if you held her close in your heart.

Violet updated Iris over tea, then told her she had to run to the Center for an hour or so to check on a case she was concerned about but hoped to be at the hospice by eight. Todd was visiting his mother in Florida with their daughters, so Iris would have the house to herself. She gave Iris directions but made her promise to take a nap before getting behind the wheel again, then sent her upstairs for a hot shower. As she headed for the door, Violet mentioned that all their sisters and brothers had been to see Auntie Rosa. Everyone but Iris and Lily.

A quarter of an hour later, Iris was enveloped in Violet's

bathrobe, her wet hair wrapped in a terrycloth turban, the phone pressed to her ear as she counted the rings, waiting for Lily to answer. Wondering whether she might have dialed the wrong number, she hung up, checked Violet's address book again, and redialed. She gripped the receiver harder as if the pressure could travel over the phone lines and force Lily to answer. After twelve rings, there was a click, but no reply.

"Hello?" Iris said. She heard no voice at the other end, only music.

"*Hello!*" Iris repeated. "Lily, are you there? Answer me!"

Clunk.

"*Answer me, darn you!*" Iris was shouting now. Lily was going to have to at least talk to her, that much was certain.

"*Heeey,*" Lily cooed, soft and dreamlike. Iris immediately regretted using such a harsh tone.

"I'm sorry, Lily," she said. "Did I wake you up?"

"I dunno." Lily sounded groggy; of course, she had been sleeping. No one but Violet would be up so early.

"Lily, it's me. Iris," she said, hoping Lily would not hang up now that she knew it was her.

"Iris … wow." Her speech was still slow and slurred with sleep, barely audible above the music in the background. "I had a dream about you, in your house over there, by the water."

"I'm here, Lily. I'm home." Why was music playing, anyway, at this hour? Lily had probably dozed off with the stereo on and left it looping all night. The thought of Lily hanging out at home killing time while Auntie Rosa lay on her deathbed infuriated Iris.

"Lily, I want you to meet me over at the Good Samaritan Hospice, on the corner of Fleming and Thomas. There's no time to waste; we have to say our goodbyes to Auntie Rosa now - this morning." She hoped she sounded firm, but not bossy. She couldn't take it if Lily attacked her again, like in their last conversation the day of Henry's funeral. Was this how it would be from now on? Would they only speak to each other when someone died?

"I'm tired," Lily grumbled. "And I have a stomachache."

"Lily, get out of that bed, get dressed, and get over there! If you

252

don't, I'll … I'll …" Iris was awful at making threats and even worse at carrying them out. What should she say? That she would never talk to her again? As if Lily cared; she would probably be doing her a favor.

"Just come, Lily. Please." Iris didn't want to confront Lily, and she didn't want to see Auntie Rosa die; she didn't want any of this. All she wanted was to curl up in Violet's cozy robe and go to sleep.

"Yeah, Iris - oh, shit!" Iris heard the thud of the phone dropping again. Lily was gone. All that was left was the music.

No stomachache was going to get Lily out of facing her responsibilities this time. She would pay her respects to Auntie Rosa if Iris had to drag her over there in person. Lily would thank her later, no matter how she felt now, no matter what unresolved issues she had with the aunt who had been a second mother to them. Iris would have to hurry, though. Her hands shook as she tore the page from the address book, grabbed the street map Violet kept in the same drawer, and threw on the least dirty clothes she could dig out of her backpack.

"Show me the way, God!" she prayed, as she pulled out of the cul-de-sac and headed to the north side of the city, in search of the house she had never visited before, and the sister who lived there.

Years of driving in Italy had provided Iris with the swift reflexes and daring maneuvers which served her well now, as she performed last minute turns, U-turns, and K-turns in the blue-collar rush hour traffic, adjusting her route according to the map spread across her lap, steering wheel gripped in one hand, cigarette and cell phone in the other. Between cigarettes, she redialed Lily's number, but the line was always busy. Spotting the green sign bearing the name of Lily's street, she cut across three congested lanes of the main thoroughfare, earning herself the baffled looks and meek toots of law-abiding citizens unaccustomed to such early morning effrontery. Iris shot up the road, slamming on the brakes when she saw a rusty blue LeMans parked in a clearing. She scanned her brain for updated information about the make and model of Lily's current car but came up with nothing more recent than the vague memory of a minivan Joe had bought after Pierce was born. She tried to imagine Lily behind the wheel of the jalopy, taking Joseph and Pierce to school, wherever that was; driving to her job, if she had one; meeting her friends for coffee, if she had any: She couldn't. A lone mailbox nailed to a stake in the ground bore two reflective stickers with black numbers printed on them: "6" and "6", with a space in between, left vacant by a third number that had peeled off. Lily's address was 626, so this could be the right place; then again, it might not. She parked next to the LeMans.

Darting up the hill to the house, Iris sent squirrels scampering every whichway across the unkempt lawn. She tried the door at the back entrance; it was locked. Searching for a bell that wasn't there, she began banging on the door.

"Lily! Are you there? Open the door!" she called, then paused to listen for a reply. The only sound Iris heard was music: the same music she had heard over the phone. At least she knew she was in the right place. "Lily!" she cried, stumbling down the cracked concrete steps that led to the lower level of the yard facing the lake. A stiff, damp wind shoved the smell of seaweed and rotting fish up her nostrils.

"Lily!" she continued to call, knocking on the door to the enclosed veranda. She tried the handle; it was unlocked. She threw open the door and hurried toward the music.

If you look inside my soul, let go of all you think you know
You'll find that I'm a lot like you,
Just someone who hopes their dreams come true.

Iris was startled to see her sister's inert form curled up on the living room couch, one bony arm dangling from the sleeve of a snagged terry robe speckled with the stains of daily routine. The cordless phone lay on the floor, inches from her fingers.

"Lily!" Iris cried, shaking her, but Lily would not open her eyes. Iris placed her hands under Lily's armpits and pulled her to a sitting position, sending a half-empty bottle of vodka rolling from the folds of her robe and crashing to the floor. The slaps she planted on Lily's ghostly pale cheeks were gentle, but strong enough to make her head loll first to one side, then to the other, before coming to rest against the back of the sofa. Her jaw dropped, and her puffy lids opened mechanically, in the manner an old-fashioned doll's, revealing the whites of eyes just as lifeless.

"My God, Lily!" Iris cried. She grabbed Lily's wrist and felt for her pulse; it was weak but detectable. "How much of that stuff did you drink?" Iris had never seen Lily drink more than a couple of glasses of wine, usually at Iris's insistence. She never thought she'd end up guzzling vodka. "Come on, Lily! Get up!" Iris slid her arms under Lily's armpits again, and pulled her to her feet, but realized that she herself had very little energy to invest in the endeavor; she simply did not have the strength to hold Lily up and make her walk without both of them ending up on the floor.

"Iris," Lily moaned. Her eyes popped open a split second before she puked. Iris instinctively pulled back as far as she could while still holding onto her, but was sprayed by the foul-smelling brownish liquid that spewed from Lily's mouth onto Iris's shirt, Lily's bathrobe, and the carpet. Lily lowered her head to her arm, wiped her mouth on her sleeve, and coughed.

"What in God's name is going on here, Lily?" Iris would have wept upon discovering her sister hiding out from the rest of the world in such a slovenly house and reduced to such a pitiful state, had it not been for the anger she felt, and the urgency for action.

"Leave me alone," Lily mumbled.

"No, I will not leave you alone!" Iris said, squeezing her arms above the elbow. "You're coming with me. We have to go see Auntie Rosa." Her voice cracked with emotion and exhaustion. "She's dying, in case you didn't know that."

"*Oow*, stop it!" Lily whined, trying to squirm out of Iris's hold. "Go away."

"I will *not* go away," Iris said, losing her grip on Lily, who flopped back onto the couch. Her total lack of cooperation made Iris furious. "I flew all the way over from Italy to see her, and you're coming with me whether you like it or not!"

What Lily needed was a dose of caffeine, Iris decided, picking her way toward the kitchen through the cardboard boxes littering the floor. She hoped she would find some leftover coffee to warm up; there was none, nor was there time to brew a fresh pot. She opened all the cupboards, looking for some instant coffee she could stir into some hot tap water, then slammed them all shut again. Not only was there no Nescafé, there was nothing, period. But if the cupboards were empty, the sink was full. Iris looked with disgust at the dirty cups and encrusted plates piled up in the basin, wondering how long they had been sitting there. She opened the refrigerator; the shelves were so empty it was easy for her to spot what she needed. She grabbed a can of Coke and hurried back to the living room, pulling the tab as she walked.

"Drink this, Lily," she said, placing one hand behind Lily's head to tilt it forward, pouring the frothing soda down her throat with the other. Lily sputtered, gulped, sputtered some more. Iris set the can down. Lily burped. Her eyes were open but did not look at Iris. Instead, they remained trained on the floor strewn with the accoutrements of a life Iris knew nothing about.

Iris pulled into the driveway of the hospice with Lily strapped into the seat beside her, clad in the clothes Iris had found in a pile on top of a dresser in an upstairs bedroom, into which she had managed to coax her sister's uncooperative appendages. An empty Coke can, the second poured down Lily's gullet during stops in traffic, sat between Iris's thighs.

Iris cut the engine, sighed, and stared at the house. It wasn't a very nice one, though less shabby than the others on either side of it. And a home, any home, was better than a hospital, or one of those nursing homes Auntie Rosa had always dreaded more than death itself. In recent weeks, she had received reports that Auntie Rosa was declining, but it was easier for Iris to believe in her aunt's remarkable resilience than it was to abandon Max and his plans. It was easier for her to appease her conscience by phoning every week; it was easier for her to feel reassured by the sound of Auntie Rosa's voice, still telling Iris that she loved her, still asking when she would visit, still pretending they had all the time in the world. But everyone – even Auntie Rosa - knew people only went to a hospice when time was running out. After all the distance Iris had traveled, after all the adversities she had overcome to get here in time, she did not want to get out of the car. She wished she could just sit there until she felt stronger. Or better yet, drive away.

"Let's go, Lily," she said, sounding more determined than she felt.

"I'll wait here," Lily said, staring out the window.

"No, you have to come in with me," Iris said. "Don't make me go alone."

Iris got out of the car, walked up to the door, and waited for Lily to join her. When she did, Iris forced a weak smile and said, "Thanks." She placed an index finger on the bell, but could not seem to press it. When the door opened, both women let out a startled gasp.

"Good morning, ladies!" A grey-haired man wearing jeans and a sweatshirt smiled at them, gesturing an invitation to enter. His kind face had a calming effect on Iris. "I heard you pull in. Something tells me you're Capotostis. There's been all kinds of brothers and sisters coming and going."

"Yes," Iris said, smiling and extending her hand. "I'm Iris, and this is my sister, Lily."

"Ah, the missing flowers! I think I've met the whole bouquet now, but it's hard to keep track. My name's Andrew," he said, pumping Iris's hand. "I'm one of the volunteers. Please, come right on in." Stepping into the foyer, Iris was immediately enveloped in the comforting aroma of freshly brewed coffee and toasty, sugary breakfast foods wafting from the kitchen. There was an undertone of lemon-scented furniture polish, and another familiar perfume lingering in the hallway, smelling vaguely out of place.

"Lily's a pretty name," Andrew said, placing a hand on Lily's shoulder. "I don't think I've heard anyone mention you, but I do recall a few things about Iris. The one who lives over in Italy, right? The one everyone has been waiting for."

"Yes." Though it never quite stopped embarrassing her, Iris had grown accustomed to having anyone remotely acquainted with Auntie Rosa know all about her alleged virtues and glamorous

Italian life without ever having met her personally. She wondered whether Auntie Rosa would have continued regaling anyone who would listen with stories about her fairytale romance had she been aware of the botched editing job Iris had performed on the ending.

"I've even seen your picture," the man said, pointing a finger at Iris. "In your aunt's room."

Standing there with her damp hair and rumpled clothes, her eyes so puffy and bloodshot it hurt to blink, Iris doubted she looked remotely like any picture ever taken of her.

"Can I interest you in some coffee?" the man said. "I just made a fresh pot."

Iris would have loved to go hide out in that cozy kitchen she caught a peek of, guzzle down a whole pot of strong coffee, and stuff herself with glazed doughnuts and bagels with cream cheese and English muffins with strawberry jam. Her mouth salivated at the thought. "I think we should go see our aunt first," she said, swallowing.

"Marianne - she's the nurse here - is with her now," Andrew said. "I'll show you to the room, and bring you your coffee there."

"That would be wonderful," Iris said. "Thank you." She walked down the hall with him, glancing over her shoulder at Lily. She was slow and unsteady on her feet, but she was following.

"Marianne, Iris and Lily are here to see their Aunt Rosa," Andrew said when they reached the front room.

Iris wanted to correct him, tell him everyone knew it was "Auntie" Rosa, and not "Aunt," but her thoughts were sidetracked, overpowered by the perfume she had sniffed in the entrance hall. It struck her with its full force here; it was Youth Dew, the unmistakable scent of Auntie Rosa.

"You've come at the right time," Marianne said. "The priest just left; he comes first thing every morning, just like your aunt requested."

The nurse, probably around Iris's age, was dressed in a cheerful floral print top and yellow slacks; her smile radiated warmth and empathy. She took Iris's hand and squeezed it, just like Auntie Rosa used to do. Iris coughed, struggling to disentangle her voice from the four decades of memories rising up in her breast, jamming her throat. Her eyes roamed the room nervously, searching for something to look at, anything that wasn't Auntie Rosa.

"As you can see, we like to surround our residents with the objects they cherish," Marianne said, following her gaze. "Your family brought these things over." Iris spotted pieces of furniture that had accompanied Auntie Rosa's orderly existence in each of the three homes that had coincided with various stages of her life: the cherry wood chest of drawers, the lacquer end table, the green and pink Tiffany lamp, Uncle Alfred's old ukulele, Auntie Rosa's glow-in-the-dark rosary beads and worn prayer book held together by a thick yellow rubber band, the framed portrait of Iris in a wedding gown, standing between Gregorio and Auntie Rosa, their three sets of eyes twinkling. There was something wrong about seeing these items here; something confusing, destabilizing, like the feeling she got when running into her gynecologist at the restaurant, or her hairdresser at the mechanic's.

But the oddest sight of all was the green velvet recliner on which was propped a wizened woman with Auntie Rosa's snow-white hair, wearing Auntie Rosa's red jacket with an embroidered hanky in the pocket and Auntie Rosa's lily of the valley brooch on the lapel and Auntie Rosa's wire-rimmed glasses and even Auntie Rosa's latest set of hearing aids. The woman listed slightly to one side, a sturdy, finely crafted vessel that had sailed a century of seas, now adrift, with no one at the helm, waiting for the benevolent breeze that would take her home.

"Your sister Violet called to say you were on your way. I knew she'd want to be dressed for the occasion," the nurse said.

"Thank you, she looks nice." Auntie Rosa had always been meticulous about her appearance and favored bright colors. But was she really still there, inside that inert form?

"How wonderful that you could both make it," the nurse added, turning to smile at Lily, who had wandered in and sat in a chair by the window.

Andrew the volunteer returned, bearing a reassuring smile and two sorely needed mugs of steaming coffee, which he set on the table by Lily, then left.

"Don't be afraid," the nurse said, placing a hand on Iris's shoulder. "She's been waiting for you."

Iris knelt on the floor in front of the armchair, resting her buttocks on her heels. She took her aunt's hands in her own.

"They're so hot!" she said, dropping the knobby arthritic hands back onto the shawl draped across her aunt's lap. Iris had crocheted that shawl for her one Christmas. Isabella had taught her how.

"She's running a bit of a fever," Marianne said. "That's normal."

"Can she hear me?" Iris asked, timidly touching the hands again.

"Hearing is usually the last of the senses to go," Marianne said. "That's why we leave her hearing aids in." She looked over at Lily, then back at Iris, and said, "I'll let you two visit with her now. Call me if you need anything."

"You're so kind, thank you."

"Your aunt worked as a nurse for sixty years. It's an honor to give something back to her." Marianne smiled and left the room, closing the door gently behind her.

"Drink your coffee," Iris said to Lily when they were alone. Lily stared out the window; Iris turned her attention to their aunt.

As she regarded the body that was preparing to relinquish Auntie Rosa's spirit, she recalled the events that had shaped this woman's life, as told in the stories Iris had first listened to as a child, and many times again as an adult. Iris envisioned little Rosa, the underprivileged and overburdened firstborn daughter of Italian immigrants, toiling in the muck farms during the Depression. She felt the burden of the little girl saddled with the responsibilities of a woman, who dared indulge in a moment of carefree frolic with her little sister along the banks of the Barge Canal. She felt her helplessness when little Teresa slipped into the murky water, and her horror when Teresa sunk to the muddy bottom before Rosa's eyes, taking both their childhoods with her.

She recalled Auntie Rosa's favorite photo album, the one bound between covers of plain black cardboard, and the ornate paper tabs glued at the corners of the faded photographs holding them in place and in time. She recalled how Auntie Rosa always wanted Iris to look at the pictures with her every time she visited, and how Auntie Rosa always lingered over the class portrait taken down in New Jersey, and how she always acted surprised when Iris recognized the dark-haired young woman in the front row proudly showing off her starched white nurse's cap and candy-striped uniform, as her father's big sister.

"Auntie Rosa," Iris said. She took a breath, cleared her throat. Thinking was so much easier than talking; it had always been that way for Iris.

"It's me. Iris." She searched her aunt's face for a flutter of the eyelids, a turn of the lips. "I told you I'd come home soon, didn't I? Well, here I am."

A rattling noise issued from Auntie Rosa's throat, followed by a trickle of foul-looking fluid that seeped from the corner of her crooked mouth. She couldn't be going already, could she? Not when Iris still had so much to say. Her hands shook as she grabbed a handful of tissues from a box on the nightstand, and mopped up the liquid before it could drip down her chin and stain her red jacket. Auntie Rosa detested stains. Iris hurried to call Marianne, who was in the sweet-smelling kitchen, reviewing the residents' conditions with the volunteers who had just come on duty.

"It's OK, Iris," she said. "It's only natural to be alarmed if you've never had this experience. Let me explain a little bit about what you can expect in the coming hours." She led Iris back into the room, showed her how to use a little sponge on a stick to swab her aunt's mouth, then motioned for her to follow her back out into the hallway.

"Your aunt's heart and lungs are slowing down, and she's too weak to cough up the fluid as it accumulates," Marianne said in a soft voice, proof of her belief in that the dying could hear until the end. Iris shivered at the thought of lying in bed, unable to speak or move, and hearing people chat about her death as if she were already gone. "We're giving her a little medication to dry up the secretions, but they'll subside gradually as her body dehydrates. When you swab her mouth, don't use too much water. She can't handle it."

"But she looks so parched," Iris said. The idea of swabbing away the gunk made her cringe, but she would do it if she had to. "Shouldn't she at least have fluids?"

"Iris, our mission here is to help terminal patients leave us painlessly and peacefully, not to prolong their suffering. Dehydration is actually a blessing at this stage. It will keep her drowsy, and probably less aware of any pain or discomfort. The human body is a beautiful machine, and so is its natural way of shutting down."

"It's just so hard to watch," Iris said. Tears filled her eyes.

"I know it is. Remember, we don't know how much she feels or hears. Her senses are growing dull, gradually severing her contact with the outside world in order to make the separation less painful. Dying is hard enough work as it is."

"How much time does she have left?" Iris asked.

"She's been at this stage for longer than anyone I've seen. She's been fighting as if she wasn't ready. I think she'll progress more quickly, now that you're here. You go be with her, Iris. Talk to her."

Iris nodded, her throat tight, her chest heavy, and went back into the room. She mustn't let Auntie Rosa hear her cry. Auntie Rosa could never bear it when her Lover-dover cried. As she knelt down again, Iris did not feel the need to raise her voice or repeat things to make sure her aunt understood. She would hear what she could hear, Iris decided, as she began her story at the place where Iris felt the most comfortable talking about, and where Auntie Rosa had always been the happiest: The Past.

Iris spoke of getting up early to attend six o'clock Mass together, and of the buttery Italian toast dunked in coffee sweetened with anisette that was her immediate earthly reward. She spoke of tomatoes bubbling in a massive kettle with meatballs and sausages, until the sauce became thick enough and the meat tender enough to meet with the approval of Grandma Capotosti, and the expectations of the Sunday spaghetti dinner crowd. She spoke of the Saturdays helping out at Uncle Alfred's guitar studio, and of the Hawaiian music that drifted from his bedroom late at night as his fingers surfed over the strings of his steel guitar, filling the house with moonlit skies and sandy beaches, while on the other side of the storm windows the snow swirled to the tune of the howling winter wind.

After several minutes, Iris paused to drink some coffee. She looked at Lily, still sitting silently by the window, blinking as though she could not bear the weight of her own eyelids, as though they relied upon the swells of sadness from some inner ocean to occasionally push them open. The coffee had cooled, but it was a tonic for Iris, and the mug warmed her hands; after a few sips, she turned her attention back to Auntie Rosa.

Iris thanked her for being in the delivery room to cuddle her just minutes after she was born, and for the new nighties and undies she snuck under the Christmas tree each year, sparing Iris's most intimate parts from hand-me-downs. She thanked her for outfitting her with her first bra, and for showing her how to rig up her first sanitary belt with a napkin. She thanked her for nursing her through peritonitis, and for accompanying her to Italy. And she thanked her for waiting. But now Auntie Rosa had waited long enough and heard enough about the past. Iris owed it to her to tell her the truth. Before speaking, she glanced over at Lily, silent and still in her chair.

"I'm sorry I haven't been home to see you in so long, Auntie Rosa," she said. "Every time I called, you asked me when I would come, and every time I told you I was too busy with work. But there was another reason, Auntie Rosa." Iris paused, half-expecting her aunt's eyes to pop open, wide with interest, like they always did when Iris had news of any kind, no matter how trivial.

"You see, things have been a little strange for me lately. You know Gregorio, and what a good man he is. An honest, reliable, family man, a good provider. Remember all the fun we had when we went to Italy together the first time, and I met him? And how tickled you were when you saw he was interested in me? And that huge bouquet of red roses he sent when I said yes to his proposal?" There was a wistful look in Iris's eyes as she stared for a moment at the framed photograph taken on her wedding day. She looked at that Auntie Rosa, plump and smiling, then at the one before her. Again, she searched her face for a twitch, a tic – some sign that would encourage her to continue. But not even Auntie Rosa's lips moved as they sipped the air in such small breaths that any rising or falling movement of the deflated chest was imperceptible.

"Well, there's something you should know, something I should have told you a long time ago, but couldn't." Iris dropped her eyes to the floor, just in case Auntie Rosa should suddenly open hers. "I just couldn't. You see, we've had some trouble. I should say, I've had some trouble. Trouble being happy. Trouble trying to live up to everyone else's expectations. I would never want to say anything against Gregorio, you know? But I felt like he was suffocating me, that his whole family was sucking the life out of me. I knew I would wither up and die if I didn't do something." Iris studied her aunt's feet, so small and defenseless in their crocheted booties. Could those feet, now so deformed by bunions and arthritis, be the same feet that had spent a lifetime hurrying back and forth along hospital corridors, running up and down the stairs of the family home, as she tended to the needs of others?

"Well, I finally did something," Iris said, glancing up. "I left. I had to do it, you see, or I would have gone crazy." There, she'd said it. Part of it, anyway. "That's why I couldn't come home because I knew I couldn't hide what I was going through if I did. I knew you would see right through me, and I didn't want to make you worry. I didn't want to disappoint you." She'd thought that talking about her separation would relieve the heaviness in her chest, but it seemed to make it worse. It seemed as though her heart would be crushed under the weight.

"But things are better now, so I want you to be happy for me. I met a really nice man." Her head throbbed as she struggled to decide how much she should say about how and when they met, about how their relationship had progressed. Maybe it would be a waste of precious time. Maybe there was no need to disclose too many details when her aunt might not even hear.

"His name is Massimiliano," she continued, "Isn't that a nice name? But he likes people to call him Max. It's easier. You'd be surprised at all the exciting things we do together." Iris's cheeks were burning; she picked up Auntie Rosa's prayer book and used it to fan her face for a moment before going on. "For example, we get to travel all over Italy. All expenses paid, imagine that! That's because Max is so talented, everyone wants to work with him. I'm working with him too, and it's so much fun!"

When Iris stopped talking, an eerie hush fell over the room; in the silence, Iris heard the unspoken question rattling behind Auntie Rosa's raspy breath.

"No, he hasn't asked me to marry him yet, Auntie Rosa. But don't worry, I can tell he will. He just has a few problems to work through first. He hasn't had an easy life. You know what that's like, right?"

Her words rang hollow and inconsequential in this room gravid with the stark truth and holiness of death. She prayed for Auntie Rosa to utter some sound of approval, to show some sign of understanding, to offer her some hint of the unwavering and heavily biased support with which she had accepted all of Iris's decisions, and overlooked all of her flaws.

"Even if you don't say anything, I know you think it was wrong for me to leave Gregorio. I vowed to make him happy, and I broke that promise. I'm so sorry, Auntie Rosa. You always said I was just like you, but I'm not. You took care of Grandma and Grandpa and Dolores and Uncle Alfred, and me, and all of us. You used to say that making other people happy was what made you happy. You used to say, 'the greater the love, the greater the sacrifice.' Why couldn't I be more like you? Why wasn't making Gregorio happy enough to make me happy?" Kneeling on the floor at her aunt's feet, Iris was swallowed by a doubt so deep, she had never been able to put it into words, not even in her most private thoughts. "Did I make a mistake, Auntie Rosa?" she blurted out. "Will I regret what I did? Will I?"

As she set down the burden of her untruth at her aunt's feet, Iris heaved a sigh heavy with guilt and grief. She had made her confession, she had said as much as she could say, but now she knew that the absolution of Auntie Rosa, or Gregorio, or Isabella, or of all the Leales and Capotostis combined would never free her of her guilt unless she forgave herself. She wondered whether she ever could, but decided her inner debate would have to wait; guilt would certainly be hanging around later, while Auntie Rosa was on her way out now. It was time to set aside her selfish concerns and give back some of the kindness and comfort she had received from the woman who had loved her like a daughter.

Iris sat up straight on her heels, pushed back her shoulders, and looked over at Lily. Her eyes were alert now, wide open and staring at Iris as if she had never seen her before. Iris rubbed her arms to chase away a sudden chill, then ran her hands over her eyes to wipe away the tears.

"My poor Auntie Rosa," she said, turning back to her. Her hand shook as she reached to caress her aunt's remarkably smooth cheek, running her fingers over her face, resting them on the glistening spot on her forehead, mingling her tears with the holy oil. "You're fed up with this body, aren't you? With those bowlegs Uncle Alfred always teased you about. With those ears that won't let you hear and those eyes that won't let you see. With those hammertoes and back pains, with the worn-out knees and arthritic hips you never wanted to replace with new ones. You made me think you were eternal. But you're ready to leave now, aren't you?" Sorrow pressed down on Iris as she bent closer, resting her cheek on her aunt's lap. She wondered whether the sound of the first language Auntie Rosa had heard as an infant would soothe her.

"*La mia cara zia,*" Iris said, terrified by the responsibility of being there at the moment of passing, yet hoping she might reassure her aunt that there was nothing to fear, that all those loved ones who had gone before would be waiting for her on the other side, ready to embrace her together with the God she had worshiped devoutly her whole life. "*Ora vai a casa. La tua mamma e il tuo papà, la tua sorella e i tuo fratelli ti aspettano. Dolores ti aspetta, e anche Henry. Sono già con Dio, tutti pronti ad abbracciarti. Ti voglio tanto bene. Ti ricorderò sempre. Accenderò tante candele per te, e spero che anche tu pregherai sempre per me.*" There were no more words, and too many words left to say. The tears streamed freely down Iris's cheeks, soaking the shawl on her aunt's knees.

Ever since embarking on this journey home, Iris had been possessed by a sense of urgency. She was acutely aware that the passing hours and minutes and seconds that had brought her to the present moment would not stop for her now; that they would keep slipping away until they had robbed her of all time left with this woman who had been many things to her; the woman who, above all things, had loved her unconditionally. On her knees, she wept: for Auntie Rosa, for Lily, for herself; for her refusal to ever let go of what was dead and gone.

"Here, Iris," Lily whispered, passing her the box of tissues.

"Oh, Lily. It's just too hard." Looking up at Lily, Iris was shocked by how small and fragile she appeared from that perspective as if all the substance and vitality had been sucked out of her. This was the shell of her sister Lily, like the woman in the chair was the shell of her Auntie Rosa.

"It's not easy for you to say goodbye either, is it?" Iris said, seeing the tears trapped in Lily's tired grey-green eyes. Pulling herself to her feet, Iris grabbed some tissues and wiped away the tears spilling from her own eyes. She must find a way to reconcile Lily with Auntie Rosa so that she could let her go. And then maybe Iris could find a way to let her go, too.

"Auntie Rosa sure adored that Hawaiian music," she sniffed, memories swirling about her like dry ice on the stage of that high school musical Lily had starred in. "Remember how she used to lean back in the rocker with her eyes closed and that blissful smile on her face when we played with Uncle Alfred?"

Lily simply nodded as the tears swam round and round in her eyes. They made Iris think of those faraway tunas circling frantically in their death chamber.

"Let me have that uke, would you?" she said to Lily. Lily picked up the instrument and handed it to her. Iris ran her fingers over the scratched koa wood, then toyed with the four pegs until the strings sounded vaguely in tune, at least with each other. She began strumming slowly, trying to recall one of Auntie Rosa's favorite tunes.

"Across the sea, where the trade winds blow
You came to me, so long ago"

Iris paused. "Auntie Rosa loved the way you used to sing that song. She said your voice gave her goosebumps. Would you sing it for her one last time?"

Lily hugged herself and shook her head.

"Please, Lily. You won't have another chance."

"I don't remember the words," Lily said. Her eyes were two salty pools on the brink of overflowing; Iris worried that the tears would corrode her to the soul if they were not cried soon.

"I don't remember the chords, either," Iris said. "But I don't think Auntie Rosa will mind. Besides, Uncle Alfred will give us a hand. He always did." Iris raised her eyes to the ceiling, pausing for a moment before beginning again:

"Across the sea, where the trade winds blow
You came to me, so long ago

Still Lily would not join in. "Please, Lily," Iris pleaded. "Do this for her. Do it for yourself. Do it for me."

"Now my love is lost, but I'll always know," Iris began again, alone, *"You'll be here with me, when the trade winds blow."*

Lily's voice was weak when she joined in, a cross between a croak and a whisper, but Iris heard it. She hoped Auntie Rosa did, too.

"Mine is the heart, that won't forget,
The dreams we shared, without regret
We'll meet again, where love will be
No Kau, a Kau, for eternity."

"Oh, my God," Iris whispered. "Look, Lily." She pointed to a droplet glistening at the corner of Auntie Rosa's eye. Iris took a fresh tissue from the box and leaned close to Auntie Rosa to dab at the tear. "Oh my God," she cried. "I don't think she's breathing anymore. Should we call the nurse?"

"You can call whoever you want," Lily blurted, "but it's not going to do any good." As soon as she spoke the words, Lily doubled over, as if gripped by a searing physical pain. Iris hoped she wouldn't be sick again, and vomit all over Auntie Rosa's red jacket. But the sound coming from behind the thick, matted veil of hair that hid her face from view was not one of retching; it was a tight, whimpering sound; it was the sound of a wounded animal. It was the sound of Lily finally crying.

"I know you wanted to talk to her too, Lily," Iris said, placing a hand on Lily's head. Her throat felt so tight she could hardly speak. "But I don't even know if she heard what I said." Iris hung her head low, full of shame for the words she had spoken, and regret for not having spoken them sooner.

After a moment, Lily pulled herself up straight. Instead of looking at Iris, she tilted her head back and stared at the ceiling. "Don't worry, Iris," she murmured. "She heard it all. So did I."

Iris's eyes followed Lily's gaze to a cobweb dangling in the early morning light, then traveled back to her face, where she thought she could detect a faint smile, despite the tears still streaming down her cheeks. Aching for the closeness they had lost, Iris placed her arms on Lily's shoulders and turned her sister around to face her. "I love you, Lily," she said.

"Me too," Lily said, her arms limp by her side as Iris pulled her close and embraced her. Iris succumbed completely to her grief, weeping with Lily over the loss of the aunt whose irrepressible love had both bound and divided them, and over the loss of the childhoods on which she had left her lasting mark. She was overcome with sorrow and awe, enveloped in Auntie Rosa's final gesture of love – reuniting Iris with her little sister - performed through the miracle of death.

Lily was the first to speak. "It's all a big mess, Iris," she said, her voice little more than a breath on Iris's shoulder. "*I'm* a big mess."

All the anger she had felt toward Lily melted away. Death overruled all, pardoned all. Iris squeezed Lily tight, and when she released her hold, Lily wavered slightly. When she took a step back to look at her, Lily stared down at the floor. Her hair, which had somehow become streaked with grey, fell in tired curls around her drawn face. Her purple paisley top hung loosely about her skinny torso, and her legs swam in the baggy green sweatpants Iris had helped her into before sticking a pair of flattened flip-flops on her feet and dragging her to the car.

"Yeah, you are a bit of a mess." Iris's chin trembled as she forced a smile. "But you're not the only one," she said, looking down at herself and opening her arms to display the striped top spattered with Lily's vomit and mottled with the mussels marinara shared with Max on another continent, the rumpled linen trousers starched with seawater, the sneakers splotched with the blood of tunas.

From: Iris Capotosti <iris.capotosti@gmail.com>
To: Lily Capotosti <lilycapotosti@gmail.com>
Sent: Sat, January 8, 2011, at 12:55 PM
Subject: The story behind the story

Dear Lily,

When I called you that morning, and you were acting all loopy on the phone, I couldn't figure out what the hell was going on with you. All I knew was that the only way you'd make it to see Auntie Rosa in time was if I dragged you over there myself. I literally had to bang your door down, and when I did, I was totally shocked to find you sprawled unconscious on the sofa.

After I recovered from the initial scare and saw that you were hugging a bottle of vodka, I remember being so furious that I could have killed you. However, as we both know, I was never great at showing anger, and worse at acting on it. That's when one of my better-honed skills kicked in, and I found an excuse for you. I asked myself: Why would Lily get herself drunk instead of going to see Auntie Rosa? Then, I answered myself: Because she couldn't bring herself to do it. She couldn't get over all her resentment and unresolved issues fast enough to go there and tell her that she loved her before it was too late. So she drank a little vodka, and then a little more. I could relate to that. But I wanted you to have one last chance with her, so I forced you to come with me. I would have felt so guilty leaving you there to sleep it off, and you would have regretted it forever.

But I could tell by the way you acted at the hospice that it wasn't all about Auntie Rosa. And afterwards, when I found out more about your life, I knew you had far more serious problems. So I still understood the vodka. Now, after reading your last chapter, the plot thickens, but my story falls apart. As it turns out, you were more than just drunk. I feel so stupid.

Why didn't you tell me that then, Lily? And while we're at it, why don't you tell me something now: Did I walk in on you trying to kill yourself?

Love,
Iris

P.S. It took all these years to ask this question, but I'm not sure I'm ready to hear the answer.

From: Lily Capotosti <lilycapotosti@gmail.com>
To: Iris Capotosti <iris.capotosti@gmail.com>
Sent: Sat, January 8, 2011, at 2:35 PM
Subject: The rest of the story

Dear Iris:

I have been a nervous wreck ever since we exchanged these last two chapters, waiting to hear from you. I knew you would ask me about that, so I've been giving it a lot of thought, trying to formulate an answer that makes some kind of sense. All I can say is that there are ways of ending your life without killing yourself. Killing seems so violent; all I wanted was to extinguish the flame that was devouring me. I just couldn't tell where the pain ended and where I began.

I may have been out of it, but I saw how pissed off you were at me that day. I wondered why you never forced me to explain my reasons for not going to see Auntie Rosa. But now I see it was because you had already cooked up and packaged your own neat little justification for me once again. How generous of you. It's sobering for me to realize what you must have thought of me, but you never said a word. I let you believe I was just drunk because I figured drunk wasn't such a bad state to be in. Even people like you got drunk for fun, right? Because you wanted to, not because you couldn't bear to live your life for another moment.

I didn't tell you the whole story because the last thing I needed at that point in my fragile life was to create another scene in which I cast myself as the screw-up and you as the savior. And yet that's exactly what happened. When you roused me, it wasn't from a state of drunkenness, but from an all-consuming despair; you pulled me back from the edge. So, I was (a screw up) and you were (my savior), and there we were. Yet again.

Love,
Lily

From: Iris Capotosti <iris.capotosti@gmail.com>
To: Lily Capotosti <lilycapotosti@gmail.com>
Sent: Sat, January 8, 2011, at 4:02 PM
Subject: Re: The rest of the story

Dear Lily,

I'm shocked to find this out, terribly saddened and hurt that you did not tell me at the time. But I'm not as scandalized as you might think. Maybe because I now realize I flirted with the same fate each time I chased down my little blue pills with a glass of wine. One day you need an extra pill or two, then an extra glass of wine - or a bottle of vodka. As we both know, people do die that way. Accidental overdose. Or not so accidental. The line is fine, almost imperceptible, isn't it? We were both lucky.

But since you brought up the savior/screw-up concept, I want to tell you something. It is harder than you think to be the "savior." It is harder than you think to be responsible for other people's happiness and well-being. It is harder than you think to know that any love that comes your way is contingent upon your impeccable virtue and unflagging willingness to live up to other people's expectations. People only love saviors when they don't screw up. And if they do, they'd better have a savior of their own in the wings.

I may have been your accidental savior that morning, but in a way, you were mine, too. If Lily "the screw-up" hadn't been by my side, I doubt I would have had the guts to come clean with Auntie Rosa. I was ashamed of covering up what I had done to Gregorio, and I never could have lived with myself if she had died before I had the chance to tell her the truth. Seeing you sit there in your wretched state gave me the inspiration I needed to open up. It struck me that if you witnessed me baring my soul, maybe you would be encouraged to open your heart to her, too. But I still couldn't bring myself to tell her the whole story. And it wasn't terribly courageous of me, anyway, when I had no proof that

274

she could even hear me. Sort of like kneeling in the confessional, and saving your juiciest sins until you hear the priest snoring.

That morning I cried out of shame for my shortcomings and out of fear for my future, as much as I cried for Auntie Rosa. Maybe a part of me wanted to show you that I could be a screw-up, too. I just needed somebody, anybody - whether it be a dying old lady or a drunk young one - to tell me that it was OK, that my happiness counted for something.

In retrospect, it was probably best that I didn't know the truth about that morning. Now that I know the facts, however, I realize that if Auntie Rosa hadn't picked that day to die, I wouldn't have rushed home like that. If she hadn't waited for me, I wouldn't have had the chance to wake you with my phone call. I shudder to think what might have happened if I hadn't. I could never have survived losing both of you. So you see, in the end, Auntie Rosa saved us both.

Love,
Iris

From: Lily Capotosti <lilycapotosti@gmail.com>
To: Iris Capotosti <iris.capotosti@gmail.com>
Sent: Sat, January 8, 2011, at 5:17 PM
Subject: Re:Re: The rest of the story

Dear Iris:

It strikes me that it is precisely because you were playing the savior and I was playing the screw-up that things turned out as they did. I mean, wouldn't it be a hoot if killing myself was the one thing I got right?

Speaking of getting things right, I have to admit that it was touching to read your accounting of Auntie Rosa's passing. From all appearances, experiencing that together created a bond between us and healed over old wounds. I could tell it was really important to you to believe that back then, so I let you. Why taint that experience for you? Why burst your bubble about who I was and how I really felt? What would have been the point? It just didn't seem worth the pain it would have caused you to hear, nor the pain it would have caused me to say.

I'm glad you brought up the "s" word. Shame is like poison. Like you, I was already under the impression that love was the reward for good performance, and as it was, I was struggling to eke out enough love to survive. I suspect that so many of the choices I've made - and am still making, quite possibly - have their foundation in that old belief that there is something basically unlovable about me. Worse, that the "something" is so vague that it can't even be identified, and therefore it can't be fixed. You were one of the only people in my life who I felt just truly loved me. Somehow you saw me as vivacious and talented and beautiful. How could I put that at risk that by letting you see the truth of who I was? I couldn't imagine how you could love that. I couldn't imagine looking into your eyes and seeing pity instead of your sweet version of me, the me I had always wished I could be.

Of course, Auntie Rosa had her shame, too. Which is probably why she grasped your love with white knuckles. If we had all just learned to let go of the shame a little, we might have seen that being the saved and being the savior are two facets of the same brilliant gem. Our vulnerability is what makes us lovable; our willingness to accept the vulnerability in others is what makes it possible for us to love.

Love,
Lily

10. LILY

"Today," said Iris, "we tackle this house." Iris stood in the center of Lily's living room, surrounded by stacks of boxes, her hands on her hips. She was dressed for action, in a pair of khaki cargo shorts and a T-shirt with an image of a lizard on it. Her hair was pushed back from her face with a black elastic headband, revealing the large diamond studs that were part of the three-piece set that Auntie Rosa had given herself for her fortieth birthday, and which she had never removed. The undertaker had carefully unscrewed the earrings and unclasped the pendant and placed them into Iris' hand. There was no need for the family to consult the will; Auntie Rosa had always made it clear that the diamonds would belong to Iris. Lily didn't bother to wonder whether Auntie Rosa ever thought about the ramifications of that.

"Ugh," groaned Lily. She kicked at a cardboard box, toppling it and spilling a pile of faded dish towels onto the floor. "It's hopeless."

"I admit, it's not going to be easy to get everything in order," said Iris, looking around. "But it's not hopeless." A shadow passed over Iris' face. "Nothing is hopeless."

Iris' voice trailed off as her gaze wandered about the room, from one pile of Lily's transported belongings to the next. There was little to differentiate the items strewn about from those that Lily had dumped at the curb earlier that morning, with the intention of separating the junk from the good stuff. Now, standing there in the middle of it, it all seemed like junk.

"Really, Iris," said Lily. "Let's not do this today. I can take care of it myself. I'm sure you have tons to do before you leave tomorrow." Lily was aware that if she could have indeed taken care of it herself, it would have been done already. It had been a week since Auntie Rosa's funeral, and every day Lily would sit on the couch, smoke, and look out the window until it was time to go to support group, where she would cry until she was exhausted, come home, collapse into bed, and then wake up and resume her position on the couch. Every morning she told herself she would get the place in order. Yet every morning, she was consumed instead with the reordering of her thoughts. Hours passed as she gazed out at the lake, reviewing the preceding week of her life - the agonizing incident with the boys, her thwarted attempt at numbing her own pain, keeping a *Reader's Digest* vigil at Auntie Rosa's deathbed with Iris. It was as though her mind were sorting through the jumble - seeking patterns, striving to make connections and sense out of what seemed like a tidal wave of confused misery. Finding no logic there, her mind drifted back further, to the months leading up to recent events. While she had been living that life, it all seemed quite believable, but from her spot on the couch, it seemed fantastic. She wondered if people really believed her account of what had happened with the boys, or if their heads, nodding in sympathy, instead shook with disbelief when they turned to walk away. She thought of Owen, of Donna, of Bethany and the women at PTW. How suddenly they all seemed like strangers when so recently they had been the buoys around which Lily's life had moored itself. It was a life that had been built on a deceptively solid set of truths: God protects the faithful, marriage is forever, love heals all wounds, children love their mothers, families care for one another... the list went on and on and on. Lily's existence had been stitched together with maxims such as these; they operated as a system and helped her navigate life. Now, like the Mousetrap game Iris and Lily used to play when they were small, one illusion bumped into another one, which toppled a third, and smashed a fourth, and ultimately Lily found herself the mouse, trapped by a contraption of her own making. She was left with the task of rebuilding the structure of her worldview, thought by thought, and she wondered whether she would ever be able to cobble it together again in a way that would enable her to move on.

"You know what Auntie Rosa always used to say," said Iris.

"Many hands make light work!" She picked up a pillow from the floor, the way a new father would pick up a soiled diaper. She let it drop onto the couch, gave it a pat, then wiped her hands on her shorts. She wore the same smile that Auntie Rosa used to apply to her face whenever she proclaimed that she loved all of her nieces the same. Her mouth feigned joy, betrayed by a darkness in her eyes. Lily considered whether Iris had inherited the smile along with the diamond studs and pendant. Or maybe she had just inherited the ease for wearing them.

"Anyway," Iris continued, "if we don't do the work, we can't have the celebration!" She pulled a bottle of champagne out of her canvas bag and set it on the coffee table. "This is for when we finish! I've had it chilling at Violet's overnight. We should put it in the fridge." Iris extended the bottle toward Lily.

"It would probably do me more good to have some of this now." A dark chuckle escaped Lily's throat, as she set the bottle down on the coffee table. It was clear Iris was intent on going back to Italy with all the loose ends neatly tied in a bow; Lily knew she would not be able to stand leaving her in this mess. The only way to get past today was to try and go along, hoping it would pass quickly.

"I know what you mean, believe me," said Iris. "But what you need now is a little inspiration - look what else I brought." Iris reached into her bag again and pulled out a *Jesus Christ Superstar* CD.

"Oh, my God! What, do you always carry that around with you?"

Iris smiled. "I borrowed it from Violet."

"I haven't listened to that since we were in high school." Not exactly the memories Lily wanted to conjure up. She was having enough trouble trying to mitigate her current disasters, without inviting past troubles to this little shindig.

"I still listen to it every Easter," said Iris. "It always reminds me of how we used to act out the whole opera, from beginning to end. I still get goosebumps when I think of you singing 'I Don't Know How to Love Him.'" Iris sighed. "Those were the days - when we spent our afternoons hanging out at the Valley Ranch clubhouse, and our nights lying in bed listening to the radio and talking."

It must be nice to have the ability to tune into the happiness of the past with such precision. Those days existed in Lily's mind as a wall of noise and confusion, of emptiness and fear, duty and drudgery. She thought about the good times once in a while, but then the sadness always hitched a ride into her reverie and rode her for hours, or even days. It was much easier not to think of those times at all. Unless you were Iris, apparently.

"Nothing gets me cleaning like a little 'What's the Buzz?'," said Iris. She reached for the boom box that sat on top of the television set.

Iris popped open the lid, extracted the CD that was inside, and read the label.

"'Lift Me Up'? Hey! Isn't this the song you recorded? Let's listen to it!"

Lily looked at Iris, then at the CD.

"No!" she cried. How could she have forgotten that it was in there? "I mean, I'd really rather not."

"Why not? Please... I want to hear it."

"It reminds me of that day - and I can't stand the thought of it."

"I know," said Iris. She sighed and shook her head slowly. "I know the song will always remind us of the morning that Auntie Rosa died."

"I wasn't talking about the day Auntie Rosa died, Iris." *Not everything that happened this week was about Auntie Rosa, believe it or not.* "I was talking about the day I recorded the CD." Lily retrieved a small glass candy dish from a box and began dusting it with one of the old cloth diapers she had held onto expressly for the purpose. Nothing better for dusting. "There was something about that night that I never shared with anyone - not even the women at support group; they probably would have thought I was nuts. Or at least more nuts." Lily hesitated as the story crouched in the back of her throat, but it was her best argument against allowing Iris to play the CD. And maybe even to purge the acrid taste of it festering there.

"I was standing there in that vocal booth," she began,

mechanically wiping the candy dish in circular movements. "Joe was sitting there, his eyes just boring holes into me... and the band was on the other side of the window, in the control room, watching me. I opened my mouth to sing, and when those first few words came out," Lily sang quietly, "'When you look at me, tell me, what do you see?' It was like I was asking them what they saw, you know? And for a split second, I was there with them, looking in at myself. Seeing Joe sitting there like he owned me made me so embarrassed. He humiliated me and shamed me. It didn't hit me until later, but that was the first time I saw the reality of my life. It scared the shit out of me, and I believe that everything that happened that night - the car chase, the cops - happened because I finally opened my eyes to the truth."

"That's good, right?" said Iris. "The truth shall set you free, as they say. And now you're free!"

"Welcome to my freedom," said Lily, gesturing to the mess all around them. "Please, really, just throw that CD away." Lily wanted to kick herself for not removing it before Iris came over. But at least she had remembered to flush the remaining pills down the toilet and get rid of the bottle.

"Lily," Iris protested. "That's all in the past now. Don't look back; look ahead. There's really no sense in wallowing in past hurts, is there?"

Spoken like someone who had no regrets, no past humiliation. Or like someone who couldn't admit them.

"I can't afford to not look back," said Lily. She set the candy dish down onto the coffee table next to the champagne. "I don't think of it as wallowing. I get the sense that I've been tripping over the same crack in the same sidewalk over and over again. If I can't figure out where it is, I can't learn to walk around it, you know?"

"I guess," said Iris.

"I mean, all that stuff you told Auntie Rosa the day she died - about what happened with Gregorio - don't you ever think about it, and wonder how things got that way? Don't you ever feel regretful or guilty about it? I even feel guilty about leaving Joe, and Gregorio adored you - bought you expensive things, took you all over the place - he treated you like a princess."

"There's something they don't tell you about being a princess, Lily. You may get to sit on a throne and be adored, but that's all you get to do." Iris removed the CD from the boom box and slipped it into the padded envelope that was lying there. Her gaze wandered out the window. "I would have traded all I had for the freedom to be myself, to get embarrassed, to make a few mistakes now and again. Get myself into a mess or two. My life with Gregorio was so... sterile. Safe, but predictable. Like he thought I was made of porcelain and was afraid the world would break me. Anyone with half a brain gets pretty darned bored with that after a while, and anyone with a mind of her own will go insane, eventually. If they don't kill themselves first."

The image of Iris as a porcelain princess locked away in an ivory tower and of Gregorio as a cold and overprotective king jarred Lily's gut.

"Isn't that weird?" asked Lily.

"Isn't what weird?"

"That we were both cut off from the world like that."

"Yes, but Gregorio wasn't like Joe. If anything, he took too much care of me."

"I guess there are all kinds of ways of controlling someone."

Iris turned from the window with a sharp sigh. "He meant well, he only had my best interests at heart, so yes, I do feel guilty, but I've learned to keep it to myself. Whenever I bring it up, Max always says regret and guilt are a waste of time." Iris smiled. "That's what every therapist he's been to says, too. They can't all be wrong. And after all, we can't change the past now, can we?"

It seemed like a rhetorical question, but dusted with hope, as though Iris thought Lily might actually know of a way. Lily wanted to mention that Joe thought he had her best interests in mind, too, that he believed he was protecting her, but she decided against it. Iris would probably get insulted at the suggestion that Joe and Gregorio were alike.

"How long were you unhappy?" Lily asked.

"It wouldn't be fair to say I was unhappy, as marriages go. What reason could I have had for being unhappy? Except, of course, the disappointment about not having a baby. It wasn't until I met Max that I realized that deep down, I *was* sad. He said he could see it in my eyes, the very first time we met."

"He could see that you weren't happy the first time he met you?" It sounded to Lily like the kind of thing a guy might say to get you into bed. Anyway, chances are that every other woman on the face of the earth had that look. Lily had seen it in her own eyes. They all had it in support group. "That's kinda strange."

"He's very perceptive," said Iris. "He knew it before I even admitted it to myself. I had no idea how messed up I was, how my sensuality was being systematically stifled, how pedestrian my tastes and habits were, how limited my view of the world was." Iris' voice began to trail off. "He really opened my eyes and showed me things about myself that Gregorio never could have." Iris reached up and touched the diamond pendant. "Well, that's enough about me!" she exclaimed. She handed the padded envelope to Lily. "We don't have to listen to this, but I think you should hold onto it. Tuck it away for now. You may want it one day." Iris ripped a sheet of paper towel off the roll, folded it in fourths and slipped it under the sweating champagne bottle. "In the meantime, we should put this in the fridge."

"To be honest," said Lily, "I can't think about someday yet... all I can handle right now is seeing the boys tomorrow. I'm so nervous - isn't that ridiculous? Being nervous about seeing my own children?"

"No, it's not ridiculous at all, given what you told me about the last time you saw them. Did you talk to your friend at the shelter about it?"

"Sophie?" Lily wanted to explain that Sophie was a counselor, not a friend. That Lily was in therapy every day, not going to tea, or for a manicure with her girlfriends. "Yes, I went to see her again yesterday. She said that no matter what happens, I should insist on keeping regular contact with the boys, but I don't even know what to say to them."

"Poor Lily... I can't even imagine what it must feel like to finally have children and then lose them. I don't think anyone would know what to do in your situation," said Iris. "What does your heart tell you to do? I think you have to listen to your heart."

"Gee, why didn't I think of that?" Lily murmured, tossing an empty box aside.

"What?" said Iris.

"Nothing."

Listen to your heart. A naive solution for simple problems. This was more complicated than Iris could ever fathom. Listening to your heart only works if you're not heartsick. Or heartbroken. Lily wished Iris would stop trying to give her advice about things she could never understand.

"I'm so hurt and angry by what they did, but at the same time, I have to remind myself that they are being coached, that somehow they think that if they make my life miserable and if they leave me, I will go back to their father and we will be a family again. When I look at them, I see Joe and his craziness, but what I want to see are my little boys." Lily's voice cracked, and a tear trailed down her cheek. "I miss my little boys."

"It's so despicable that anyone would manipulate innocence that way," said Iris, setting down a stack of books, and going to place a hand on Lily's shoulder. "You know, take someone who doesn't know any better and mess their mind up like that. Makes me sick to my stomach." Iris' gaze again wandered out the window.

"I know, me too," said Lily. "And I refuse to put them in the middle or use them that way, but of course if I insist on taking the high road, I'm afraid I'll lose them forever. But I do know that I'm just so sick of all the drama, you know? I just want to rest; I don't want to fight or struggle anymore right now."

"So maybe tomorrow you should just do that," said Iris. "If you think you're confused, imagine how Joseph and Pierce feel. Personally, I think it would be better if you guys just tried to have some fun together, you know? Don't drag them down by talking about what happened. Give them some fun. Maybe spread a blanket under that huge old oak tree out there in the yard and have a picnic." With a clap of her hands, she added, "Yes! In fact, when we're done here, I'm going to go down to that little grocery I passed on my way - the one by that bike place just over the bridge - and get you all set up for a picnic. It will be my gift to you and the boys."

"I don't think that's such a good idea," said Lily.

"Why not?" said Iris, the smile draining from her face.

Because. Because this can't be fixed by forcing them into a scene from a Rockwell painting. Because they are my children and this is my mess. Because I can handle this on my own. Just because.

"I've already got something in mind," said Lily.

"Oh," said Iris.

Lily shook a Merit from the pack and offered one to Iris.

"No," said Iris, turning her back. "But thanks."

Droplets of condensation ran down the sides of the champagne bottle, forming a ring of moisture around the base.

"We should put that champagne in the fridge," said Lily. She drew on the cigarette and blew a series of smoke rings. "It's getting hot in here."

"And late," said Iris, cranking open the window. "We'd better step it up - we have a lot to do and not much time to do it. You know me, I like to get the work out of the way first. Max, on the other hand, is all pleasure before business. *Carpe diem*, that's what he always says."

Iris placed the *Superstar* disc into the boom box and listened as the "Overture" began to play. She worked her way through the maze of debris with a white plastic garbage bag, tossing packing paper, food wrappers, and empty soda cans inside.

"So tell me more about Max," said Lily. "What's he like?"

"What do you want to know?"

"Like, what kind of personality does he have?"

"He's pretty hard to describe," said Iris, lugging the garbage bag to the back door.

"Try," said Lily, when she returned with a new bag.

"Basically, I'd say he is everything Gregorio was not," said Iris.

"Which is?" said Lily.

"Which is exactly what I needed. What I need. Max is adventurous, he's bold, he takes chances - he isn't confined by the rules that keep people trapped."

Max sounded a lot like Indiana Jones. "What does he do for a living?" Lily asked.

"Well, right now he actually shoots films for Italian TV, documentaries and stuff, but he's really a filmmaker. He's working on this big project, trying to find backing."

"What kind of project?" said Lily, emptying an ashtray into a garbage bag.

"It's a screenplay, for a feature film. It's highly artistic, and he won't settle for anything less than some big names. That's why it's taking so long to get off the ground.

"Cool," said Lily. "So you're working as his assistant now?"

"I wouldn't exactly call it that," Iris said. "But I help out with some things. He has a whole crew working under him, and his own personal assistant. He doesn't speak much English, so he'll need me to help with the film project, as soon as he has some time to dedicate to it," Iris kept moving as she talked, never coming up for breath, never pausing for thought, as though reciting from memory. "He's amazing at what he does, which is why he's always too busy to really focus. Meanwhile, he got me some work writing copy for the documentaries and the English voiceovers, that kind of thing. That's what makes it so fun, I get to travel everywhere with him, and my trip pays for itself."

"You have to pay?"

"No, of course not! You have to understand how these things work, though. Max usually finds a way to pass me off as one of the crew, but if some things aren't covered, like for example if we're in a very exclusive resort and decide to stay on and enjoy it for a few extra days, I can pay for my share out of the money I earn. But that doesn't happen often. Max has a way of dealing with hotel and restaurant owners, and once we're there, they are usually the ones who offer us free hospitality. I know how it is because I've been at the other end, dealing with the media, journalists, travel agents - anyone that has the pull to promote a property. That's how I met Max in the first place. When he came to my hotel."

Still, it seemed to Lily like the least he could do was let Iris keep the money she made. "Speaking of your hotel - don't you ever miss your job? Sounds like you were really good at that."

"I got as far as I wanted to go with that career. The hotel was beautiful, but the job sounds more glamorous than it actually was. The hours were grueling, and the responsibility was dragging me down. I even had to start taking Xanax. When I left Gregorio, Max opened my eyes for me. He told me I wouldn't really be free unless I cut all my ties. I mean, what sense did it make for him to be traveling to all those beautiful places on his own, while I slaved away, pandering to the bourgeoisie, not to mention the owner of the hotel ... 'yes sir, no ma'am, right away sir...' God - I was little more than a glorified servant. Working with Max, well, he is just amazing to watch. And his friends are so accomplished and interesting; he's opened up a whole new world to me."

"You took Xanax?" Lily had to stop herself from adding "too" to the end of her question.

"For a while, said Iris. "It helped take the edge off. Hey - Maybe I'll take that cigarette, after all, if you've got one to spare."

"What about your friends from the hotel?" asked Lily, offering the pack to Iris. "Do you miss them?"

"I didn't have any friends there. I had staff. You have to keep your distance when you're the boss, you know." Iris picked up the bottle of champagne by the neck. Tiny rivulets of water ran down the side of the bottle. Iris passed a dust cloth over the surface of the coffee table. "Here, Lily - take this," said Iris, holding the bottle out. "We have to get this into the fridge."

Lily took the bottle. "I will," she said, "in just a sec... I'm trying to figure out if this is a stain or a burn mark in the carpet. God, I hope it's a stain." She set the champagne down on the end table next to the couch and returned to scrubbing at the carpet.

"So what's it like to be assistant to a filmmaker?" said Lily. "That sounds like a fun job."

"I told you, I'm not his assistant," Iris snapped.

"Geez Louise, Iris. What's the big deal?" "I'm sorry. It's just that Max hates it when people call me that. And so do I," said Iris. "After all, I am his companion, Lily."

"I'm sure you are," said Lily, although she thought that Iris sounded a bit like a groupie. Then again, what did Lily know? She obviously had no idea what it was like to be with a man like Max.

"My main job is to give him support and encouragement. He is so sensitive, and so - I don't know - tortured, I guess. He needs me there to keep him grounded, you know? Everyone says he's so much more centered when I'm around – even a lot nicer. I go on location with him, and then at the end of the day, I am there to help him unwind, relax a little. And of course, I'm in charge of entertaining when we're in Rome, or whatever. He has to throw lots of parties in order to make the kind of connections that are so crucial in his field."

Entertain for him, encourage him, help him get along with others. Now Iris sounded more like his wife, really. Or his mother.

"Rome? Do you live there now?" asked Lily, wondering how many other pieces of information Iris was keeping to herself. They weren't exactly minor details, either. Leaving her husband for a new relationship, quitting her job, moving to another city.

"Max has a place there, from back before we met."

"I guess it made sense for you to move in with him since you left your house. It sounded like Liguria was beautiful, though."

"I haven't left Liguria."

The edge to Iris' voice alerted Lily that her sister was losing her patience. "So you and Max got an apartment there?"

"Look Lily, it's not like Europeans live the same way as Americans. They don't all have their nice little houses, and their nice little families, you know? I have an apartment, and Max has an apartment, and sometimes we're in one, and sometimes we're in the other, sometimes we're together, and sometimes we're apart. That's how modern relationships work. Like Max says, I've been married once, for half my life. We both need a little breathing room, at least for now. You should know what it's like."

"Yeah, OK," said Lily, fighting back tears. Just because Lily didn't know how things worked in Italy, it didn't mean she was stupid. She'd had a modern a relationship. Sort of. Anyway, if Iris was so sure that her set-up with Max was so perfect, why did she seem so irritated by it?

"Do you think you and Max will ever get married?"

"I don't know, we've never talked about it. Men as unconventional as Max, with such an unhappy family background, naturally shy away from the subject of marriage."

"I thought I heard you tell Auntie Rosa he would marry you."

Iris sighed. "Yeah, well, what was I supposed to say? When someone is dying right in front of you, it's kind of hard to tell them things you know they wouldn't want to hear."

True. Or when they are living right in front of you.

"Hmm. If you ask me, that's the perfect time to spit out the truth."

"Look, I'm not even divorced yet. It takes three years in Italy. So let's just say we'll cross that bridge when we come to it, OK? Can we talk about something else now?"

"With pleasure," said Lily. This whole sisterly bonding experience wasn't exactly turning out the way Iris had likely imagined. No surprise there. Not much ever did. Too bad Iris didn't notice that more. Maybe they should just stick to cleaning and talking about the weather.

Judas finishing belting out "Heaven on their Minds" as Lily tied up the ends of her garbage bag. "One down, one thousand to go!" She wiped her brow with a paper towel. "You want a Coke?"

"Is it diet?" asked Iris, her voice still shaking. "I've been taking in way too many calories since I got here."

"Diet is all I drink," said Lily. That, and the occasional bottle of Smirnoff.

Lily disappeared into the kitchen and returned with two cans of diet Coke.

Iris popped the tab on her Coke and held it up in a toast.

"To crossing that bridge when we come to it," she said, her smile marred by a quiver.

"Or burning it down," said Lily.

The house throbbed with heat as the two women made their way from the great room to the dining room, to the kitchen, continuing their work long after the music stopped. Even with all the doors and windows open, the stifling air hung heavy around them. Lily's rickety old oscillating fan measured out a steady *click-click, click-click* when it should have been sweeping the room with air. Like a metronome, it inspired rhythm in their movements as Lily dragged a broom across the kitchen floor and Iris wiped down the cupboards with oil soap.

"That stuff smells like the pews in church," said Lily.

"I know," said Iris. "That's why I like it. I always liked being in church, you know? The candles, the incense, the ritual, and pageantry. Oh, Lily, you have to come see the cathedrals in Italy - you would just love them!"

"Yeah," said Lily, letting the word drop like a guillotine on the conversation. Iris may as well have told her she should go to Mars; even a trip to the grocery store seemed like too much right now. The mere thought of going back to work on Monday nauseated her.

Lily had called in sick the entire week previous, leaving messages on Mrs. Windham-Childs' machine in the middle of the night in order to avoid having to actually speak with her. What could Lily have told her? That she couldn't come in because she went off the deep end and drank half a bottle of vodka and almost killed herself? Or that her ex-husband had been dragging her through hell, and all that was left was skin and bones, and it was all she could do to keep breathing? She could have blamed it on Auntie Rosa, which would have been true in part since Lily needed to attend the wake and the funeral services. She may even have gained favor with Mrs. Windham-Childs for that because taking a certain amount of time to honor a family member who has passed would have been regarded not as time off, but as a proper and necessary family obligation. At the time, she hadn't cared much about what Mrs. Windham-Childs thought of her reasons for missing a week of work. But with Monday looming on the horizon, she was reminded of what Sophie had told her - that she could be dismissed without explanation or warning if things didn't work out.

"Lily - look at this!" Iris cried. She held up the Porky Pig glass from the kitchen window sill that held the lavender clippings. "They've got roots!"

Lily didn't even remember caring for them over the weeks - she barely remembered caring for herself.

"I wouldn't plant them today, though," said Iris, wiping her brow with a paper towel. "It's just way too hot. Give them a little time. Wait until it cools off a bit, so they have a fighting chance." She added an inch of water to the glass.

"Believe it or not," said Lily. "We are down to our last box."

"Wait! Let's open it together!" said Iris. "On the count of three. One, two,..."

"Honestly, Iris," said Lily. "You are the only person I know who can make an event out of opening a box." It was hardly a victory; this was just the beginning of a long road for which Lily felt categorically unprepared. It was the part that Iris would not have to deal with.

"Three!" cried Iris.

Together they pulled open the flaps of cardboard, revealing two small beige cotton afghans, done in a simple shell stitch.

"What do we have here?" said Iris. She held up one of the afghans and shook it out. Rather than square, it was shaped was more like a trapezoid, with one edge longer than the other by a foot.

"Oh, those are awful!" said Lily, with a laugh. "I crocheted them a few years ago, but they are so bad, I never put them out. I am just going to have to admit that I do not have the patience - or the talent - for needlework. Just one more thing I tried to master along the way."

"I know just what to do with these!" Iris brought the blankets into the great room and laid one across the back of the couch and one across the back of the love seat, strategically placing them to hide the spots where the fabric on the furniture had worn through.

"They're lovely," said Iris, as though trying to convince herself. She ironed them out with her hands, gently tugging at the edges in an attempt to square off the corners. "They will come in handy in case you get chilly."

"Hard to imagine ever feeling chilly after today." Lily plucked a paper napkin from the holder on the dining table and swabbed her neck. She took a second napkin and used it to wipe the last remaining moisture from the bottle of champagne. Drenched in sweat, together they finally hauled the last of the empty boxes out to the back porch.

"We did it!" shouted Iris, taking Lily's hands in hers and jumping up and down in place. "We got them all unpacked!"

Lily didn't feel quite feel like jumping for joy. She would celebrate when it was all over. Whenever that might be. And where did Iris get this indefatigable sense of joy and optimism? Would Lily ever be able to rediscover a bit of that in her life? Had she ever had any? Still, she only had to pretend to be cheerful for a little while longer. Then she would be left again in peace.

"Now," said Iris. "You go take your shower, and I'll run these bags out to the curb."

"Iris - you've done enough, really, you can take off now."

"Go get into the shower." Iris pinched her nostrils closed between her index finger and thumb. "You stink."

Lily let the cool water spray down over her head, allowed it to trickle into her ears, run down her back. She watched the water swirl down the drain, wishing the toils of her life could so easily be rinsed away. She stood under the stream until she heard the back door slam, unaware if a minute or an hour had passed, and wishing she could pause life just long enough to get her bearings.

Lily cinched the belt of her robe around her waist as she stepped down into the dining room, exhausted, but refreshed. Four side chairs rallied around the little round table that had been transplanted from the kitchenette on Trevi Way. A large glass vase filled with purple and white wildflowers stood at its center.

"Where did those come from?" Lily asked.

"I found them behind the garage - can you believe it?"

"They're beautiful," said Lily.

"Beautiful things are everywhere," said Iris. "You just have to be willing to look for them – sometimes in unexpected places."

It sounded like something Lily had once heard on *Mr. Rogers' Neighborhood*.

"Now, the first thing I want you to remember when you come down those stairs tomorrow morning," Iris told her with a catch in her voice, "Is that *you* are a beautiful wildflower. Never let anyone tell you otherwise."

"OK," said Lily. "I'll try." She bent forward to sniff the bouquet, then jerked back in repulsion at how bad they smelled. Maybe Iris did see her as a wildflower - beautiful from a distance, but if you get too close, you'll get a snoutful of stink. If Lily were a flower, she'd want to think of herself as a white Easter lily, exuding the strong and unmistakable fragrance of the hope for redemption. Lily couldn't recall if she had ever actually smelled an iris.

"And the second thing I want you to remember," said Iris, tears forming in her eyes, "Is that if I ever catch you with plastic flowers in your house, I will fly across the Atlantic Ocean and personally pound you."

Lily envied Iris her sentimentality, and she felt guilty that she did not feel the same sense of sadness over their parting.

Iris opened the refrigerator. "Hey- where's the champagne?" she cried. "I thought you put it in the refrigerator."

"I thought you did," said Lily.

Iris scurried into the living room, returning with the champagne. "Now it's warm! I can't believe we didn't put this on ice."

Lily looked from Iris' face to the bottle, and back to Iris. She shrugged. She didn't much care to celebrate anyway.

"That's alright, Iris," said Lily. "It's no big deal."

"Of course it is!" said Iris. "We have to mark this occasion - today is the first day of the rest of your life! God knows I've done worse things than drink warm champagne. You want to do the honors?" Iris offered the bottle to Lily.

"You go ahead," said Lily, shoving her hands into the pockets of her robe. She was embarrassed that she didn't know how to open champagne, that she'd never had the occasion to learn.

Iris peeled the foil from the neck of the bottle, pointed it towards the windows overlooking the lake, untwisted the wire cork restraint and then looked at Lily.

"Are you ready to launch your new life?"

"Yes," said Lily. "I am."

"I'm not convinced," said Iris.

"Neither am I." Lily laughed weakly, hoping it sounded like a joke, yet relieved at the chance to speak the truth.

"C'mon, Lily," said Iris. "Say it like you mean it."

"Yes, yes!" said Lily, hoping to infuse her voice with enough enthusiasm to meet Iris' expectations so she would open the fucking bottle of champagne.

Iris placed her thumbs against the cork and worked it free.

"*Evviva!*" she cried.

With a *pop!* the cork flew across the room, and a puff of smoke erupted from the bottle like a magic genie. Lily would like three wishes, and her first wish would be for an unlimited number of wishes. She had a feeling she would need them.

Iris handed Lily a foaming glass of champagne.

"Wait!" cried Iris. "Before you drink it, let me get my camera - I want to capture this moment."

Iris left the kitchen and returned a moment later with her bag. She reached in and pulled out a camera.

"Wow, nice camera," said Lily. "I don't know you were interested in photography."

"Isn't it cool? It's a Canon EOS Rebel. Max has so many, and he wasn't using this anymore, so he gave it to me. He's teaching me how to use it," said Iris. "Just a second while I find the right setting - I want to immortalize this moment. Now hold up the glass like you're making a toast, Lily."

Lily obliged.

"Now say *evviva!*"

"*Evviva,*" Lily mumbled.

"Oh, come on!" said Iris. "Can't you at least try to look happy? I want something to remember you by when I go back home."

You could just remember it the way it actually was. Lily smiled. The camera clicked. Iris poured herself a glass of champagne.

"Try to enjoy yourself tomorrow, Lily. Don't be so worried about what you're going to say or do with the boys. They might surprise you."

"That's what I'm afraid of." Lily took a long sip of champagne. "I keep wishing there was an instruction manual or something, you know? I could flip to the index and look up 'children, what to do when they abuse and leave you' and then I could turn to page twelve or whatever, and there would be a diagram of a mother and two little kids all smiling and happy, with text that read, 'Step one, step two, step three.' Wouldn't it be great if you could look up stuff like that in manual?"

Iris covered her face and burst into tears.

"What is it, Iris?" said Lily. "What's wrong?"

"I don't know what's wrong with me." Iris smiled through the tears that ran down her face. "It must be the champagne... the idea of leaving ... I'm just tired... it's been a long week - but look who I'm telling!" Iris blew her nose on the towel.

Lily just looked at her, not knowing what to say.

"Oh! I almost forgot!" Iris dug into her bag and pulled out a small silver box. "This is for you."

Lily opened the box, to find Auntie Rosa's lily of the valley pin inside. "Auntie Rosa's rhinestone pin?"

"I'll have you know," said Iris. "That those are real diamond chips."

"No kidding..." Real diamond chips. The pieces that fell to the floor as the whole diamonds were cut.

"Everyone thought they were imitation, but that's because they never bothered to really look at them - see how they sparkle in the light? Just like you."

"Thank you, Iris," said Lily.

"Dolores gave that pin to Auntie Rosa, and I know they would both want you to have it. I was hoping it would be a reminder to you of how much you are loved, Lily. Dolores loved you, Auntie Rosa loved you, and I love you."

"I love you too, Iris." That part was true, despite the rest. She put the pin back into the box.

"Don't you want to put it on?" said Iris.

"I'm in my robe," said Lily.

"Oh, I know, but just to see how it feels - let's pin it on!"

"No thanks," said Lily. "I think I'll save it for a special occasion." Iris heaved a deep sigh, drained her glass, and gathered her things into her bag. Lily knew that she had disappointed Iris by not putting the pin on. Perhaps Iris thought that receiving a diamond chip pin *was* a special occasion - or at least that it should have been regarded as one by someone as down on their luck as Lily. But in that moment, Lily realized that getting diamond chips instead of two-carat earrings wasn't okay with her anymore, nor could she keep pretending that it was. Why should she revel in being second best? Why should she accept survival as a cause for celebration when life was so much more than that?

The sisters said their final goodbyes, and Lily watched as Iris walked down the driveway. As her car disappeared around the corner, a wave of relief mingled with remorse passed over Lily. She could give up the charade of optimism now that Iris was gone, but now, Iris was gone. Lily hated that it was so difficult to be around her, and still so difficult to watch her drive away.

She picked up the bottle and poured the rest of the champagne down the drain. One more drink might take the edge off, but it might also blur the new image of herself that was just coming into focus.

Lily woke the next morning to a gentle breeze that draped itself across her bare breasts like a cool washcloth. With a groan, she pulled the white cotton sheet up over her shoulder and rolled over onto her stomach.

She had dived head first into a deep sleep the night before, exhausted from the work she and Iris had done, lightly relaxed by the champagne. As she rose to full wakefulness, she remembered how lovely the great room had looked when they'd finished, how much it had seemed like a real home, and then she remembered that today was the day the boys were coming. She quickly rolled back over, unwrapped herself from the sheet and jumped to her feet. She slipped into the nightshirt she'd abandoned to the floor during the stifling night and went downstairs into the kitchen to make a pot of coffee. She wandered into the great room, cranked the windows all the way open and closed her eyes as the refreshing morning breeze flowed past her face, displacing the stagnant air still trapped inside from the day before. She sat by the window in the rocking chair, which had been a birthday gift from Joe the year she was pregnant with Joseph. It was the only gift of his she'd kept.

Lily watched a thick, dark shelf of clouds being pushed across the sky by a lively northwestern breeze. She was disappointed to see that it was probably going to rain. After Iris left, Lily had decided that a picnic sounded like a good idea (especially since she hadn't been able to come up with an idea of her own), and had taken a trip to the corner grocery to buy some food, a frisbee, and a bottle of soap bubbles for blowing.

The boys would be arriving in an hour. All those years, they were never more than a few feet from her side. Now she had to wait for them, receive them like guests. When they'd left (was it really just last week?) it was as though Lily had lost a part of herself, but already, the space where they had been was different somehow. It felt smaller, quieter. She missed them terribly, but she had to admit that she was enjoying the respite from the chaos. Her stomach twinged with guilt. She would use this time to get her strength back - then she would be able to provide them with the kind of home they wanted.

Lily finished her coffee, got dressed, and then sat in the back hall watching for Joe's car. As thunder rumbled and lightning flashed she was grateful that at least she did not have to drive across town to pick the boys up, even though she knew this was one more opportunity for Joe to mess with her. He could drop the boys off late, pick them up early - even "forget" to bring them by at all. But of course, her house was on the way to the track, so this arrangement worked out for Joe, which meant that it would have to work out for everyone.

Joseph and Pierce's mad dash from the car couldn't save them from getting drenched in the downpour. Lily greeted them at the back door with two fresh towels.

"Good-bye, my sons!" Joe poked his head out through the open car window. "I'll call you later to say good-night!"

Lily wanted to shout back, "Don't call them later! They can go one day without talking to you!" You'd be surprised, in fact.

Yet Lily trained her eyes on the ground, unable even to look at Joe, his face the very gateway to horrifying memories and searing pain. It was the face with whom she had shared daily life for twenty years, the face for whom she had labored and borne two sons, the face that accepted her virginity and stole her innocence, once the face of a passionate boy who made her heart pound and her body call out in desire. Now, she couldn't even bring herself to look at it. How long would it be before she could raise her eyes to his and not recoil? How long before his face would mean nothing to her? How long before his would become a face she used to know?

"Who's the best Daddy in the world?" Joe called out through the teeming rain.

"You are, Daddy!" shouted Pierce.

"Hey you two," Lily delivered a kiss to each of the boys as they stepped into the foyer. "I have some fresh clothes for you. Give me your wet things."

"Mommy, I'm soaped!" said Pierce.

Lily laughed. "*Soaked*, my love. You're *soaked*."

Joseph grabbed his towel and the dry clothes and went into the bathroom, closing the door without saying a word.

"I was hoping we could go on a picnic today," said Lily. She pulled Pierce's T-shirt off over his head. "But it looks like we're going to have to go to Plan B."

"What's Plan B?" asked Pierce. He pulled his white socks off one at a time and flung them across the foyer.

Good question, thought Lily. "Well, maybe we can go down to the video store and rent 'A Fish Tale.' I heard that's good."

"My Daddy just rented it for us last night," said Pierce. "We stayed up until eleven a-clock and watched it three times!"

"Oh," said Lily.

Joseph emerged from the bathroom, dressed in his dry clothes. "Where do you want these?" he asked flatly.

"You can leave them here, honey."

Joseph let the bundle of wet clothes drop to the floor.

"Well, how about if we go to the mall?" said Lily. "We can ride the Carousel, maybe get a hamburger..."

"We just came from the mall," said Joseph as he headed for the stairs. "Samantha forced us to walk around all morning, shopping for clothes for our vacation."

"Oh," said Lily. "OK."

Joseph headed down the stairs. Pierce followed.

"Well then, go on downstairs," said Lily. "I'll put your things in the dryer and then I'll come down, and maybe we can play some Gin Rummy or something."

"Do we like Gin Rummy, Joseph?" Pierce asked.

"No," Joseph replied. "Card games are gay."

"Yeah," said Pierce. "Card games are gay, right, Joseph?"

Lily tossed their clothes in the dryer and hung their coats on the rack. She headed down the stairs and called toward the great room. "At least I know you must be hungry, right?" She didn't wait for a reply; she needed time to think. "I'll make some sandwiches, and then we can decide how we'd like to spend the afternoon." So far, this was not going very well.

Lily grilled up three cheese sandwiches and pulled three containers of chocolate pudding, three juice boxes, and three apples from the refrigerator. She placed everything on an aluminum tray.

She noticed the Porky Pig glass and the sticks that she hoped would one day be lavender again. "I'm sorry you've had to wait so long – and I know you don't belong in there – it's so undignified. Hang on just a little while longer. I'm dancing as fast as I can." She opened the faucet and added an inch of water to the glass.

"I know!" she called in to the boys. "I'll get a tablecloth out of the closet, and we can have our picnic right here in the house! What do you say?"

When she didn't hear a reply, she went to check on them and discovered that they had both fallen fast asleep - Joseph on the couch, and Pierce on the loveseat. She'd never seen them pass out so quickly. She stood and watched them sleep, then closed her eyes and listened to the sounds of their breath. In and out. In and out. The rain had tapered off and was gently *tap-tap-tapping* against the house, tiny rivulets of water trickling through cracks in the rusted gutter. A cool breeze followed on the heels of the downpour, gushing in through the mesh of the window screens. Lily pulled one afghan first over Joseph, then gently laid the other one over Pierce. They both stirred. Lily held her breath, silently praying that they would stay still, for just a while longer.

As quietly as she could, Lily turned the rocking chair away from the window and toward her sleeping children. She slowly let her body down into the chair and began rocking gently, adding the creaking of the wood to the sweet symphony that played. The *tap-tap* of the rain droplets on the window pane, the *crick-crick* as Lily rocked, the hissing and rumbling of little boy snores and slumbers.

She missed them so much. Whenever she'd called them over the past week to check on them and say hello they had been on their way to a baseball game, or just coming in from Sea Breeze amusement park, or had been in the middle of putting together a new trampoline, or focused on conquering the most treacherous villain that stood guard at the final gate of the latest video game. Apparently, it was exhausting to be entertained twenty-four hours a day. The ransom for their loyalty left them too tired to enjoy its spoils.

Lily rocked to and fro, unconsciously keeping time with the boys as they breathed in and out. She could sit there and watch them sleep all day. They did not need more fun, additional activities, greater thrills. Perhaps they just needed a place to rest. Admittedly, peace wasn't as exciting as buying new clothes, or as seductive as staying up until all hours getting hopped up on sugar and fairy tale philosophy. Lily could not - would not - give them that. But if they needed a place to sleep in a crazy world where all the grownups were frantically competing for their affections and vying for their loyalty, where their own fledgling sense of fair play could be no match for their fear of losing their father to death by loneliness, she would give them that. Even though she had little more to offer than a threadbare couch, a crooked afghan, and a cool breeze, it was enough. It was what they needed, for now.

Lily's mother had tried to give her what she needed, and Lily hadn't made that easy for her. Lily had wanted sympathy, not strategy. In the end, her mother was right – what Lily really needed was to find a way to face her predicament with strength and wisdom. That's what she had tried to give Lily. She was finally starting to see that. After the boys went home, Lily would call her. Maybe go over for a visit.

Lily bowed her head and gave thanks for all the women in her life who had tried to give her what she needed, all those who had nurtured her, who had birthed her, who had saved her. Or tried to save her soul, like Donna. Sweet, simple Donna who thought a plate of cookies and a Bible verse could solve almost anything, and even when it couldn't, would be sufficient to at least numb the pain.

She thought of Iris, and of all the ways in which she'd loved Lily over the years – from sharing the candy she'd bought with her saved allowance long after Lily had squandered all of hers, to pushing Alba Ichberg into the duck pond in Lily's defense, to putting aside her own grief and giving up her last day in town to help Lily create a home for her children. Poor Iris seemed so sad and displaced when she'd left last night, knowing that she was forever leaving Auntie Rosa behind. Lily had never realized before how dear Auntie Rosa had been to Iris, how much they had loved each other. A pang of envy sliced into Lily's sense of peace. Maybe one day she would understand, would learn to truly forgive Auntie Rosa – for Iris' sake, and for her own.

Iris had seemed so different yesterday. She looked like the sister that Lily had always known and loved, but not much else about her seemed familiar. The Iris that Lily knew was conventional, demure, timid, even. Lily smiled as she remembered how Iris used to tremble when she had to call the doctor to make an appointment, the way she would write down what she wanted to say and then rehearse it over and over again. She sure wasn't shy anymore. Iris wasn't the fainthearted young girl she used to be any more than Lily was the starry-eyed dreamer she once was. Iris was a sophisticated and worldly woman who used to be a little girl that Lily once knew.

Different could be good; grown up and mature she understood.

But Lily couldn't shake the nagging feeling that the changes she saw in Iris were something else. Lily could even understand about Iris leaving Gregorio. As much as she'd always thought she would have died to have a husband like him, there were lots of women along the way who probably thought that about Joe. You can't tell what goes on behind someone else's front door - let alone their bedroom door - and you can't turn on happiness with the flip of a switch. As far as Lily could tell, neither could you beg it or cajole it or tease it or chase it. Happiness seemed to have a mind of its own. The best you could do was look out for it and hope you recognized it as it flit past.

More than Iris' past, it was her future that disturbed Lily. Max certainly sounded exciting, intelligent, talented, popular... Iris had done a thorough job of painting a picture of what kind of a man he was. Who was she trying to convince?

Lily's thoughts travelled on to Sophie and Kitten and Claire and Edie – all the women at the CBW support group who gave her the space and freedom to cry and scream, whose pain reflected Lily's past and gave her a place to lay it all down.

She prayed for wisdom as she faced her own uncertain future as a mother, and considered the work of delicately carving out what that meant for her now.

Lily rocked and the rain tapped and the boys slept. No matter what came next, they would always be her children. No one could ever take that away.

"I love you guys," she whispered.

Lily stashed her purse in the broom closet and set a pot of coffee to brew in the kitchen. She stopped in the bathroom to check out her hair and make-up. She readjusted Auntie Rosa's lily of the valley pin, which she had fastened to the lapel of her jacket to cover the stain there. Besides, Mrs. Windham-Childs would surely appreciate both the style of the pin and the fact that Lily had gone to the extra trouble to look nice. She needed all the help she could get this morning. She took her seat at her desk a full half an hour early, hoping to appear the model of punctuality and cheerfulness when Mrs. Windham-Childs breezed in through the front door. In her own way, she was caring for Lily, too, teaching her about life's finer points and giving her a peek into the world of privilege.

"Good morning, Mrs. Diotallevi," she chimed as she passed. "Welcome back."

"Thank you!" said Lily. She heaved a sigh of relief. Maybe she had worried for nothing. Lily picked up the first envelope from the stack of unopened mail on her desk and sliced through the top with a letter opener.

"Mrs. Diotallevi," Mrs. Windham-Childs called from inside her office. "May I see you for a moment, please?"

Shit. Lily's eyes stung. *Stop that. Just stop. Pull yourself together and just get your story straight. But whatever you do, don't cry!*

"Yes?" Lily said, poking her head in the door.

"Please," said Mrs. Windham-Childs. "Come in and close the door."

Lily complied, but her heart sank. This was not a good sign.

Mrs. Windham-Childs was wearing her glasses, reading a letter. Without looking up, she motioned to Lily to sit down and asked, "How are you feeling this morning?"

"Better," said Lily, taking her seat. "Much better, thanks."

"You must have been quite ill to miss an entire week of work." Mrs. Windham-Childs removed her glasses and sat back in her chair, placing her folded hands in her lap. It was the closest thing to a dare allowed by a woman of such stature.

Lily had been completely prepared to reassert her claim that she'd had the flu. She had gone over the story again and again in her mind, complete with tales of being up all night, and of sleeping in a feverish stupor all day, which would explain the late night phone messages. Of course, as ill as she was, she hadn't been able to get to the doctor's office, and so she didn't have a written excuse to provide. The story made perfect sense. It wasn't a fantastic tale, and there was no way that Mrs. Windham-Childs could prove that she was lying. Yet the story suddenly seemed thin and vain; the unformed words tasted sour in Lily's mouth. Half-truths and excuses had been the tools of the life she'd left behind. Or was trying to, at least.

She looked at Mrs. Windham-Childs and saw a woman, herself a mother, an educator, a champion of the underprivileged. Could it be possible that she, too, would help if she only knew what Lily was really going through? Lily certainly could use an ally and a mentor right about now.

"Yes, well, about that -" Lily began. She shed her story about the flu, savoring the sweet taste of truth on her lips as she explained to Mrs. Windham-Childs what had been going on in her life. Without going into great detail, but being careful to touch on the key points, she told her about the trouble she'd been having with the boys, about how Joe took them from her, and how her dance of despair had taken her so close to the edge. She told her about Auntie Rosa's death and her reconciliation with Iris. She spoke for a full five minutes; it felt so good to be who she truly was, to be honest about her life in all its gruesome glory. It felt good not to cry about it, but to accept it for what it was: one hell of a bad week - one hell of a bad decade, in fact. And the best thing about getting to the bottom was that there was nowhere to go but back up again.

When Lily finally stopped speaking, she and Mrs. Windham-Childs sat and looked at each other for a moment. Mrs. Windham-Childs did not move, except to raise her eyebrows.

"So that's where I was last week," said Lily. "And things are still kind of a mess, really, but I think I'm going to be OK. I'm ready to try, you know? I'm going to do my best." Lily's throat burned as she fought back tears of pride and determination.

Mrs. Windham-Childs sat up in her chair, shifting her weight forward, placing her folded hands on the desk.

"I must say," she began, "That is quite a lot to take in."

"Tell me about it," Lily said with a giggle.

Mrs. Windham-Childs cleared her throat. "Mrs. Diotallevi, if you should find yourself in a similar position in the future, one in which you find it impossible to come into work and perform your duties, I would suggest that you attribute such an absence to a head cold, or, in the case of extended periods, perhaps the flu. That might be most comfortable for all concerned. At the end of the day," she continued, "honesty and decorum don't always complement each other." Mrs. Windham-Childs' red lips formed themselves into an icy inverted arc. "I'm quite sure you'll find a sufficient amount of work at your desk. Perhaps it will serve you to distract yourself, taking you beyond thoughts of your recent tribulations."

"OK." Lily was confused, and a sense of shame and embarrassment began to creep over her, like the shadows of a fast approaching rain cloud. She had bared her soul, had opened up in the spirit of trust and honesty, and now Mrs. Windham-Childs was acting as though Lily had just vomited on her desk.

"Thank you, Mrs. Diotallevi. That will be all for now." Mrs. Windham-Childs placed her glasses back atop her nose and resumed her reading.

Mechanically, Lily returned to her desk. She finished opening the mail, but the quiet *zip-zip* of the opener slicing through paper was no match for the crescendo of humiliation that rose within her. Lily saw herself sitting in the chair in Mrs. Windham-Childs' office, going on and on about Joe and the boys and how awful it all was, about her despair, about Auntie Rosa's death, all the while thinking that she was garnering empathy and support, mistaking Mrs. Windham-Childs' non-responsive countenance for respectful listening. It was clear now that her reticence was actually an attempt at restraining her repulsion first at the details of Lily's disclosure and then at her vulgar display of intimacy.

Mortified, Lily tried to lose herself in the tasks at hand as Mrs. Windham-Childs had suggested, but the more she tried to suppress her thoughts about the conversation, the more insistent they became.

Lily imagined Iris shaking her finger and saying, "You are a beautiful wildflower - and don't you ever let anyone tell you differently." Lily remembered the way the wildflowers at home had smelled. Maybe that's the price they paid for freedom, and maybe that's why florists didn't sell them. Still, better to be a stinky wildflower than a plastic rose. That's what Mrs. Windham-Childs was like; a plastic rose. Flawless and invulnerable. Beautiful to look at, but not real.

"If I ever catch you with plastic flowers in your house, I will personally come here and pound you!" Lily smiled as she recalled her sister's attempt at being threatening; the one thing that Iris just couldn't quite pull off.

Gradually, Lily's feelings of shame and self-recrimination retreated, their hold on her loosening as she became emboldened by advancing forces of anger and indignation. Who says that honesty and decorum are not always complementary? That only applies if you think that maintaining appearances is more important than being real. Wasn't that the system of thought that had perpetuated Lily's suffering all these years? She had invested so much time and energy trying to uphold the appearance of things, trying to protect herself and her children from the ugly realities of their life, trying to spray perfume on a plastic rose. All that did was delay the pain and divert the suffering for another day.

Lily set the letter opener down on the desk and looked over at Mrs. Windham-Childs' closed door. She - not Lily - was the one who was acting inappropriately. She - not Lily - lacked a sense of what was good and right. Truth always trumps appearances. At least it should. At least it would in Lily's life - from now on. Starting with today.

Lily stood and tugged on the hem of her jacket with both hands. She would knock on Mrs. Windham-Childs' door and ask for a few minutes of her time. She would tell her exactly what she thought about the conversation they'd had. She would tell her that she couldn't understand how a human being with blood running through her veins could listen to Lily's story and not be moved to compassion, that a person who presumes to educate children should be ashamed at her own lack of empathy, and at her preference for deception as a defense from getting spattered with life.

As Lily took her first steps toward Mrs. Windham-Childs' office, her bravado wavered.

If she carried out her plan, Mrs. Windham-Childs could just fire her, right then and there. She thought of Sophie and her box of index cards; she could get another job. Maybe she could even get a real job, and not one whose only qualification was desperation. Besides, even if she didn't, what could happen? She wouldn't be able to pay the rent, for starters. Well then, she would just call Curtis' lawyer and tell him that it didn't work out; that part wouldn't be a lie, for sure. She had taken the house for its three bedrooms and its beach and its sledding hill; it was a house for children to live in, and hers were only visitors there.

Speaking of which, what about the kids? Lily chuckled to herself. Well, unemployment was one way to get out of paying child support. The women at support group used to complain about that all the time. They would get a child support decision in their favor, and then their ex-husbands would mysteriously get fired from their jobs and move in with a family member. If Lily found herself without a paycheck, the boys certainly wouldn't suffer. Samantha would have to do with fewer manicures. Lily could live with that.

Trembling, she took another step toward the door. Her heart pounded. *What would Sophie say when she found out? What would Mom say? What would Iris say?*

At that moment, Mrs. Windham-Childs opened her door and nearly collided with Lily, who was now standing just on the other side.

"Mrs. Diotallevi - you startled me!"

What would Lily say?

"Is there something I can do for you?" Mrs. Windham-Childs asked.

No, Lily thought. *There's nothing you can do for me. And there's nothing you can do to me, either. Nothing I don't allow, anyway.*

"I quit," blurted Lily.

"I beg your pardon?" said Mrs. Windham-Childs, with a *humpf.*

"Yes," said Lily, feeling as surprised as Mrs. Windham-Childs looked.

"I. Quit." Lily was exhilarated. She felt as if she were floating two feet off the ground. "I don't want to work for you anymore." She opened the broom closet and retrieved her purse.

"I would hardly call this mature behavior," said Mrs. Windham-

Childs.

"I'm sure you wouldn't," said Lily. "All the letters there on the desk are opened. Have a good day." Lily placed her hand on the front door.

"Mrs. Diotallevi, need I remind you that it is customary to provide two weeks' notice before vacating a position and that failing to do so will result in a loss of a positive reference from me?"

"Well the way I see it, *Gloria*, I don't actually have anything left to lose, and I definitely don't have two weeks to waste." Lily turned to walk out the door. She stopped, turned around one last time and said, "And by the way, it's Capotosti. My name is Lily Capotosti."

Lily hadn't been to the park since the day she met Curtis. She drove directly to Hava Java's coffee shop in Charlotte where she bought herself a large coffee with cream and sugar, and one copy of each of the four different newspapers stacked by the register. The table she chose was littered with sugar granules and stained with dried coffee, but it sat in a sunny window with a view of the lake. She took a pen from her purse, spread the papers out on the table, and began her search for a new job. Every listing presented a challenge - either it was too far from home, didn't offer a high enough wage, or required more experience than she could offer. Two refills and three trips to the ladies' room later, Lily began to wonder whether she had acted too rashly. Maybe quitting on the spot like that hadn't been such a good idea. If she had played her cards right (a favorite saying of her mother's), she would have found a new job first, before walking out as she had. But Lily never did things the same way as everyone else. Why start now? Besides, walking out like that was fun. It was a beautiful summer day, and she still had two paychecks coming, so there was time. She folded up the newspapers. The only thing left to do that made any sense was to go home and plant the lavender.

Lily drove up through Charlotte, across the Stutson Street bridge, and past the industrial park. Mounted on the sculpture of the bike that sat in front of the Kendall Company, there was a sign that read, "We're on the move! Applications now being accepted!"

"Why the hell not?" Lily asked herself. It seemed to be the day for trying new things. A factory job would be boring, but it would at least be something to tide her over. She didn't have any other prospects, and she was already dressed in what she lovingly referred to as her "big girl clothes," suitable for Sunday Mass, job interviews, and, apparently, speaking one's mind. She flipped her directional on and turned into the parking lot.

"Good morning!" said a young blond woman at the front desk. "I'm Wendy. How may I help you?"

"Hi," said Lily. "Are you taking applications?"

"Yes - we sure are! Have you ever applied here before?"

"No, no, I haven't ever applied here before," replied Lily.

The walls were covered with photographs of an assortment of people - men, women, old, young - posing with their bicycles. Many of the photos were accompanied by letters from customers raving about their new bikes and thanking the Kendall Company.

"I love your pin," said Wendy. "My Grammie used to have one that like. She died last month, and she wore that pin every single day of her life. But hers was a rose - which I always thought was funny because her name was Lillian."

Lily touched her fingers to the pin. "Would you believe it if I told you that this had been my aunt's – who died just last week - and that her name was Rosa?"

"Get out!" said Wendy, slapping the desktop with a laugh.

"Really," said Lily. "Not only that, but my name is Lily!"

"Well, if that doesn't take the cake! I bet that my Grammie Lil and your Aunt Rose are up in heaven right now having a good laugh."

"That's a nice thought," said Lily. "I hope you're right."

"Here's the application, and there are pens right there on the table," said Wendy.

Everything about this place was gentle and sweet. The receptionist, the smiling faces of happy customers, and pens that were not chained to the desk.

"You can just have a seat and take your time," said Wendy. "And let me know if I can get you anything."

"An interview would be nice," quipped Lily.

"You fill that out, and I'll see what I can do!"

They both laughed.

Not much of a resume, thought Lily as she reviewed what she had written. High school education. One minimum wage job a hundred years ago, and three months at a job under which "reason for leaving" Lily had penned, "temporary." Still, how much experience do you need to work on an assembly line? She was breathing, and she could show up every day. It was a relief to not face greater requirements than that.

"Here you go," said Lily, handing the application back to Wendy. She turned to walk out.

"Wait a minute!" said Wendy. "I thought you wanted an interview."

"You were serious?" Lily asked.

"I said I would try, didn't I? Just wait right there, give me a minute or two." Wendy winked and then disappeared through the door behind her desk.

"Thanks," Lily said, tilting her face to the ceiling. "I needed that."

Wendy's face appeared in the doorway. "Lily!" she said softly, gesturing for Lily to come close. "Can you wait about fifteen minutes?"

"Yes, sure," said Lily.

"Great. Our Human Resources manager is going to speak with you."

After twenty minutes, a silver-haired man wearing a shiny gold watch stepped through the door.

"Ms. Capotosti?" he said.

Lily walked over and extended her hand. His handshake was warm and firm. He looked into Lily's eyes and smiled.

"Wow," she said, "You pronounced my last name perfectly - that hardly ever happens!"

"I'm Vincent Papandreas, Director of Human Resources."

"That would explain it," said Lily.

"If you have a few minutes, we can go into my office and chat."

"Sure - that'd be great." She had all day. In fact, she had a lot of all days.

Lily took a seat across from Mr. Papandreas directly opposite a print of Hawaii that hung on the wall. White sands, palm trees, blue water, and a line of hula dancers wearing bright pink leis. Lily smiled. Vincent smiled back.

"So tell me, Ms. Capotosti, what made you come in and fill out an application with us today?"

"Please, call me Lily. To answer your question, I'll have to say that I was passing by on my way home and I saw the sign out in front of the building that you were accepting applications, and here I am."

"So you live in the area?"

"Yes, I do," said Lily. "I live in Summerville."

"No kidding?" said Mr. Papandreas. "I grew up in Summerville." He scribbled something on the application. "So tell me what you know about the Kendall Company."

"To be honest, sir, not much. I know that you make bicycles and that you have an entire wall of photos from customers who really like your bikes, and I know that Wendy is a doll. But that's about it."

Wrong answer for a job interview, she knew that much. You can't just go in and order a job like it was an envelope of French fries. You have to know the company you're applying to, do your research. That was the first bit of advice Sophie had given her, and in her haste, she hadn't followed it.

"Then let me tell you a bit about us," said Mr. Papandreas. "Our company mission is to promote cycling as an eco-friendly, family-friendly activity. We see cycling as a healthy way to bring communities and families together. To that end, we make a high-quality, low-cost bicycle that we call the 'YouBike.' One of the ways we keep our costs down is by standardizing most parts and then shipping them partially assembled. This reduces our labor investment and also enables our cyclists to customize their bikes - they can order the frame they want, the seat they want, the handlebars they want - the way competitive cyclists do - which makes each bike unique, as you may have noticed on our 'Wall of Frame' out in the waiting area."

"Oh, wait -" said Lily. "I know those bikes! I didn't realize you made those here!"

Mr. Papandreas chuckled. "We are the best-kept secret in Rochester - but that's because we do ninety-five percent of our business out of town, especially in places that have a climate more suited to year-round cycling."

"When I worked at SaveMart they used to sell them there. I actually used to put them together for people who didn't want to have to do it."

Mr. Papandreas' face lit up. "You did?" He flipped Lily's application over and scanned her previous work experience.

"It was a while ago," said Lily. "But I had the assembly down to a science. I used to make a game of it, with the goal of trying to break my own records to see how fast I could go. I guess that must sound silly -"

"Hold on one second," said Mr. Papandreas. He wheeled his chair toward his computer and punched some keys on the keyboard.

"One of our biggest initiatives right now is to provide better support to our customers by improving the written instructions we include with every bike - we know we need to make them friendlier, easier to follow. So we're looking for a technical writer - someone who knows our products and can explain clearly and simply how to take what looks like a crazy collection of parts and pieces, and make some sense out of them. Does that sound like something you'd be interested in?"

"Mr. Papandreas," said Lily. "You just described my life."

11. IRIS

Iris maneuvered her red Vespa around the silver Porsche Boxster and the black BMW SUV, both bearing Milan license plates, both illegally hogging the parking area reserved for two-wheelers. She doubted the cars would be fined, but even if they were, their owners would probably just curse, then chuckle, then tear up the ticket. When Iris was fresh from a visit from America, she had very little tolerance for the way Italians just did whatever they wanted, regardless of the rules, and without a thought for others or the consequences. A part of her would like to take matters into her own hands and use one of the several blades of the Swiss army knife she carried in her backpack to hit the bastards where it hurt, right in the shiny metal doors and high-performance tires of their ostentatious vehicles. But Iris just shook her head in disgust, slipped her scooter into a spot between the slanted trunks of two umbrella pines, hoisted it onto its stand, and locked her helmet in its case. Backpack slung over her shoulder, she headed down the steep stone steps, ignoring the silly suggestion from her creaking knees that she was no longer a teenager, and should perhaps modify her behavior accordingly.

Sure-footed in her rubber-soled Menorcan sandals, Iris trotted down the narrow passage under a colorful canopy of purple bougainvilleas and pink oleanders growing on opposite sides of the high stone walls. She had already put the question of ill-mannered drivers out of her mind when she was stopped in her tracks by a slow-moving couple blocking her path.

"Give me a break," Iris grumbled in English, at the sight of the tanned redhead in a yellow halter dress struggling to stay on board her sling-back high heels by clinging to the arm of a companion better equipped for the walk in his spiffy deck shoes. In addition to the accessory on his arm, the man sported a pink Lacoste polo shirt tucked into plaid Bermuda shorts of the style that make short men look shorter, tall men taller, and all men ridiculous.

Six dozen steps later (she counted them every time, each step marking the name of a Capotosti sibling, of which there would always be twelve in her heart), she paused for a few moments at the bottom, where the curtain of vines and branches parted, revealing a scene of breathtaking beauty. The sea was perfectly calm, shimmering with the light of the late afternoon sun slipping to the horizon, bathing the city of Genoa and the entire gulf in an enchanting golden haze. This was the same view she used to spend hours gazing at from the balcony of the little flat Gregorio had provided for his young bride, and it was the same view she shared with Max from the apartment up in Ruta. Same view, different perspectives.

"*Scusi,*" a voice came from behind her. The guy with the redhead on his arm and the crocodile on his shirt and the mirrors on his eyes landed next to her on the last step.

"*Scusi lei,*" Iris replied, hopping to a slab of rock to her right, and allowing the couple access to the walkway on the left. They were obviously not going for a swim, but were headed for the seasonal bar which returned to its perch above the rocks every Easter and stayed put as long as the summer did. She watched the couple totter toward the row of white umbrellas fluttering above a dozen painted blue tables lined along a blue railing, wondering how they had discovered the spot that for years had only been known to locals, including, of course, Iris.

Picking her way across the craggy rocks, she found a flat spot on which to leave her towel and backpack and quickly stripped down to the two-piece bathing suit she wore under her sundress. A shudder escaped her as she lowered her body into the cool seawater, hoping it would neutralize the nagging negativity that had plagued her since her return.

Though her swimming had improved over the years, Iris was reluctant to venture too far out on her own, especially since most other bathers had already abandoned the rocks in favor of mojitos.

She wondered whether any of the people chatting and drinking up at the bar would even notice if she drowned. She wondered how long it would take before anyone at all would. She had no husband waiting for her at home, no job to report to, no family checking in on her, no neighbors knocking on her door.

If the sea wanted to take her, she would let it, Iris thought, as she rolled over in its salty embrace, her face upturned to the sky. The sounds splashing in her ears whispered that she was not alone, that the sea would help bear the burden of her troubled soul. After a few moments, the tears began to flow, mixing with the water that washed over her eyes, making her one with the great and powerful body that buoyed her.

Extending her arms and legs to form a star, she opened herself to the sky and sea, feeling their energy pulsating above and below and all around her. She pictured herself from high above, a minuscule speck on the immense cobalt surface of the sea. Soaring on the wings of her imagination, she flew to the Strait of Gibraltar, leaving behind the placid Mediterranean for the rolling waves of the Atlantic Ocean that took her to the eastern seaboard of America. From the Gulf of St. Lawrence, she sailed into the mouth of the river that flowed between Kingston and Cape Vincent and followed its course until it she reached Lake Ontario, on whose shores Lily's house stood. Knowing exactly where Lily lived made her seem closer, but imagining her sister there all alone, struggling to cope with the challenges of her life, filled Iris with frustration and regret. It seemed that no matter how hard Iris tried, she would never be able to bridge the gap that had opened up between them. Her words always came out wrong, and her actions were misconstrued. That day Iris had gone over to Lily's armed with good intentions, music from their high school days, and a bottle of champagne to celebrate their new lives as single women, had left her feeling awkward and aggrieved. There were so many things she had left unsaid, so many others she had been desperate to hear.

Iris's innermost thoughts and feelings bobbed to the surface as she floated on the water, gazing up at the sky, feeling all around her the presence of those she had loved and lost. In a cumulus drifting across the setting sun, she saw her father's face the day he walked her down the aisle; in the lapping of the water she discerned the notes of Uncle Alfred's Hawaiian melodies; in the cawing of the gulls circling above, she heard Auntie Rosa's raucous laughter; and in the deep, dark water which both sustained and frightened her, she felt the tragedies of Dolores and Henry. She felt closer to all of them than to the families over on the main beach, whose shrill voices were carried to her on the breeze, or to the crowd socializing at the bar above the rocks. Or to Lily, in her impenetrable shell of self-absorption. Or to Max, who had sent her a message saying that he would not be returning from Ponza tonight after all.

Thoughts of Max made her muscles twitch. She flipped over onto her belly and began to swim, her legs kicking furiously, her arms slicing through the water. Back and forth she splashed between the rocks and the open sea, swimming through waves of conflicting emotions: hope and fear, liberation and guilt, love and doubt. When she was out of breath, she found a foothold and boosted herself out of the water. She was standing at its edge, still dripping and panting, when she heard a voice call her name in the Italian pronunciation she had grown accustomed to. "*Eeerees!*" She looked up, trying to figure out where the voice had originated. "*Eeerees!*" she heard again, this time spotting a woman standing by the umbrellas up at the bar, waving both hands over her head.

"Bea!" Iris waved back, recognizing the slender silhouette in the long skirt. Beatrix made a circling gesture with her arm, and Iris raised her hand in an "OK" sign. She could use a friend right now, and didn't have many to choose from; her old "friends" were Gregorio's and her new ones Max's. She just wasn't sure whether in her current state of confusion she could handle the crowd scene at the bar, or Bea's *Sex and the City* psychology. But she was deeply fond of her, and they had not seen each other since before Iris had left on her trip with Max over a month ago, a lifetime ago. She wrapped her towel around her, wriggled out of her wet bikini and into her sundress, wrung the water from her hair, and made her way back up the rocks.

"It's so good to see you, Bea," Iris said, leaning over to kiss Beatrix's cheeks.

"Yuk! You're dripping all over me," Beatrix said, holding her at arm's length, and kissing the air instead.

Iris couldn't help but smile at her friend's theatrics. "I thought you were still in Milan," she said.

"I get the impression I still am," Beatrix said, flipping a wrist at the Friday evening cluster of young men and women dressed to happy hour perfection, talking loudly in their Milanese accents, laughing and smoking and sipping on trendy cocktails, while the locals sucked beer from bottles and nibbled on focaccia.

"I had a feeling I'd find you here when you didn't answer your phone," Bea said.

Iris had actually seen the call before leaving home, and felt a little guilty about not answering, but she knew Bea would never understand how thirty minutes squandered on conversation would never equal the same number of minutes spent swimming in the setting sun.

"As you can see, I was swimming," Iris said.

"I figured as much," Bea said, with a note of resignation in her voice. Iris had long since stopped asking Bea to go swimming with her, and Bea had finally understood that Iris would rather shoot herself in the foot than spend a day with her on the beach, chatting and roasting on lounge chairs. Despite their differences, it gave Iris a good feeling to know so much about another person, and to have another person know so much about her. By now, Beatrix knew more things about her life than her own sisters did.

"How are you doing?" Bea asked, taking Iris by the hand and leading her to the table she had staked out for them. The concern in Bea's voice tickled her tear ducts, but Iris resisted; she had cried enough on this lovely summer day.

"Oh, all right, I guess," she said, as they sat down. "I'm still reeling, though. Too much travel and too much emotion packed into one week."

"I'll bet everyone was glad to see you," Bea said.

"I suppose. I know I was glad to see them, especially my sisters.

Even though it wasn't exactly a happy occasion. I still can't believe Auntie Rosa is gone."

"You should have stayed longer," Bea said. "You should have taken the time to work through your grief with people who really know you, people who care, people who share your feelings."

"Maybe. But once the funeral was over, everyone disbanded pretty quickly. They all had their own lives to get back to: their jobs, their kids, their houses. Sometimes I feel like I don't really belong, like no one really knows me anymore. The Iris who flies back and forth to visit is not the same twenty-year-old girl who left."

"Has it ever occurred to you that they don't see who you really are because you won't let them?" Bea asked. Talking to Bea, especially when they hadn't seen each other in some time, was like going to a restaurant famished and immediately being served a hearty entrée. Iris took a moment to digest her comment before answering.

"I know I haven't been very good at sharing the things that embarrass me," she said, speaking with some difficulty. "I can't help worrying about what people will think when they find out Iris hasn't always been such a good little girl. I never really admitted that to myself until one day when I was talking to Lily."

"Wait a minute - you talked to Lily?"

"Yes, I did. We were with Auntie Rosa together when she died. It was a very intense experience. But I don't feel like getting into that story just yet - not without a drink." Iris gazed at the horizon, just as the last glowing speck of sun dipped behind the hills, leaving in its wake a gouache of pinks and purples that spilled from sky to sea, coating the water in a violet sheen, its reflection making everything and everyone look smoother, softer, more mysterious.

"We'll take a bottle of that Corsican rosé - nice and chilled," Beatrix said to the server, who had appeared as if on cue, clad in his usual attire of shorts, T-shirt and sandals. Bea glanced at Iris for approval; Iris nodded. No sense pretending a glass or two would see them through a conversation of any substance.

"Anyway, family matters aside, I did have to get back," Iris said when they were alone again. "I literally just ran off on Max, you know."

"Speak of the devil. I was just going to ask you about Max. Where the heck is he, anyway?"

"Ponza," Iris said, hoping Bea would let her leave it at that.

Bea arched her eyebrows. "Is he planning on gracing you with his presence anytime soon?"

Knowing Bea would keep pestering her until she provided a satisfactory explanation, Iris accepted one of the two cigarettes her friend had taken from her cigarette case and lit for them. Iris choked on the first puff, wondering for the umpteenth time why she bothered smoking.

"Max has a deadline to meet," Iris said. "Which is why he hasn't been able to get away." She took a deeper drag this time and held it in her lungs before exhaling. "I was thinking of going down there, but I haven't exactly been in the right frame of mind. And Max agreed that I should just stay put and recover. He said he didn't want me to get exhausted traipsing back and forth since he has to come up to Milan soon anyway."

"What a dear boy," Beatrix said, tilting her head and blowing smoke slowly into the air. "What's going on in Milan?"

"Max has been looking for a chance to get a foot in the door with those Mediaset people. It's all connected to that film project of his. He's been trying to set up a meeting, and he says it's only a matter of days now. As soon as that's confirmed, he'll head up to Milan, then back here, and after that, we'll take a ferry from Genoa and pick up where he left off." It sounded like a good plan to Iris; logical, convenient. She searched Bea's face for a reaction, but couldn't see her eyes through the lenses of her sunglasses.

"How is he ever managing without you?" she said.

"Oh, that assistant of his didn't waste ten minutes getting her pretty little ass down there to take my place," Iris spit out the information, before deciding whether she wanted to. Bea just shook her head and laughed.

"And what about the work you were doing? The writing?"

"Between you and me, this so-called job of mine seems so bogus. I've been giving it my best, and I always submit my work before the deadline. I even managed to finish the piece on Carloforte while I was away." Iris recalled the tear-filled days of the wake and funeral, followed by the sleepless nights in Violet's guest room, her head propped up on a pillow, her laptop warming her thighs. That was one benefit of suffering from insomnia and not having any drugs around - the days were twice as long.

"And to think you have been accused of having no sense of duty," Bea said, a sardonic smile on her glossy lips.

"For all the good it does me," Iris said. "No one ever acknowledges anything. I don't even know whether anyone reads what I write, whether they like it, whether they'll ever use it. I don't even really see why they pay me. Max tells me to just take the money and stop worrying."

"You don't sound like the optimistic Iris I know and love," Bea said, raising her Gucci sunglasses from her nose and parking them on her head. As the waiter approached, the two friends leaned back in their chairs: Iris with her soggy mop of curls and the one-size-fits-all sundress purchased at the market in Rapallo; Beatrix with her professionally styled hair brushing the collar of her linen tunic, her crossed legs and pedicured feet peeking out from the slit in her fashionable wrap-around skirt. They smoked in silence as the waiter set down the bottle without showing them the label, opened it without sniffing the cork, poured out two full glasses of pale pink liquid without suggesting they taste it, set down a plate of focaccia squares and mortadella cubes. His only concession to his role was the slight bow he performed before retreating.

"Is there something else I should know?" Bea continued after they had performed their ritual of touching glasses with a *"cin cin."*

"Oh, it's not only about the work, it's just - " Iris wasn't really sure she wanted the conversation to take this direction, but she was tired of holding everything inside.

"It's just what?" Bea prompted her.

"Well, if Max lost someone he loved, I would do everything in my power to stay close to him. He knows I have no one else here except you, but he didn't even ask whether you were around."

"Did you tell him you need him to come home?"

"No," Iris said, taking another sip of wine. "It would only make him feel bad. He can't just drop everything and leave because of me."

"He can't?"

"Of course not. He's on a tight schedule, and everything's all set up weeks in advance when he films those segments." It was true; Iris had seen it for herself, she had even helped make the arrangements.

"So what would you like him to do?"

"Well, there are ways of being close to someone without being physically in the same place. You can talk to them about their feelings on the phone, for example. You can console them. But I know that's not fair of me, either."

"What's not fair?"

"Expecting Max to get over his past as if it were a case of chicken pox. I have to keep reminding myself how traumatized he was by his parents' death. He simply wouldn't be able to cope with seeing me all weepy and sad, but it's not because he doesn't care about me. It's because witnessing my grief would trigger a whole series of mechanisms that would throw him completely off balance."

"So he keeps his balance by working, leaving you to deal with your mourning all alone?" Bea leaned toward Iris and stabbed a cube of mortadella with a toothpick.

"I can handle it; Max can't," Iris said, her voice strong with resolve as she ground her cigarette butt into the ashtray. "Now that we've talked it over, I realize it's for the best he couldn't come back today. This will give me a little more time to get myself together. I've been such a downer."

"Whoa! Hold on. Let me get this straight. You're expected to tend to all his needs, put up with him when he's depressed, change your plans - not to mention your entire life - to suit his, but then you have to play the smiling muse and nursemaid even when you have shit of your own to deal with?"

"Well, I wouldn't exactly put it that way."

"What other way would you put it? Honestly, Iris, what are you, some kind of Florence Nightingale? Are you on a humanitarian mission to save the weak and troubled? Are you hoping to reap your rewards in another life? Because I'll be damned if you are going to see any in this one unless you learn how to demand what you are entitled to. Entitlement. That's the keyword. Learn it."

Either Iris wasn't able to explain herself, or Bea wasn't able to understand. And she was irritated by her friend's gratuitous advice, the same way she had been irritated when Gregorio made her ask for Sundays off and a week's vacation before she had even started her new job; and when Max pestered her to demand more money from Gregorio, from Signora Mangiagallo, and even from the people at RAI. She didn't want to demand anything from anyone. And all she wanted from Bea now was a little support – if she wanted to give it.

"Maybe you could go easy on me tonight?" she said.

"I'm serious, Iris."

"I know you are. I appreciate your concern. But can we give it a rest for now? Please?"

"So when will Max be home?"

"As soon as he can," Iris said. "He promised. Enough about me, though. Tell me what kind of trouble you've been getting yourself into lately."

As the women sipped and talked, a lopsided moon rose over the promontory of Portofino and began inching its way up and across the sky. *Gobba a levante, luna calante, gobba a ponente, luna crescente.* Iris always resorted to the rhyme to figure out whether the moon was waning or waxing, coming or going. She wished there were a rhyme that could help her figure that out about herself.

A procession of small fishing boats was setting off from Camogli, complacently allowing the lead *gozzo* to tow them out to sea, the lights of their *lampare* blinking as the boats rocked to and fro on the waves. Beatrix took Iris up on her suggestion and began chatting about a revelation that had come to her during a recent session with her shrink, but Iris was far away, lost in thoughts of her own, scrutinizing the darkening horizon in search of something she thought might be out there, but couldn't quite see.

"Ciao, Capo! Sono arrivato!"

Iris was squatted over the plants in her terrace when Max's voice broke the sleepy afternoon silence. The unexpected intrusion knocked her off balance and straight into the arms of a prickly pear plant.

"Yikes!" she squealed, as the thorns stabbed her in the butt. The terrace had seemed so spacious when she signed the one-year lease for the apartment, and indeed there was plenty of room for the sage and basil and rosemary plants, as well as for the potted lilac bush and lemon tree, which she hoped to plant in the garden of a permanent home one day soon. It was the growing colony of cacti for which Max had a passion that made her feel cramped; no matter how cautiously she moved about, she was always getting jabbed and pricked and poked at.

"Max!" she cried, her heart lunging as she rushed to greet him, wiping the sweat from her brow with the hem of her T-shirt. "I can't believe you're here!"

The loneliness and anxiety that had plagued her during their separation vanished at the sight of Max standing there in the hallway, doused in the golden afternoon sun streaming through the windows, his rumpled clothes and mocha skin lending him the intriguing aspect of an adventurous traveler hailing from some exotic corner of the globe. Grinning that smile she had missed so much, he dipped a shoulder to lower his dusty backpack to the floor. He looked every bit as happy to see her as she was to see him, and the moment she felt his arms around her, all those nasty little doubts that had been nagging her in his absence flew right out the open door.

"Why didn't you tell me you were coming today?" she said.

"I thought you liked surprises," Max said.

"Of course I do!" Iris said. Of course she did. But she also liked to be physically and psychologically prepared for things. She would have taken a shower, for example, and dressed in a cute outfit, and done something with her hair. She would have put on a little make-up, and some nail polish. All those little touches that Max liked. But none of those things were really important; the important thing was that Max was home.

Iris nuzzled her face in his chest, blinking back tears of emotion, drinking in his familiar scent. "I missed you so much!"

"I missed you too, Capo," Max said, taking her chin in his hand and tilting her mouth to his. The warmth of his full, moist lips and the slightly sour taste of his tongue made the blood rush to her head and her body throb with desire. When he released her, and they stood facing each other, she knew he felt the same way. They needed each other, and they would satisfy each other but first, they had a lot of catching up to do.

"*Permesso?*" A grating female voice announced a pair of skittish brown eyes, an aquiline nose and a crooked mouth peeking through the door Max had left ajar. Iris's lips twitched, determined to hold her smile in place, as she tilted her head inquisitively at Max.

"*Vieni avanti, Silli!*" Max said. "Come on in, don't be shy." Shy was not the first word Iris would have used to describe the compact brunette who bounced into her living room within a nanosecond of the invitation. "Silli, this is Iris," Max said.

"Silly?" Iris said.

"Well, it's really Silvana," Max said. Silli's just a nickname I gave her."

Iris was used to Max bringing unexpected guests over for dinner, or for the weekend, or for an impromptu party. One day it was wrap day, another day it was a birthday, another day it was have fun with your friends day. Today was different, though. Today she wanted Max to herself. She wondered who the woman was (in addition to being Silli) and why and when Max would give her a nickname. But not wanting to embarrass Max or his friend with such blunt questions, she extended her hand politely, and said, "*Piacere.*"

Tolerant, or even sympathetic, was perhaps a word Iris could use to describe the smile on the face of the woman Max called Silli as she shook her hand, but certainly not friendly. Quickly dropping Iris's hand (noticing the potting soil under her nails, Iris couldn't blame her), the woman's attention was directed to her surroundings. Iris followed the shifty eyes as they inspected the apartment, making her feel self-conscious about the mismatched pieces of furniture that had settled in like homeless relatives. Iris wondered why she felt the impulse to explain to this stranger that at one time she had owned finer furniture and that she certainly would again in the future, once she and Max moved to a permanent place of their own.

The afternoon was hot and still, and the air in the sun-filled room was quickly overpowered by Max's body odor and the woman's musky perfume. Iris felt sticky, and her butt throbbed from its encounter with the cactus.

"How can you stand it like this?" Max asked as he went around the room, closing all the windows, and switching on the air conditioning full blast. Iris detested air conditioning, but unfortunately, it had come with the apartment. The thin layer of perspiration she had worked up on the terrace instantly froze on her skin; she sneezed.

"*Cazzo*, that's a Vanesi, isn't it?" the woman said, pointing the manicured index finger of an arm bejeweled with bangles to the giant unframed canvas hanging on the wall behind the sofa. That this nicknamed visitor was no stranger to Massimiliano Vanesi was obvious, but that she could recognize Max's pathos in a painting made her wonder even more about their connection.

"*Colpevole!*" Max laughed. "I plead guilty; it's mine."

Iris averted her eyes from the painting; the dark forms lurking beneath the wild spattering of acrylic angst reminded her of Dolores's last paintings and filled her with a sense of doom. Her only consolation was that it would be gone before long, as soon as Max fell prey to another bout of depression, and produced a new masterpiece to hang in its place.

"Do you have more canvases here?" Silvana whatever-her-last-name-was asked Max as if nothing in the world could interest her more. Perhaps that explained her presence here; maybe Max had convinced her to buy or barter a painting; maybe she owned a gallery.

"Sure. If you're a good girl, I'll show them to you later. There are plenty down in the storage room."

The mention of the storage room made Iris cringe; every time she went there to look for something, she was irked by the way Max had buried her belongings under all the paraphernalia he had brought from Rome and dumped there: defunct movie equipment he couldn't bear to part with; musty camping gear from the summer after high school when he had hitchhiked to Morocco; the fishing tackle he still hadn't used; the bicycle he had ridden once down to Camogli, but couldn't pedal back up the hill; and, to top of the tottering piles of crap, the prolific manifestations of his most recently discovered artistic talent.

Though Iris was disturbed by his work, painting seemed to be an effective form of therapy for Max during his tumultuous mood swings, so she had done what she could to encourage him. She had bought him an easel, and a plastic sheet to cover the terracotta tiles on the terrace where he liked to paint. But when inspiration grabbed Max, it did not waste time on preparations; he grabbed his tubes of paint and brushes and began his unrestrained splashing and smearing. When Iris arrived with the plastic sheet in hand, Max waved her away, saying that any interruption would spoil the spontaneity of the creative process, that it would be like trying to put on a condom in the middle of an orgasm. She wondered if she would be able to explain that to the landlord when it came time to move out.

"OK, later it is, but you have to promise!" Silvana said to Max, as she plopped down on the sofa. Iris wondered what Max intended by "later," and what the woman was planning to do at her house between now and then besides act like she owned the place.

"Capo, I know you have lots to tell me," Max said, sitting down next to Silvana. "But first you gotta hear about this amazing coincidence!" It was as if he could read her mind, and by now, she knew he actually could, to some extent. She hated to be cynical, but she had noticed that Max was very good at knowing how and when to dole out the information, the attention, the praise, and the criticism he gave her, in order to lead her where he wanted her to go.

"Aren't you curious?" Max said.

"About what?" Iris said, distracted by her reflections.

"About the coincidence I was telling you about."

"Yes, sure. The amazing coincidence. Go on."

Max grinned. "I was getting my visitor's badge at the Mediaset reception area, and I heard this voice calling my name. A voice I hadn't heard in ages, but recognized instantly!"

"This voice, let me guess, belonged to, um … " Iris searched for a way to avoid pronouncing her name without being rude, but couldn't. "Silvana?" she said, immediately regretting it, as she perceived the status of the woman on her sofa shift ever so slightly, but irrevocably, from that of stranger to acquaintance.

"How did you know?" Max said, slapping his knee.

"Female intuition?" Iris smiled.

"Anyway, Silvana works right there, at Mediaset. How fuckin' amazing is that? She introduced me around to a few people after my meeting. While we were having lunch, she told me she just bought an apartment in San Rocco!"

"Oh, you had lunch? How nice." He had time for lunch, but not time to call her and tell her he was coming home. Or that he would be bringing a visitor.

"Did you hear what I said? An apartment in San Rocco! You can walk there from here!" Max chuckled as he looked from Iris, to Silvana, to Iris again.

"How convenient," Iris said, not sure why or for whom it might prove convenient, but afraid to find out.

"She was planning to drive down tomorrow to check on the contractors - the place is being totally renovated – but I told her why not come with me today? Who wants to stick around Milan on a Friday night, you know?"

"Of course," Iris nodded, her mind busily fitting together each tidbit of time-released information. A house undergoing renovations … a capacious shoulder bag on the floor by Silvana's feet … a foot in the door here, a foot in the door there. A clear picture was forming. She knew how to recognize the signs by now.

"I figured why not let her sleep on the sofa bed?" Max finally spit it out. "Silli wanted me to check with you first, but I said you wouldn't mind. Especially since the sofa bed *is* actually mine."

Silvana made a little bouncing movement on the sofa and laughed. "It still has a good spring to it."

"Cut the shit, Silli, or you'll get me in trouble here," Max said, punching her playfully in the arm, then turning to Iris while Silli made a show of suppressing more giggles. "Don't pay any attention to her, Capo. In case you're wondering, Silli and me are just old friends."

Iris had already met several of Max's "old friends" in Rome and knew that at some point in time each of the females had taken a bounce or two on some bed with him. Whenever Iris remarked on the frequent occurrence of the phenomenon, Max told her she was old-fashioned, that she'd been a married lady too long, that the past was the past, and that the rest of the world was living in the Third Millenium now, anytime she cared to join in.

Iris just stood there, letting the air conditioning spit cold air in her face. Max stared at Silvana, Silvana stared at Iris, Iris sneezed.

"Why don't you go change, Capo?" Max suggested, turning to her. "And while you're at it, have a look in the mirror; you have dirt all over your nose."

Iris wished she were witty enough to tell him that the dirt on her nose was nothing compared to the pain in her ass, and not the kind caused by the cactus needles. Instead, she apologized. "Sorry, I was doing a little gardening," she said, brushing her nose off with her hand. "I'll grab a quick shower. I'm sure you'll see to it that Silvana gets whatever she needs."

"You'd better close the door," Iris said to Max several hours later, watching him strip off his shirt without unbuttoning it and dropping it to the floor. In the soft light of her bedside lamp, she noticed that his torso was as deeply tanned as his arms. Either he had been working without a shirt on, or had taken plenty of swimming breaks; probably both, judging from her experience on the road with him. Max shut the door, unbuckled his belt, unbuttoned the fly of his white jeans. He lowered them to his knees, then stepped out of them, stomping on the cuffs to free his feet. Iris was already in bed, lying naked beneath the sheet she had slipped under while Max was in the bathroom.

Ever since the promising kiss Max had planted on her lips that afternoon when he breezed through the door, Iris had felt a desperate desire rising inside her, despite her disappointment that they were not alone, despite the stabs of jealousy caused by Silvana's presence - or perhaps in part because of them. Iris had spoken little as the three of them strolled from Ruta to San Rocco, stopping at the historic Nicco's bar for an *aperitivo* before Silvana showed them where her new house was, then stopping again on their way home for a plate of *pansotti*. Throughout the evening, she had been constantly distracted by the scenes conjured up by her fidgety imagination, first picturing Max and Silvana making love, then imagining Max and herself making love later. Max had been fondling Iris in front of Silvana all evening, resting his hand on her buttocks as they walked, nipping at her neck, caressing her bare thighs as they chatted over Americanos and watched the sun set. Each time Iris caught Silvana watching Max touch her, she felt a strange thrill. By the time she pulled out the sofa bed for Silvana and retreated to her room, Iris no longer felt like the helpless little mouse being pawed at by the cat, she felt like the cat.

"You still have to tell me about your trip," Max said, standing in front of her. She knew he wanted her, too.

"Not now," Iris said. The time for sobbing and seeking solace in his arms was over; she had survived without his sympathy, and now she needed his substance. She needed passion to crush her loneliness. She needed joy to squelch her sadness. She needed to reconnect with Max; she needed him to convince her that she belonged in Italy, that they belonged together, and that nothing else or no one else mattered.

Max slowly pulled back the sheet, exposing Iris's nudity. Thanks to her loss of appetite combined with her obsession with running and swimming, her body was tanned and thin. Just the way Max liked it. The intensity of his gaze made her skin burn, and her hips rise in invitation. Max slipped a hand between her thighs and spread them apart. She was hot and slippery and his fingers had barely touched her when she arched her back, biting her lip to silence her cry of pleasure. Max entered her with a hard thrust, a loud moan escaping him as the bed frame was pushed up against the wall.

"Shhh!" Iris whispered, but Max pushed harder, the banging of the bed frame growing louder and faster with each of his guttural grunts and groans. "Silvana will hear us!" she said.

Max grabbed Iris by the hips and flipped her over onto her tummy. When he shoved himself inside her, the bed slammed against the wall, and Iris cried out in pain. Max howled, shuddered, and collapsed on top of her.

"Well, good morning, Capo," Max said to Iris as she stumbled into the kitchen. She wondered how long he and Silvana had been sitting on their stools chatting.

"Rough night?" Silvana said, raising her eyebrows over the demitasse from which she sipped espresso.

Iris blushed, recalling Max's bedroom antics. She had crashed after their lovemaking and slept better than she had in days, but this morning she felt a vague sense of lack rather than a sense of satisfaction. She was probably just suffering from emotional overload; she would probably bounce back after a cup of strong coffee.

"Beautiful day, isn't it?" Iris said.

"It sure is," Max said. "In fact, it's so fucking beautiful that we hatched a great idea while you were sleeping."

"Can I have some coffee first?" Iris said, lifting the lid on the Bialetti. Empty. She unscrewed the coffee pot and dumped out the used grounds.

"You know what I was telling you yesterday? About those people Silli introduced me to?" Max said.

"At Mediaset?" Iris asked, refilling the bottom section of the coffee pot with water, then dropping in the filter basket.

"Yeah - well, it would be a huge push for me if I got to know them better," Max said. "There's a few of them in particular I need to feel out - for my movie project." She sniffed the aroma of the coffee as she spooned it into the basket, passed her index finger along the outer rim to clean it, then screwed on the top. She put the pot on the burner and turned on the flame, wondering who would spew it out first, Max or the coffee pot.

"Silli texted them all, and we already got twelve answers," Max said.

"Really?" Iris said, looking up at him and smiling. "They're interested in the project? That's fantastic!" She had been hearing him talk about his film project for so long she was beginning to have serious doubts it would ever get off the ground. But the few times she had tried to ask Max for more specific information about the status of things, he had brushed off her questions and accused her of not believing in him.

"Well for now, at least we got them to come!" Max said.

"Come where?" The hairs on her forearm tingled, sensing the danger before her brain did.

"Here, that's where. For a party! Tonight!"

Iris looked at Max, then at Silvana, then at Max again. "You invited people over for a party here? Tonight?" Her head was throbbing; she hoped the coffee would start bubbling up soon.

"All thanks to Silli," Max said. "She's goddamn amazing." Silvana beamed.

"How many people, Max?" Iris said, her voice flat. Trying to talk Max out of a plan once it was set in motion was like trying to scoop live eels into a bucket.

"Oh, no big deal, I'd say about twenty, tops," Max said, glancing at Silvana, who shrugged.

"Most of them will probably bring someone, a girlfriend, a husband - whatever," she said. "Maybe forty, maybe thirty. Maybe more, maybe less. These guys are unpredictable." She laughed and shrugged, the way the lenient mother of a rambunctious boy would dismiss complaints of his tomfoolery in the classroom.

"Iris knows what to do," Max said to Silvana. "It's not exactly our first party, and she did use to manage a hotel, you know." Turning back to Iris, he said, "So Capo, here's the plan. You take care of the food since that's one thing you're good at it. Remember, this is not a dinner party. No one's really coming to eat, so don't go overboard like you always do. I'll drop Silli off at her place, then I'll go stock up on the booze."

Coffee gurgled on the stove, filling the kitchen with its rich aroma. Iris took a mug from the cupboard and poured herself the entire pot, feeling guilty, but only moderately so, for not offering any to the others. It was going to be a long day.

Cooking was one of the few things for which Max complimented Iris, and he was right about one thing: She *was* good at it. Years in the hospitality business had taught her whether fish came before meat in a menu, which wines to serve with each and all kinds of other useful information. But the joy of cooking for a crowd stemmed from the times when there was only one course to choose from when appetites needed no goading, and no matter how many people crowded around the table, there was always enough food for one more. She recalled the fun she and Lily used to have in the kitchen, getting dinner started for their mother when she first stepped out of her domestic domain and into the working world. But from the day their mother stepped away altogether, cooking became a daily chore for the girls, and Lily soon lost all interest.

Cooking never bothered Iris, though, even when it was a duty. She remembered the last time she had prepared a meal for a large group of people, not very many days ago. It had been at Violet's house, after Auntie Rosa's funeral, when she had pulled out the biggest pot in the pantry and cooked up some pasta for the entire Capotosti clan. While the brothers drank beer and talked in the backyard, the sisters all pitched in to help. Jasmine and Violet, Marguerite and Iris chatted and sipped wine as they shared tasks and tears and laughter, secrets and truths and anecdotes. Lily had been unusually silent, though, drinking diet Coke as she chopped celery for the salad. Their mother, who had sat in a back pew at the funeral and hugged Iris afterwards, had gone home with her soft-spoken husband, possibly no longer capable of coping with so many Capotostis in one place.

The family reunion had filled Iris with such joy, that if it hadn't been a funeral, it would have been a fabulous party. The contrast between then and now saddened her as she cooked for the unspecified number of strangers who would soon invade her home. Today there were no peals of laughter or comments from people about how good the food smelled punctuating the sounds of her slicing and dicing. Her vision blurred by welling tears (she blamed the onions on the cutting board), Iris misdirected the knife and chopped off a chunk of skin from her middle finger instead.

"Shit!" she cried, sticking her finger under a stream of cold water, watching her blood swirl down the drain with an odd sense of loss and detachment. She wrapped a paper towel around her finger and went to get a bandage from the medicine cabinet.

As she was leaving the bathroom, she noticed Max's backpack sitting on top of the washing machine. Between Silli and the party, she had not yet had the opportunity to discuss travel plans with Max, but knowing he was not likely to give her much advance notice about their departure date, she thought it wise to get a head start on preparations and throw his clothes in the washer before getting back to her cooking. Dumping the soiled garments onto the floor, she wrinkled her nose at the ripe bouquet of odors and began frisking the items with pockets, where she discovered wads of used tissues, handfuls of sand, a small collection of seashells she assumed were for her, and various crumpled receipts and notes, which she set aside for him. While patting down his favorite khaki shorts, she came across a small, rectangular object she immediately identified as a mobile phone. Shaking her head and tsking her tongue at his absent-mindedness, she removed the phone from the pocket, cringing to think how upset Max would have been if she had run it through the wash. She started the machine and returned to the kitchen, where she set the phone and the other salvaged items on the counter and resumed her race against the clock with the added handicap of a bandaged finger. She was interrupted by the ringing of her home phone.

"*Pronto?*" Iris said, picking up the cordless.

"It's me, Capo!" Max said. It made her happy to hear him in such high spirits. But she would be curious to know how much of his cheerfulness could be attributed to their reunion, how much to the prospect of a party which might also lead to new business, and how much to the presence of a one-woman fan club by the name of Silli. It was probably a three-way split. "I just wanted to check whether you were already home from the market," he continued. "But since you picked up, I guess that answers my question. Do you need anything else while I'm out?"

"No, thanks. I found everything I needed at the market, and I'm already cooking," Iris said, cradling the phone on her shoulder as she stirred the cubed eggplant frying in one skillet, and the onions, celery, tomatoes, and capers in the other. Caponata always went over well, and it was a convenient dish to prepare in advance. "Are you with Silvana?"

"No, I'm picking her up in a few minutes because she wants to see where I buy the candles and torches. Why?"

"I was just wondering where you're calling me from."

"What are you talking about? From my phone, no?"

The vegetables were starting to stick; she grabbed the olive oil to add some, but the bottle slipped from her hand and crashed to the floor.

"Oh, no!" she cried.

"What's going on?" Max said.

"Nothing, I'm just making a big mess. I have to go. I guess you'd better pick up some olive oil. *Ciao.*"

"Sure, Capo. *Ciao.*"

Iris tossed the phone onto the table, spread paper towels over the oily floor, and was about to combine the contents of the two skillets before they burned when from the corner of her eye she saw a light flashing on the counter. By the time she finished what she was doing, the flashing had stopped. By the time she wiped off her hands, it had started again. She glanced at the silently flashing cell phone and saw the name "PonzaLor" on the display. She stared at the device for a moment, trying to decide whether or not to answer. If Max had his phone with him, and she had found this one in his pocket, it must belong to someone else, and maybe that person had lost it. Something about the name flashing on the display was familiar, though; it had something to do with the system Max used when storing his contacts' numbers, according to location. In this case, it would mean that the caller was in some way connected with his work in Ponza, while "Lor" would be an abbreviation of that person's name. Which in turn would mean that this caller – perhaps a man named Lorenzo, for example - was looking for Max, not for the device. When the flashing stopped again, the screen updated the tally: 6 missed calls, 12 new messages.

It was possible that this was a work phone the production people had provided Max as a fringe benefit, and if so, maybe she should let him know someone was trying desperately to get in touch with him. Or maybe she should check what this person wanted, to save him the time and bother. Or maybe she was just giving herself an excuse to pry.

Growing up with a total lack of privacy had made Iris appreciate it as a sacrosanct right. She always respected Max's privacy, but there had been some instances of his behavior in the past – the enigmatic expressions and truncated conversations when she walked into a room, the sudden solo trips to Rome to "check on things" - that made her vaguely uncomfortable, but which she did not question out of fear of being considered jealous or old-fashioned. Whether prompted by a surge of female intuition, or a sarcastic remark of Lily's, or an eye-roll of Bea's, or a whisper of Auntie Rosa's, Iris's index finger began pressing keys on the cell phone. All six missed calls were from "PonzaLor," as were all the unread messages. The information was not enough to satisfy her curiosity, but more than enough to arouse her suspicions. All she needed was to read one message then she could forget about it and get back to her cooking before she burned everything. Of course, she would then have to cancel the message if she didn't want Max to know it had been tampered with, but she had to do what she had to do. She would cross that bridge when she came to it. She tapped on the most recent message:

Max!! Why aren't you answering my calls??

The message certainly couldn't be considered compromising. All it confirmed was that this phone Iris knew nothing about did indeed belong to Max. Maybe PonzaLor was some guy connected with his assignment. She'd have to read another one to be sure.

When are you coming back to finish what you started?

That made sense. Max had rushed off when he got the OK for the Mediaset meeting, and he must have left some unfinished business. She felt reassured. Sort of. But maybe she should read another.

The moon we shared that night has vanished. But not the memory of what happened.

What moon? What memory? What happened? Iris held her breath, her fingertip poised over the next message.

The thought of you with another woman is driving me insane.

Her racing heart throbbed, her rushing blood pounded in her ears together with the sizzling, bubbling, and boiling sounds of the vegetables screaming for attention. She turned to the stove, switched off all the burners and, weak-kneed and shaking, leaned against the refrigerator for support, realizing that she, Iris, was the other woman. Her back slid down the cold steel door, her feet slipping and sliding in olive oil until she found herself on the floor. She sat there, curled into a ball, tears rolling down her cheeks, spasms gripping her gut, as with trembling fingers she searched the phone's memory for evidence that this Ponza woman was delusional, that she was misinterpreting Max's harmless flirtation, that it was all a big mistake.

Iris quickly reviewed her options and decided she should do nothing, at least not for now. She abhorred melodrama, and it was too late to call the party off without creating a scene. She would pull herself together, keep a close eye on Max, then confront him tomorrow, when they would finally be alone. There still might be a logical explanation; after all, there was no trace of any sent calls or text messages from that phone. Iris had taken too many risks, made too many sacrifices, caused too much pain, invested too much of herself in their relationship to throw it all away over a misunderstanding. She hid the phone in a cupboard, then went to the bathroom and splashed cold water on her face. A pair of frightened red eyes blinked back at her from the mirror, as she patted her splotched face with a towel then opened the medicine cabinet and took out her box of little blue pills. She popped one out and put it in her mouth, bending and tipping her head under the faucet to gulp the water that dribbled down her cheek and chin, then went back to the kitchen to clean up the mess on the floor, and finish preparing for the party.

Out on the terrace, Silvana giggled and sputtered, waving a hand theatrically in front of her face, while Max fanned the charcoal he was attempting to ignite in the grill. He had bought both on a whim while out shopping with Silvana after they had been struck with the brilliant idea that barbecued pork ribs would be a fun addition to whatever Iris had planned. The living room and kitchen were filling with smoke, and Iris had already spotted a few of their neighbors leaning out from their balconies to see where it was coming from. Although Iris knew she could do a better job negotiating with both the neighbors and the grill, she was determined to let Max deal with it. She wanted no part of his porkfest, and besides, every American woman knew that grill duty fell to the man of the house. As for her duties as hostess, Iris had managed to fix everything on time, including her appearance. Cooking always calmed her nerves, and with the help of another pill or two, her internal organs seemed to be under control again. Congratulating herself on her composure, she poured herself a glass of the wine Max and Silvana were already drinking, just as the first guests rang the bell.

Throughout the course of the evening, no one - not even Max, who was busy entertaining the new circle of friends gathered around his half-charred, half-raw pile of pork - seemed to notice Iris's silence as she slipped in and out of the kitchen setting out trays of food on the buffet table while making sure bottles were uncorked, glasses filled, soiled dishes cleared. No one seemed to expect that she would participate in the animated conversations revolving around television programs and personalities, soccer players and politicians, love affairs and upcoming vacations.

Despite not giving a damn about any of the people milling around the buffet and heaping their plates with the food she had prepared, it gave Iris a certain satisfaction to watch the expressions on their faces as they gorged themselves. Sometimes it was interesting to step back and observe from a distance; it helped you see things you wouldn't notice close up. Take Max, for example. She wouldn't call his style of flirtation harmless; lascivious would be a more accurate adjective. And the crude jokes he exchanged with the men were idiotic and vulgar. As the alcohol flowed, the voices around her grew louder, the behavior more deplorable. Though she herself could not eat a thing, she gripped her wineglass tight all night. It reassured her - and also prevented her from being mistaken for hired help.

She tried to remember a comment Lily had made that day at her house, something about looking at people through a window or something. That was sort of how she felt now, as she watched Max and his buddies. Sort of detached, like she wasn't really there, like she was on the outside looking in. But that wasn't quite what Lily had said. It was hard to remember now, what with all the talking, and the music, and the wine.

Iris detested getting up to a mess in the morning, but Max held the view that cleaning up was a downer after a good party. In the end, they each always did as they liked. Iris squeezed one more glass into the dishwasher, and started the machine, not caring whether it disturbed anyone's sleep. She glanced over at Silvana, sprawled on her back and snoring, having conked out before she could change out of her clothes or pull open the sofa bed. Max had still not satisfied his desire to play with fire and was amusing himself by the grill, having rustled up enough embers to ignite the used paper napkins and any other burnable waste.

Now that she was alone with him, Iris knew she could not wait until the next morning to confront Max, though she had no idea what she should say or do. The only thing she knew for certain was that she could not share her bed with him until she discovered the truth. "Play it by ear," Auntie Rosa would say. "We'll cross that bridge when we come to it," her mother would say. "Things always work out for you," Lily would say. "What's the worst that could happen?" Iris would say. Plenty, that's what.

Her stomach in knots, Iris retrieved the cell phone from its hiding place in the cupboard; there were new messages and unanswered calls showing on the display, but she had already seen enough. She activated the ringer, and hid the phone in the palm of her hand, then joined Max on the terrace. She approached him slowly, her movements weighed down by the disturbing impressions and uncouth behavior she had glimpsed on many occasions, but chosen not to see until tonight, and by the sobering realization that she may have placed her heart upon an altar of shifting sands.

Max smiled an inebriated grin as she neared, his eyes twinkling with that mischievous glint that had both attracted and agitated Iris from the moment they first met. A pile of smoldering napkins flared, the lights and shadows distorting Max's features. Iris lowered her gaze, waiting for the blaze to burn itself out, and darkness to shield her face. Cigarette butts littered the floor of the terrace and stuck out from the soil of her potted herbs. Pigs! This time they were from Milan instead of Rome, but that's all they were - just another herd of disgusting pigs. A sense of revulsion made Iris jerk up her head and face Max, just as he unzipped his fly.

"Can't be too careful," he snorted, as he pulled out his penis and began urinating on the grill. The glowing embers sizzled, and a final puff of smoke rose in the warm night air.

"Max!" Iris gasped.

"It's just water, Capo. It's good for the plants, too," he said, slurring his words, drawing circles on the ground with his pee before directing it into the pot where her little lilac had recently lost its first and only bloom.

"Stop it! That's my lilac!" she cried.

Max laughed. "If it were in a park, dogs would be pissing on it, wouldn't they?"

Anger and disgust roiled deep inside her like molten lava but lacked the force to break through her crust of fear. She stared at Max with clenched fists and burning cheeks as he finished pissing on her lilac, his face turned toward the night sky, his mouth open in a gaping yawn. As he shook off the final drops of urine, Iris set his phone beside the grill then rushed to the kitchen, where she picked up her own cell phone. She pressed the redial key to call the number she had stored by calling herself from Max's phone, then returned to the terrace just as Max was zipping up his fly, looking startled to see a phone flashing and ringing at him in the night.

"I think that's for you," Iris said.

"What the fuck?" Max said, staring at the phone as if he had never seen one before.

"Aren't you going to answer it?"

"That's not mine. My phone's in my pocket." Max reached into his back pocket, took out another phone and waved it in front of Iris's face. Iris pressed the "end call" key on her phone, and the other one fell silent. Max looked disinterested as he picked up the phone. "One of those assholes probably forgot it. I'll have Silli find out who it belongs to."

"Right. Maybe Silli can also tell me how it got into the pocket of your shorts?"

"You found this in the pocket of my shorts?" Max asked, his eyes now dark and dull under half-closed lids.

"Yes, Max." Why couldn't she just accuse him outright? Maybe because she didn't really want to force a confession out of him. Maybe because she wanted to give him time to come up with one of his highly creative but plausible excuses.

"Oh – now I know what happened. This phone," he said, waving in the air the phone he had taken from his pocket and held in his right hand, "is mine. Only I lost it somewhere on the way to Ponza. So I had to get a new one. This one." He waved in the air the phone in his left hand. "Only then my assistant found the one I lost in one of the equipment cases, so now I have an extra. A spare always comes in handy, you know?"

If Iris hadn't seen those messages, she would have left it at that. In the time she had known him, Max had dropped, smashed and lost more cell phones than most people would own in a lifetime. But she had seen the messages and read them. She needed to know what they meant.

"Especially for all those other women who need to call you and text you?" she said, annoyed to hear her voice sounding so thin and uncertain.

"What women?"

"Women who go by the name of 'PonzaLor.' for example?"

"I don't know what you're talking about."

"Look, Max. I found the phone when I was doing the laundry. It kept ringing, so I looked at it. I didn't mean to, but I happened to see there were all these messages and calls coming from this person. Who is she? What's going on?"

"This is so wrong! You had no right to go snooping around like that! What are you, the fucking CIA?" Iris had heard Max raise his voice before, but never with her. It scared her.

"Max, I'm your ..." Iris began, her voice cracking. What was she to him, anyway? His girlfriend? His woman? His partner? "I'm your companion. And I need to know what this is all about."

"It's not about anything," Max said, his voice reverting to a drunken slur. "It was probably just that Lorella woman, pestering me for advice again. We all stayed at her bed and breakfast, and I was giving her some tips on how to promote the place. It turns out she's from Rome, too. We found out we have some friends in common. That sort of thing."

"That's not the only thing you have in common, is it, Max?" Despite the Xanax and the wine, she could not forget the words she had read. "Don't you have in common this thing that you started and have to finish? And something that happened by the light of the moon?"

"Oh, come on! I can't believe you're making such a big fucking deal out of a couple of text messages!" His words rang with the indignant shrillness of the unjustly accused.

"It *is* a big deal, Max. If a woman is writing those things to you, I can only imagine what you've been writing to her!" Iris felt ready now. She wasn't interested in reasonable explanations anymore. She knew there were none; she had known it from the start.

"Like what?" Max shouted. "Give me an example. Go on."

"There weren't any messages from you. You deleted them all."

"Get your story straight, Iris!" Max yelled. "First it was an accident, and now it turns out you spent the whole day snooping through my stuff!"

"Once I saw what she wrote, I had to know the rest!"

"How about asking me, Iris? Huh?"

"That's what I'm doing. And please lower your voice before someone calls the carabinieri."

"Go ahead, ask me what you want to know," Max hissed. "Go on."

Why was he making her do this? Why couldn't he just deny it all, or admit it all, and be done with it? It wasn't fair for him to force her into the role of interrogator.

"Did you go to bed with her?" she blurted out.

"You *left* me, Iris. You don't know what that did to me when you flew away like that," Max said.

"I didn't 'fly away' from you, Max!" Iris cried. "How can you say that? I went to bury an aunt who was like a mother to me!"

"You abandoned me," Max said. His accusation was laced with that pathetic tone of vulnerability Iris knew so well. Instead of clearing things up, everything he said just confused her more.

"Please, Max!" she pleaded. "Just tell me. Did you go to bed with her?"

"So what if I did?" Max shrugged his shoulders. "It was no big deal."

"Nothing's a big deal to you, is it, Max?" she cried, her jaw quivering. "How could you do that to me? How could you?"

Max threw back his head and laughed. "How could *I*? So it's all right for *you* to screw around on your old man with a rich guy twice your age, huh? And it's all right for *you* to screw around on him again with me. But if *I* make one little slip up, you're suddenly some kind of *saint*, and I'm a fuckin' *sinner*!"

"That's not how it was, and you know that!"

"Yeah – it was worse. You were married, and I'm not. Why don't we just call Gregorio and tell him the whole story, huh? Why don't we see what he thinks?"

Iris couldn't believe this was happening, she couldn't believe the things she was hearing. The anger and hurt were already crushing her, without adding the guilt. It was too much to bear; too much. She hunched over in a stance of defense, her hands on her head, her forearms shielding her face, her chin tucked to her chest. She couldn't stand the sight of him standing there. She couldn't bear the sound of his voice. She couldn't listen to another word.

"*Stop! Please!*" she said, tears streaming down her face.

"The fact is, you're no better than me," Max shouted, pulling her head back by the hair, shoving a finger in her face. "And you know it!"

"Shut up!" Iris screamed, her fists beating the air. "Get out of here! Leave me alone!"

"I'll give you a little time to think it over," Max said, releasing her.

Iris crumbled to the floor, her ears so filled with the sound of her own sobbing she didn't hear him slam the door.

"Feel free to leave anytime," Iris said, her red-rimmed eyes burning and her head throbbing from a sleepless night spent crying in her bed. "But now would be good." She kicked an empty wine bottle across the living room floor just to hear the noise it would make when it slammed into the wall by the sofa. "Bitch," she muttered, walking out onto the balcony. The sea far below was a deep shade of blue, and the air clear enough in the early morning light for her to make out the shape of Genoa's *lanterna* in the distance. She would count to twelve, and if Silvana wasn't gone when she went back inside, she would grab her by the hair and drag her out to the street.

"Learn to live with it!" a voice croaked from the living room. "That's just the way he is."

Iris was picking cigarette butts out of her plants when she heard a slam. She ran to the door and locked it, securing the safety latch for good measure. She grabbed a broom, dustpan and garbage bag from the kitchen, and went back out to the balcony, where she finished cleaning up the litter, then filled the watering can from the outdoor tap. She sprinkled the lilac, filled the can again, then poured more water on the plant to flush it clean. The whole story of the phone, the whole scene with Max seemed like a bad dream. Staring out at the sea, she wondered whether she had been wrong to confront him right after the party when neither one of them was clearheaded. She wondered whether things would have gone differently if she had waited until morning as she had planned. Maybe they would have been able to talk things over, work things out.

Sniffling and wiping her tears from her face with the hem of her T-shirt, she went back inside the empty apartment, where less than forty-eight hours earlier her now broken heart had danced with joy at Max's unexpected reappearance. Though she had removed the bulk of the dirty dishes and glasses while the last of the lingerers were still shooting shots of liquor down their gullets, the living room was a shambles. But as much as it disgusted her to see the whiskey and rum and vodka bottles scattered around the room reeking of smoke and booze, Iris was dying to set to work purging her house of the filth.

She raised a liter of vodka to see how much was left, but remembering she had seen a couple of slutty looking girls and a bald guy with a beard swigging it straight from the bottle, she took it to the kitchen and poured the rest of the liquor down the drain. A wave of nausea made her grip the edge of the sink, as images of finding Lily passed out drunk on her couch flashed through her mind.

Splashing cold water on her face, Iris wondered whether she would be living alone in this house from now on, with no job, no family, no friends. Would she end up like Lily, and Dolores before her, guzzling vodka on her sofa, too?

What if it was over with Max? Would she stay in Italy, or move back to America? Despite two decades of living and working in the country, she knew she would never be Italian; she would never understand certain nuances of its multifaceted culture. How could she, when a Sardinian couldn't really understand the workings of a Venetian's mind, or a Sicilian that of a Milanese? And because of the ways she had changed over the past two decades – as had her family, friends and native country - she never felt truly at home when she went back to America.

Iris had not spoken at length about Max to her sisters, but she had no doubt what they would say if they knew about his little lark. They would dismiss him as an asshole and tell her to kick him out. But she was pretty sure the people she knew here would react differently. The men were likely to chortle and brush it off, maybe even congratulate him when she wasn't around, while the women would adopt their usual boys-will-be-boys attitude, and with a roll of their eyes and a shrug of their shoulders, tell her to get on with it.

For now, that was the only thing Iris could do. Armed with dust rags, furniture polish, and glass cleaner, she went to tackle the living room. The mess inside her and all around her reminded her of how she had tried to put up a good front for Lily when they had cleaned her house together. Stupid Iris, with her stupid illusions that she could turn the project into something fun when even a fool could see Lily didn't even want her there. Lily didn't need Iris or her optimistic platitudes; she didn't need her stupid housecleaning music, or her warm champagne and foolish fixation with celebrating.

Iris wished she could give it another try. She wished Lily would materialize instantly, and they could try cleaning house together again, on her turf this time. Maybe as they worked, Lily could repeat those questions she had asked Iris about her life with Max. Maybe Lily had been filled with good intentions, and not resentful, as Iris had assumed after seeing her eyes dart from Iris's ears to her neck, where Auntie Rosa's diamonds had come to rest.

Even if Lily wasn't around to help clean house, Iris remembered that something else was. She dropped her dust cloth, went to her bedroom, and rummaged through the canvas shoulder bag Violet had given her to use around town, then let her keep for the trip back. She hadn't yet found the courage to empty out the bag, because it contained a few of Auntie Rosa's belongings – her Italian prayer book, her rosary beads, Iris's wedding photograph which no one wanted, but which Iris did not have the heart to simply throw away – in addition to the copy of *Jesus Christ Superstar* she and Lily had listened to while cleaning. Hearing that Iris had lost her copy during a move, Violet had insisted that she take hers. Reaching into a zippered compartment, her fingers found the CD, and behind it, a padded envelope. She opened the envelope, and pulled out another CD, with a note wrapped around it. The sight of Lily's handwriting brought tears to her eyes.

Dear Iris,
You wouldn't let me throw this away, but I don't even want it in the same house with me right now.
Hope it doesn't bring you the same bad luck it brought me.
Love,
Lily
P.S. Thanks for coming over. Really.

Iris knew that listening to Lily's voice, that beautiful voice Iris had always known was meant to be heard by the multitudes, would wrench still more tears from her. But that didn't matter; it was a small price to pay for having Lily there with her. She went into the living room and popped the CD into the cheap portable stereo she kept hoping to replace. She punched the sofa cushions until the indentation left by Silvana's body was beaten out of them, and lay down.

When you look at me, tell me what do you see?
Would you be surprised to learn that in my heart desire burns?
If you look inside my soul, let go of all you think you know
You'll find that I'm a lot like you,
Just someone who hopes their dreams come true

I know I may not have all that it takes
To reach those dreams alone
But with open hearts and open arms
I feel your strength become my own

The sound of Lily's soulful voice carrying a message of hope and dreams quickly melted Iris into a puddle of tears. She thought of her little sister's ravaged dreams, and she thought of her own lost dreams, of the faded fantasies of motherhood and happily ever after that had eluded her during her marriage with Gregorio. She thought of the dreams of a fun-filled future of travel and romance and adventure she shared with Max. Sensuous, spontaneous, Max. But Max was weak, at times fragile. It was her strength that kept him balanced when he was depressed, and her hope and freshness that kept his cynicism in check. He had told her that himself many times, even recently, on the ferry to Carloforte. Like in the lyrics, he felt her strength become his own. Together, maybe their dreams still had a chance.

Lift me up, take me higher
Feel the power; feed the fire
Lift me high above the clouds
Up to a place where dreams come true
Lift me high enough to touch the sun, the stars, the moon

Lily's words kindled enough inspiration in Iris to make her stop sniveling. She might not be in a position to reach for the moon right now, but maybe once she pulled herself together, she could start by lifting herself off of the sofa, then figure out how to lift herself out of this situation she had created. She should have known by now that Max was too complicated to be handled like most men.

Still, there was something Max had said that hurt her more than anything - probably because it was true. She had regretted telling him about her previous affair the moment she had blurted it out one night over their second bottle of wine when they had been playing a game of dare, each of them taking turns sharing their darkest secrets. Max and his stories were starting to make the Iris feel like Snow White, and even the chocolate-stealing episode at Sacred Family and the pot-snatching scheme with Lily and Frances had done little to impress him. That was when she had surprised him with the story of Claudio Olona.

Max was right. She was no better than him. Nor could she blame him for turning her into a cheater. She wasn't being fair, holding Max to a standard that she herself had failed to live up to. She tried to imagine what would have happened if Gregorio had discovered her affair with Claudio Olona at the time. Wouldn't she have deserved the opportunity to explain things? Wouldn't she have begged for a second chance?

Another thought occurred to her: If she had sought certain things in other men, it was because she wasn't getting them from Gregorio. By the same token, if Max was turning to another woman, it must mean that he wasn't getting what he needed from Iris. It was just as she had always feared since the night of that first party in Rome. She wasn't sexy enough, or wild enough, or successful enough to keep a man like him interested.

Max may have plenty of alternatives, but what about Iris? What men could she possibly meet around here, who could share her enthusiasm for living new experiences in new places? Who could make her laugh away the sadness of the past and dream away the boredom of routine? Could she perhaps go skinny-dipping under a full moon with a bank clerk? Could she ride bikes around the Circus Maximus in the pouring rain at three in the morning with an accountant or an engineer? Weren't all men either Gregorios or Maxes?

You hold the power in your hands
To touch what most don't understand
So trust your heart, you'll know just what to do
Lift me up, I'm reaching out for you.

Iris rummaged through her pocket for a tissue to catch her dripping snot, but they were all soggy and shredded. She picked up a dust cloth and blew her nose into it. She had told Lily to trust her heart when she saw her little boys, and now Lily was telling her the same thing with her song.

Don't shed a tear for me, I don't need sympathy
I may bend, but I won't break
You'd be amazed what I can take
I have learned along the way
To find the beauty in each day
So until the wells of faith run dry
I will set my sights upon the sky
And whenever hope begins to fade
My spirit all but gone
I can feel the angels here on earth
Giving me the strength to carry on

Iris could feel the angel here on earth, too, speaking through Lily, encouraging her, supporting her. She must call Lily right away and tell her what a beautiful job she had done, tell her that the pain and suffering she had endured to record the song had not been in vain.

"Hello?" Lily said, picking up on the third ring.

"Hi, Lily! It's me, Iris! I know it's early over there. I hope I didn't wake you."

"Iris!" Lily cried. "Don't worry, I'm wide awake. In fact, I was just thinking about you, if you can believe it."

"It must be telepathy!" Iris said. She walked with the cordless phone out onto the balcony. "I just found your note and the CD. I can't believe you sneaked it into my bag!"

"I felt bad that I refused to let you play it that day, but I just couldn't handle it," Lily said. "I was kind of in a bad place."

"I know, don't worry," Iris said, brushing away a stray sniffle with the back of her hand. "Anyway, I just listened to it. Your song really moved me. I couldn't wait to tell you what a beautiful job you did."

"Well, thanks, but all I can hear when I listen to it is the fear in my voice."

"That's funny, because to me you sound so positive, so full of hope."

"Speaking of which," Lily said. "Are you OK?"

"Sure, I'm fine," Iris said, clearing her throat. "Why do you ask?"

"I don't know," Lily said. "You sound strange... different..."

"Maybe it's the connection."

"Yeah, that must be it - the connection."

"Plus, I didn't really get much sleep last night. We had a party."

"A party?"

Iris scanned her brain for something positive to say about the horrendous evening without actually lying but came up with nothing.

"Are you still there, Iris?"

"Sure, of course."

"You know," Lily said, her words fraught with reluctance, "I really feel like I have to tell you something."

When they were little girls sharing the same bed, Lily could always tell when something was bothering her, or one of their big brothers had made her cry. Could she still pick up on that even now, even over the phone, even from thousands of miles away?

"I've always admired your ability to bounce back," Lily continued, "And I can only imagine how hard it was for you to lose Auntie Rosa. I want you to know that I did appreciate your help and moral support that day when you came over, and it did make me feel better to have a nice clean house when the boys visited. It was an awful time for me, and you were trying so hard to be cheerful. I know I didn't make that easy for you."

"That's OK, Lily," Iris said. "I was glad to help." That was good to know, and it was also good to know that Lily was blaming Auntie Rosa's death for making her sound "strange."

"But you couldn't hide your sadness from me, Iris. And why should you? You don't have to prove anything to me, or anyone else. You don't always have to be all bubbles and champagne. Give yourself time to grieve. What was the big hurry to start throwing parties?"

Iris was struck with a vision of how dreadful she must appear to

Lily's eyes, breezing into town from her exotic island just hours before Auntie Rosa died, turning up at Lily's with a bottle of champagne so soon after the funeral (and so soon after Lily's drinking binge), then jetting back to Italy with her new diamonds when the drama was over, all ready to party it up.

"The party was actually Max's idea." she blurted out.

"Oh," Lily said. "Well, I guess that was nice of him, to try and cheer you up. I'll bet he just couldn't stand to see you sad - no one who knows you can. All your friends were probably glad to have you back, too. You're lucky to have them help you through your mourning."

Right. That's exactly what I told Bea, she wanted to say. Max couldn't stand to see me sad. That's why he never came home until yesterday. As for friends, of course, there's Bea, always good for a glassful of wine and an earful of advice I could live without. Or by "friends" do you mean that crass crowd of strangers who spent the night here, stuffing their faces and smoking and drinking? The ones whose vulgar, meaningless conversations about more people I don't know made me feel like an outsider in my own home, while inside I was dying?

"Well, most of the guests he invited were TV people," she said. That should end it.

"How exciting." Lily's voice sounded anything but excited. "Are you on close terms with them?"

"Not really. They all work in Milan. Max is trying to get a foot in the door with them, feel out their interest for that project I was telling you about."

Iris waited for Lily to comment, but all she heard was some background static and then a cough.

"You know, the film project." Iris could hear her own voice bouncing back over the line, her own words echoing tinnily in the earpiece. The connection seemed to be getting worse.

"Right. I remember you mentioning that." Lily said.

Lily wasn't really holding up her end of the conversation. But if Iris didn't want to talk about the friends she didn't have, maybe Lily didn't want to hear about a bunch of TV people. Maybe it resuscitated her regrets about not having pursued a performing career. Lily was probably irked that Iris, and not she, was hobnobbing with show people. Iris was tactful enough to avoid mentioning certain subjects, but what was she supposed to do, if Lily kept badgering her?

"Anyway, everyone was having such a great time, I thought they would never leave. But to be honest, I was glad when they did," Iris spoke quickly, hoping Lily would finally let it drop.

"Why? Weren't you having fun?"

Lily's insistence on hearing about the party was really starting to confuse her. Now that things were finally patched up between them, it could be that she was making an effort at some casual conversation, trying to show a sincere interest in Iris's daily life. But on the other hand, maybe she wanted to hear how marvelous it was, just to feed her old resentments and make Iris feel guilty about the life she led. If they were to ever get over that, Lily would have to realize that it wasn't all about the glamour and glitter and that Iris did not spend her time at parties just standing there and looking pretty in her diamonds while liveried waiters kept her flute filled with champagne. Especially not last night's party.

"Well, it was late when they left, and I was exhausted from all the cooking and setting up," she said, immediately concerned that now it might sound like she was complaining. It was easy to get the wrong idea over the phone, especially with the static on the line complicating matters. "Not that I minded," she added. "You know how I've always loved to cook."

"And where was Max all this time when you were cooking and running around?"

"Oh, he was busy, too, out buying supplies - wine and candles and all those things." Iris recalled those hours home alone, plagued by the pulsating presence of Max's secret cell phone. She stepped out from under the awning and into a ray of sunshine, hoping it would chase away a sudden shiver. "He was also helping out a friend of his he invited to spend the night."

"Is his friend a good house guest, or is he one of those guys who leaves the toilet seat up?" Lily said. It came as no surprise to Iris that she and Lily shared the same preoccupation with men's treatment of toilets. What woman wouldn't, after growing up with so many brothers?

"Well, actually, it was a she," Iris said.

There was a moment of silence broken only by an annoying crackling sound before Lily spoke.

"He had a female friend stay overnight at your house?"

"Sure, we have people stay over a lot," Iris said. "She and Max are old friends." Lily would never understand the intricacies of certain types of male-female relationships. How could she, if she had never experienced or been exposed to them? Still, Iris felt compelled to offer some sort of explanation. "She was the one who contacted all those people, just to help Max out. She works with them."

"Are you telling me that she invited all those people to your house and then she and Max left while you did all the work?"

"Well, Max manned the grill all night."

Iris glanced at the grill, still full of ash and half-burnt rubbish, still full of images of Max's face flickering in the flames as she fought back tears of hurt and anger. She walked from the balcony and into the living room, pacing the floor, wondering why Lily refused to just let it go.

"Let's not talk about her anymore, OK? Anyway, she's gone already."

"Oh, that's good. I hope she helped clean up first." Lily said. "So now it's just you and Max?"

"More or less," Iris swallowed. She was good at sifting out information she did not want to share, but lying was another story altogether. Especially to Lily.

"More or less," Lily repeated. "So either there are more people than just the two of you, meaning you still have guests or less people than the two of you, meaning you're alone. Which is it?"

Iris collapsed on the sofa, exhausted. All these questions were wearing her down. Maybe she should just hang up and go to sleep. Or maybe she should talk to her sister. Wasn't that why she had called?

"No, it's just me. Max is gone too."

"What do you mean, Max is gone?"

"We had a little difference of opinion," she said. Given Lily's history with Joe, Iris hoped she wouldn't blow things all out of proportion. "It was no big deal."

"He left because you had a difference of opinion?"

"It was late, we were both tired," she said. "It was just one of those things. We'll work it out."

"So you two had a fight?"

"It wasn't a fight. We never fight."

"Why can't you just call it what it is, Iris?"

"You call it what you want to, Lily. Whatever makes you happy. But I was here, and you weren't, OK? And he wouldn't have left if I hadn't asked him to. I needed some time to think, you know? I needed to make some sense out of certain things that were bothering me before we both said things we might regret."

"You mean you kicked him out? Wow - what did he do?"

"I didn't kick him out." Iris stood up again and resumed her pacing, trying not to step on the cracks between the tiles as she walked back and forth, wondering why Lily, who had spent her entire married life skirting the issues and making excuses, was suddenly so interested in spelling things out.

"He pissed you off so bad that you had a fight and then you asked him to leave, right? That's kicking him out."

"He got mad because I was criticizing certain things that he had done," Iris gesticulated with her free hand as she spoke as if it could help get the idea across to Lily, who didn't seem to be understanding anything. "And then he pointed out that maybe I wasn't really one to judge, and then..."

"You keep talking about 'certain things' - what certain things?"

"It doesn't matter, really. It'll be OK."

There was no sense getting into the whole story; it would just give Lily an even worse impression of Max, and prompt her to grill her with more questions.

"Why don't you let me tell you why I called?" Iris said, trying to get the conversation back on track. "That will explain everything."

"I'm listening."

"Well, I wanted to say that after our disagreement last night, that song of yours really helped me sort out my thoughts."

"How did it help you do that?" Lily's voice finally sounded calmer, more reasonable. Now if only Iris could recall what she had wanted to say before Lily's line of questioning befuddled her thoughts.

"It made me realize that I need to keep reaching out to Max, even though sometimes it's hard, and sometimes he says or does things he doesn't mean. I always have to remember he doesn't see things the same way I do because he doesn't have the same background as I do. And he's actually very fragile, because of what happened to him as a child. He relies on my strength. He looks to me for certain qualities he doesn't possess." Iris paused, doubting her answer was specific enough for Lily. "You see, I thought I was giving him everything he needed, but I realized I may be wrong. I think I have to take an honest look at myself, and give a little bit more if I really want it to work."

Why did all those things that she had been thinking in the privacy of her own head now sound like they were spewing from the mouth of an idiot?

"And that's what you got out of my song?" The edge was already back in Lily's voice.

"Yes, you know when you sing about the need to reach out and lift up?" she said. She'd need to concentrate to get this right. "Of course, I do my best to lift Max up when he's depressed. But I know it has to go beyond that. If I try harder, I know I can lift him up to a higher level - to a level where he can reach out and touch those dreams of his." Iris felt the heat climbing up her neck and into her cheeks as she walked from the living room to the kitchen, then back out onto the balcony. "You know, like the film project, for example."

"I don't know what you're smoking over there, Iris, but that is *not* what that song is about," Lily snapped. "That song is about redemption, about leaving an old self behind, about finding the courage and the faith to reach beyond the limitations we put on ourselves, the chains that weigh us down."

Iris was thrown off balance by the reproach in Lily's voice. Lily had always been the one to take her cue from Iris, and now here she was, suddenly telling her what to think.

"Well, that may be your version, but if that's the message I got, it must be in there," Iris said. "You can't really believe that the creators of any song, any story, any painting or other work of art get to dictate how it is interpreted. Each artist follows his or her own inspiration, but once the work is out there, everyone will see different things in it. To sum it up in a nutshell: Beauty is in the eyes of the beholder."

That was one of Auntie Rosa's favorite adages, but even in her muddle-headed state Iris realized it had nothing to do with what she was saying. Fine, maybe it would confound Lily, too, and make her relent long enough for Iris to collect her thoughts. She took a deep breath, and continued, "What I wanted to say, is that your song helped me see some things."

"When I wrote those lyrics, I didn't even really understand them completely - not the way I do now. You are totally twisting the meaning around. And yes, I do get to say what the lyrics mean - and especially what they *don't* mean - because *I* wrote them. And I will not let you use that song to make excuses for Max."

"Why do you think Max needs anyone to make excuses for him?"

"He doesn't - not as long as you're around. You are already doing it all the time. From what you've told me, you quit your job, you travel all over the place taking care of him. He brings a woman to sleep over at your house, invites a bunch of people over for you to cook for - that makes me crazy! You keep telling me how much he needs you, how exceptional he is, how tortured. You talk about being Max's strength, taking responsibility for his dreams... I hate to tell you, but every one of the women in my support group at the shelter said those same kinds of things about their abusers. Hell, I used to say the same things about Joe."

"What are you talking about? What does that have to do with me?"

357

"Iris, I may not know a lot about a lot of things. I don't know which wine goes with fish, or how to uncork a bottle of champagne. But there are a couple things I do know about. First of all, I know what bullshit is, and I'm hearing a lot of it from you. I also know about abusive relationships. And believe it or not, you are in one."

"How can you say that? You don't even know Max!"

"I don't have to know Max. I know *you*. You keep saying there are 'certain things' that are going on, but you won't tell me what they are. When we talked at my house, I could tell you were avoiding issues you didn't want to discuss, because I used to do the exact same thing. And now you're doing it again! All you talk about *his* life, *his* dreams, what you can do to support and encourage *him*. That's typical textbook behavior - they call it 'battered women's syndrome,' you know."

"Good God, Lily! Now you sound like Mom!"

"Yeah, well, Mom knew a thing or two, as it turns out. Iris, in support group they used to tell us that we had an obligation to expose abuse when we see it in the world. You are displaying all the classic behaviors: you're glossing over your problems, minimizing your own pain, making excuses for Max all over the place, taking responsibility for his lack of ability to cope with the world, running interference for him. Every other word that comes out of your mouth is about Max, and all I keep thinking is, 'What about Iris?'"

Iris felt like throwing up. "Listen, Lily. This connection is getting really bad. There's all this static and feedback on the line. Maybe we should hang up, and I'll call you back in a little bit?"

"That's not necessary. I can hear you well enough. And I'm waiting for an answer. What about Iris?"

"Yes, what about Iris?" A rush of hot saliva filled her mouth. "I haven't been such a saint either, you know," she said. "Max isn't the only one to blame here."

"And I'm sure he is an expert on your flaws and failures, isn't he?"

Iris recoiled from the words as if they were a snake at her feet, not a question asked by her sister three thousand miles away. Max had never before spoken to her with such cruelty as he had last night, but she was the one who had started it. Sure, he had joked about her infidelities on a few occasions - even in front of his friends, which she didn't appreciate. And sure, there had been times, especially back in the beginning, when Max had made all those digs at her for being content with her sheltered life as Gregorio's wife, for being such a slave to rules and convention. But that had been for her own good, hadn't it? Hadn't the purpose been to expose her to new ways of thinking, to encourage her to get out and grab some happiness for herself before it was too late?

"No one is perfect, Lily," she said. "Not even me. You should know that by now."

"And I bet Max is all too happy to remind you of that. Throwing past mistakes up in your face is a classic tactic of abusers."

"He doesn't need to remind me of anything! I made my mistakes on my own, and I can remember each one perfectly well on my own, thank you very much! All I seem to do is make mistakes! Even calling you was a mistake!" Iris cried, bursting into tears.

"Love forgives mistakes, Iris," Lily said, her voice soft, but firm. "Abuse makes you live your mistakes over and over again. I've always looked up to you, you know? You were the closest thing to perfection I knew, flitting around in your tutu, always so graceful, always so ready to dispense help and smiles and love. I refuse to just sit here and listen to you demolish my role model. You are not weak, but you have been systematically duped into believing that you are. Strong men want their women to believe in their own strength; they want them to pursue their own dreams, to challenge them, and to demand respect. Controlling men need women who are insecure, who lack confidence and conviction, who think poorly of themselves and who will do almost anything to stay in their good graces - including betraying themselves. Just ask yourself one question, Iris: What kind of woman are you when you're with Max?"

"Lily, please. Stop it." Iris sobbed.

"I won't stop. I can't. You can hate me, you can scream at me, you can hang up on me if you want, but I am going to stay on this phone until you ask yourself that question."

Iris could never hate Lily, she could never hang up on her, and she didn't have the strength to scream back at her. All she wanted was for her to leave her alone. All she wanted was to catch her breath and end the conversation. Then she heard that Lily was crying, too.

"Iris, abusers don't wear a sign around their neck, you know?" Lily said. "They don't all live in Gates, wear grimy muscle shirts and throw things and scream. They don't walk around kicking puppies. And abused women aren't all somewhere else, standing in some welfare line with runny-nosed children. They don't all turn up in the emergency ward in the middle of the night with broken bones and lame excuses. Abuse happens in Italy, too. And it happens to wealthy women, to educated women, to sophisticated women. In fact, when I was in counseling at the shelter, they used to tell us that women like you have a much harder time recognizing and accepting that they are in abusive relationships because their partners are wealthy, slick, popular, successful - whatever. It's much easier for someone like me who has suffered in a more obvious and worldly way - like not having any money or any personal freedom to see friends. Can you see that, Iris? Can you answer my question: Who are you when you are with Max?"

Iris sat down on the sofa, holding the phone in one hand and her face in the other. She was so utterly confused, she didn't even know how to answer. But by now she did have a pretty clear idea of who Max wanted her to be: the clever organizer, the indulgent mamma, the reckless teenager, the innocent sex toy in high heels.

"When I'm with Max," Iris struggled to gain control of her voice. "When I'm with Max, I always feel insecure, like I'm never beautiful enough, or smart enough, or interesting enough."

"Iris," Lily said through tears, "The whole time we were growing up, I just adored you. I dreamed that one day I would be as graceful and beautiful and sweet and intelligent as you were. As you are. You have always been my idol, the one person I wished I could be like. It breaks my heart to know that you believe those lies about yourself. And it makes me raging mad!"

"Lily, I'm not who you think I am. I'm not worthy of being anyone's idol. The only thing I ever knew how to do was smile. That was how I defended myself. That was how I got attention. That was the only reason anyone wanted to be around me. For my idiotic, stupid smile. Look where it got me."

"Oh, Iris. I saw that smile fade from your face when I asked you about Max that day, and I haven't been able to stop thinking about it since. Don't let him steal that smile any longer. I know how it happens. They take a little bit here, a little bit there, and before you know it, there is only empty space where you used to be. I am not going to sit here and watch you do that to yourself."

Iris knew there was something to what Lily said. She thought of all the bits and pieces of her that had been chipped away over the years, how willing she had been to let them all have a go at it. Not only Max, but Claudio, and Gregorio, and her high school boyfriends, even her very own father. They had all served themselves with what they needed from her and lopped away what they didn't like. But not one of them had ever loved her enough to give her the one thing she needed: the freedom to be herself.

"But how do you stop it from happening?" Iris asked. "What am I supposed to do?" How strange it was for her to be asking Lily for advice. Lily, the little sister she hadn't been able to protect. Lily, who somewhere along the way had lost everything, but found her true voice. Iris gripped the phone, waiting in silence for Lily's answer, hoping to feel a surge of the strength she so desperately needed flow from her sister through the receiver and into her.

"You do it one breath at a time, Iris. One word, one thought. You begin by honoring yourself in all that you say and do."

"But how do I do that today? How do I do it right now?"

"You do it by being Iris," said Lily. "She will show you the way."

Iris picked up the dust cloth from the end table, and swiped it across her swollen eyes and runny nose, wondering whether she even knew who Iris was anymore. The sound of a key turning in the lock made her jump to her feet.

"Lily!" she said. "He's at the door!"

"Who is? Max?"

"Yes!"

"Can he get in?"

"He has the keys. But I locked the safety latch." The knocking on the door turned to pounding, accompanied by the insistent buzzing of the bell.

"What are you going to do?" Lily asked.

"What should I do?" Iris wished he had given her a little more time to think. She was a wreck, not nearly calm enough to confront him.

"Are you afraid of him, Iris? Don't let him inside if you are afraid of him. Go outside to talk."

"I'm not afraid of him." Lily probably thought Max was violent, that he might try to hurt her, like the husbands of those women at the shelter. He wasn't like that at all, but she was nervous just the same. "But I am nervous about facing him. I don't know what to say."

"Think of what we just talked about. Be strong."

"OK, Lily. But will you wait here? Will you stay on the line while I open the door?"

"I'll be right here."

Iris set the phone down on the table, walked to the door and unlatched it. When she saw Max standing on the landing, she did not see the monstrous manipulator Lily had described. She saw an unshaven man with bags under his bloodshot eyes, who looked at her and heaved a deep sigh. His appearance told her he must have suffered just as much as she. Iris wondered where he had spent the night. The only thing that stopped her from throwing her arms around him was the thought of Lily on the phone.

"I'm glad you came, Max," Iris said.

Max brandished that grin of his. That grin. That condescending grin of a man so magnanimous as to put up with her quirky foreign viewpoints and provincial morals. That self-serving grin of a man who despised the constraints of conventional relationships and kept her vacillating between a constant state of worry and want. That ridiculous grin of a man on a mission to liberate her from the slavery of family values and religious beliefs and secure paychecks.

362

That vile, disgusting grin of a man who pissed on her lilac like an animal while pointing his finger at her, accusing her of thinking herself so much better than him. Who the hell was he anyway? A wannabe filmmaker? A freeloading fraudster? A pig who had betrayed her and coerced her into betraying herself?

"I'm glad I came, too," Max said. "I knew you'd come around."

"And I can finally see that you never will," Iris said through clenched teeth, her gut roiling, her muscles quivering. "Lily was just talking to me about that."

"What the fuck would Lily know about anything?"

The grin was still there. That goddamn shit-eating son-of-a-bitch grin was still there.

Her heart pounding, her face burning, Iris stared wide-eyed as her arm flew through the air and whacked her open palm against Max's cheek with such force it knocked him off balance. If it weren't for the stinging in her hand and the stunned look on his face, she never would have believed such a gesture could have come from Iris Capotosti.

12. LILY

Click-click, click-click. Lily tilted her face into the sunshine's embrace as she pedaled her way across the Stutson Street bridge toward home. She relished this Indian summer afternoon, knowing that it was one of the few remaining. Soon, it would be too cold and dark to bike back and forth to work, a routine she had grown to love. It had become a precious form of meditation, giving Lily space at the beginning of each day to pray for guidance and strength and at the end of each to offer thanks.

So much had changed about Lily's life over the past few months. The boys remained with Joe, but every interaction Lily had with them was a new chance to help them navigate the confusion she knew they must be feeling about their new life and about the twisted family dynamic firmly planted at the center of it all. They could never understand the complexities of emotional manipulation, of alienation of affection, of psychological blackmail. Even after months of counseling, it was hard enough for Lily to understand. But one day, the boys would see. One day, they would come home to her again. On her best of days, Lily held onto that hope; it sat with her during dinners for one, walked beside her during her lone evening strolls on the beach, and acted as a salve to soothe the sting of the indignation she could see in the eyes of people who couldn't fathom how any mother in her right mind could give up her children.

On her worst of days, Lily planted herself on the grass at the base of the massive oak tree in her yard, looked out over the waters of Lake Ontario and wept until the tidal wave of sadness passed. Sometimes, that took hours. Sometimes, it took days. It amazed Lily how many tears she could hold, how many her body could manufacture. Where did the sadness come from? Where did it go when she released it? She wondered if there would come a time when a week would pass without sorrow again dismantling her fledgling sense of optimism.

Regardless of her struggle to keep a positive perspective, there were two things to which Lily remained doggedly dedicated: Her attendance and performance at work - whether she wanted to be there or not - and her twice weekly visits with the boys, whether they wanted to be there or not.

As a perk of her job at the Kendall Company, Lily received a bike for herself and for each immediate family member, along with a comprehensive guide to the local bike paths and trails. Taking a family ride had quickly become the routine when Joseph and Pierce visited. The boys had excitedly designed their own YouBikes– Pierce's in red and blue like Superman - and Joseph's in silver, "So it will match my Dad's car." Lily's bike was purple and white.

Bicycles were not the only gifts Lily received from the Kendall Company. Her work as a technical writer was so totally absorbing that it helped her to get through those early days when all she could think about was how much she missed the boys, and how angry she was at Joe. But as she spread out the parts and pieces of the latest YouBike model on a large table before her, her mind became consumed with the order of the steps, the tone of the language, and the illustrations that were best suited to support customers as they approached what had the potential to be a frustrating experience. It gave Lily great comfort to know that some things really did work out the way they were supposed to, and even though she might not be changing lives in her work, if she could help people experience that kind of certainty - even in a small way - maybe they would be comforted, too.

Lily and Iris had promised to stay in better touch with each other since the previous summer. Lily had always been terrible at sitting down to write a response to a longhand letter and was even less inclined to initiate one. She'd spent so much time trying to free herself from the prison of her thoughts, that the last thing she wanted to do in her spare time was record them on paper. Maybe

Lily would have felt different about staying in touch with Iris if she ever had anything interesting or happy to share. So often, there was nothing to report but the latest run-in with Joe, or the most recent nightmare that the boys were drowning in the lake, with Lily unable to reach them in time. It was so much simpler to write about putting peg A into slot B.

Email eventually rendered longhand letter writing and two-week delivery times obsolete. Still, it was easy enough to mark an email for response by placing a little red flag next to it – and just as easy to ignore the flag. They finally settled on using chat, which afforded them a way to stay in touch in real-time, at any hour of the day or night. Iris said it would be less like writing a letter, and more like having a conversation. Lily wasn't convinced that was going to make it any less burdensome. It wasn't the medium that was the problem. After all, when had they ever had easy conversation? Still, in the spirit of wanting to want to stay in touch, they made fairly regular plans to meet online. Sometimes both of them even remembered to show up.

> *So tell me about this promotion*, Iris typed.
> *They want to make me a communications associate.*
> *What does that involve?*
> *Instead of just writing tech manuals, I'll get to write some ad copy, some company newsletters – that sort of thing.*
> *Sounds like fun! See?* typed Iris. *I'm not the only one who recognizes your talent!*
> *Working all the time is better than coming home to an empty house*, typed Lily. *I think my boss confused my desperation with dedication. Still, I'll take the promotion – and the raise.*
> *Congratulations, Lily – you deserve it!*
> *What I deserve is to get my kids back.*
> *I know you do.*
> *Every day I pray for that. I figure by getting ahead at work, I will be able to give them a better life when that time comes.*
> *I know, Lily. I pray for it too.*

It was from the seat of her bicycle that Lily began to rebuild her relationships with her sons. Cycling was an activity that they could engage in together, but that also allowed each of them to experience their own challenges and victories. For Joseph, that entailed finally making it to the top of the hill on Lake Avenue without having to get off and walk, and for Pierce, it was being able to keep pace so that Joseph and Lily did not have to stop and wait for him to catch up.

Lily's first real challenge was deciding whether she should ride in front of the boys or behind them. Riding at the back, she would be able to see them, know that they still had their helmets on, that their tires had not gone flat, and of course, that they were still there. But riding in front afforded her the opportunity to block their way should a car fail to notice their brightly colored bicycles or the flashing reflectors and neon streamers with which Lily had decorated them. Riding in front, she could also alert them of broken glass or other debris in the road while they still had time to avoid it. It gave her the chance to protect them, providing a buffer between them, the traffic, and sometimes their own naïve enthusiasm. Each approach provided its own benefits and its own drawbacks. The only thing that was certain was that she couldn't do both.

Together, Lily and the boys devised a system whereby she would ride in front, and then every few minutes she would call out to them to make sure they were doing alright, and they would respond. The boys understood that it would not be considered a joke to purposely remain silent when Lily called "Check!," and they assured Lily that she could trust them in this regard. This system enabled Lily to lead the boys and clear their way, without sacrificing their independence, their safety, or Lily's peace of mind - a commodity she'd come to regard as more precious with each passing day.

Even though her dreams were still sometimes peppered with frightening images of her sons in peril, over time the weekend rides helped her to understand that just because she couldn't see the boys, it didn't mean that tragedy was sure to befall them. She came to see that keeping her eyes on them was more for her own benefit than it was for theirs. It was out of this that her trust in their abilities grew, which in turn inspired appreciation in them for the latitude she offered.

The crusted black snow of March gave way to purple crocuses of April, which yielded to daffodils and lilacs. Lily, Joseph, and Pierce celebrated the new cycling season by taking a bike tour of Charlotte. They stopped at the beach to walk the pier and feed the ducks with leftover bread crusts. As they approached home, the trio rounded the corner, picking up speed, in anticipation of tackling the steep hill onto which Lily's driveway emptied. Blasting up the hill and sailing into the garage was the crowning glory of each ride.

"Check!" Lily called.

"Check!" replied Pierce.

"Check!" echoed Joseph.

"OK, boys!" shouted Lily. "Full steam ahead!"

With grunts and groans, they crested the hill - Joseph passing Lily on the way, Pierce chugging along behind them both.

"C'mon buddy!" shouted Lily from the top of the hill.

"Go PJ!" cried Joseph.

With a face red with exertion and a grimace of determination that exposed the large gap where his front teeth used to be, Pierce cranked out the final few revolutions of his pedals, and as he glided past the mailbox and toward the open garage door, he raised his hands overhead and shouted, "I did it!"

Lily and Joseph clapped and cheered.

"Great ride, you two," said Lily. "Please put your bikes away and let's go inside and have some dinner. I am starving!"

Lily wheeled over to the mailbox, opened the door, and retrieved a brown eight-and-a-half-by-eleven envelope, exactly like the ones in which her Order of Protection, Separation Agreement, and Child Support orders had been delivered. Her heart jumped as she tried to imagine what else Joe could possibly have in store for her. Things had just started to settle down, to feel normal. Maybe too normal for his tastes. She turned the envelope over to discover the name, "Orvitz and Kramer" stamped in the return address area. It was from Curtis' lawyer.

As soon as the boys left the next day, she would open it. Today was too perfect, and if Lily had learned anything during this ordeal, it was the skill for savoring a moment of perfection and for appreciating and protecting its frailty.

Just after lunch the following day, Joe pulled into the driveway and tooted the car horn.

"Your Dad's here!" Lily called down to the boys. She collected the pile of dirty clothes from the floor of the bedroom and shoved it into the duffle bag they brought with them every Friday.

"Tell Samantha I'm sorry that I didn't get time to wash your stuff," said Lily. She handed the bag to Joseph.

"Mom," said Pierce, using the tone that children use when they are about to reveal to their parents how little they really know about life, "We don't have Samantha anymore."

"You don't?!"

"No," said Joseph. "She moved out like *two weeks* ago," indicating that this was a very, very long time and that perhaps Lily should be concerned that she was so behind on the latest news.

"Why did she leave? What happened?"

"I dunno," said Joseph. "My Dad says she's crazy. They were screaming and yelling one night and then the next day she was gone."

Good for you, Samantha, Lily thought. "That's too bad," she said. "I know you really liked her. And I know she did a lot to help your Dad take care of you guys and the house."

"That's OK, Mommy," said Pierce. "We have Annette now."

"Annette?"

"Yeah," said Joseph. "My Dad says they just don't make 'em like Annette anymore."

I bet they don't, thought Lily.

Joe honked the car horn a second time.

"Kisses!" said Lily.

The boys kissed her and then headed for the car. Joe extended his arm out the window and waved. Lily waved back.

"Good luck with that," she said as she turned and closed the door behind her.

By afternoon, Lily still felt unprepared to deal with whatever news was inside the envelope; good news rarely came in eight-and-a-half-by-eleven envelopes with a metal clap on the flap. She booted up her computer.

Iris, are you there?

Hey there! Yep, I'm here. You just caught me! I was getting ready to run out and get a few things for a trip I'm taking on Monday.

Oh. You're taking a trip?

It's for work, typed Iris. *It's just Venice.*

Just Venice, thought Lily. *I was going to go to Venice, too, but I thought I would cut the lawn instead.*

What's up?

I got an envelope in the mail from Curtis' lawyer yesterday, but I haven't had the nerve to open it.

Want me to be here with you when you do?

Yes, that's what I was thinking.

Sure! Go ahead and open it and tell me what it says.

It's just what I thought, Iris. Poor old Curtis. He died. Last week.

I'm sorry, Lily. I know he was really an angel to you.

Yes, he was. Whenever I've felt overwhelmed – which has been a lot, believe me – I've remembered the night I met him. It reminds that somehow, somewhere, someone cares, is looking out for me. Lily sniffed.

So what's the deal? Did he name you in his will? :)

Lily scanned the document. *Actually, he sort of did.*

What?!

Don't get too excited. He named me because he said I could stay here until he died, at which time the house would pass into probate and I would have to leave.

But I don't want you to move! I love to think of you there, knowing that I helped you set it all up, remembering that day we cleaned and

370

sang along with "I Don't Know How to Love Him." It makes me feel like I'm still there with you, in a way.

It was good to know that Iris was still Iris... still focused on the good times, still endowed with the vision to see beauty even when beauty would hide. It must be wonderful to remember the good times with such clarity, but it also must make it really hard to let go and move on.

> *To be honest, I am not that sad about this,* typed Lily. *I'm actually kind of relieved.*
> *You are?*
> *Iris, I have lots of memories of this place. Not all of them are good.*
> *But some are, right?*
> *Yes, some are - that's true. Every evening when I curl up on the couch with my tea and pull one of those sorry old afghans over my knees, I think of you and how you came over to try and help that day.*
> *I'm so glad.*
> *And I think of all the sleepy Saturday afternoons when the boys conked out watching TV or resting after a long ride, waiting for dinner.*
> *Sounds so cozy.*
> *But you know, every time I go up the stairs to the second floor, I also remember when Joseph locked me out, and I kicked the door in.*
> *God, that must have been so awful...*
> *I can still feel the pain shooting through my foot, I can still hear Pierce crying, and I can still feel that sense of death when they walked out the door. Maybe it's time to let those memories go, you know? Maybe it's time for me to get a new place that doesn't harbor painful ghosts.*
> *I completely understand that, Lily. Promise me the next time I come there I can stay with you in your new place?*
> *Only if you help me find it! Are you going to be around tomorrow? I'll go down to the grocery store and get a copy of the Sunday paper and then maybe we can check out the listings online.*

Sure! Call me on the phone around two-o'clock your time; I'll just about be ready for a glass of wine by then. And don't you buy any cigarettes at the store, young lady. I quit for good, and you can too. Don't worry - I'll definitely have to stay off of them if I'm going to keep up with those boys on their bikes!

The next day, as Lily placed the staples of her weekly diet onto the conveyer belt at the grocery store – cereal, milk, eggs, wheat bread, sliced turkey from the deli, five frozen entrees, and a twelve-pack of diet coke – she felt grateful. It was simple fare, but it was hers, and she was able to pay for it with money she earned from a job she got on her own. She tossed a newspaper and a pack of gum onto the belt. She drove home on a full tank of gas, and hope swelled in the warmth of the shining sun. She spent the morning doing her laundry, and getting ready for the new week at work, giving thanks for everything she touched – it wasn't so long ago, she reminded herself, that life was so painful that she couldn't imagine going on. Today was better. Today was a good day.

At two o'clock, Lily brewed a cup of tea before sitting down to call Iris.

"It's been *a whole day* since we chatted," said Iris. "Did you miss me?"

"Yes," said Lily. She had. "It's nice to be able to hear your voice." It was.

"I know - the connection is great! OK, so how do you want to do this?" Iris asked.

"Well, some agents only list stuff online – so why don't I start with the paper, and you can start online. I sent you the link on email earlier. Let me know if you see anything interesting."

"Are you going to rent, or buy?"

"Probably rent for now, but maybe I'll buy - I don't know. There are some good government loans out there for first-time buyers. Depends on what we find."

"You want two bedrooms, or three?" Iris asked.

"Three is better if I want to stay for a while... but many of the three bedrooms are too expensive for me."

"Do you want to stay on the east side?"

"I think so," said Lily, turning the page of the newspaper. "I want to give the boys a chance to live somewhere else besides in their father's shadow."

Lily turned the pages as Iris clicked through the listings.

"Oh my, God!" shouted Iris.

"You are not going to believe this!" cried Lily.

In unison they cried, "Chestnut Crest is for sale!"

"What does your listing say?" asked Iris.

"It just says, 'Circa Nineteen-eighteen. Rural living on the bus line. Suburban farmhouse with one-and-a-quarter acres. Save this timeless beauty from foreclosure! Immediate occupancy.'"

"Mine says pretty much the same thing," said Iris.

"Any photos?" Lily asked.

"Only of the outside."

"I can't believe it's for sale," said Lily.

"You should go look at it," said Iris.

"I hope you're kidding me," said Lily. "I would never want to live there again."

"Not to live," said Iris. "But aren't you curious? Oh, Lily, you *have* to go see it!"

"I just told you yesterday that I'm trying to leave my ghosts behind," said Lily. "And now you want me to go chasing after them?"

Over the next week, the thought of driving by the house on Chestnut Crest - just to take a peek - kept creeping into Lily's mind, and she kept pushing it back out again. She had to admit, the idea did hold appeal for her, but perhaps not in the same way as it seemed to for Iris. Iris idealized the old house, the way you might romanticize a former lover that you have no chance of ever seeing again and so run no risk of remembering the pain around why you broke up in the first place. For Lily, going back to Chestnut Crest was more like facing an old demon - which was an argument both for and against doing so.

As Lily walked up the long empty driveway, she passed a red, white, and black sign that had been pounded into the grass: For Sale - Call Jackson Guardiner. One apple tree was now only a stump, but the other was still there, its tiny blossoms dreaming of September. The memory of the apples' tartness and of the way her jaw tingled whenever she bit into one made Lily's mouth water, but the sensation was chased off by a wave of nausea, as she recalled the smell of the rotting fruit, and of the dead bird she had found among it as a child. Now that she was here, it seemed senseless not to try and take a peek inside. She stepped up onto the back porch, balanced herself on the top step and cupped her hands around her face as she peered through the window glass. From inside the house, she could hear strains of "Dust in the Wind" being played on the guitar.

"Oh, shit!" she cried, and losing her balance she fell against the aluminum door with a clatter.

The music stopped, and the door between the kitchen and the porch opened. Lily turned and walked away as briskly as she could without breaking into a run, hoping to reach her car in the street before whoever was inside could discover her.

"Hey - hey there!" shouted a man's voice. "Did you want to take a look?"

Lily stopped, her heart pounding. Slowly, she turned around. "Oh - hi."

"Hi." The man was about Lily's age. He had a guitar slung over his back with the strap stretched across his broad chest. "Did you want to check it out?" He walked toward Lily. His blond hair was pulled back into a ponytail.

"Check it out?"

"The house... did you want to see the inside?" The look of expectation on his face made Lily feel bad for him. She had the sense that prospects on this place were hard to come by.

"The inside?"

"Yea. Or, you could just stand there all day and repeat everything I say." He extended his hand toward Lily. "I'm Jackson

Guardiner, the listing agent."

"I'm Lily," she replied. She shook his hand and looked up at him, using her free hand to shield her eyes from the sun.

"This is a great old house," said Jackson. "I'd be happy to give you a quick tour." He walked back toward the door and motioned for Lily to follow.

"OK," Lily said, not sure at all if it was, but she couldn't bring herself to disappoint this guitar-playing real estate agent who was obviously dying to show the place to someone.

Lily followed Jackson onto the back porch. She automatically kicked off her shoes and left them by the kitchen door.

"Don't bother," said Jackson. "The place is vacant."

"Where are the owners?"

"Technically there aren't any - unless you count the bank. The people who lived here are divorced. The husband got laid off from his job, and then he just took off. The wife kept up with the place for as long as she could, but this is too much house for one person. After a while, she just gave up, so the mortgage went into default, and now it's headed into foreclosure."

"That's too bad." Lily had never thought about how her father had managed to keep this place going after her mother moved out. And after she followed.

Lily allowed Jackson to lead her into the living room. The old stained and worn green carpeting had been replaced with a wide-slat cherry hardwood floor. The yellowed wallpaper was gone, and the walls were now simply covered in a flat paint in soft eggshell. The rickety windows and grimy light fixtures had been replaced by new ones at some point, but those had also grown old and worn in the ensuing years. There was no vomit stained furniture, no ash-covered smoking stand, no lingering voices.

"This," said Jackson, flinging open the French doors leading into the sunroom, "Is my favorite room in the whole house."

"Mine too," said Lily, drawing a quizzical look from Jackson.

The room was awash in afternoon sunlight, and greenery sprouted and flowed from pots of all shapes, sizes, and colors, which lined the shelves of the bookcases and filled every corner.

"Wow - how are these plants so beautiful, with no one living here?" Lily asked.

"I come by every day or two and water them," said Jackson. "She - the wife - was going to toss them into the dumpster when she moved, but I couldn't stand to see them get trashed."

"Why didn't you just take them to your place?" Lily asked.

"They were an awful mess," said Jackson. "I was afraid they would die if I moved them. Anyway," he said, leaning in toward Lily. "I'll tell you a secret: it's so nice and quiet in this neighborhood - the plants give me a reason to come here so I can practice. It's secluded, so I'm not bothering my neighbors like I do when I play at my apartment. Plus, I don't have to be self-conscious because I know no one can hear me."

"Is there such a thing as a self-conscious guitar player?" asked Lily. She would have backed away to balance out the personal space between them, but she was enjoying the quality of his eyes. They were a crystal-clear blue, grazed by the glint of the sun. "I thought you guys were all about putting on a show as if God gave you an extra 'look at me' gene."

"I must've stepped out of the showmanship line to get stoned or something," said Jackson, "because I did not get that gene at all. Probably why I'm playing to a room full of plants. But they do really seem to like it." He scanned the array of pots with a smile as if they were loyal and adoring fans.

"I heard you playing when I was outside," said Lily. "Kansas, right? It was very nice."

"Thanks." Jackson smiled. "So, if you don't mind my saying so, I noticed you're not wearing a wedding ring. It's strange that a single person would be interested in this place; that lawn alone is practically a full-time job - not to mention what it would take to care for the fruit trees."

"As long as we're telling secrets," said Lily, "I should come clean and tell you that I'm not interested in buying." She waited to see signs of anger or disappointment on his face, but Jackson just nodded his head. Lily added, "See, I grew up here. We sold this place after my father died in the early eighties. I came because -

well, I don't really know why I came to tell you the truth."

"No kidding?" said Jackson. "Man, I remember the house I grew up in... I'd love to go back and see it. Why don't you just go take a look around? I'm sure you can find your way without me."

"Really? You don't mind?"

"Not at all. The philodendron - I call him Phil - he wants me to run through that last tune again anyway." Jackson reached back and swung his guitar around to his chest. "You have fun."

The house was much smaller than Lily had remembered it, and every room had been redecorated. Someone else's memories now covered over the sights of Lily's childhood. The little boy smells of sweat and dirt were gone from the room that Charles, William, and Ricci had shared; the big boy smells of stale pot smoke and sandalwood incense were gone from the room that Louis and Henry had slept in together once Alexander and John had left for college. Lily entered the bedroom she and Iris had shared after the older girls had moved out. She held her breath in anticipation of the onslaught of emotion she expected, only to find that there was nothing there. No peeling butterfly wallpaper, no wistfulness of dreams long forgotten, no Venetian blinds coated with a film of congealed dust, no overwhelming nostalgia. There was only the vague recollection of two distant little girls who tumbled and fumbled their way down the stairs and out the door.

Lily found her way back to a stirring yet unfamiliar tune coming from the sunroom.

"Back so soon?" Jackson paused his playing.

"Yeah," said Lily. "I think I've seen everything there is to see. Hey - I know you don't like people listening to you, but I have to ask: what was that song you were just playing? It was beautiful."

"Seriously?" said Jackson. "It's a new tune I'm working on."

"You wrote it?"

"Not yet, but I hope to. Songs come to me in bits and pieces, and this one sure is testing my patience. It's kind of like being schizophrenic, except I hear music instead of voices."

"What do you do with them, after you've written them?"

"Depends," said Jackson, adjusting the guitar strap across his shoulders. "I record them mostly, send them out to LA or New York, hoping to get an agent, or get something licensed. One day, I'd like to stop pretending to sell real estate."

"I know what you mean," said Lily. "I'm pretending to be a communications associate."

"You're also pretending to shop for a house."

"Yes, I am," said Lily with a chuckle.

"So technically, we're not even really here right now."

"Now I'm thoroughly confused." Lily laughed.

"Hey - before you go - what's with that cool barn out back?"

"The chicken coop?"

"Is that what it is? I wondered why it was so long and narrow. Hmmm... chickens. Interesting. She - the wife - gave me a key to it and offered me a couple hundred bucks to clean it out."

"What did they use it for?"

"Nothing," said Jackson. "The wife said it was one of those things they'd always intended to do, you know? They thought it might be a playhouse, but when their kids were small, they didn't have the money to convert it. She told me that later on, they thought about turning it into a guesthouse, or a game room, but as the kids grew up, I guess the marriage got kinda shaky. The rest is divorce court history."

"That's too bad," said Lily. "But if they never used it, what is there to clean out?"

"She told me that when they bought this place, it was still full of junk, but the sellers - I guess that would be your family now that I think about it - the sellers knocked a few hundred bucks off the asking price if she would take it with the contents intact."

"I have a vague recollection of that," said Lily. The final act of Capotosti neglect: leaving the mess of memories for someone else to clean out. "We were all kind of discombobulated back then."

"Discombobulated?" said Jackson. "What a fantastic word. Discombobulated."

"Word of the day email," said Lily.

"Discombobulated," repeated Jackson. "I wonder if I could use it in a song. Would be tough to find a rhyme."

378

"Wait just a second," said Lily. "Are you telling me that my family's junk is still in that chicken coop after all this time?"

"Hard to say," said Jackson. "But as far as I can tell, yeah. I have the key here somewhere."

Lily clenched the tiny skeleton key in her fist as she walked toward the chicken coop. The row of windows across the front that used to taunt Lily with its Jack O'Lantern sneer now only sighed and bore a toothless grin. As she approached, the building seemed to get smaller rather than larger, its perspective skewed by the intervening years. Lily worked the key into the rusted lock on the door, jiggling and shimmying it until the latch popped open. Finally free, the stale, dusty air inside lumbered past her, like a stunned and confused prisoner stepping out of solitary confinement. Late afternoon sun poured in through the windows casting spotlights on forgotten boxes and piles of junk that looked immediately familiar: a collection of mismatched ice skates, two bicycle pumps, and a moldy box containing the miniature lean-to from the old family Nativity set that the children put up every year - complete with ceramic figurines of shepherds, sheep, oxen, wise men, and of course the Sacred Family. As a child, Lily had spent hours every Christmas season staring at the tiny scene, playing with the figurines, telling baby Jesus that she loved him and that if she had been there, she would have brought him inside and he could have been born in the sunroom, or even on her bed.

When Lily lifted the box, the bottom fell out, and the pieces - sheep, angels, Joseph - all came tumbling out. Baby Jesus rolled away and disappeared between two stacks of boxes against the wall, and as Lily moved them to get to him, she noticed a distinct and unmistakable shade of blue peeking out from behind the boxes. Quieter than royal blue, but deeper than powder blue, it was the color of the open sky on a July afternoon. She slipped Jesus into her pocket and stretched out to retrieve Iris' blue valise.

Without regard for the years of grime coating the concrete, Lily sat down cross-legged and placed the valise on the floor in front of her. The sketch of a young man and woman standing in front of the Eiffel tower was still clearly branded in the lower right corner.

Lily pressed on the latch, and the cover of the valise sprang open. It appeared empty, except for the pink satin lining which was still intact, though faded. Lily raised the valise to her face and inhaled deeply. Beyond the mold, it still smelled like Saturday morning dance class, like freshly toasted Italian bread dunked in coffee the color of caramel. It smelled like Iris.

Strange that this little valise had sparked Iris' imagination so long ago. She'd always been captivated by it, and by the idea of faraway places where boys and girls could lustfully wander, have great adventures and see amazing things. Just as strange was the way the valise had always created a sense of abandonment in Lily. How did this tiny construction of plastic, vinyl, and satin become imbued with such power as to send one sister forth and hold another back? If Auntie Rosa had not given Iris the valise, where would she be now? Or, what if she had bought two of them? Would Lily also be living another life in an exotic and remote place, or would she have remained deaf to the beckoning that Iris so clearly heard? Would Lily have escaped the misery of her life with Joe? Would she have missed the ecstasy of carrying her sweet babies in her belly, and giving them birth? Would she have been spared the agony of watching them walk away? Would that life have been a better one?

She remembered a time when a little girl she knew had lain in that spot, confused and powerless. Why hadn't she just walked away that day when Henry had first brought her here? Why did she so often seem to stay in situations when anyone else would go, would run and not turn back? And where was that little girl now?

Lily knew that even if she overturned every box, she would not find that child. She was past, disappeared into the folds of time. She existed only because Lily sustained her with thought and memory. She was real once, perhaps, but now she was just a story of what used to be - a story that Lily had nurtured and told herself again and again throughout her life. It was a story that she had used to explain mysteries and rationalize decisions, as though the idea of that child was a discrete and volatile thing with a will of its own, steering Lily this way or that.

She closed the lid of the valise and held it to her chest as she lay back on the cool concrete and drifted off.

"Hello?" Jackson's voice startled Lily awake, and in the moment before she realized that decades had passed since she last found herself lying there, she bolted upright. Jackson stood in the doorway, his body a silhouette against the setting sun.

"Whatcha got there?"

"Oh, hi," said Lily, gathering her composure. "Can you believe it? This used to be mine." She held the valise up, hoping to distract him, as though he might otherwise see the memories suspended in the air all around her. "Actually, it was my sister's."

"Wow... " said Jackson. "What was her name?"

"Iris."

"How did she die?"

"Oh! She's not dead. She lives in Italy." The thought of Iris dead sent a chill up her spine. She would send her a message as soon as she got home. There was suddenly so much to say.

Jackson extended his hand toward Lily and helped her up.

"May I?" asked Jackson, pointing to Lily's head. Without waiting for her to answer, he extracted a long sticky cobweb from her hair and held it up to show her. "How long were you in here, anyway?" He laughed.

"A lifetime," said Lily.

"I hate to disturb you, but I gotta close up shop here," said Jackson.

"No - not at all - I'm sorry if I held you up." Clutching the valise to her chest, Lily asked, "Do you think I could keep this? I mean, technically it belongs to the house. I don't want to steal it."

"Clearly, it's yours."

"I could pay you for it if you want."

"I tell you what," said Jackson. "Have coffee with me sometime, and we'll call it even."

Lily felt a flush to her cheeks. "Deal."

They stepped back outside into the oblique sunshine.

"Have you ever been?" Jackson asked, locking the chicken coop.

"Where?"

"To Italy. To see your sister."

"No, not yet."

"I've heard it's gorgeous," said Jackson. "I've always wanted to go - Italians are best at three of my favorite things: wine, coffee, and bicycles." Jackson tugged on the padlock, to ensure it was locked. "So how come you've never been?"

"I guess I never had the time, or the money, or the freedom... I don't know; maybe those are all just excuses. It's a long story."

"Stories are fun," said Jackson. "Maybe yours has a chapter with a trip to Italy, but you just haven't gotten to that part yet."

"Could be," said Lily. Holding up the valise, she added, "At least now I have a suitcase."

Lily and Jackson walked back toward the house, a flurry of insects and dandelion tufts dancing toward dusk, the blue valise gently swinging to and fro at Lily's side.

13. IRIS

Iris stepped into her denim overalls, slipped the straps over her shoulders and hooked up the bib over her T-shirt, feeling quite American indeed. Max would have considered the dungarees the epitome of un-sexiness and made some disgusting remark about how he wouldn't get an erection (only he would call it a hard-on) for a week after seeing her dressed like that. Gregorio, not to mention Isabella and dear Cinzia, would have thought them an abominable garment for anyone of a certain social standing, let alone a woman, to be seen in. But Iris felt right at home in her OshKosh overalls; she had been thrilled to stumble upon them at a used clothes stall at the *Festa di Primavera*, a little country fair just down the road from her house, where she had also bought some plants for her garden. It had been on the first of May, a day which commemorated different things for different people, among them May Day, Labor Day, and Bea's fiftieth birthday. Iris wondered whether she would be as self-assured and independent as Beatrix when she turned fifty herself. She was working at it, and fortunately still had a few more years to go. Like her mother always said, she'd cross that bridge when she came to it. Over the past several months, her mother - perhaps finally finding an opening for more closeness now that Auntie Rosa was gone, perhaps because she had learned of Iris's struggles through Lily - had also suggested more proactive ways for her to deal with the challenges of rebuilding her life. Betty Capotosti was always ready to come to the aid of a struggling woman - even it was her own daughter.

The sun was beginning its descent behind the hill as Iris stepped out the door of her little stone house, pausing to drink in the sweet scent of the jasmine climbing over the wrought iron gate, and to allow her computer-weary eyes to rest on the view of the terraced olive groves across the valley. She loved the freedom of working from home but sometimes forgot when to quit, especially when she was immersed in writing about hotels that enthused her. She took pride in capturing the atmosphere of the properties she inspected in her descriptions, while respecting the three-hundred-word limit – not a simple feat, given her tendency to write on until she had covered every single aspect that might spark an interest in readers. Her goal was to make them crave the deep sense of inner peace and timeless beauty inspired by the Fiesole hills when admired from the rooftop terrace of a particular hotel in Florence, for example; to make them succumb, heart and soul, to the overwhelming romanticism of a fiery sunset over Capri as viewed from the restaurant of a certain charming resort on the Sorrento coast; and, ultimately, to book their accommodations at any of the hotels in the Delightful Hotels and Resorts Italian Collection.

She reached her arms to the sky in a stretch, then touched her fingers to her toes, before sitting down on the steps leading to the garden to lace up her sneakers. Two cats approached: one tiger-striped, the other black and white. They stopped by their empty bowls, crouched on their haunches, front paws daintily composed in front of them, and stared at her.

"Sorry, you two. It's not time yet," Iris said, holding her hand out in the vain hope of caressing one of them. The cats spent their days roaming freely about the stone paths and country gardens of the sleepy little neighborhood, stopping by for their fill of food and compliments when they felt like it. "Come on, I'm not asking for much," Iris said to the pair, who simply looked back at her and blinked. A little love and affection were not easy to come by these days.

Ready to set to work, Iris fetched a pair of clippers from the tool shed and headed straight for her lilac bush. The plant had survived tough times while confined to a pot on the terrace in the hostile company of Max and his cacti, but Iris had continued caring for it throughout the summer and autumn until her move the past winter – a move in which neither Max nor his prickly pears were included. Since sinking its roots into the soil of its permanent home, the lilac had begun to finally thrive and repaid her with the generous gift of five fragrant blooms.

Iris was conscientious about providing all her plants with proper water and nourishment, but as she carefully clipped away bits of dead wood and suckers from the lilac, she realized that she was not a good pruner. Because she had a hard time recognizing the difference between growth that benefitted a plant and growth that was detrimental to its long-term wellbeing, her clipping was more conservative than recommended by the manuals she consulted. She wondered whether that tendency was part of an ingrained behavioral pattern of hers which might also be responsible for her difficulty in making a clean break with the past.

Sniffing a pale purple bloom, she closed her eyes and thought of Lily, who had emailed her a picture of a grinning Joseph and proud Pierce on their bicycles as they toured the Lilac Festival in Highland Park. The lone bush in Iris's garden was no match for the scores of varieties that flourished in the park, but its presence helped Iris keep alive some pleasant recollections of her childhood. On more than one occasion, Lily had remarked on Iris's knack for cultivating the good memories and weeding out the bad, another trait that made it difficult for her to have an objective view of the past. Iris could never see the point of dwelling on past memories that upset her, but at times she wished her tendency was inverted. If, when glancing over a shoulder at the past, Iris could see nothing but pain and disappointment, wouldn't that inspire her to run headlong into the arms of a more promising future, and never look back?

Since that day when she kicked Max out - Iris still did not like to think of it in such brutal terms, but Lily insisted she force herself to; it was "empowering," she said – one of her greatest challenges had been to overcome that very tendency. Whenever she thought back on her relationship with Max, her mind inevitably selected memories of the romantic dinners, the spectacular sunsets, the travels, the freedom from rules and routine, and, let's face it, the hottest sex she had ever been party to. Granted, those mental incursions into what Lily referred to as Iris's la-la-land usually occurred after a disastrous date with some divorcee who had moved back in with mamma after the breakup, or some hopelessly boring engineer (Liguria was crawling with them, in particular, naval engineers, possibly the most tedious sub-species of the profession).

After providing Iris with no news of his whereabouts for nearly a month, Max had begun sending her messages and emails telling her he had "so much" to tell her. But because he never progressed beyond that preface, she never knew whether he was sorry, or suffering, or missing her, or making a new life without her. At least, not until the day he turned up at the apartment in Ruta to pick up some clothes and took the opportunity to inform her that his lady friend in Ponza was pregnant. So she had been right all along. This Lorella woman - whom Iris, with the help of Bea and the Internet, had since identified and viewed photos of in various poses and situations, determining that she appeared even more beautiful and successful than Iris had imagined - was definitely giving Max something Iris could not. Something another woman, in another set of circumstances, was also giving Gregorio. As soon as his divorce from Iris was final, he had plans to marry the demure elementary school teacher with two small children he had met at the Policlinico, where she had entered the respectable and pitiable state of widowhood following a risky surgical procedure unsuccessfully performed on her terminally ill husband.

With quivering lips, Iris had asked Max to hand back his keys (Lily had been bugging her to change the locks, but Iris thought the measure rather drastic), and told him to send over a van for the rest of his belongings within a week. She then threw herself on the sofa for a good cry, the duration of which was further prolonged by her realization that soon the sofa itself would also be gone.

Iris sighed, wishing that the painful memory of that moment could be prolonged, at least enough to prevent her from wondering whether Max's baby had been born yet, whether it was a little boy or a little girl, whether he would take his family with him when he traveled, or whether he would leave them behind so he would be free to pursue fresh prey at each new destination.

Shaking her head to chase away such thoughts, she strolled over to the climbing tea rose, whose thin branches were weighed down by dozens of bright pink flowers and hosts of tight, new buds. She stopped to tie some wayward stems to the rudimentary trellis she had constructed from canes, then looked around to see what else needed tending. The grass of the gently sloping lawn was a bit wild, but she liked it that way, especially when it was swimming with little daisies like now, or earlier in the season, when the generous sprinkling of violets had discouraged her from cutting until it had almost grown too high for her to tackle with the rusty-bladed manual lawnmower left behind by the previous owners.

She wandered over to a spot near the old apple tree, which was her favorite corner of the garden. That was where she had found a cluster of irises, and where, in honor of Lily, she had planted the bulbs of the calla lilies, choosing them over the sweet-smelling lilies of the valley which were so dainty they would have been overshadowed by the taller flowers. Leaving plenty of room for both to grow, she had planted the lily bulbs near the dormant irises and waited impatiently for them to blossom. It filled Iris with joy now, to see the fanciful purple flowers and the essential and elegant white blooms standing side by side on their sturdy green stalks, in a safe place, where no one could trample them.

Her eyes roamed over to the fig tree raising its tender new leaves to the sun on crooked arms, to the lemon and orange trees, which bore both fruit and blossoms at this time of year, to the olive trees her mother had taught her to dream about decades ago, simply by placing one outside the kitchen window. The simple plants and flowers of her childhood home in America and the more exotic flora of her adoptive home in Italy surrounded her, fostering the realization that her home was neither here nor there, but the place where she was free to live and grow according to her nature.

There was still plenty of work to do on the little *rustico* she had found not far from Camogli, but she had moved in as soon as the plumbing and electricity were in working order, anxious to escape the memories (and junk) left behind by Max in the apartment in Ruta, which she could ill-afford once she became jobless. As soon as she laid eyes on the simple stone structure that had been standing in the sunny valley long before the sumptuous villas and overpriced condominiums had overcrowded the Riviera, she had felt an unexplainable flutter deep inside, as if some dormant part of her were stirring to life. The two-room house, once a shepherd's cottage, had belonged to a retired boatswain living in Rapallo, who spent his days tending to the small plot of land that had been in his family for generations. When the man died, his widow was anxious to sell the house, but the modest property was too small to accommodate the material needs of a modern family, too simple to encourage the expectations of a young couple, too fraught with architectural barriers for an older person, too isolated for singles so used to living in a densely populated area that they felt uncomfortable without the noise of neighbors living above, below and beside them. For Iris, it was perfect. The old woman had agreed to rent it to her until she could come up with the money for the purchase and then it would be hers.

Iris had been apprehensive about taking the leap with so little financial security backing her and such a foggy future looming ahead of her. She had only recently started her freelance job inspecting hotels all over the country and writing reviews for Delightful Hotels and Resorts, the same representation company with which she had collaborated as manager of the Dimora Baia dell'Incanto. When she emailed Lily the photos of the neglected home and overgrown garden, Lily had written back immediately, telling her the house looked like it needed her just as much as Iris needed it. Backed by Lily's encouragement, Beatrix's string-pulling with the director of her bank's mortgage department in Milan, and all her savings, Iris managed to close the deal by Christmas. When she had devised the four-point recovery plan to help her get back on course after her breakup with Max, Iris had never imagined that the resolution to "follow your heart" (point 1), and "be daring" (point 4) would entail indebting herself up to her eyeballs, but then again, she never would have imagined most of what had happened to her in life.

Iris gazed regretfully at the sun as it slipped behind the hill, knowing it would still be shining in Camogli. These were the longest days of the year, and she was struck with the idea that this might be the perfect time to fulfill another challenge she had put to herself but postponed for far too long with the excuse of waiting for warmer weather, and which would also have the added benefit of satisfying her "stay physically fit" requirement (point 2).

Excited by her newly hatched plan, Iris put away her tools and skipped into the house, where she changed, stuffed a few items into her backpack, including the book she was reading in Italian, to "pursue mental stimulation" (point 3)". She hopped on her scooter and headed up the hill; within minutes she caught up with the retreating sun.

"Diecimila," the aging beach boy in a Speedo said, and Iris placed a banknote in his hand. He stashed the bill in the money pouch strapped around his waist, then tucked two lank strands of sun-bleached hair behind his ears and lifted a yellow kayak from a rack. Iris was hoping he would give her the red one but said nothing. Balancing the kayak on his shoulder, he pranced nimbly across the pebbly strip of beach and placed it at the water's edge. He told Iris she could leave her backpack with him, and in exchange handed her a long wooden paddle.

"What about my life vest?" Iris asked the guy, as she peered at the immense blue looking-glass stretching across the gulf, and out into the open sea.

The guy cocked his head and looked at Iris as if she had asked whether there was a fully stocked bar on board. "It's smooth as oil," he said, pointing his chin at the sea, "but there's probably one behind the seat if you need it. These things are unsinkable. If you flip, just hang on and swim."

Iris forced a nervous smile as she lowered herself into the cockpit, then made a surreptitious sign of the cross as the man launched her with a shove and a grunt. She focused on her breathing and balance as she floated past a group of shrill-voiced children throwing stones in the shallow water despite mothers nagging them not to get wet, then maneuvered awkwardly to avoid a group of boisterous teenage boys tossing a water polo ball back and forth. Few swimmers ventured farther out into the deeper, colder water, especially at the beginning of the season, leaving Iris feeling quite alone in her kayak. Looking over her shoulder to gauge the growing distance from the receding safety of the beach, her courage wavered, and she fancied she could see past images of herself shimmering on the surface of the water: a younger, inexperienced Iris following Gregorio's lead, each movement of hers meticulously monitored, patiently corrected, as she paddled behind the husband who was poised to rush to her rescue should she stray from the safety of the course he had charted for them both. A breeze rippled the water, dissolving the image, and a more recent version of Iris emerged, an Iris trembling with determination to prove her worth to a smirking Max who goaded her on from behind, challenging her to paddle faster, daring her to adventure farther, his constant prodding confusing her to the point that she lost sight of where she was heading. When she finally turned around to ask for directions, she saw him zigzagging off in another direction.

She reminded herself that today she was finally the captain of her kayak; she set her own course, her own speed, her own goal. She turned her gaze forward, knowing she must not look back again if she were to succeed. Taking a deep breath, she focused on the distant view of Punta Chiappa, lurking low on the water like the humped back of a mighty sea creature. She had hiked overland from San Rocco to the agglomerate rock outcrop many times, but this was her first time venturing there on her own by sea. Knowing that reaching her destination depended solely upon her own abilities and determination was both a fascinating and frightening feeling. Her strokes were hesitant at first, their rhythm erratic, as they thrust her into the unfamiliar dimension she had decided, of her own volition, to explore. Her sense of vulnerability was not allayed by the fact that both sea and sky were calm, nor could she dismiss as irrational her concerns that stealthy currents and whimsical waves might at any time pounce upon her and overturn the kayak just for fun, the way a playful pup might topple a toddler.

"What is the worst that could happen?" she asked a seagull

bobbing on the water, as she imagined the scene of the capsized kayak. She might be able to swim back, as long as she didn't panic. Or, she could hang onto the kayak until someone came looking for her, praying not to freeze or drown in the meantime. Staring down into the deep blue sea from the flimsy fiberglass shell that suspended her above the abyss, Iris imagined her legs dangling beneath the surface of the water as she clung to the kayak. Thanks to those dreadful killer shark movies, she could visualize perfectly how tender and juicy her white flesh would look to the eyes of the fish that were certainly lurking beneath her. She paddled cautiously, watching with increasing dismay the rocky coast to her left rising to form craggy cliffs too steep to provide a place to land. Iris was stranded in her shell, her paddle her only defense against the fickle elements. She knew she was free to turn back at any time, but she also knew she couldn't. She wouldn't.

Counting each stroke as it sliced the water, concentrating on the coordination of her movements, she gradually relaxed, and soon found her rhythm, alternating her arms, right, left, right, left, each dip of the paddle sprinkling her bare back and shoulders with cold seawater. She managed a smile when she spotted a shoal of silvery anchovies glittering just below the surface of the water, and frowned as she glided past the orange buoys which marked the fishing nets of the *tonnarella* that were dropped in the same spot each spring. The nets reminded her of her trip to Carloforte just a year ago, of the bloody rite of the tuna kill, of the phone call warning her of Auntie Rosa's imminent death, of Max's total lack of understanding, of his lighthearted betrayal.

Iris reached Punta Chiappa just as the passenger ferry on a stopover from the isolated hamlet of San Fruttuoso en route to Camogli reversed its engines and pulled away from the jetty. A young couple with a camera and a child waved their hats at her; she smiled and waved back, though her heart was pounding as the kayak rocked wildly on the waves caused by the ferry's wake. Iris imagined what comments the tourists might make about the woman they saw in the kayak, so brave to go out on the sea all by herself. Vowing to be as fearless as they must think her, she rubbed her white knuckles, took a deep breath, and set off for her return trip to Camogli.

As she paddled, Iris felt a sudden surge of courage. It seemed a uniquely feminine form of courage, filling her with equal doses of physical and emotional strength, daring and caution. It flowed into her shoulders and arms, propelling her forward, infusing her with determination.

"There's no looking back, Iris," she said out loud, ever aware of the abyss below still threatening to undermine her confidence. "Just stay your course." She recalled the dark sea of emptiness into which she had plunged after her break-up with Max; how bitterly she had regretted giving up the security of marriage and the safe haven of a family for him, how foolhardy she had been to toss aside her financial independence and professional identity to follow him around like a stray mongrel, licking up his crumbs, hoping for a pat on the head; how terrified she had been to discover herself all alone, with no one to share her life, her dreams, her failures.

"There's nothing to be afraid of!" she called out. Lily had repeated those same words to her many times since then. "You're doing great on your own!" The louder she spoke, the more convinced she felt, and the more convinced she felt, the harder she pushed herself. She was amazed at her ability to achieve such speed and maintain such a steady route.

"Did you really need a Max to prod you and push you?" she cried to the open sea. "Did you really need a Gregorio to tow you and guide you?" she demanded of the sky. She thrust her pelvis forward in sync with each movement of her shoulders and arms, feeling her anger grow with each stroke. She unleashed her fury at the men who had designated themselves her leaders and superiors but was even more outraged at herself for falling into their traps, for not having had the courage to try and find out who she really was, instead of letting others decide for her.

"You will not do that again!" Her voice rose to a shout as she pressed on. (*stroke-breath*) "I'm talking to all you Gregorios out there!" she yelled. (*stroke-breath*) "I'm talking to all you Maxes!" Water sprayed over her shoulders and back as she oared, her palms burning, her shoulders aching. (*stroke-breath*) "And I'm talking to you, Iris!" She had never forgotten Lily's words: *What kind of woman are you when you're with Max?*

"I was a stupid woman! (*stroke-breath*) A blind woman! (*stroke-breath*) A weak woman!" (*stroke-breath*) Seawater splashed her face as Iris jettisoned the fear and insecurity that had been the ballast of her life. "I'm not that woman anymore!" she yelled, as the kayak glided over the water, light, and swift. "I never want to be that woman again!"

Just be Iris had been Lily's simple words of advice. "I'm Iris. You hear that?" She filled her lungs and thrust the paddle into the water, harder and deeper. Raising her face to the sky, she was shouting, "I'M IRIS CAPOTOSTI!", when she felt rather than heard a heavy thump reverberate through the thin hull. The kayak shook and swerved, nearly capsizing before Iris managed to recover her equilibrium.

"What the heck?!" she cried, holding the oar across her chest, her heart pounding as she scanned the water for the tip of the submerged rock or trunk of driftwood or frightfully large fish that might have caused the impact. Whipping her head around to check her wake, she was horrified to see a pair of human hands attached to a pair of human arms floating just below the surface of the water.

"Oh, my God!" Iris screamed. She lowered the right end of the paddle into the water to veer the kayak around. As she rowed over, a head emerged, sputtering and coughing. Like the hands and arms, it was attached to the body of a man! An alive one, praise Jesus, Mary, and Joseph!

"Oh, my God!" she cried again, instinctively continuing in the mother tongue of her madwoman monologue. "Are you hurt?"

"*Are you crazy?!*" the man screamed, pressing a hand against his skull. At least he could still speak, and in English at that.

"Oh, my God!" Iris yelled a third time, horrified to see blood dripping from the man's head, down his hand and into the water, where it disappeared together with Iris's newfound courage. What had she done? What if the guy lost consciousness? What if he drowned, right there in front of her?!

"I can't believe this is happening!" she cried, her voice trembling, her insides quivering.

"*You* can't?!" The man tilted his head up to look at her. She tried to check for signs of concussion in his eyes, but all she could see in them was the molten orange glaze of the setting sun reflecting off the water.

"Are you all right?" she cried, hoping he would say something to contradict her impression that he was on the verge of passing out.

"What does it look like to you?" he barked.

His tone of outrage was reassuring, anyway, but it also rekindled the still smoldering anger Iris had been venting out at sea. Who did this man think he was, talking to her like that when she was only trying to help? She might be at fault for paddling into him, but really, the guy must be crazy to be swimming so far out on his own. Why, he could have been struck by a motor boat and chopped to pieces by the propeller! And if he didn't care about his own safety, he should be more considerate of others. Because of his stupidity, she was the one sitting there feeling guilty and helpless all over again.

"What are you doing way out here, anyway?" she said, determined to assert her new self, but instead of replying, the man slipped silently beneath the surface of the water again and stayed there. Wasn't he ever going to come up for air? What if he didn't? What if he had lost consciousness after all?!

"*Hey, you!*" she cried, pushing herself closer with the kayak. She watched in horror as his thick dark hair swirled in the bloodied water around his submerged head. "Don't do that! *Come up! Right now!*" She inched closer, until the kayak was almost on top of him until she could reach into the water and grab a fistful of his hair. She tugged at it so hard, the kayak listed to one side and a wave splashed over its edge, flooding the cockpit with water.

"*Ooowww!*" the man popped to the surface with such force, he rocked the kayak in the opposite direction, causing it to take on more water. "Are you trying to scalp me, too?" he screamed.

Iris was flooded with relief at the sound of his voice. Let him insult her and curse her and even sink her if he wanted. Anything, sweet Jesus, as long as he didn't drown! The man then gripped the side of the kayak, steadying both of them. At least he had the strength to hang on, that was a good sign. As she stared down at him, trying to get a better look at the wound, the man cocked his head up at her, and their eyes locked. She leaned slightly to one side so that her body would shield his face from the sun's glare. He blinked once, slowly, as if his vision were blurred, and when he reopened his eyes, the orange glaze was gone. If it weren't for the fact that the man must be in pain, she might have mistaken the glimmer in his warm brown eyes for a flicker of recognition, or a glint of amusement, or even - as absurd as that may be - a twinkle of admiration.

Though she knew she should immediately find a way to transport the man to safety, all she could do was stare at him staring at her, and wonder why he looked so familiar. Maybe it was the classic shape of the man's head that gave her that impression; she could picture such a head on the statue of a Greek or Roman god. But marble didn't split open that easily, she thought, panicking again at the sight of blood gushing from the long gash on the man's forehead.

"Oh Lord, what have I done?" she cried, cupping a hand over her mouth, realizing that her oar had missed his eye by no more than an inch. She could have easily blinded him; no doubt that would be only one of the many accusations he would flail at her once they were back on land and he recovered from his shock.

"Does it hurt?" she asked, afraid of his answer. She wondered whether he was one of those macho types who actually enjoyed brandishing injuries but never admitted to pain, or one of those who blew any form of suffering way out of proportion whenever he saw the opportunity to squeeze some extra attention out of a woman.

"Not really," the man said, still treading water with his legs and holding onto the kayak with his left hand, as he splashed seawater over the gash with his right. "It just stings like hell." Of course it did; and he'd be sure to feel more pain later when a nice bump and bruise settled in over the cut.

He probably couldn't wait to scream and rant at her, but some male instinct was probably advising him to wait. After all, she was in the more powerful position, bobbing safely above him in her kayak and armed with a deadly oar, while he was in the more vulnerable position, injured and dog-paddling in deep water. The thought of what he might say to her later made her want to row away as fast as she could.

"Why don't you hang on there?" she said, annoyed at the tremor in her hand when she pointed to the handle at the aft of the kayak. "And I'll row you to shore."

"No offense," the man said. "But I'd rather swim." His lips parted, revealing a gap between his two front teeth. The hint of a smile made her wonder whether she had been too quick to cast him in the role of the menacing male; he was far more believable as a little boy who loved splashing around in the water and had simply wandered too far from shore. Again, she was struck with a feeling of familiarity, as if she had known him back when he was a child. He was probably around her age, and they might have known each other, had they grown up in the same place. But they hadn't, that much she was sure of.

"But you're in no shape to swim!" Iris said.

"I doubt my swimming could be any worse than your kayaking."

"I'm not that bad!" Iris said. Of course, she wasn't; expert kayakers clobbered swimmers on the head all the time.

"No, I'm sure you're not bad at all," the man said, looking up at her. His irises were hazelnut, with flecks of dark chocolate. Oddly, she had felt more sure of herself before, when the eyes were glossed over by the sun.

"Seriously, I can pull you," she said, wondering whether she actually could. "You just have to hang on."

The man smiled again, shook his head. "Really. I'll swim," he said.

"I'll follow you then, to make sure you're all right."

The man nodded, then set off without another word, the muscles in his back and shoulders rippling as his arms cut through the water with strong, even strokes. She wondered how much effort it cost him to swim like that in his condition and whether he was just doing it to impress her. Part of her was irritated at the display, but another part wished she could ditch the kayak and jump into the water with him. She felt cumbersome in her kayak as she began paddling again, but soon overcame the resistance of the water, and found herself gliding - at a safe distance - behind the first victim of the new, improved Iris.

If she hadn't been so upset by the accident and so worried about the anger and insults she still may have to endure once the man was safely ashore, she would have sat back and congratulated herself on the successful completion of her challenge. She would have delighted in the golden rays of the setting sun warming her wet back and bathing the tall, multicolored houses clustered along Camogli's seafront in a glowing mélange of pinks and oranges and yellows. Instead, Iris kept her apprehensive gaze trained on the man as he stepped out of the water; he had swum well, regardless of what he wanted to prove, and seemed to be steady on his feet. Seeing him in such good shape was encouraging; she'd soon be able to rush home for a sorely needed glass of wine and a hot shower, then she could try and put the incident behind her. But first, she had the duty to make sure the man didn't need any assistance. After all, she did slice his forehead open with her paddle. She landed her kayak by the rental kiosk, grabbed her backpack, and made a dash across the pebbly beach toward him in her bathing suit, her sandals dangling from her hand.

"Hey!" she called, slightly short of breath, wincing from the discomfort of hopping barefooted over the stones.

The man was holding a towel to his head, blotting his cut. Water dripped from his hair, which curled into soft black locks around his square-jawed face. Spotting Iris as she approached, he raised his hands in front of his face. "Hold it right there!" he said.

"Don't worry. I come in peace." Iris opened her arms, dropping her backpack and sandals. "How's your head?" The man was a few inches taller than her, forcing her to crane her neck and stand on tiptoes for a closer look. "It's still bleeding," she said. "You might need stitches. Can I take you to the hospital?" She had never driven a passenger on her Vespa, let alone an injured one. What if he started swooning and swaying behind her, and caused them both to fall?

"You're quite the Florence Nightingale, aren't you?" he said with a laugh, revealing that little space between his front teeth again as he slung his bloodied towel over his shoulder.

"No!" Iris blurted out. Was it that obvious? Had she changed so little despite all her months of trying break old habits? "I mean, what kind of person would just leave without making sure you're OK?"

"I'll be fine, don't worry," he said, dropping his towel and bending over to pick up a black T-shirt from a small pile of neatly stacked garments. His balance seemed quite good, but Iris was distracted from making further clinical assessments when he raised his arms over his head to put on his T-shirt. She had just enough time to admire his well-formed chest and taut abdomen when his head popped through the opening. It was still bleeding. She unzipped her backpack and took out her towel.

"May I?" she asked, pressing the towel to the cut on his head.

"Ouch," he said, wincing, then fell silent. After a moment, he waved her away. "Thanks."

"It's the least I could do," she said.

"So, your accent tells me East Coast," he said. "Did you kayak all the way across the Atlantic? You were traveling at a pretty fast clip."

"No," Iris smiled, relieved. Apparently, he was going to spare her the insults. "The kayak was only mine for an hour. I live here." She waved her hand in the general direction of the hill beyond which lay her hidden valley. She was curious to know why he spoke such good English, too. "And how about you?"

"I always have a hard time saying where I'm from. But I live in Italy, too. Most of the time, anyway. Sometimes Milan, when I have to, but preferably by the sea."

Iris nodded. She understood completely; she disliked it when her job forced her to spend more than a day in any city. She was curious about his accent but didn't want to sound nosy. "I can tell you didn't learn English in Milan, though." By not phrasing it as a question, she would leave him free to drop the subject or volunteer whatever information he felt like sharing.

"My father was born in Chile, my mother in Australia, both children of Italian immigrants married to locals. They met in New York."

"Amazing! What were the odds of that happening?" Iris said.

"Quite a long shot," the man said, smiling. "About as likely as me colliding with an American at the helm of a kayak in the Mediterranean."

"I'd say." Iris laughed, slowly shaking her head. "By the way, I'm Iris."

"I'm Martin," the man said, holding out his hand.

"Nice to meet you," Iris said, extending hers. "Nicer than before, I mean." He nodded slowly, clasping her hand a few seconds longer than necessary.

"You know, Iris," he said. "I can't shake this feeling that we've met before."

"You mean before the catastrophe at sea?"

"Yes, way before that."

She felt the same way, too. So much so, that she felt a pang of loss when he finally released her hand. Iris could already imagine herself telling Lily about this strange encounter; she could already hear Lily scolding her for being intrigued by such a stupid line. ("Geez, Iris! *Haven't we met before?*' How original, really!") But the fact was, this man, this Martin, did not seem a stranger at all. Except for the fact that he quite obviously was.

"Well, I think we would have remembered each other," Iris said before her imagination could start weaving fabric from material that wasn't there.

"Sure, and I don't suppose I can trust my memory right now, anyway," he said. "Maybe I just need another whack on the head." He looked at her with disarming directness, but there was nothing at all in his gaze that would make her categorize him as the type of man who undressed women with his eyes. She had become all too expert at reading that expression in the past. Here she saw subtlety in the directness; curiosity, intelligence. Still, Iris blushed, suddenly feeling too naked in her bikini.

"So, you're sure you'll be OK?" she asked, knotting her towel around her waist, somehow not minding that it was stained with his blood. She wondered whether she was insured for accidents like this, but couldn't imagine what kind of policy she would need to have. She cringed to think what might have happened if she had whacked a lawsuit-happy American tourist instead. Still, she felt she should give him her telephone number, so he could call her in case he suffered complications. She worried how she could offer the information, without him taking it the wrong way.

"I'm sure," he said. "How about you?"

"What do you mean?"

"I mean, out there on the water, you sounded rather, let me see, how should I phrase this ...?" He paused, raising the thick, arched brows that gave his face a permanent look of surprise. "Intense, I think is the word I'm looking for. Who were you screaming at?"

"Oh, that," Iris said, the heat in her cheeks flaring. "I was just talking to myself." She looked down at her bare feet plastered with pebbles, wondering why they refused to walk her away.

"I hope you're a good listener." He smiled again.

"Yeah, I'm learning." The compelling need to do or say something else anchored her in place. But what? She looked up at him and said, "Anyway, it's Capotosti."

"What is?"

"My name. Just in case, I don't know, if that injury turns out to be serious. Iris Capotosti. I'm in the phone book." There, it was done; if he wanted to claim any damages, he could find her. Now that she had appeased her conscience, at least in part, she really couldn't justify standing there any longer. She raised her hand in an awkward wave, smiled politely, and said, "*Ciao*, then."

"*Ciao*, Iris Capotosti," he said, as she turned and dragged her heavy feet away. She glanced over her shoulder, just once, and saw he still stood facing her, with his back to the sea, his solid shape silhouetted by the setting sun.

"How could I be so dense!" Iris repeated aloud, slapping her forehead with the heel of her hand. Always encouraged by her presence in the kitchen, the cats observed her from their post on the threshold, tails wrapped around their paws, as she set a pot of water on the stove. A gentle breeze billowed the filmy white curtain hanging across the open doorway, one minute hiding the cats from view, the next exposing them.

It wasn't until she had emptied out her backpack the previous evening after returning from her kayaking adventure that Iris made the connection. The book had landed face down on the table, with the author's photograph on the back cover staring straight up at her. The same dark, curly hair, the same arched eyebrows, the same look of intelligent curiosity and amusement. "Martin Casagrande!" she had gasped. "That's who you are!" All that evening, she had repeated the name over and over again, to the cats, to herself; silently, aloud, in a whisper. The man she had clobbered over the head with her paddle was a writer! Iris had never read any of his novels before, but had just recently started *Navigazione a vista*, a book recommended to her by Beatrix.

Spurred by curiosity now that she had met, and nearly killed, the author, Iris had read into the wee hours of the night, not stopping until she reached the back cover. Closing the book, she had studied his photograph again. The eyes seemed a shade darker and deeper than she recalled, but were illuminated by the same mixture of directness and curiosity she had noticed out on the water. Looking into those eyes, she decided that this was no typical male author, this was an uncommonly sensitive man who had a deep understanding of others, and a remarkable ability to interpret the thoughts and feelings of women. Iris felt as though he had dipped his pen into her soul, and scribbled her sentiments across the pages in the form of words. If only she had read the book before meeting him, she would not have been so wary; she would not have heaped upon his battered head the sins of the men who had hurt her.

She was trying to conjure up the image of his smile, trying to decide whether she would define it more as friendly, or amused, when she was summoned back to the present by the cymbal clash of the steel lid vibrating over the pot of boiling water. She drizzled a bit more olive oil into the mortar, working it into the bright green blend of basil and garlic and pine nuts and cheese. She dropped a few handfuls of trofie into the pot, uncorked a bottle of Rossese di Dolceacqua, fed the cats, drained the pasta, and dressed it with a generous dollop of pesto. She carried her dinner out to the garden, and sat at the table she had fashioned from the old wooden door she had replaced, and set on a pair of sawhorses left behind by the Albanian handyman she had hired by the hour to plaster some cracks and help her paint. She lit herself a candle and looked around the garden contentedly as she savored her food and sipped her wine, wishing she could share the moment with Lily. Iris had talked to her recently about the possibility of visiting, and for the first time, instead of changing the subject, Lily had laughed and said Iris had better be on the lookout because she had already a suitcase.

As Iris ate, she reflected on how she had risked allowing the unfortunate incident at the end of her kayaking adventure to compromise the entire experience. She thought back on the rest of the journey, leading up to that moment when she had been paddling bravely back to Camogli, and realized that the hour she had spent alone in the kayak was comprised of many moments, each with its own significance, each offering its own revelations. She made an effort to isolate her feelings of guilt for injuring an unsuspecting swimmer and grasp the importance of what she had done. She had been perfectly capable of piloting the kayak, once she detached herself from her previous perceptions of Iris, and released her grip on the fear of things she could not see. She knew she must have more faith in her abilities, and truly embrace the concept that her only real limitations were those she set herself. Only by letting go of what was behind her, would she be able to face what lay ahead; only by distancing herself from the safety of familiar shores would she be able to embark on new adventures.

Yet try as she may, Iris could not isolate her sense of accomplishment from images of the blood trickling down Martin Casagrande's face, which had immediately triggered in her feelings of guilt, even though once he recovered from his shock, the man had not been in the least concerned with placing the blame on her. Perhaps the character given to her at birth and forged in the kiln of her childhood could not be changed. She might have to accept that she would suffer from bouts of fear and guilt and insecurity throughout her life. But she had no doubt that Lily's three simple words of advice, the same ones she had yelled out to herself at sea, should be her most trusted guide: Just be Iris. And perhaps the key to interpreting the sensations and revelations that had come to her out there on the water was to stop trying to separate the paddle-whacking incident from the rest of the experience; to accept it as one of its organic elements.

Iris sealed the thought with a sip of wine, then rose to bring her empty plate inside. The cats, having licked their bowls clean, paused their postprandial ablutions in mid-action to observe her as she pushed aside the curtain and went through the doorway, then came out again a moment later with the old ukulele she had brought to Italy after Auntie Rosa's death. She couldn't see herself ever playing in front of strangers again, as in the old luau days, but enjoyed her after-dinner habit of playing for the cats, who seemed to appreciate - or at least tolerate - Hawaiian music. She walked back down the stairs to the garden, inhaling the night air heavy with the scents of jasmine and honeysuckle and pittosporum. She sometimes wished the plants would bloom at different times of the year so the inebriating scents would be spread over a longer span, but also knew their simultaneous explosion was what made spring so magical.

Iris upturned her face to the indigo sky, admiring the velvet backdrop it offered to a silver sliver of moon. Again, her thoughts turned to Lily, and a poem she had sent Iris recently. Lily said they were actually the lyrics to "Halfway 'Round the Moon," a song written by a mysterious friend that Lily had promised to tell Iris more about soon. Every time Iris gazed at the moon and thought of the words, she fantasized about meeting Lily up there in the sky, if only long enough to touch fingertips.

"*Gobba a ponente, luna crescente,*" she said aloud, staring up at the perfect crescent. A waxing moon, with summer almost upon her: what could be more promising? She began strumming softly on her uke as she strolled among the olive trees, stopping to admire the lemon and the orange trees, the kumquat and the pomegranate, the lilac and the lawn, the irises and the lilies. Like her, each had a reason for being where it was, the way it was; each brought her joy with its unique offering of fruit and flower.

"A firefly, that's what could make it more promising!" she said, spotting the first one of the season blinking in the laurel bushes, beneath which she had once spotted the pair of hedgehogs that sometimes ventured forth at night to clean up any leftover cat food, but not before the uke playing ceased.

Her spirits soared on the wings of the beauty that surrounded her and the feeling that she, too, was finally where she needed to be. The intensity of her strumming increased until she became so lost in the music, she had the impression she could hear Uncle Alfred accompanying her. At a certain point, the second set of strings sounded so real that she interrupted her playing, and cocked her ear. Silence. What did she expect to hear? Uncle Alfred and his steel guitar? An angel with a harp? Yet as soon as she resumed her playing, she was certain it was the sound of another instrument she was hearing, not an echo of her own.

"*Chi c'è?*" she called out to the darkness.

The snappy arpeggio of a string instrument replied. Could it be a banjo? No, the sound was bright and woody, not twangy and flat. It must be some sort of mandolin. Iris crept toward the sound of the notes that seemed to come from the path flanking her garden. Hiding behind the jasmine vines that draped the gate, she peered into the darkness, where she discerned the shadow of a man.

"*Chi è lì?*" Iris asked, very curious, slightly alarmed. Even in her wildest state of paranoia, she couldn't fathom a mandolin-wielding homicidal maniac strolling the countryside, but just the same …

"*Mi scusi!*" a man's voice replied from the shadows. "*Spero di non averla spaventata."*

Iris didn't think it wise to admit to this stranger that he did frighten her, at least a little. *"No, figuriamoci,"* she said.

"A volte suono mentre cammino, o cammino mentre suono, non so esattamente come inizio," he replied. *"Mi rilassa."* She could understand that he liked to relax by walking and playing, just as she had been doing, but that didn't explain where he had come from, or what he was doing here. Instead of telling her, he said, *"Che strano, sentire un ukulele da queste parti."*

If he thought it was strange to hear a uke in her garden, what should she think about hearing a wandering minstrel with a mandolin there?

"La musica era deliziosa, non potevo resistere," he said. At least he didn't criticize her playing; in fact, no one had ever called it "delightful" before.

"Grazie," she said. Maybe it was time for her to ask a few questions of her own. *"Abita da queste parti?"*

"Non proprio. Però sì, anche, almeno per un po'." What did that mean, that he didn't really live in the neighborhood, but also that he did live there, at least "for a while"? Like just long enough to stalk women, or long enough to show his face and introduce himself?

Iris was starting to feel ridiculous, talking to a face she couldn't see.

"Vuole entrare?" she asked. *"Può venire in giardino un momento, se vuole."* Letting him into the garden wasn't exactly like letting him into her house. If he had evil intentions, he would have already burst right in without waiting for an invitation. Still, she gripped her ukulele by the neck, just in case. Not that the tiny instrument would provide much defense; it would smash to smithereens if she tried to clobber someone over the head with it. But just standing there on her turf, poised to defend herself made her feel strong. She could handle this.

"Certo che mi piacerebbe," the voice accepted. *"Grazie."*

Iris pulled open the wrought iron gate slowly, taking care not to damage the jasmine. The lock had never worked, and she had never bothered to have it repaired; she just closed it at night, out of some vague sense of propriety.

"*Permesso*," the man said, pushing the vines gently aside with his right hand, holding his mandolin in his left. "*E' che quella musica era così angelica*," he said, bowing his head as he brushed some blossoms from his dark curls. "*Mi ricordava…*"

"Oh my God!" Her surprise was so great, Iris instinctively switched to English, interrupting the man's greeting the instant he raised his head. Placing her free hand over her somersaulting heart, she waved her uke at the gauze patch taped on the man's bruised forehead, just above his right eye.

The man shook his head and laughed, his gap-toothed smile instantly flooding her with tenderness. "Well, that's a shock. The Lone Kayaker is also a Pied Piper!" he said, in English. "Am I safe here?" He pointed to the uke she wielded in her hand.

Iris laughed. "At least this time, you're armed, too," she said, pointing to his mandolin.

"But I come in peace, Iris Capotosti," he said.

"And I welcome you in peace, Martin Casagrande," Iris said. "We all do." She made a sweeping gesture with her arm, to encompass the little stone house, the family of plants and flowers gathered in the simple garden, the cats sitting on the steps, the fireflies glowing in the hedge, the crescent moon on the rise.

From: Iris Capotosti <iris.capotosti@gmail.com>
To: Lily Capotosti <lilycapotosti@gmail.com>
Sent: Mon, February 21, 2011, at 5:07 PM
Subject: Glad that's over!

Dear Lily,

After making it through these final chapters, I'm relieved we decided to stop our story here. I don't know how much more of this reality I can take.

When we started out, I imagined how much fun it would be to write down a bunch of anecdotes about growing up as such close sisters in our crazy family. Then I imagined it all ending with some universal statement about the fact that the bond between sisters is stronger than all the evil forces of the world, and that sisters always understand and support each other, no matter how bad they are at staying in touch or expressing their true feelings.

But things didn't turn out quite the way I imagined. There was an awful lot of ugliness in your life that I didn't even know about, and a lot of unpleasantness in mine that I myself never took a close look at before. It's been tough, but I'm glad we've finally faced the truth.

I don't know what comes next, but for now, I just want to tell you how thrilled I am that we've made it to the end and that we've found each other again along the way.

Now, I think a celebration is in order. Martin is taking me out for dinner to that little restaurant by the sea in Camogli where we shared our first bottle of bubbly rosé. Then tomorrow, it's off to London for a few days. But I'll see you online - don't think you're rid of me yet!

Love,
Iris

From: Lily Capotosti <lilycapotosti@gmail.com>
To: Iris Capotosti <iris.capotosti@gmail.com>
Sent: Mon, February 21, 2011, at 12:05 PM
Subject: Surprise! There's an epilogue

Dear Iris:

I really can't believe we stuck with it all this time - and that we didn't grow to hate each other in the process. (I will admit, I had my moments...) Seriously, when we started this, I did a lot of what I had conditioned myself to do - suppress my real feelings, deny my experience of our loosely shared past, smile, and nod. Ironically, it was in remembering those times, in reliving the sweetness of our relationship as children, and in recalling in detail all that we'd faced together that I was emboldened to be honest. I have grown to trust you with my deepest secrets.

Now that we are looking back over all of that, I discover that I am standing at a crossroads. Just as we are approaching "The End," I find that I am asking myself if I want to make nice-nice and tell you, "Yes, it's over, and all wounds are healed." Or, am I willing to take this exchange one step further?

You know me well enough by now to know my answer to that question. So before we close the back cover on this story, I feel I must share one more secret.

I am sitting here, trying to get this letter written during my lunch hour at a job I can't stand, while intermittently peering out an icy window at the falling February snow, which might actually even be kind of pretty if I weren't stuck in this igloo of a cubicle, huddled up to my space heater, dreaming of spring. The clock is ticking out my sentence a second at a time, and I don't even get excited about five o'clock because I know I'll just have to come back here again tomorrow. So when you wrote about your dash down to Camogli for a fancy dinner and a bottle of champagne, followed by a trip to London, it was all I could do to keep from screaming.

Even after all we've been through, and even after all the growth I've experienced as a result, I still find myself resenting that things have worked out so well for you, while I am trapped in the ramifications of the choices I made when I was someone else. Whose life is this, anyway?

Over the course of my life, the only way I knew to cope with my perceived shortcomings and bad luck was to blame others. I felt like someone needed to be punished. I often blamed you. My interpretation of life as predator with me as its victim was simply the attempt of a powerless girl to give meaning to what she could not understand. But now I know things she did not; I can see what she could not.

One of the most valuable things I've learned is that while I may not be able to control everything that happens, and I may not be able to purge the residuals of my past choices as quickly as I'd like to, I can control how I respond to my life. And I can make a new choice and refuse to define our relationship according to the same terms that stole so much away from us in the first place.

That much, I can do. And maybe that's all there is to it.

Love,
Lily

From: Iris Capotosti <iris.capotosti@gmail.com>
To: Lily Capotosti <lilycapotosti@gmail.com>
Sent: Mon, February 21, 2011, at 8:04 PM
Subject: Surprises are not always surprises

Dear Lily,

I was just getting ready to go out the door when I decided to check my email one more time. I sort of wish I hadn't.

What you wrote comes as no surprise, and I doubt what I have to say will surprise you, either. But since you've stepped forward, I suppose I should follow your lead.

You have always believed that I am the lucky one, and maybe I am. But I have never been able to fully savor most of the good things that have happened to me because they are turned sour by the taste of guilt always lingering in the back of my throat.

I can't tell you how many times I have stopped myself from sharing a joyful moment with you, knowing that although you would never fail to respond, "How nice!" or, "I'm so happy for you!", I would always sense resentment in your words, which in turn would only make me feel more guilty. If my mentioning plans to go to a place ten minutes from home for a bite to eat is enough to make you scream, I wonder about all the rest.

When I read your comment about blaming others for your perceived shortcomings and bad luck, it struck me that maybe blaming myself has been my way of coping with my successes and my good luck. The only problem is, I don't know what I am blaming myself for. We all grew up feeling undeserving - of love, of attention, of material possessions. Maybe I have a sense that I've received more than I should have as if in doing so, I was stealing blessings from others.

I don't know whether I'll ever be able to get rid of my guilt, but I do know that I am sick of it letting it dictate how happy I am allowed to be, and how I should behave toward you.

I think we are entitled to move on, Lily. And I think that after all we've been through together, we are entitled to an honest relationship. We've earned that much.

Love,
Iris

PS Can I still go out to dinner, or do I have to worry about you wishing I would choke on a fish bone?

From: Lily Capotosti <lilycapotosti@gmail.com>
To: Iris Capotosti <iris.capotosti@gmail.com>
Sent: Mon, February 21, 2011, at 2:28 PM
Subject: NOW we're done

Dear Iris:

At least now we know what we are dealing with. And I feel like we can finally be genuine and honest with each other. I'm so grateful for that.

Love,
Lily

PS: I don't wish for you to choke on a fishbone, but I wouldn't mind if you got some spinach stuck in your front teeth.

.

In honor of our mother Marion,
who gave the most any mother can:
her best.
We love you.

MORE FROM AUTHORS
ANGELA AND JULIE SCIPIONI

For the complete story read the entire *Iris & Lily* novel series.

Iris & Lily is also available in ebook and audiobook form.

The songs in the novel are featured in the *Songs of Iris & Lily* CD.

Visit IrisandLilytheNovel.com

Made in the USA
Middletown, DE
30 July 2020